Sons of the Order

Book Two of the Sons of the Order Series

Clare SM Keating

This book may not be reproduced or used in any manner without the express written permission of the copyright holder. This story contains explicit content that is intended for adult audiences only. All characters involved in sexual situations are 18 years of age or older.

This book is a work of fiction.

Names, characters, places and events of historical mention are all products of the author's imagination and are meant to be fictitious. Any resemblance to persons, living or dead, actual events, locales or organisations is entirely for plot purposes and are not intended to offend.

This book is dedicated to everyone who brought the first volume and of course my ridiculous love of writing this stuff!

Also special thanks to my Patrons...

Lucy

Casey

John

And Badger

Thank you for your support!

One: The Coming Change

Pagan Prussia 1230

The Castle of Vogelsang upon the edge of the Vistula River was a curious fortress, it was nearly complete thanks to the hard work of the squires, the men at arms, the seven knights and whatever resources the Duke of Masovia granted to aid them. Considering it was so young a castle, already its mix of stone and timber seemed to echo with a strange hollow doom in the night that was assumed, by the fearful squires, as caused by the story that the duke's initial attempts to build this castle nearly a year before had been massacred brutally by the pagan Prussians from the other side of the river. It was becoming a new ghost story that the squires were enjoying teasing each other with and each evening, someone always ended up knocking on the door of the tiny closet-like room where the knight Meinhardt Lehenman had staked his claim and it was no exception tonight.

Tentative hands wrapped against the wooden door, the light from Meinhardt's candle gleaming under the doorway to alert anyone passing in the halls that he was indeed awake. Hearing the knocking, Meinhardt gave a soft growl and then sat himself up off the bunk, shifting the worn layers of fabric from his form and stepping up in his scratchy and thick woollen nightgown, he reached the door. He was trying to ponder which of the youngest gaggle of squires it could be, especially when the fourteen-year-olds were always the more reactive and to be fair, needed the most encouragement. They ordinarily did not irritate Meinhardt when they came to him for help, but to his great frustration they had chosen the one moment where it had been so quiet, but for the cold wind, that Meinhardt had dared to try and read a letter he had received along with the recent information from Rome, where the Hochmeister was busy discussing the movements of the Order up here with the Emperor.

Gently pulling the door inward, Meinhardt gave a groan when he found that it was none other than the skinny little big-nosed wimp, Christian, from a lower-class family just like Meinhardt but had been named with where they hoped the excess child would go, only for the Teutonic Order to open its doors for the rather irritating brat. Christian was nothing like the other squires or indeed the other knights that Meinhardt had ever known, he did not have the best patience to begin with, but Christian had a tendency to be arrogant, question everything and then assume he knew better than anybody else because he was completely literate. However, Christian had a terrible cowardly streak, wetting himself each time battle started to the point that Meinhardt had a fondness for leaving him the task of helping the servants with the laundry. But on this occasion he looked rather concerned and Meinhardt was just not in the mood to get upset when he needed solitude.

"Whatever it is, you have to the count of ten to speak so make it clear." Meinhardt was not actually going to count to ten to make the point as he scrubbed his hand across his face with a grimace. He was making a point that he was tired, that he needed to sleep but of course that was not the truth at all. Christian though began to look about anxiously and then stretched forward, whimpering one word… ghosts. This made Meinhardt's face seem to pull to one side, his eyebrows raising and his eyes squinting against the shadows of the hallway torches to stare at Christian. Now Meinhardt was going to lose his patience as he gave a groan and then grabbed Christian by his awkwardly cut crop of hair and spun his head around to the rest of the hall. Christian's brown eyes swirled in confusion before Meinhardt stretched a finger and gave a firm snort. "You'll want Brother Bertholt in the next room… he deals with the spiritual, I deal with things I can jab with a sword."

"He won't open the door and you're awake." Christian stated in his nasally way that made Meinhardt roll his eyes before stepping forward and closing his door. He then shrugged his shoulders, allowing Christian to beckon him to follow him down to the barracks where the squires were all sleeping along with two of the brother knights and most of the sergeants. Christian brought him over to his bed, which was a double bunk where another young squire was snoring away above him. Meinhardt was rubbing at his head in frustration as Christian then pointed towards a door that led down some stairs into areas where there was still some construction going on. The cold late winter winds were making the wood creak and moan and the hollow stone passages whistle. There was also a strange sound of flapping and this was what seemed to be making Christian concerned. "That sound, something's moving about there and every so often I hear a strange moan… everyone else is asleep!"

"Uh… give me a few moments." Meinhardt stated with a snort, hopping the door open and then slumping down the freezing staircase, shaking and trembling with the cold as he slapped his hands together, muttering and snarling to himself. It was too cold for him to be wandering around looking for trouble and he had to pause when he spotted a set of pikes hanging from the wall, shifting one out of its holder ready to bash whatever was annoying him. As he padded down the stairs he could also hear a moaning sound, but the closer he got the more it sounded like a whine or a whimper and Meinhardt dropped to the bottom of the stairs only to see one of the sheets stretched over the building materials was slapping about.

He groaned, grabbing the sheet and tying it back down, after-all the sheet was to stop the ice getting on the building material and rotting the wood used for the frames, but then he heard the whining sound. As he looked out, he spotted that there was one of the rather wolf-like sheepdogs padding about, looking confused and upset because no one was letting it in. With the wind so cold and the winters here enough to make the horses drop dead from the temperature, Meinhardt gave a swift whistle and the dog turned about to look at him with an expression of delight. He patted his thigh and the dog bolted over, it reached him, lapping at his hands and wrists, whimpering and whining as Meinhardt shook its chilly pelt and then padded back up the stairs, clicking his tongue for the dog to follow. He put the pike back up, opened the door back into the barracks and the dog trotted in at his side.

"There you go… a ghost."

"Ah…" Christian stated, there were a few sudden sniggers to indicate that a few people had been woken up by the sound of the door opening and they were all amused at Christian's stupidity. As the squire clambered back into his bed, he gave a grunt of surprise as Meinhardt pointed his hand to him and the dog suddenly leapt on him. Christian was then being bathed in licks and nuzzles before the dog slipped under the blankets with him and settled down to sleep. Christian gave a gulp of frustration, about to state he was going to stink but Meinhardt wagged a finger, patting the dog's head and then patting Christian's shoulder.

"The dog will tell you if there's something to worry about, these boys are good for guarding and it will lunge into the jaws of death to save you, so give it some cuddles. This is your punishment for waking me up… goodnight. Goodnight everyone." Meinhardt grunted as Christian growled about the dog lapping his ears, but the others that were awake stated their goodnight to the fourth knight-in-command as he padded back towards his room. He was frustrated, he felt like thumping Christian about the head but hopefully the dog would wet his bunk and give him a taste of his own medicine. Meinhardt was not very good with dealing with some of the squires, that was not supposed to be his job, he was the one that could speak to the Poles, speak to the locals and they all trusted him because they looked at him and could see either his older brothers or his father. In fact, his own father had been present upon their initial meeting with Konrad of Masovia to be useful and Meinhardt had been so happy to see his father after so long! But it was not family that had sent him a letter that he was desperate to read, but rather a message from someone more important as Meinhardt finally reached his bed and, within trembling hands, opened the letter.

Steir,

If you can read this than your skills are improving. Things have been going well here in the training grounds and I have been made rather busy helping deal with dysentery and spider bites... I miss watching you dancing about like a fool because you got bitten on the toe! But things are changing, a group of us are being called up to Rome for a meeting with the Hochmeister and Deutschmeister... I've got a feeling we're going to be reshuffled around with the situations going on in Armenia and Acre. I'm looking forward to it though but not travelling by boat to the mainland!

Reinhard's growing well, he'll be four soon enough and I'm being permitted to visit the family as my mother is very ill and she had requested to see me. I have a feeling that it will be the last time I see her and I am thankful to my master and his talk with the others to allow me to do so, my mother it seems is leaving all her remaining possessions to our order so I will be visiting the Bailiwick too. It will be pleasant to see Reinhard again and to see how Esther and Kirk are doing... last I heard they had actually married.

I miss being around you, stubborn ox.

-   Hengst

"Oh Dietrich..." Meinhardt growled softly in frustration as he realised that his ability to read had improved but as always Dietrich had left his letter as brief as possible. But it only made Meinhardt want to weep, he gripped the scrap of paper and pulled it to his chest, glad that he had kept the nicknames and made a point to their meaning to the others, at least a non-explicit meaning. Meinhardt then slouched on his side in the bed, blowing out the candle and then nuzzling his face against the piece of paper, feeling is tears start to fall from his eyes and down his cheeks as he tried to wipe his face and not damage the paper before he rolled onto his back and then gave a grunt. "Uh... wait... the Rome meeting? But... but I'm being sent there to talk about the work here..."

Meinhardt sat up suddenly, looking suddenly very excited as he looked to the paper and then thought about the orders his Komtur Konrad had informed him of that day. Meinhardt would be going to Rome to represent the situation here and get help to improve their efforts and that meant... that meant he would see Dietrich again! Meinhardt gave a shrill but squeezed sound of delight as he settled the paper down and then gave a sigh as he rolled about on the bed for a little while, squeaking in utter delight. He gave a sigh of joy, he was so very happy to think that he would be able to see his beloved husband again, hold his hand and maybe even more. Meinhardt gave a groan as he rolled within his sheets once more, their secret marriage known only between them and witnessed only by God, it had kept them both going the past four years of bouncing back and forth between staying in the same Kommende and being separated completely. Meinhardt then licked his lips before pinching them together, pinching his legs together for the sudden excitement he felt in his body over what had happened the last time they were together.

It had been about nine months ago, just before being deployed out here and they had been in Sicily together, watching Dietrich train the youngsters and work in the hospital. He'd been getting more practice in the hospital and Dietrich had been helping him learn to read again and they'd been sharing a room with two other knights, one of which had been good old Leonhard, whom Meinhardt had replaced in Konrad's group. Their other companion Meinhardt could hardly remember but he'd been on the night watches most of the time and Leonhard had often come to bed late and at a rather predictable time. For four months they'd shared that room, kissed each other goodnight every night, held hands and on a few nights when that mood in Sicily had seemed just right and they had the time, they'd indulged in a little more passion. Although, Meinhardt almost laughed as he remembered that one night they'd been kissing and writhing against each other, getting very excited when Leonhard had come back early and Meinhardt had suddenly stuck his hands around Dietrich's neck to stop any suspicion, only for Leonhard to smack them both about the head for it.

It had been worth it... and Meinhardt settled for bed with a sigh and snuggled into the sheets thinking of Dietrich and how much he hoped the pair of them would be lucky enough to have a room together again. But then he sniggered to himself and thought about another incident, when they'd both been in Tyrol the pair had managed a daring stunt in kissing each other in one of the libraries when they had been reading to candlelight and well, he'd remembered throwing Dietrich onto his back on the table, practically climbing onto it with him until it had flipped and they'd landed in a heap on the floor. When they had been checked on, Meinhardt had insisted he'd gotten overexcited for completing a passage and punched the wall, only to cause the incident. Indeed, Meinhardt sighed heavily in delight as he thought about it all and then he stroked at his stomach with a sigh and then a blush. He wondered what on earth Dietrich looked like now, whether he'd managed to let his beard grow out a little more and sniggered at the thought of that damn moustache he'd grown that he'd constantly scratched and complained over!

With another sigh, Meinhardt settled back down to sleep, letting his dreams guide him through the bitter cold of the night towards the warm nights in Sicily with his arms looped about Dietrich and his face buried against Dietrich's shoulder....

Morning came and as always Meinhardt was up the moment he heard the movements in the room next door where Brother Bertholt was preparing for the morning sermon. Meinhardt swung himself out of the bed and swiftly stripped down before pulling his raiment. He then stomped out of the room and towards the chapel at the end of the hall where Bertholt was already standing beside Komtur Konrad von Landsberg as they were discussing a few matters before they spotted Meinhardt and straightened up. The ordained brother, or rather the former monk come to be a warrior of God, with his bald head and soft greyed eyes beckoned him in. Meinhardt stepped out to them with a soft grin of delight as he then bowed before the altar, kneeling down and preparing for the sermon before Konrad gave a soft chuckle in his curiously gentle voice.

"You know Meinhardt… you may come across as tough with them, but you are actually quite soft with the squires. I would have told Christian to go back to bed…" Konrad was stroking at his mouth gently, one of his odd little quirks when he was amused and Meinhardt gave a soft snort in response before deciding not to acknowledge the statement. He refused to be called soft by any other man in the order but his Komtur and well, he and Konrad knew each other well and Meinhardt could not say anything to him about it. As the sound of the other members of the order echoed around the stone hallway in gentle marching steps as the lieutenant was keen on everyone getting used to marching in order, Meinhardt and Konrad settled themselves down for the sermon and soon the large hall that echoed with silence was filled with the fifty strong members of the order.

The sermon was short and simple, the usual in the morning and when it was done they were all pleased to smell the porridge being made by the servants, the best thing on a freezing morning when frost could be seen clinging to the stain glass windows and even within the breath steamed. The convent stomped down the staircase to the dining hall, still a building made predominantly of wood with one stone wall and it was the current point of construction for the day as everyone settled to eat. They were eating quickly and heartily but in silence broken only by the shifting of plates and the occasional bad manners of slapping jaws or belches. Belches irked everyone to pause and look to the offender, shaking their heads from the disrespect before they would pause and make a brief apology to their comrades before saying a few quick prayers before continuing their food. It was patient and pleasant... it came with a definite sensation of home.

As Meinhardt continued to eat his porridge, he suddenly realised that a large black nose was probing his elbow, butting him gently for attention and lapping at the table with their tongue. It was making some of the squires chuckle to see although they got fierce eyes from the elder knights. Meinhardt pushed the nose away with his hand, hoping that would put the animal off, but it only worked a few minutes as the dog came back. Clearly, for rescuing him last night, the dog had decided that Meinhardt must be the soft touch and it started to lap at his elbow again. When Meinhardt pushed away again, the dog then sat down beside him and began to whimper and whine, pulling its ears back and sounding pathetic as Meinhardt scowled and continued to have his breakfast. Considering what had been said by his master before the sermon, Meinhardt knew he had to prove that he was not that soft and then, to his relief, Konrad gave a soft whistle and the dog trotted over.

Konrad's hands then stroked gently at the animal's cheeks and sides, the dog's tongue lolling and looking up at him lovingly. Konrad gave a soft smile and then lifted a hand to the bowl of porridge that he'd half-eaten and tenderly he brought it down to the dog to eat up. Everyone watched in awe, considering how bloodthirsty and cruel Konrad could be to any of the pagans that refused to convert, with those he felt were his allies, he was nothing but kindness personified. Indeed, Konrad chuckled at the dog gently before he turned to Meinhardt who was giving him a funny expression and Konrad just lowered his eyes gently, in a manner that one could almost say was coyly as if he were perhaps excited and embarrassed all at once to be given such an expression. Konrad though then stood himself up, everyone stopped and stood up as if to salute him stepping out of the room.

"Come along Meinhardt, I've got the letters to give you a brief… are you sure you will be willing to travel this evening? It could indeed be a difficult journey." Konrad stated calmly as he stepped over to Meinhardt's side and the other knight gave a grunt before standing up and marching with his master. There was no fear between them and the relationship was so very different from what Meinhardt had experienced with Heinrich, indeed Heinrich had been akin to a father or an uncle to Meinhardt, teaching him and disciplining him… turning him into a man ready to be a knight. Konrad of course had known Meinhardt since childhood and practically been another older brother, except that he understood the religious devotions of his companion and there was little they could not talk about as they paced the cold stone halls towards the stairs and Konrad's office. "I believe you received a letter from Dietrich yesterday… I was always amused by your tendency for nicknames with each other, calling you a bull for being stubborn and you calling him a stallion for… well, I have to admit you and your brothers always did have a weird tendency to joke about that kind of aspect. I'll be honest, if it were not for the fact we must maintain a brotherhood about us, I might have been concerned that you were still mocking someone's anatomy. It's the actions of a child and yet, Dietrich seems to bare it well."

"Ah… ja… Dietrich and I can only cope with each other for having that kind of joke together, rather than me calling him a Swabian Pig. To be fair, it has me in hysterics each time I say it and his face goes bright red and everyone just shakes their head at him." Meinhardt stated with a soft chuckle, his usual 'kse-kse' sound as it was always more of a snigger or a cough perhaps than a real laugh. But as he sighed and then stepped into the office, Meinhardt was rather startled when Konrad's arms suddenly gripped about him and pulled him into a tight hug. Meinhardt gave a gasp and then scrabbled about in frustration to try and get free before Konrad sighed and then rubbed his knuckles violently against Meinhardt's head, making him growl and pull away in frustration. Then

Konrad let him go and Meinhardt gave a growl as Konrad then shook his head very gently.

"Just a warning not to cause trouble when I send you to Rome. Considering Dietrich is likely to be sent there too, as you two both seem to have a curious level of luck in always ending up together, please do not try to throttle him for something ridiculous." Konrad stated and then Meinhardt seemed to blush as suddenly Konrad gripped his shoulder and smiled down at him like a proud big brother. Konrad had seen how Meinhardt had changed in the order and how it seemed Dietrich, more than anything else, had made this change happen and Konrad gave a soft chuckle of amusement. "I do not know what the influence he has over you is… but I hope you do indeed see him there because it gives you all the more encouragement in our cause."

Meinhardt was startled, he almost had a funny sensation that Konrad had some idea on what was going on between the pair of them and he did not like it at all. But Meinhardt just shrugged his shoulders, grumbling that Dietrich was just a good healer and helped Meinhardt remember to be humble. He hoped this would have helped, but upon looking at the way Konrad was thumbing his neat black moustache again, Meinhardt grimaced. He hated the way it always felt as if Konrad knew exactly what he was thinking and then, thankfully, Konrad patted his shoulder and gave a soft chuckle.

"I have a mountain of reports for you to take and there will be a few men and servants sent with you. But, if my hunch proves correct… you won't be returning alone." Konrad stated with a soft chuckle as he turned towards a wooden chest on the table where the reports were kept. Meinhardt curled an eyebrow in fascination; no doubt there might be a few more squires or even some mercenaries sent their way, but he doubted it would be anything on a larger scale. He grumbled his thoughts to Konrad but the Komtur settled down with a soft sigh and then rested his face into his hands before giving a soft, almost silky kind of chuckle. "I do believe it will be far more than what you may be expecting."

With that, Meinhardt grasped the chest and bobbed his head before giving a salute and then turning to leave to prepare himself for the journey. Konrad watched him go and then gently lay his hands to the other letter that remained on his desk. He pulled it out and read over it with dark, tired eyes before heaving a soft sigh of relief and yet dismay. He had hoped that he would be given more time to stay in control, but his success had proven of interest and though Konrad would have preferred to keep to this castle as its commander… the decisions of the officer were different. But he was humble and would never refute the thoughts of the Hochmeister, though he would certainly ponder just how Balk would do out here, let alone how he would talk with the Sword Brothers… but such was the life of a knight… it was in God's hands no matter what.

Castle von Hohenflacherstein

Dietrich von Hohenflacherstein had not been hoping to return to the castle of his childhood until after the meeting in Rome, but an urgent letter regarding his mother's health had been sent and he'd ended up being switched with Leonhard to go and do recruitment before coming back down for the meeting in Rome. He had been thankful to have been accompanied on his journey by a familiar young friend who had finally stepped into the position of a knight, Siegfried. The pair had ridden hard on their journey, the crossing from Sicily to Italy had led to Dietrich's customary vomiting over the side to feed the fish in the Straits of Messina, before they'd travelled to Tyrol and gathered up lists on areas and administrators to talk with. Then they had travelled through the Alps towards the familiar mountains of the Swabian Jura and on towards that strange and lonely looking patch of bald land that he'd grown up in.

Dietrich's return had been thankfully well timed for some better news that spring; though he was aware that his mother was not long for this world a miracle had seemed fit to happen. Bertilde had in fact fallen to Friedrich and the baby would be born later in the year. No matter the gender, the church had recognised Reinhard as the heir of the household and though at first he'd been filled with a bitter sickness to hear that time would have permitted it to happen between them, he was grateful all the same. Besides, aside from having brought the beautiful Reinhard into the world, he had taken Esther to a family where she was happy and by happy circumstance, Esther had married Kirk the previous spring and had a little bundle to present to Dietrich upon his entrance into the castle and Siegfried had almost bowled over in surprise when Esther had called out his name in memory.

"Well now… I was not expecting such a wonderful surprise to greet my return, oh Esther… and what have you named your little girl?" Dietrich had been swift to step over and swing his arms about Esther's now plumper looking form but to be careful of the baby. Once his body heat had met with theirs, the baby had given a soft groan and begun to writhe in complaint for the knight's attentions and Dietrich had pulled back. Esther had beamed at him, stating the girl was named Agnes and then gently ushering Dietrich to hold the baby in his arms. Though Dietrich was a little cautious at first to hold her, Esther took the moment to run out and tackle Siegfried as he bellowed that they were not supposed to hug and Dietrich snorted. "Sorry… but she seems to have a selective translation on that rule… I'd be honoured she remembers you though Siggi, you were such a scrawny little squire when she met you!"

"Ziggi all manly now." Esther snorted in amusement, patting Siegfried's cheek before she turned back to look at Dietrich holding onto Agnes. Dietrich was glad of the luck of experiencing holding Reinhard when he was a year old, although this baby was smaller and more delicate, his arms automatically cradled and rocked the baby with a soft sigh. To know that he had held a baby without dropping it before gave him a little more confidence as he rocked her gently and then noticed she was looking a little unpleasant as if she might be doing unpleasant baby things in his arms. Esther noticed the way Dietrich was looking and swiftly she stepped over with her arms open to take the baby and she grasped her and pulled her in, carrying her close and with such ease that Dietrich had to shake his head. He could hardly believe that Esther was a grown young woman with her own baby now and of course, Kirk's wife. "Dietrich is better with the baby… you should go upstairs to your mother; she won't see anyone but you and the priest now."

"Thank you, Esther." Even grown her voice still held the strange sounds of the scarring to her face and her tongue, even if the scars were faded with age. Dietrich bent forward to give her a gentle kiss on the cheek before giving the baby a similar kiss and then beckoning Siegfried to follow after him. Siegfried still stood nervously in the hall, not sure whether he needed to greet the baby as well or whether this was simply because they were in Dietrich's household. But he padded to the stairs after Dietrich and together they padded to the main hall that was still as small as ever and filled with hunting hounds that rushed out to meet Dietrich and were fussed gently before Friedrich stepped over to grab his brother in a tight embrace.

It rather startled Dietrich each time he was permitted to visit and his brother greeted him with an embrace, especially since their father's death not long after Reinhard's birth had given him total control and he had given even more land

and money to the order. Dietrich gripped his brother back in a gentle hug and then suddenly there was a thud into Dietrich's leg as Reinhard came galloping over to cuddle his uncle with a squeak of delight. Dietrich bent down, hooking up the brown-haired boy firmly in his arms and pulling himself straight up, Reinhard hooking around him tightly. The boy's eyes were a vivid green like both his father and uncle, his face was round and beaming with a happy smile and podgy cheeks that were rosy as Reinhard grasped his uncle's nose and then pinched at it. They cuddled together tightly, Siegfried staring in fascination at the sight of Dietrich's son let alone how Friedrich truly was his twin with the same sandy-blonde hair, tall muscular form, green eyes, soft skin and both now having grown a matching beard that Reinhard grasped at.

"Uncle Dieter grew a beard! How do I tell you and daddy apart?" Reinhard squeaked, a cheeky grin upon his face to say that he would always tell the difference but wanted to be cute. Dietrich nuzzled is face against him and Reinhard made a sound as if it were disgusting before begging to be put back down. As soon as he was released, he rushed over to Siegfried and rather than greet him, grasped at his scabbard of his sword and then began to tug at it as Siegfried gave a grimace of surprise and tried to pull away. Dietrich was not sure he should say anything to tell him off and make things awkward, but Friedrich gave a stern grunt and Reinhard spun around and just looked stubbornly towards his father. "I just wanted to see what a knight's sword looks like."

"Much the same as my own sword… it just has heathen blood on, so you shouldn't touch it!" Fritz barked to his son and Reinhard turned about to look at his father again before rolling his eyes and then padded off to go and wrestle with the dogs for a bit. Friedrich shook his head at his rambunctious young son, he saw more of his mother in the child than of either of them and yet Fritz beckoned his brother to follow after him and Siegfried to sit himself down. Siegfried did so, grimacing as he found himself sitting down and getting suddenly smothered in excitable dogs as Reinhard sniggered and wrestled with a mastiff. Dietrich was amused all the same by the child and then he knew the grim task of seeing his mother and saying his goodbyes was to come. When they walked up the next set of steps to the corridor that had held their parents' rooms but now was the sleeping place of Bertilde and Friedrich, Dietrich felt a cold chill run down his spine as he spotted the lonely room at the end where their mother was now dying.

He did not want to go in, he did not want to step inside and then step out and know that she was gone for good and the woman to have been his happy mother would indeed no longer exist. He should be happy, relieved that her suffering would end, and she would go into God's embrace, but when it came to death, sometimes it was still too terrifying to really accept and come to terms with. Killing the enemy was different though, when they died you did not think how sad it was they had passed on, you were just thankful it was one less person trying to cut you down. Dietrich gulped heavily as his brother beckoned him to go to the door and Dietrich's body was shaking as he stepped to the tiny little arched doorway and tenderly tapped on the door, hearing the weakened voice and the heavy cough of his sickly, dying mother.

Dietrich stepped into the room and immediately there was an audible smile in his mother's voice as she called to him and shifted her arms up for an embrace. With her so sickly she was practically strapped into the bed, her legs barely of any use anymore and Dietrich could see where they had withered beneath the bed. Her arms were just as slim, her whole body skeletal and he did not know what her ailment was, although there was the talk it was of a kind no one could ever hope to cure that the old suffered greatest of all. Dietrich knelt down beside her, letting her arms wrap about his head as her fingers then felt cautiously for the pale graze against his scalp where he had been wounded five years ago for rescuing Esther. His mother then stroked at his cheeks, grasping at the coiled hairs of his beard and giving a soft chuckle.

"You finally managed to let it grow out past the sores… its best you leave it to keep growing now, if you shave it the sores will come back. Aren't you still so handsome and looking healthier now you've truly matured… your father would have been amused to see your hair looking so rough and unkempt." The frail woman mused softly as she lay there, her hands still clasping her son's face. There were tears in her weakened eyes, her skin was sallow and seemed as fragile as the rest of her and it made Dietrich sad. He was glad she still held her wits, but to see her shrinking away to nothing was heart-breaking and he wanted to howl out at this sight. She noticed the tears in his eyes and she stroked beneath them gently with a slightly scared look as she almost whispered to him. "You… you will promise me that, that no matter what you will always refer to me as your mother. You can call the order or the church your father… but please, promise me you'll never forget me, Dieter."

"I promise… I know you did not wish for me to return to the order, but I am glad you did not fight it in the end as I am much better off there. But I have never once referred to anyone but you as my mother… and I swear upon God and my position as a Holy Knight to always think of you as my mother." Dietrich stated kindly, sadness gripping him to be asked such a thing, how could she ever think he could say otherwise? Though he still held a great hatred in his heart for the family he felt he had done penance for time and time again, it did not mean there was not equal amounts of love. His father's death in a hunting accident had taken them all by surprise and Dietrich had been permitted back at the request of the Swabian Duke to pay his condolences and then he had been sent back once more when Friedrich had taken his position as lord of the land and offered land and money to his Order. There had only been one brief visit between that time, a simple stop over for recruitment in the Swabian Court that had proven successful and then this visit. "Do you wish me to read from the Bible for you mother or to perhaps read you some of my hideous poetry?"

"Your poetry always made me worry about you… but I'm quite exhausted from hearing the passages over and over from the priests and I would rather my son did not repeat them. I want to hear you speak from the heart." She sighed softly as she released his head and then Dietrich settled onto the floor and shifted through his robes to find his poetry. He was startled when he looked through to see just how many were his rather more passionate poems he'd written for Meinhardt that had got him a few tugs to the ear for reading naughty things, but he doubted his mother would understand and so he felt it safe to pull one out and start to read it as his mother settled down to listen. Dietrich did not know how much longer she would have but they would only have this night to be around each other and then he would have to leave again… but it was precious time all the same….

Two: A Night in Rome

"How did we end up being relegated to a barn? We're in Rome! There should be some kind of fortification or barracks for us all to live in!" The group of squires that Leonhard had brought over from Sicily and were relegated into his, Siegfried and Dietrich's care were a rather fussy bunch to say the least. New to the system but old enough to know how to enter battle, they had been rather used to the barracks in Sicily and a fortress lifestyle and suddenly being taken over to Rome and housed in buildings outside the main city was practically insulting. But too many knights going into Rome at once could panic the locals and the meeting was not to be held until tomorrow evening to allow knights time to settle.

"Could be worse… at least you don't have to build it or sleep in mud. There are bunks set up in the barn and it'll be warm with all of us in there, at least you're not getting stuck in the monastery apartments like Dietrich and a couple of the other knights." Siegfried scoffed at the youngsters, all ten of them looking miserable as they gathered up the scraps of cloth left on the makeshift bunks with expressions of dismay. It would be a good lesson in humility and the poverty vows of the order as well as a good training exercise for wherever they were sent next. Considering the men-at-arms were to be sleeping in the camps outside, literally bundled up in tents, the squires were getting off lightly and they would only be sharing with a few more knights that were due to arrive in the morning, so it would be a brief squish and tonight would be calm.

"The monastery doesn't sound so bad… why is it?" One of the squires questioned as they looked towards Dietrich's tired expression as he looked across from the barn to the nearby monastery that was willing to be of help and put them up, if only they kept to the rules within. It was those rules that bothered Siegfried and Leonhard at least, rules on silence and sleeping in an apartment with another knight on the same bed they'd probably never met before. When Leonhard grumbled that it would mean Dietrich would have to sleep with one of the old knights snoring in his ear, the squires grimaced and then Dietrich gave Leonhard a gentle flick to the ear for teasing as he rubbed at his back and dismounted his new horse.

However, this new horse was little more than a fresh colt just getting used to a saddle and when Dietrich dismounted, the pitch-black and heavily built animal was suddenly bucking and screeching in relief as the men rushed to grasp at him and the other beings pulled back in anxiety of the animal's fury. Calling the horse Verbrecher had not been Dietrich's choice but his Komtur's since Stanzi had popped the colt out and he'd done nothing more than bully every other horse that met him. He was a huge animal, one to rival most of the other knight's mounts and at three he was just on the cusp of maturity. They pondered whether to castrate but his father had been a prized stallion given to the order as a gift by a wealthy duke, it would seem a bit rude to geld the brute. But when Verbrecher was pulled down, he barged over to the grass and began to nibble at the lush herbs in ignorance to everyone staring at him and Dietrich just rubbed the back of his neck… he'd seemed to have gained a stallion to rival Meinhardt in stubbornness and temper!

A few of the monks suddenly appeared out of their little monastery, wearing dark cloaks and looking rather eager to be of assistance. Outside of the monastery they were able to speak and they marched right up to Dietrich, looking at his face in fascination for the fact it must have reminded them of someone and yet Dietrich ignored it as he turned about and greeted them. His Italian was better for having been in Sicily for a few years and the monks appreciated it as they beckoned for him to follow and bring his stallion. Dietrich thanked them then turned about to leave Leonhard and Siegfried to settle with the youngsters as Dietrich grabbed Verbrecher's rein and gave him a firm tug. The black stallion pulled his head up, looking as if he were about to rear up and then attack his master until Dietrich just continued to march on and found himself being tugged along. The stallion was certainly going to be a handful going into battle and Dietrich just hoped that he was not going anywhere extreme as the orders to go to Rome had seemed to suggest there were plans to shuffle people around.

The monks had no issue taking the horse's reins and leading him to a stall that was situated next to a nice-looking chestnut filly. Immediately Verbrecher was ignorant to the humans and doing his best to try and flirt with the filly, making Dietrich shake his head gently in frustration as he then padded after the monks and was reminded of the rules that the order he was staying with appreciated silence. Before they entered the building, Dietrich insisted he would pay attention to their vow of silence and offer his own silence in appreciation to their kindness. They were thankful of the words and they led him to the kitchen where there was some food he could have left over from their own meal, he made a bow of his head in thanks to them and then he was left to eat before they beckoned him to join them in prayer. Dietrich did so, rather quick to settle into the idea of total silence as the soft shuffling of people seemed far more appealing than the constant quibbles of squires with saddle-sore backsides!

When the prayers were done, Dietrich was then escorted to the room left aside for him and to his great frustration, there was indeed just one large bed prepared that he was expected to share with another. Dietrich thanked the monks with the same gesture as the door was closed and then he settled down to say some prayers of his own before he began to remove his tunic in preparation for what he hoped to be a long sleep. Tired after all the riding and saddle-sore because that damn colt never knew how to stay still and not keep trying to shrug Dietrich off, Dietrich was just relieved to have whatever brief time there was to himself in order to fall asleep and ignore whoever was going to come in and join him on the bed. Once into just the long shirt, he lifted the parchment-thin sheet and gently shifted himself into the bed before closing his eyes and then hoping he would get some rest.

The bed was little more than a thin layer of straw lying over hard boards, so hard that there was no give as Dietrich lay back. He gave a soft grunt, feeling as if he'd just dropped from a horse onto the bunk before he gave a soft groan and then tried to relax his body onto the bed, only to find his eyes wandering towards a very fat spider that was observing him from the ceiling. Dietrich grimaced, there was no light in here but the lone candle they had lit for him upon a lonely desk and though tomorrow night he might dare to sit up and write a poem or a letter to Meinhardt, tonight was just about sleep. The quiet made it peaceful at least but somehow, just listening to his own breathing made Dietrich feel a little uncomfortable as he lay on his side and tried not to feel like he was just sleeping on stone! But no sooner had Dietrich just managed to settle than the door had opened and suddenly he sat up to see who was being brought in with a jug of water.

At first the knight that came in had his back to Dietrich, so he was left to just assume it was someone that he probably did not know from Thuringia, almost every knight seemed to be coming from Thuringia, but when the figure was barged in by the monks insisting for quiet, Dietrich almost sniggered. He knew that growl in the throat and the scowling expression upon the figure that turned into the room, clearly upset that he would have to be sharing quarters with someone he did not know either. However, when his ice blue eyes locked upon Dietrich's form on the bed, he was about to bleat the name before Dietrich motioned for quiet and then the figure gave another growl and clenched his teeth in frustration. When the monk closed the door, the figure hopped the jug onto the desk, marched to Dietrich's side and firmly grabbed his beard.

Dietrich almost yelped in pain, but managed to smother his mouth as he stared up at Meinhardt in irritation, only for his husband to give a vicious grin. Meinhardt's fingers then stroked along the edge of the thickened beard, it was not long but it at least covered Dietrich's neck and chin as well as about his lips. Dietrich rolled his eyes at Meinhardt; yes, he knew he was going to get a lecture in the morning about having a beard but oddly Dietrich was suddenly quite worried. He wanted to speak, he wanted to say anything to Meinhardt, he was so elated to see his secret husband again and yet he did not want to lure in the monks with the noise. Meinhardt also looked like he wanted to say things too, but instead he just let go of Dietrich's beard after tilting his chin upward. When Dietrich lifted his head up, Meinhardt gently lowered his lips to Dietrich's, their lips clasping for one another in a gentle and sweet kiss that made Meinhardt suddenly almost giggle as he grabbed his mouth and rubbed at it.

Dietrich scowled, he knew that was a comment about how his beard felt 'ticklish' and he breathed a low snort of irritation before Meinhardt then pressed forward again for another quick kiss. Then, Meinhardt sat himself down on the edge of the bed next to Dietrich and dropped his hand to stroke Dietrich's shoulder, glad to see him and hoping he would understand that. Dietrich gave a soft smile, grasping Meinhardt's hand and pulling it to his face, kissing at his knuckles gently to remind him he was glad to see his 'husband' and Meinhardt gave him a scowl this time. It was that penetrating one he always managed, and Dietrich was grinning, almost wanting to laugh as Meinhardt then pushed his shoulder gently before Dietrich noticed something and sat up properly to stretch out his hand and gently stroke the edge of Meinhardt's neck. He shuddered suddenly in delight at the touch, grasping Dietrich's hand feverishly and holding it to his neck as he turned his head into it, kissing the softer palm gently and lovingly as Dietrich gave a soft sigh of pleasure, but still stroked along a scabby line upon Meinhardt's neck, questioning what it came from.

Meinhardt eased his hand away, gently making the gestures of a fight and a sword narrowly missing taking off his head and Dietrich gave a grimace although Meinhardt grinned. Then Meinhardt gently grasped his tunic and began to pull off the cloth, as Dietrich gave a curious grin and watched in amusement. He got a lovely display of Meinhardt's neat muscles and could see there were new ones although it was clear Meinhardt had lost weight again and there were also new scars. Meinhardt gave a sudden jump of surprise when Dietrich's cool hands suddenly wrapped about his torso, the beard rubbing against his bare back and making him grimace at the bristly sensation. Dietrich paused, planting a gentle kiss to one of the new scars before sitting up with an apologetic expression as Meinhardt's sneered at him. Meinhardt then straightened up off the bed, removed his trousers and then was about to grasp his long nightshirt when a resounding clap filled the room and Meinhardt jumped. He then spun around ready to punch Dietrich and his partner gave him a playful wink.

For that, Meinhardt ignored putting his clothes on and quickly hopped onto the bed, pushing Dietrich back with a growling sound, their hands locking as they wrestled slightly and Dietrich gave a grin to be seeing Meinhardt in his underwear. They wrestled a little, just pushing their hands against each other, but then they paused and Meinhardt rolled off Dietrich and onto the bed, only to realise his mistake and give a sudden grunt. Dietrich almost burst into laughter, he knew that Meinhardt had just bashed his backside on the hard bed and swiftly Dietrich turned about with a soft expression to make a motion of his hand as if to rub at Meinhardt's backside. But for the expression and the fact Meinhardt could not ask a question to finalise exactly what was going on, made him growl again and shift about to get the cover onto himself as Dietrich lifted it up and then rolled onto Meinhardt who gave a soft groan of irritation.

Meinhardt certainly did not like being on the bottom for any reason, but with Dietrich lounging over him and nuzzling at his nose tenderly with his own, it was far too comfortable for him not to nuzzle back and sigh lovingly. Dietrich buried his head against Meinhardt's chest, giving a soft and loving little moan that made Meinhardt snort and bring his hands up to Dietrich's head. He stroked his fingers through the hair, finding that pale ragged line from years before where he had almost thought he'd lost Dietrich. Meinhardt heaved a sigh of utter relief to know that his love was with him again. Then the pair were kissing one another again, their lips dragging and pinching, clasping as their tongues then stroked and twirled against one another as the pair gave sharp little moans before freezing. They feared for a moment that someone might come to check on them, but instead everything seemed quite calm and they continued to kiss just a little more.

Then Dietrich rolled off Meinhardt, lying his head onto his husband's shoulder and gripping his arm, heaving the most adoring sigh he could. He snuggled to him tightly as Meinhardt pulled the sheet up around them, urging Dietrich to roll onto his side. Then, to Dietrich's great surprise, Meinhardt hooked his arms around Dietrich's shoulders and then shuffled up against him, practically forcing Dietrich to almost sit into his lap and Meinhardt nibbled softly a Dietrich's neck to make him give a little giggling sound. They then shuffled into the position a little more, their hot bodies pressing together as Meinhardt just heaved a soft sigh and then whispered very, very quietly to Dietrich.

"I've missed you, Hengst."

The meeting was miserable, the most boring situation that they could have imagined finding themselves within although Meinhardt was happy to see Leonhard, Siegfried and even old Udolf as he had grabbed Meinhardt under his arm and slapped his back pretty hard. But there had been another pair of knights present that Meinhardt, Dietrich and the others were not so pleased to see, Sigmond and his brand-new lieutenant, Franz. It shocked them to see that Franz had been put in such a position, but Meinhardt had been happy to greet Franz as his friend, though Sigmond was immediately irritated at the sight of the Northerner. Of course, when Leonhard mentioned that Sigmond had been saying that Meinhardt was dead, the northerner had scoffed and insisted the chaos of that fire had meant information was easily mixed up. Dietrich and the others though had still felt uncomfortable about it, but they'd settled near Udolf and some of his new companions and then found themselves coming face-to-face with *the* Hermann Balk!

He had been the Deutschmeister, the head of recruitment and well, all matters within the empire until three years ago when he'd been pulled back and forth like most of the higher ranked members of the order to discuss what was to happen. He'd been in Rome for at least a month now, apparently holding meetings from Konrad of Masovia and conversing with the Hochmeister, who was stuck in Rome again to play diplomat between the emperor and the pope. Balk was a very tall man, there were rumours he'd been a canon in Hildesheim, but all the older men to have joined the order in the Holy Land never spoke of their life before then. But with a thick beard like most of the elder knights, a total intolerance for pagans, a nose that had been crushed down from constant use of a helmet and bashes during war, there was such a dominating aura about the figure that everyone, even Udolf, shrank as the figure stepped into the room. He was followed by several other knights, totalling their number to twenty-one and then the familiar but worn looking form of Hermann von Salza himself stepped into the room.

It should have been a moment of excitement to see the broad figure with his stern looks but gentle eyes again, a figure that of course held total authority but for those who had served under his cousin Heinrich, a familiarity that eased them. However, his first statement was regarding issues with the pope and the emperor and the usual political nightmares of in-fighting back home affecting recruitment drives and the availability of mercenaries for what tasks they had in mind. Immediately the mention of heading into the Baltic regions, territories filled with pagans, Danes and the cantankerous forces of the Order of the German Sword Brethren, not to mention the Polish princes caused a ripple of displeasure amongst all present. Meinhardt sat straight though, he listened and then to his own shock he was called up to give his assessment of the capture of Vogelsang and indeed his experiences with dealing with the pagans there.

Meinhardt had been more than a little worried, he was not used to being asked to give information to such noble peers, let alone to an audience of knights that were all more experienced than himself. He did not know how to explain this all to them, but Meinhardt kept it simple in informing them of von Landsberg's tough reactions to the pagans, giving only help and security to those that converted and slaughtering those that did not. There had been a mention that later hit and run tactics in the winter had been far more useful in damaging the villages and by setting fire to those enemies, they had captured a decent number of slaves to send back and be sold. This Balk nodded his head over, pointing to a series of parchments at his table that tallied information on money gained from this incursion. It had been something he'd needed for his discussions with the Duke of Masovia, especially with the information he was about to present to the knights as Meinhardt was beckoned to settle back and thanked for his work thus far.

Meinhardt sat beside Dietrich again, wishing he could hold his hand and thank him for just being there to give him some kind of strength for having needed to speak up, but Sigmond sat behind them, glaring at them. With this explanation given, Balk then pulled out a parchment bearing several seals for the Hochmeister to view and nod his head wisely to, before it was explained to the knights present. Where the Hochmeister had gained permission for the order to go and deal with the northern pagans in a Golden Bull from the Emperor four years before, Balk had assisted in the negotiations with Konrad of Masovia to gain a new treaty. The treaty was not accepted just yet, but the draft in his hand was the current proposition that Balk and some of the other knights present were going to present to Konrad and it would mean that Culmerland would be for the Order and not be given to Masovia.

As the ideas were given out, it brought a bitter taste back to the knights to have been in Burzenland, recalling the agreements with King Andrew of Hungary that had fallen through. The Hungarians were still making claims that the order had never had such an agreement with them, it was five years since their expulsions and an additional reason for the Hochmeister to have a headache and more work to deal with. The fact this treaty had not yet been signed and was going to be presented to the Duke only made them all anxious that there was going to be similar aggression for any of them moving forward in the region. Meinhardt though had confidence in this matter, he had spoken with Konrad of Masovia and his advisors, they were all rather trusting of Meinhardt and of von Landsberg and they had been thankful for their efforts thus far. Konrad would probably accept the treaty to ensure there were allies sitting near him instead of pagan enemies, but part of him was still aware of the frustration caused by the jealous boyars in Burzenland and finally, von Salza cleared his throat and everyone turned to him.

"You have all been summoned here because of your experiences in Burzenland and in the Holy Lands and that you have been bouncing frequently throughout our holdings, working mainly in recruitment whilst I have been arranging a new place for you. This place is the north, the regions above Masovia in the pagan-infested reaches known as Culmerland and its surrounding territories. Our Emperor has already forged an agreement granting us autonomy in removing the pagans from this place and its surrounding areas where our fellow brothers, the Order of the Sword Brethren, are already fighting to secure Christendom in the Baltic. Konrad of Masovia has requested our presence to aid him, but as with the matter of Burzenland we will ensure we have a secondary agreement with him to prevent any such expulsion. Already our work in the region has proven useful and with firm tactics we will do as much good there as we did in Burzenland. But the terrain is harsher, the land more dangerous and at this time of Crusades in the Holy Land I cannot send a massive force of knights. All you see within this room, is who will accompany you… Balk here at the head and Konrad von Landsberg beneath him until you have suitable ground enough to create new convents and hold them against pagans. Squires, men-at-arms, servants and religious brothers will accompany you, but your journey will begin tomorrow from Balk's camp and you will travel to Masovia to meet with Konrad's approval. That is all." Firm, direct and yet with a tired air because he knew that there would be frustrations for those not returning to the Holy Lands, Hermann von Salza straightened up and then turned to Balk. The pair nodded their heads in agreement to the situation before Hermann then settled onto his seat and then permitted Balk to start barking out his orders and ideas for what was going to happen as the soldiers listened in silence. Dietrich could not believe his twisted luck, not only was he going to join up with Meinhardt again, but Sigmond was going to be in the north with him as well and he had to hope that Konrad was smart enough to keep the pair separated!

When the meeting was over, the men were given a copy of their orders to present to their groups and the usual requests to pick up stock for the journey northwards. It was going to be an awkward journey northward and there was already thought that using the rivers to travel could be affective, but for the horses. Once Dietrich had given the orders to the squires and the men, they entered the main city of Rome to collect what was needed and then met back up near the monastery on the outskirts. This was in time for an evening mass all together, a meal provided by the monks that was just bread and water, before everyone was to settle for sleep. Leonhard and Siegfried had wanted to chat with Meinhardt some more and make a point of their frustrations over Sigmond being sent north with them, but it was clear that Dietrich was far too tired and he and Meinhardt went to go check on their horses before they were to enter the silent order and well, Meinhardt had a thought in his head.

"You know… Dieter… I'm pretty sure we can keep ourselves quiet… it's been nine months and… and last night was bad enough a temptation it was just lucky we were both so tired." Meinhardt whispered gently to Dietrich's ear, his eyes spinning about looking for any kind of spies and finding none. The pair of them were standing beside Klobig, the massive gelding still plodding on and quite used to the life in the northern marches and the pagan lands. With no one able to see them and Dietrich looking towards Meinhardt with an almost dumb expression, Meinhardt knew he had to make himself quite clear. He stretched his hand across to stroke at the bottom of Dietrich's stomach, making him give a sharp gasp before they quickly hooked their hands together as they both looked around for someone in fear of being seen. But with no one looking, Meinhardt could see the excitement written upon Dietrich's face and he gave a soft chuckle before patting Klobig's side. "I'll let you sort yourself out first."

With that, Dietrich left and knew exactly where to go and what to do, something he'd been learning from medical books and, though being a monk gaining an item like antimony was awkward to keep hold of, Dietrich had something just as useful that he'd been pleased to see that these monks had the items on hand for a swift purging. Though Meinhardt did not believe that purging the body was necessary for the health, it had been a growing fad with laxatives being used in preference to bleeding with leeches and well, anything that meant he did not have to have a hideous blood-sucker upon him was good enough for Dietrich. Not only this, but he had learnt that after such a purge, when he and Meinhardt had become a little… passionate, it had made it a lot less painful despite the amount of time between and Dietrich had enjoyed it even more than usual, though Meinhardt still could not quite understand, he just wanted Dietrich to be comfortable.

After a while cleaning Klobig, stroking the horse and playing with his mane whilst the grey animal had just been chewing away in boredom, Meinhardt had realised he had not seen someone else. He quickly hopped to the kitchens where the monks were and made a reference with shadow puppets, of all things, to explain what he needed. The monks just shrugged, willing to give him whatever and swiftly he stepped to where there was a few scraps of stinking meat and a big bone left over from the meals. He padded back out to the stables in search of his other companion that he knew Dietrich was going to love as much as Meinhardt and everyone else loved him. Meinhardt clambered into the back of the stables where a large tan coloured dog, mastiff like but leaner with long legs and almost the size of a horse, was lying on the ground with a miserable expression, chained to the nearest wall. The moment the dog saw him, it stood up, snuffling and wagging his tail, panting and whimpering towards Meinhardt with its big thick black muzzle suddenly lounging against Meinhardt's hand as it whimpered lovingly towards him.

"There we are Igel… I haven't let you meet your other daddy have I? But don't you worry, you'll meet him tomorrow and he's going to love you just like me. Isn't he? How's my little boy huh? My little hunter?" Meinhardt knelt down, setting the food down but the dog was far more excited at the idea of trying to nuzzle his master and get a good cuddle. Meinhardt sat on the straw and then suddenly the massive dog leapt onto his lap, whimpering and fussing as Meinhardt gripped him tightly, hugging him and patting him gently as the dog lapped his forehead and gave a whimper of utter joy. Meinhardt snuggled with his dog for a little while longer before encouraging him to have his food, patting him lovingly and saying his goodbye before leaving to go wash his face at the nearby fountain before turning and padding straight towards the rooms.

Dietrich had made sure to clean his whole body with a damp rag, excitement tingling at the base of his spine. It was perhaps a little pride, but more that he did not like Meinhardt to think that he was not looking after himself and of course all thoughts of lust had long since departed from the pair. With the firm understanding that they believed themselves as married in the eyes of God if not within each other's eyes, they felt no more fear that their actions were the sin of lust. At least, Dietrich had forgotten all such anxieties, knowing only that the occasions were rare and sacred to him, moments where he and Meinhardt could indulge in something that was now becoming the proof of the pair of them recognising themselves as married to each other. Meinhardt still had his anxieties, but he never spoke of them and often he was far more desperate for the embracing of their flesh than Dietrich could ever have believed.

As Dietrich stepped into the bedroom given to them by the monks, silence echoing about the corridor as if to remind him that care was needed, Dietrich stepped to the bedside. He pulled off his underclothes, arranging his knightly garb upon the desk and then gently slipping under the covers of the bed. He settled within the sheets, pondering over how on earth he was going to keep himself quiet enough as they made love? It was hard enough any other time when the accommodations were not silent and often it was all down to Meinhardt kissing Dietrich at the right moment to smother his cries. Sometimes Dietrich had to bite his own arm or put some scrap of cloth in his mouth to bite down on, he'd even pressed his face into the pillows before to stifle his cries and well, perhaps that was what he should do now. He might be prepared for his partner, but if Meinhardt was feeling particularly excitable, Dietrich was quite sure he'd need to bury his face because otherwise the monks might believe he was being murdered with the great bear-like bellows he made into the fabric when he reached climax in such times.

Meinhardt had gone to wash very briefly, but as precisely and carefully as possible, grumbling under his breath despite the request for silence about the lack of snow. Having been in the north so long during the freezing winter, Meinhardt had learnt that using snow to rub against his naked body was not only good for giving him a quick wash but making him warmer. He'd grown a curious fondness for it and he nearly giggled aloud as he thought about grabbing Dietrich and then washing his body with snow as the other screamed over the cold. Meinhardt's sense of humour was still rather wicked, but Dietrich loved him for it all the same. When Meinhardt stepped out of the bathroom in his undershirt and breeches, the rest of his garb folded up neatly within his arms, he watched the monks heading out to prayer in the chapel on the other side of the courtyard and he almost cackled to himself. He bowed his head to them in greeting, forcing a yawn to make them understand that he was very tired before he stepped into the room with Dietrich and then hurriedly sat on the end of the bed.

He began to gesture with his fingers, swinging his index around to indicate all the other people in the building before walking two of his fingers across his knee to then bring them together in a gesture of prayer before grinning. He looked to Dietrich, hoping the message that they had the area to themselves was passed along, but Dietrich just stared at him for a moment in utter confusion. He got the idea that someone was walking somewhere, but he assumed that it meant they needed to be careful and so very carefully, Dietrich lifted up the cover and beckoned Meinhardt into the bed. Meinhardt assumed he understood the message and so sat on the edge of the bunk, gently jerking off his breeches and then pondering as he grasped the edge of his nightshirt... did he really need to pull it off? Dietrich grabbed the edge of the nightshirt and gently teased it up as Meinhardt grinned and pulled his way back out of it before suddenly leaning forward to kiss Dietrich and stroke his bearded cheeks with amusement.

"Meinhardt..." Dietrich whispered very softly as Meinhardt's generally cold blue eyes seemed to be shining with utter love and gentility as he sighed and brought his lips to Dietrich's with a gentle clapping sound. They kissed softly again, pulling back to just smile and blush at each other, still so curiously nervous each time they were together as Meinhardt stroked Dietrich's arms gently and he stretched a hand to caress Meinhardt's thigh. They leant closer to each other, kissing softly once again and then nuzzling their noses, Meinhardt trying not to laugh to feel the beard tickling at him and he had to grab Dietrich's cheeks to grin at him. Then he dropped a hand to stroke and rub at Dietrich's neck and shoulder, making him give a soft moan and lean gently against it, sighing softly as he grasped Meinhardt's hand and then pulled it up to his mouth, kissing those calloused fingertips lovingly before he then bent forward and gave Meinhardt a gentle expression. He was asking permission to touch and Meinhardt gave him a sceptical expression with a curled eyebrow before Dietrich leant forward and pressed his mouth to Meinhardt's neck.

"Nei... nuuu... huhuu..." Meinhardt was suddenly wrinkling his lip, trying not to giggle too loud, suddenly slapping a hand to his mouth as Dietrich held him gently as he seemed to buck and writhe upon the bed. The sudden sensation of Dietrich's warm lips upon his neck, where he was so sensitive was lost quickly by the tickling scratching of the beard. After a while, he got used to it a little more, Dietrich dragging his lips across the sensitive skin, trying not to scratch him with the beard though Meinhardt was still trembling and gritting his teeth with a wicked grin. Dietrich sighed softly as he then pulled away, a firm blush on both their faces as Dietrich noticed the red rub his beard had been making and the way Meinhardt suddenly scratched at it with a grunt. "Maybe I should shave the beard, keep the moustache..."

Swiftly Dietrich clapped his hand about Meinhardt's mouth, emphatically making the reference for their need to be quiet and Meinhardt looked at him with confusion for a moment before rolling his eyes. Clearly Dietrich had not gotten his message about the monks having disappeared to pray, so he gently pushed Dietrich's chest to knock him back on the bed and then scrabbled over him, quickly bending down to give him a firm kiss on the lips before giving a soft growl and then kissing down the centre of Dietrich's chest, making him stiffen and his breath shudder in embarrassment for a moment before he gave a low sigh as he felt his lover's mouth pecking gently down to his navel. Meinhardt then stroked gently at Dietrich's thighs, feeling their excited heat with a soft grin as he also felt the phallus swelling alongside, but he drew his lips back up, laying his slimmer body along Dietrich's as he then lay is arms comfortably about Dietrich's sides, the bed supporting his weight as he lay his head to Dietrich's chest.

He heaved a soft sigh of relief, listening to the trembling heartbeat beneath as Dietrich stretched out a hand to stroke at Meinhardt's pale blonde hair. He was bemused by how brilliantly light it was and how terrifying it must be to see him emerge from the snow in his white garb with those icy eyes piercing into his foes. Dietrich gave a soft, loving sigh and then a sudden sharp tremble, his back arching as Meinhardt turned his had and then pinched his lips firmly around one of Dietrich's nipples. Meinhardt then lifted his head up to look at his lover, producing a wicked grin before stretching his tongue out and then slowly rolling it in circles around the crinkling areola. Dietrich's breath caught in sharp little hiccups, making him blush brightly, his stomach starting to churn with that nausea and hunger such actions elicited. Then his warm, damp tongue slid over the elastic flesh of the nipple, strolling in playful circles, pushing the flesh this way and that as it strained out and hardened. Dietrich gave an almost despairing sound of anguish, feeling such shameful pleasure at the sensation as Meinhardt smiled and then moved to do the same to the other nipple. The burning in Dietrich's loins began to feel more urgent, a molten tossing of desire and anxiety making his whole body feel wretched and yet perfect all at once before Meinhardt then straightened up along him, kissing his lips tenderly.

As their bodies lined up over one another, Dietrich's body relaxed as Meinhardt gently lay over him, dropping his arms down to hold Dietrich's shoulders as he kissed his lover's lips again. They moaned softly together, their arms then shifting about onc another's body, Meinhardt's hands grasping and groping at Dietrich's warm hips and soft skin with a sigh. Dietrich moaned as his hands slid down to grasp at Meinhardt's hips, stroking the middle of his back and then up towards his shoulders with a sigh as they continued to kiss lovingly. Their bodies were so hot and pleasant just lying together and then, knowing he could not help himself, Meinhardt dropped his head against Dietrich's chest and kissed at his nipples to make Dietrich give a soft sound of pleasure as he grit his teeth. Then Meinhardt began to shift his hips, rubbing his body comfortably against his lovers, their groins pushed together and suddenly both their bodies starting to burn with excitement as Meinhardt gave a soft groan into Dietrich's chest as he gripped him tightly and continued to rub himself up and down his lover.

Dietrich gasped, feeling the soft, hot flesh rubbing against his own, pushing and tugging at him, the friction urging their lengths both to stretch out and harden as Meinhardt continued to grind his body against his lover's. Meinhardt was making soft little cries, almost of pain or upset that he was getting so excited for such a motion, but Dietrich was sighing and moaning with pleasure, feeling their heat mingling and their flesh practically stroking and even clapping at one another. They were both enjoying it more than perhaps they would have liked, if only because it was not the main event and just proved how much they had been desperate to be with each other. Then, with a sigh, Meinhardt stopped and kissed Dietrich's Adam's Apple, pinching it between his lips to make his lover give a slight hiccup before Meinhardt then sat himself upwards onto Dietrich's body. Dietrich grimaced at the shift in weight, feeling Meinhardt leaning his groin into Dietrich's as he seemed to straighten up and then began to rock his hips back and forth again. Dietrich gasped loudly this time, his eyes locked onto the sight of their swollen lengths straining and even starting to glisten with excitement and he quickly grasped for Meinhardt to stop, feeling a fizzing in his belly that begged to be filled as Dietrich gave a grunt.

"Back or knees?" He whispered softly and Meinhardt paused in his rubbing and his thrusting, suddenly realising that he had been getting overwhelmed by the situation and he made a swift apology before shifting back and off his lover. But then Meinhardt pondered over what to do, not sure which one was the best for them both and as he stretched his hand forward, gently stroking Dietrich's hard length to make him moan and keep them both in the mood, he then gave a soft snort and pondered it over. If he wanted to kiss Dietrich, it was better this way, but then Dietrich might make too much noise and so Meinhardt motioned for Dietrich to go on his knees. Then Meinhardt stretched his arm out, grasping the pillows and pulling them under Dietrich's chest before making the motion that they needed to keep quiet. Dietrich gave a soft smirk as he cuddled into the pillow, his legs spread and then he gave a soft jolt of shock as Meinhardt's hands pinched tightly about Dietrich's backside, stretching his cheeks as far apart as he could before bringing his mouth to the spot in loving kisses. "Stier…"

Meinhardt gave a soft growl, he was not going to be interrupted as he licked and kissed and even sucked at his lover's body, even if it made Dietrich go bright red even to the ears. Dietrich was moaning softly, gripping the fabric with his teeth as his body quivered for such a curiously pleasant sensation. He never spoke of it of course or asked questions on why Meinhardt did it, it was too taboo even for Dietrich to question, but he liked it and Meinhardt had become quite insistent that it was needed. When Meinhardt stopped, Dietrich's passage quivering in expectation for more, Meinhardt leant over Dietrich's body and then nipped his ear playfully before kissing the back of his neck and whispering low, hot and slowly.

"I love you, Hengst." Meinhardt almost cackled to use that nickname as

Dietrich gave a groan that was quickly replaced by a sharp little squeak as Meinhardt brought their flesh into union. His arms hooked around his lover, his legs intertwining with Dietrich's as his mouth then peppered Dietrich's shoulders and neck with kisses. Dietrich mumbled softly in pleasure, turning his head to the side slightly to take in a few clear breaths as he gave a soft moan as Meinhardt prepared himself. When Dietrich was more relaxed, Meinhardt pushed his hips firmly into Dietrich, penetrating him fully as Dietrich gasped and bit into the pillow, then he pulled back, making Dietrich moan loudly with joy. Meinhardt kissed him gently, glad the fabric smothered the sound as he gave his own moan of pleasure as he gently rocked himself back and forth against Dietrich.

Their motions were slow, their bodies became fiery, sweaty and Meinhardt moaned as quietly as he could as his arms grasped and groped Dietrich's body as he thrust slowly in and out. Dietrich was moaning and crying happily into the pillow, his body quaking and trembling, pleasure and ecstasy filling every part of him from every caress by hand or lips or phallus to his form. Dietrich moaned loudly, his body suddenly clenching as Meinhardt gave a sharp gasping, almost thinking to bite Dietrich as his lover reached a climax and then Meinhardt reached his own. But he still lounged over Dietrich, kissing him and moaning in pleasure and Dietrich gave a groan… apparently Meinhardt felt they could do a little more tonight….

Three: Heading to the North

In the morning Dietrich had a bad back and a sore throat; he was quiet as he gathered his horse and thankfully the stallion kicked about in excitement so anyone could understand why he was feeling so uncomfortable. He'd brought the damn animal out of the courtyard, giving thanks to the monks before meeting up with his companions then had been waiting for Meinhardt to join them. Dietrich had yet to mount his horse, waiting patiently to see that Klobig was joining them and this he was about to regret as they were all made suddenly aware of a heavy, booming bark and something ran at them. At first Dietrich could not tell if it was a horse or deer of some kind, the animal having long legs and galloping so fast out of the stable, but the spiked collar made it clear something was wrong. Indeed, this beast had his mouth open, his floppy jowls slapping in the air, his tongue hanging out and a line of drool streaming in the wind behind him as he charged right into Dietrich and reared up.

Dietrich remembered making a sound like a grunt but feeling something slam into him like three men brawling in a bar. He was suddenly upon his back, his face being caked in a hideously sticky substance as the creature stood panting over him with breath that smelt of rotten flesh and shit, its big black nose twitching and its whole form shaking as its tail was wiggling about in delight. Dietrich was not sure what had happened to him, but he was quite sure the monks had not owned a war dog like this and even Leonhard and Siegfried were utterly frozen upon their horses just staring. Suddenly there was the sound of a holler, someone calling out for a hedgehog in German and the dog suddenly straightened up and gave a funny grunt. Then, when it heard the call again, the dog gave out a loud booming bark that made Dietrich jolt beneath it before the dog brought his head back down to snuffle at Dietrich in affection. The group then recognised the voice and Leonhard hollered out that the dog was with them as Meinhardt hurried over, dragging Klobig by the reins behind him and carrying a slither of stinking meat in his hands.

"Igel! Igel! Ig… look at you, silly boy… did you find Brother Dietrich? Yes, you did! Who's a good boy then, huh? Who found daddy's friend?" Meinhardt chuckled in delight, hurrying over and plopping the meat down as the big fawn coloured animal with his dark muzzle pulled off Dietrich and then ran into Meinhardt's open arms. Dietrich gasped in relief before pulling himself up into a sitting position, glowering at Meinhardt as he snuggled and tickled at the big loveable pup. Even Leonhard was confused, he'd certainly never heard Meinhardt speak so lovingly about anything before, let alone to snuggle a massive dog that was lapping at his ear as Meinhardt giggled. He then straightened up, passing the dog the meat before he noticed Dietrich and gave a snort. "What do you think then Dieter? I got a curious little gift for the order in this dog, his parents are terrible war dogs, powerful beasts trained not only to rip boar, bear and wolf to shreds but grab the enemy by the ankle when they're riding and pull them off the horse. They can even attack horses and they've got no sense of fear. Isn't he a good boy, he knew exactly who the weakest was amongst the three of you, but recognised your scent, my scent and your uniform so he didn't eat you!"

"Yet with such power you called him Igel? Why not call him Ringer or Krieger? Why'd you name him after something small and pathetic?" Leonhard called out, utterly startled to hear this praise and see Meinhardt giving such affection when he'd never seen Meinhardt give affection to anything much but Klobig and maybe Dietrich. But when he noticed the way Meinhardt was looking at him as if he were the idiot, Leonhard's eyes shot to Dietrich for some kind of reaction or agreement. Dietrich was still trying to wipe the drool off his face, but he was just as startled when Meinhardt then grabbed the dog by its spiked collar and pulled it over to Leonhard, the dog jumping and jolting in excitement before Meinhardt leant against it in a firm hug and pointed to his big twitching nose.

"That's why... he's got a big nose and makes a snorty sound in his sleep like his namesake snuffling around in the woodlands. I actually used to have fun picking up those beasts and bringing them into the household, used to petrify the cook into thinking we had an infestation... I only learnt my lesson when I got bitten by those horrid white bugs that live off them..." Meinhardt stated, sighing away in memory of happier but still rather obscure childhood moments as he patted the dog lovingly and the other knights just looked between them. They were starting to wonder if Meinhardt had been given a kick up the arse by the Holy Spirit with his attitude seemingly more pleasant, but within a flash he was up and barking orders at them. "Come on, round up the squires already and let's get going. I'm itching to get back and show you all how difficult but utterly fulfilling our mission north is!"

"Oh joy..." Was the sound in unison from the knights as they looked towards Meinhardt with heavy hearts and yet humour was still written upon their faces. In a time when politics made everything about them change and even the households of their families shift alliances and power, it was nice to know that somethings never changed, even if it was just Meinhardt's attitude! They steered their horses over towards the gathering gaggle of anxious looking squires before Meinhardt had stepped over to Dietrich, patting his shoulder hard in delight before mounting Klobig. Dietrich was just left staring at him for a moment, until Meinhardt's encouragement for Dietrich to mount up already caused a frightening and booming bark from the canine, urging Dietrich to do as he was told. Somehow, he had a feeling that this dog was going to be causing him grief on the journey!

Mounted up and the squires and men-at-arms all gathered about them, the impressive caravan shuffled over to where the main body of the knights were waiting under the command of Balk. They were all eager to get going, waiting for Dietrich's band to join them before they were beckoned to stand still or remain mounted and say their prayers. After a sermon, in which a priest from the papacy's services itself arrived to grant them a blessing and splash their armour with holy water, Balk gave a very brief statement on how he saw everything would work under his command and it was clear to see that he did not take slackers. He was going to be a very tough commander in order to keep certain boisterous or overly ambitious young knights in their positions.

"Let's get one thing straight upon this journey and this campaign, our duty is to purge the north of the heretical views of the natives… those Christians we will protect and those willing to convert we will embrace. There will be no middle ground as there is in the Holy Land… you're either a follower of Christ or a pagan and my sword knows the difference. Now, our journey will take time, we have to travel through disputed territories and when we reach Thuringia, we will have our first proper encampment and time to gather up extra supplies. From then on we move close to the Kingdom of Bohemia to Masovia where we will engage in talks with their leader whilst Brother Meinhardt and a selected small squad go to replenish the supplies for Brother Konrad. Is that clear?" It was indeed very straightforward with no room for grey areas and when there were a few simple quibbles, Balk gave a sudden snort of irritation. His hand slid onto the hilt of his sword hanging from his waist almost as a reflex to any such insubordination and it quickly silence the crowd. However, he had recognised the concerns and his more Christian side perhaps, his more amiable side at least came to the fore with a gentle tone that was fatherlier to them all, proving perhaps the rumours of his past in the priesthood. "All relevant authorities have been informed of our movements through the landscape and we will, by the grace of our Lord God, face no aggression from our fellow Christian nations. Our duty is not to a flag born by any land, it is to the infinite wish of our saviour to save all non-Christians with baptism and redemption. We will not engage in any struggle with any being upon the road and any quarrels will result in immediate expulsion from the order, the stripping of garb and weapon, to leave you a naked pilgrim upon the path of penance... an unnamed hermit. Is that understood?"

For most of the squires it was a terrifying prospect, given up by their families they were too young and too unaware of the world beyond their training and their cloister-like life to know the dangers out there. They knew no other life after-all, they had been abandoned by their families to the church and that was all they were prepared for. But for those well-versed in the life of a warrior, having to tent out in the desert or find shelter in the wilds and hunt, this was nothing fearful, just shameful. The knights all saluted before informing their master that they would obey him, the Hochmeister, the Emperor and the Papacy... those two having to be shoved in together... in order to aid the followers of Christ and spread the true nature of God. It was the usual departing holler before everyone gathered up and then the marching began. Meinhardt was pulled near the front with his ridiculous canine, which Balk seemed to pat and muse over its daft face and Dietrich rode beside Leonhard and the youngsters.

The first hour of marching was oddly quiet, aside from the occasional Ordained members choosing to break the seeming determined nature of the march with some light preaching to remind them of their purpose. After this first hour, the squires began their usual quibbles, chattering amongst themselves over what to expect or grumbling about how long they were supposed to march carrying everything with them! They were going to be incredibly frustrating for the rest of the day and Leonhard warned them all that men on foot would do better to check their breathing than anything else. After three hours the squires were really grumbling, and the knights and their men were all grumbling as well about how many days they would be travelling for.... They would probably be unhappy to know it would be as good as a month of travel if not more because of the mountains. For a knight riding with two horses, it would be half that time almost, Meinhardt had done it in twenty-one days because of various stops, but he tended to only rest as long as his horses needed and with the dog it probably had reduced things a bit. All the same, the first break was a chance to share water from a fresh stream that was running nearby, let the horses graze and of course dismount.

There was the usual bolt towards the latrine and as usual, the squires had to be reminded not to urinate near the river or they'd be drinking it. A few squires had still bolted towards the river, but Meinhardt had sent Igel out to chase them off and they obeyed before the dog rushed through the brush. There was a series of calamitous barking, the other dogs came rushing over and then there was an ear-splitting shriek and everyone emptying themselves were nearly bolting into the river or up trees. Backsides and bits were on display as Igel came galloping towards Meinhardt with a shrieking boar piglet in his mouth and its mother charging out after him. It was enough for a real riot until Udolf grabbed a spear and in one slamming thrust the sow was down and he whistled for the rest of the hunting dogs and their men to gather the rest of the piglets for their evening meal.

Balk was not exactly pleased for the disruption, but the food was welcomed and as everyone prepared to walk on, the boar were gathered, stuck and then put in a cart pulled by some very bulky looking horses that snorted as they dragged other supplies on. Igel though got the ear from the sow to race around and show off to the other dogs before he lunged onto Klobig's back, sitting perfectly upon the big fat hips of the old gelding a panting with his bloody maw looking right towards Dietrich further back. It was hardly a pleasant sight but, that was only one of Igel's little quirks as they marched on until dark and then made camp, everyone ate and then were settled to their tents and Dietrich and Meinhardt had a tent to themselves!

"Another night together… we must be getting very lucky indeed, Husband." Dietrich whispered softly into Meinhardt's ears as the sounds of the other knights and men-at-arms scowling and grumbling about blisters filled the air. He kept his voice low and snuffed out their candle as Meinhardt had shuddered in excitement. They could not do much in this sort of situation but to be able to sleep beside each other in a private little spot again was precious and whenever Dietrich referred to Meinhardt as his husband, you could see the hairs of his body lift and he was quite sure he heard the sound of blood flushing to

Meinhardt's organ. It seemed to be their cheeky little trick with one another to entice and Meinhardt had barely pulled off his tunic before he rolled right onto Meinhardt, pinning him beneath him. They were glad the candle was out, no one could clearly see what they were doing and Meinhardt could easily grab something and make out he was trying to strangle Dietrich again, but instead his body began to grind against Dietrich's as he grasped his shoulders. "I didn't mean to set you off like you were in rut!"

"I'm in rut whenever I'm with you… Hengst…" Meinhardt nuzzled his face into Dietrich's chest, kissing and nipping at the top of his chest where garments would cover their marks. He continued to grind his hardened body against Dietrich's watching his partner's face clench up softly as he stifled his breath to stop himself moaning out in pleasure as they pressed their bodies together. When Meinhardt then paused to bend forward and kiss his lips firmly, Dietrich's hands wrapped about his blonde crop of hair, holding Meinhardt to him in soft, snorty kisses as they trembled against one another. Then Meinhardt slid his hand down to grasp at Dietrich's thick form, squeezing at his balls to make him gasp before gently pushing his hand to Dietrich's mouth so he could lick and suck and bite if he needed as he whispered to him. "My turn to be a little dangerous…"

Dietrich made a mumble about him being a bastard, knowing full well this was about a situation in Sicily where they'd been at a latrine at night on routine marching missions and Dietrich had been a little ridiculous. Meinhardt had gone with the light to help keep watch for trouble as Dietrich had relieved himself against a tree before kneeling into a bush. When a cold wind had knocked out the light on the candle and Meinhardt had fumbled to the bush, he'd been grabbed, his hose yanked down and Dietrich had made him feel not only good but they'd almost been caught by the next person. Meinhardt had needed to pretend he was pissing in the bush because then no-one could leap out at him! It had been very risky… very stupid and Dietrich had been punched in the gut afterwards and Meinhardt had stormed off, leaving him to wander in the dark and Dietrich had found a delightful cactus to walk into! Meinhardt had a good memory for these things and as he kissed Dietrich's eyes to make him sigh, he slid his hand down and began to slowly squeeze and stroke the form below, grinning down to see Dietrich drool against his hand and feel his pulse quickening thanks to the throbbing within.

They could have been enjoying themselves quite a while with the way

Meinhardt teased, paused to kiss and grope before massaging again to make Dietrich's face go red, but for a sound by the tent. Meinhardt's hand was yanked away and he rolled onto his front, Dietrich forced to do the same and grimace in agony. There was the familiar sound of Siegfried at the tent, he asked if he could come in for a second and as Meinhardt grumbled they'd been sleeping, the young knight let himself in and brought with him… Igel. Rather than greet his master, the big dog barged onto Dietrich, snuffing at him firmly and then barging his nose somewhere he was not wanted. Dietrich's response was automatic, thumping the dog so he gave a squeal and launched sideways into Siegfried, pulling the tent clean over. As it collapsed, Meinhardt was up in a flash to chase his upset dog, yelling that Dietrich had been very unkind and Siegfried was left flat on his back, only to have Dietrich throw a blanket over him with a grunt.

"I think I hate that dog…"

The next ten days of marching was focused and harsh, during this time they came to their first set of mountains to cross and wild winds meant there was little sleep and a risk of losing people. But the crossing was swift as pained feet were forgotten ahead of getting out of there as fast as possible. By the end of a fortnight, they were in sight of more familiar mountains and roads that passed through to Bavaria and Thuringia, then northward towards Bohemia and Masovia. Thuringia was their stopping point, wedged alongside the two other kingdoms and where they would reach a good deal of supplies and a chance to heal up any wounds and give the squires a little more calm before they were taken to the chilly north. Thankfully, as it was spring the passes through the mountains were clear for the most part, but rain made some areas treacherous and thick mist had clung about so some parties had been separated and some fellows had made the mistake of falling to darkness.

It was during this time that Igel ended up the favoured beast of the entire march; when people were missing, he was sent to fetch them and he'd drag horses back by the reins or nipping their heels, pull humans back too. Thankfully, aside from a few accidents to cut down some of the number of men-at-arms and squires, the unit was not separated, and that dog could find any prey in the wilderness and would carry it back. He was also an excellent guard dog, when wolves howled out in the darkest part of the night, he would bark back ferociously until the howling stopped and everyone was sure that they were safe with him on watch. He also had a fondness for licking blister-covered feet and this had a curious habit of making them less painful and heal just a tad faster, not to mention he'd mark any hard boots he found so blisters and sores from harsh boots were practically forgotten. He was very useful and everyone adored him… except Dietrich.

During the journey, Dietrich had been very glad that Sigmond and Franz were leading the men-at-arms on so that he was not working with the squires and separated, but it meant he was separate from Meinhardt too. Balk was in constant conversation with him, brushing up his Polish and asking for more details on the situation with the natives. Meinhardt was never lonely with Igel and barely went to look to Dietrich unless there was an issue with the squires. It made Dietrich very disconcerted that the damn dog was getting far more attention from his husband than he was! Most of the time Dietrich was sleeping huddled beside some of the more terrified of the squires who were practically children and would cuddle up to him for some extra warmth and strength. Leonhard and Siegfried would do the same beside him, the group all huddled together against the fierce winds until they broke out to the areas of the mountains into Bavaria. Here there were wider patches for proper campsites and the farmers and hunters were German and eager to greet *their* knights and even join the sermons that occurred eight times a day as usual, although with soldiers still marching as they were spoken to by a priest riding a mule.

On the evening when they were about to break out of the strong shadow of the Alps and follow a common road through to Thuringia, Dietrich and Meinhardt had their own tent together again and this time they were the only men in a tent as a nearby woodsman had offered his household and his barn for their use. Balk had settled the squires here with Leonhard and Siegfried and Udolf in charge of them. He'd sent Sigmond and the men-at-arms further down the pathway to reach the road ahead of them and everyone else was settled down, but for a few of the knights who were on guard with one or two squires joining them. Dietrich and Meinhardt however were just uphill from the barn, a little group of squires not too far away around a fire keeping watch with Igel and the horses. As always, the pair dropped into their underwear and pulled the blankets tightly about themselves before knocking out the light and waiting until they knew there was the sound of settling down and that no one was walking near their tent and then, they were quickly holding onto one another and kissing and groping each other with low moans of utter delight.

"You were really quite adorable with the squires... it makes me sad we could not have children together... but we will raise these squires as our own... oh, and we have Igel." Meinhardt purred in a soft whisper as he nuzzled against Dietrich's broad chest, looking as if he might just fall asleep then and there, he was so comfortable. Dietrich had to admit that they were both refreshingly warm lying next to each other when the spring air was still so bitterly cold, but the mention of that dog made his face slip into a sneer. There was no way on God's earth that Dietrich would ever look at a dog as anything but a servant... certainly not as a substitute child after all the chaos he'd caused. Even during the mountains he'd appeared out of nowhere, his face leaning against Dietrich's side when he'd been on foot and smeared his body in drool. He'd also constantly appeared whenever Dietrich had been relieving himself and seemed to want to use the same patch... clearly, he thought Dietrich was Meinhardt's property! Meinhardt though just leant upward to kiss Dietrich's lip in a neat little peck as he gave a soft chuckle. "It's quiet, it's getting late and I think it might be safe..."

"And you're still in heat..." Dietrich muttered softly, only to receive a soft clap to the shoulder before suddenly Meinhardt was up and turning about upon him. Dietrich gave a few soft mumbles and grunts as suddenly Meinhardt's knees were bashing his face and he was trying to angle himself upon Dietrich in a way they could both enjoy. Dietrich gave a few growls as he got a knee to his chin to make him bite his lip, Meinhardt though turned about to hiss at him to be quiet and just stay still, which was easier said than done! Meinhardt then shifted his breeches down, only to smother Dietrich's face as he almost spat the fabric out and then Meinhardt turned about to grunt at him as he growled. "Get your drawers off, I'm not going to rest my head in cloths that haven't been changed in a week! They stink!"

"And you smell like a spring blossom I'm sure... fine, just, if anything happens I was airing them, alright?" Meinhardt grunted, lifting a leg that prodded at their tent posts and made Dietrich grimace in fear he might just knock the whole thing down. Thankfully he did not, but with his breeches thrown across the tent, he was blushing hideously as a cold breeze from the flap seemed aimed perfectly to tickle his bared and vulnerable backside. He made a few complaints about Dietrich always getting his head by the tent opening as he then jerked Dietrich's breeches down and teased his fat length out. Dietrich was soon sighing in pleasure as he felt Meinhardt stroking his body again, luring the shaft up to full height with his hands before he began to lather it with his tongue. Meinhardt moaned rather loudly, enjoying the tingling in his body from kissing at this form and sighing as his mouth engulfed it and irked a sharp little sound from Dietrich. He worked away, his own form rigid just from having this much control and contact with his lover again and Dietrich tried not to just stretch out and moan away.

Clearly there was a reason for this awkward positioning and Dietrich's hands stretched under Meinhardt's squatting form and gently began to stroke and squeeze the exposed jewels of his lover. It caused a sudden jolt in Meinhardt's longer form, making his arousal clearer as Dietrich slid his hand down to the shaft and then began to tug and tease it free from the covering flesh. Meinhardt moaned in his throat, pushing his chest further against Dietrich's body, pushing his mate's length further into his throat as Dietrich's hips twitched in reaction. Dietrich's hand slid down to the head of his husband's length, feeling the dew already spitting out to say Meinhardt was so aroused he would not need too much work to give pleasure to, and so Dietrich continued to stroke at him whilst lifting up his groin and gritting his teeth with each moan.

As Meinhardt's mouth made strange moaning sounds that were almost hollow, his face so flushed his cheeks looked to be burning as he sucked strongly and moaned pitifully, Dietrich groaned. He could feel his end coming much quicker than he could control and with it his senses as his head felt dizzy and his throat felt wet and dry all at once as if he might just choke on air. He knew these signals, but he needed to give Meinhardt just a little more and so he stroked at his lover, pulling his form downward rather than upward, urging it to sit back though Meinhardt grimaced and then shifted his legs, trying to pull his body back a little more so he could be closer to Dietrich's face. Dietrich grimaced, bending his chest forward, feeling Meinhardt's body awkward to navigate with as he strained forward with a grunt and then just strained out his tongue, lapping at whatever flesh he could reach, which seemed to only be the bottom of Meinhardt's thighs, but was enough for Meinhardt's hips to jiggle with pleasure.

"Dieter…" Meinhardt whimpered softly, pulling the slippery form of his lover from his mouth as he continued to squeeze and rub his thumb against the tip all the same as Dietrich's hips jolted, rubbing his form up and down within the grip of his hand. Dietrich moaned as he leant to lap more at Meinhardt's body, his own hand still stroking and grasping at his lover. When Meinhardt then managed to regain enough composure to suckle at his lover again, Dietrich managed to lean his mouth forward and then, just as he reached his climax, he gave a clumsy motion to stifle his cry and accidentally bit the bottom of Meinhardt's backside. It could not have been a luckier point for Dietrich, his lover's mouth drowned as he choked his yelp and his own excitement caked Dietrich's chest. Dietrich flopped back with a funny moan, almost groaning like he was ill and hoping that Meinhardt was not going to kill him for this, but he heard that hideously deep growling sound.

Meinhardt swung his body away from him, his backside now bearing a bright red pinch that was stinging enough Meinhardt was crying, but his fury was overtaking the whimper of pain. His face was messy but in the darkness Dietrich could not see it as his husband prowled over to his side with his body taking on the curious stalking mannerisms of a wild cat. He pushed his hand to Dietrich's throat, grasping him and making him give a gasp before Meinhardt then smashed his mouth to Dietrich's, spitting something into it to make Dietrich suddenly want to vomit before Meinhardt then let him be. He made a show of swallowing what was left in his mouth before yanking his breeches back on and turning his body away from Dietrich. Dietrich had sat up, choking and trying to decide whether to spit or swallow or just vomit, knowing he deserved that for biting Meinhardt and yet quite sure he did not. He dropped a hand to his chest, realising it was stained and he gave a swear, shifting up to grab some old rag he could spit into until he heard the soft footfalls of a creature and the tent open behind him.

Dietrich slowly bent his head back, unable to see in the dark but hearing the familiar grumbling snuffles of that damned dog. No sooner had he spotted the outline of the dumb head, then suddenly the dog's tongue and lips were slapping over Dietrich's face. He groaned in horror, seemingly smothered as Igel thought to lap his face and Dietrich was forced to swallow so he could cry out for help, only to open his mouth and get drooled upon. As he choked and gurgled, Meinhardt sat up and then grabbed some cloth, wiping the slobber from the dog's mouth and pulling his head away as he babied at him and Dietrich was left trembling and mentally scarred by this wretched beast. Dietrich soon gained enough traction to wipe his chest, jerk up his breeches but make a show as he left the tent to find a latrine, only to vomit whilst he was out there and find himself being brought some watered-down wine from a squire; he made it clear it was the dog. The squire had chuckled at him and Dietrich had then settled back to the tent, only to find the dog lounging on his bed, Meinhardt snoring in sleep and the dog's tail wagging in delight to see Dietrich returning.

"Oh no… we're not sharing…" Dietrich grabbed the leather collar, jerking the dog out and Igel followed with a heavy pant and wagging tail as he let him go. Dietrich then stepped right into the tent again, only to find Igel follow him in, then he pushed the dog over towards Meinhardt. The dog stared at Dietrich like a harlequin or court jester, that same dumbfounded expression that knew exactly what it was doing and just waiting for Dietrich to crack. When he pointed to the end of the tent, the lanky dog marched over to Meinhardt's feet, snuffing at his toes as Meinhardt snorted and then Dietrich gave a groan. He slumped back under his blanket, cuddled close to Meinhardt and then gave a grunt of agony as Igel stood up, stood on Dietrich's thigh and then flopped onto his back right between them. The dog made a few groans, wiggling his great long legs about and automatically Meinhardt threw his blanket over the dog and tickled at his chest. The dog turned his panting face about, blowing his stinking breath into Dietrich's face and expecting him to stroke him too. Dietrich groaned, pulling the blanket over his head and snarling as he rolled to the other side, only to have the great long legs of the dog flop onto his back to make him grunt. "I hate you, dog."

The morning came and everyone was up fast, Dietrich had bags under his eyes and was looking utterly exhausted as he mounted his horse and the stallion seemed to be giving him a funny expression as if he was humoured. As they all began to move and Meinhardt was back at the front with Balk, the squire to have spotted him that night dared to ask how he'd slept. Dietrich had opened his mouth and was about to say something, when out of nowhere the dog lunged up onto the horse and lay himself like a dead doe across Dietrich's lap, his tail wagging and his tongue lolling. The horse turned back, nipping Dietrich's kneecap in punishment as Igel just continued to wag his tail and look up at Dietrich lovingly. All thoughts on being Meinhardt's property was now replaced with the thought of being Igel's property instead as he shook his head in frustration and they continued on.

The next few days were far more comfortable for marching and the squires felt refreshed to be back within the Empire, just as Dietrich and the others were content breathing in the familiar scent of their homelands. The music of the wind through the trees was like the laughter of children, joyful and greatly loved as they travelled on with relief to be somewhere that seemed so familiar and so beloved. They felt happiness and there were few complaints over blisters, instead about having to leave familiar flowers and good-looking women behind, which only meant they were rather beaten about the head by everyone from Sigmond to Dietrich to Meinhardt to Balk for suggesting such a thing. It was upon arriving within Thuringia that everything seemed to have a brighter ray of sunshine for Dietrich as they were welcomed in by the household of the duchy to have produced the Hochmeister and Heinrich. Here there was a lot of food offered, a lot of friendship and a lot of moments where everyone felt like they were in the bosom of family rather than just friends of the Order. It was pleasant and joyful and then, Sigmond approached Dietrich in the night when he was alone in a room given to him that he was preparing for himself and Meinhardt. The dog had chosen to follow him in, in fact Igel was sitting on Dietrich's bunk annoying him as Sigmond had come in and slouched against the doorway, closing the door behind him and making Dietrich jump.

"You've got some curiously bad luck, Dieter… everyone else is being allowed to stay here longer to build up their strength and resources and gather mercenaries but you and your Northerner get tonight. Then you're both bolting off with no one else to go and bring news to von Landsburg that he needs to meet us in Masovia for the meeting and proper treaty. How am I supposed to fulfil my debt to you if I can't fight beside you?" Sigmond was looking rather sickly, there were rumours from the men that had travelled with him that he'd been up to his usual bad deeds and dared to claim some 'old toy' for the locals in some God forsaken village that had born strange markings on her body that were linked to a sickness… one linked to the vice of lust. Sigmond looked unpleasant and was bearing one of these strange red marks upon his shoulder and he stank of festering, he was due to be given treatment from the surgeon for it, but it was enough of a smell to make Dietrich feel sick, though he was happy for his assignment.

"You've given me the message, Meinhardt's fetching the documents and that's all I need from you, Brother Sigmond. Do yourself a favour and leave now, you do not need to protect me… I would rather you pay your debt by leaving me alone." Dietrich grimaced in frustration, but as he continued to adjust the bedding for Meinhardt, Sigmond stepped forward and put his hand to Dietrich's back. He pushed him firmly right onto the bed suddenly straddling him and pushing Dietrich's face into the cloth to muffle his sounds as Sigmond growled at him to shut up already.

"You just never keep your mouth shut, do you? I'm taking what you owe for my silence… then I'll leave you alone…" Sigmond hissed in frustration as he pushed Dietrich so firmly into the fabric, he could not breathe for the cloth fibres filling his mouth. His hands were flapping and slapping back, trying to push Sigmond away, kicking about with his legs as Sigmond growled and grasped at Dietrich's breeches, jerking them downward as Dietrich pulled his head up to cry out just a simple 'N' before his face was smacked back into the pillow. But this was enough for Igel to realise that Dietrich was in danger and he stood right up and let out the most aggressive booming bark at Sigmond. He barked three times, growling between and then even making a howling sound, alerting everyone to danger and Sigmond pulled back immediately, not sure what to do but quick to hear feet marching towards them and Meinhardt calling out to the dog. Sigmond moved towards Dietrich, testing what the dog would do but the animal lunged at him with a snarl and Sigmond got the door open and fell onto the ground as the dog jumped him, barking into his face furiously.

"Igel! Igel! Get off, go on get back inside. Sorry Brother Sigmond, Igel must have thought you were trying to steal his bed. He didn't bite you? No… off you go then, the surgeon's come to look at your… wounds." Meinhardt spoke calmly and softly, almost wickedly as the dog relaxed and sat back into the doorway. Udolf came around the corner with another one of the more senior knights and they overheard the conversation as Sigmond insisted that they were both fine. As the knight then left, Meinhardt stepped into the room, listening to Dietrich panting in relief as Igel then bolted to him, whimpering and lapping at Dietrich's hands lovingly as Dietrich looked up at him with a groan before patting his nose. "Dieter… did he hurt you? Your… your face is pale and your… by the Devil your clothes… he tried to… he tried…"

"And this blasted dog saved me when he realised it was not a game. Ugh… I refute everything I've said about him… you're a good boy Igel!" Dietrich rolled onto his backside, sitting on the floor and accepting the cold stone to his bared flesh with a sigh of relief before the dog nuzzled his face and gave a joyous bark. Meinhardt then flopped onto his knees, hooking his arms around Dietrich and nuzzling against him as he kissed his ear. "I hope Sigmond gets ripped apart by wolves!"

Four: An Unruly Introduction to Culmerland

"We've passed through Masovia and you've done nothing more than shove us into the middle of a very large marsh and I'm blaming all of this on you." Dietrich groaned, waist-deep in a steaming, stinking swamp with Meinhardt also stuck upon his front, but sniggering into the moist, squelching mess over it all. On the grassy edge of the quagmire, the two horses were grazing calmly and Igel was dragging about Dietrich's sword within its scabbard, trying to find somewhere suitable to bury it. Dietrich was miserable, muddy, soggy and thankfully he was able to breathe but his arms could not stretch close enough to the shore to pull himself out and to be fair, he was fuming. Meinhardt had insisted he could navigate this bog and it was the safest route to get through to the castle without the natives attacking them, but it had all gone awry when Dietrich's stubborn stallion had decided he had not wanted to move. When Dietrich had charged ahead through the squelching mud, dragging the stallion by the reins, the animal had pivoted and bolted back, dragging the already sinking knight through the muck until he was chest-deep and the horse was grazing.

Meinhardt had been fine at first, coming over to the safe edge of the swamp and taking Dietrich's sword and belt to try and give him a boost out, only for Igel to assume it was a game. The dog stole the sword, but only after bouncing off Meinhardt and sending him face-first into the mud. Meinhardt had been in uncontrollable hysterics for the past ten minutes and thankfully, fury over his amusement was enough to stop Dietrich from panicking. The horses were still content and finally, as the giggling subsided, Meinhardt pulled his own muddy body up from the ground… his back might be white but the front of his uniform was all brown now as he sniggered. He then whistled gently to Klobig and the big old gelding lifted his head, staring at Meinhardt in boredom as he chewed away on his grass before he was beckoned over. With a seeming shrug, he plodded forward and then barged his face into Meinhardt's shoulder as his master loosened the reins.

"I know… you can blame me, Igel hasn't been here before and he didn't know you were in trouble… he's just excited because it stinks of wolves out here. There you go, take both of Klobig's reins and when I start pushing him back, try and walk upward out of the mud. It'll take a little bit of strength, but if the worst happens, I'll get the reins, tie them to you, then to your stallion and scare him!" Meinhardt snorted as he swung the leather bonds to Dietrich, and he grasped them with a sneer. This marsh stunk; it was no wonder conversions were not going well when this was the kind of terrain they were dealing with. Elsewhere it was springtime, but here there seemed a permanent misty rain, the flowers were dull and hidden amongst the thick woodlands in tiny meadows and there was an ungodly feel to the place. It was not like home, those forests were alive and bright and sung with birds, here it seemed oddly silent but for the distant sound of the Vistula and the occasional clacking, throaty call of grouse. "Alright, you've got it? Let's go!"

Dietrich groaned as he tried to lift his heavy legs, glad Klobig was helping as the old bulky horse just paced back steadily, one hoof at a time without too much strain so that Dietrich could slide and slip upward. Meinhardt steadily barged himself into the front of the rather stubborn old animal, it did not really need the coaxing but liked to think that it was getting some kind of payback for having to walk so long. As Klobig stepped further and further back, Verbrecher lifted his head from grazing nearby and spotted Dietrich emerging from the muck and was fascinated. The stallion stepped over, his soft velvety muzzle snuffing and sniffing about Dietrich's ears before then nipping at his cloak, making Dietrich grumble that the horses were enjoying his predicament far too much. Eventually one foot made it to the edge of the mud and he flopped forward and bumped into the side of the big grey, which produced a soft snort of boredom before turning back to graze as Dietrich patted his hip in thanks before marching to his stallion.

"You... you... you are as much a pain in my arse as Meinhardt..." Dietrich grunted as he grabbed the reins, the black horse rolling its eyes to show the whites in a sign of disrespect as Meinhardt gave a grunt. The stallion though behaved when there was a sudden sound of rustling in the reeds and scrub nearby and both Dietrich and Meinhardt froze in anxiety. Last night they'd both been alerted to the close howling of a wolfpack and Dietrich's struggling could easily have drawn in such predators, besides... Igel had disappeared off bouncing away after dropping Dietrich's sword and it meant he was not properly armed. As they stepped together, the pair of them turned about slowly with Meinhardt's hand to the hilt of his sword as they heard the familiar drawing of bowstrings and they both gulped. Their eyes peered through the low-lying evening mists and they spotted the shifting figures of men within the edges of the quagmire and Meinhardt gave a soft gulp, alerting Dietrich to the fact they'd walked into a pagan trap. "Oh well… at least we die together…"

But perhaps God was not quite done with the pair just yet and had a few ideas left for their destiny as something rather startling happened. There was the hideous squealing, screeching roar of something hideous within the woodlands approaching and suddenly the bows were dropped and the half dozen or so natives stood up to see what was coming. Every human present was soon screaming in horror at the sudden squealing, charging swarm of boar rushing straight into the quagmire as fast as possible. They were aimed straight at the pagans and as the figures gave grunts and swears of shock, the boars rammed into and threw them to escape whatever danger had driven them out of the woodland. Dietrich leapt from Meinhardt, grabbed his horse and launched onto the horse just as Meinhardt copied and the pair kicked their terrified horses straight back into the cover of the woodland, hurrying deep within before they dismounted and dropped down amongst the bushes. They were both glad now to be coated in mud as their white raiment was less visible and the horses wandered off to find somewhere to graze, which would steer the enemy away from them.

They waited patiently, expecting the creature to have chased the boars to appear from nowhere and devour everything in its paths. There were stories of dragons haunting these regions and other hideous monsters that the pagans worshipped, but even the natives had appeared stunned. Grabbing their wounded companions and looking as petrified as the knights had been, the group had thought to cut their losses and head back to where they felt they were safe. Clearly there must be an encampment nearby and when Dietrich and Meinhardt continued waiting for the monster, they were both rather confused by the sudden reappearance of Igel. Indeed, the big mastiff trotted right to where Dietrich was lying under some thick brush and sat firmly over his hips, panting and looking like he'd been up to something as Dietrich gave a grunt and then Meinhardt gave a groan.

"Hey now Igel… the only one allowed to sit on Dietrich is daddy… come here puppy… did you chase the boars out and save us? Yes, you did, didn't you?" Meinhardt was cooing as he sat up and patted his thighs, the big dog bolting off Dietrich to make him give a grunt as he hurried to his master.

Suddenly he was pulled into Meinhardt's arms, snuggling the great animal as Dietrich rolled onto his back and then began to cackle for a little while over the stupidity of this dog and yet his amazing ability to just be useful. Then Meinhardt pulled himself upward and beckoned for the horses to come back with a soft whistle, Klobig plodding over to his side and that damn black stallion plodded over as well with a hideous snort of irritation. Dietrich stood up and grabbed him and then gave a soft groan of concern.

"We need to get out of here as fast as possible Meinhardt, those pagans will be back very quickly I'm sure, so we need to get on and find somewhere safe to camp for the night!" Dietrich grumbled as he mounted his horse, only to feel a horrid damp squelch in the saddle and a hideously cold sensation settle within his groin. It reminded him very hideously of when he had dysentery and he grimaced in frustration as he looked towards Meinhardt and then suddenly Igel launched onto his lap again, making the stallion snort and spin his head around to try and bite either dog or man. Meinhardt nodded his head, urging Klobig over and then giving Dietrich a firm pat on the back with a grin of delight before encouraging him that he knew the perfect place. Then, to Dietrich's relief, Meinhardt took his reins and lashed them to Klobig's saddle so he could teach the colt a thing or two about being a better-behaved horse whilst Dietrich grasped the dog as they charged on.

After two hours at a steady canter through the woods, the darkness of the night was starting to close in around them and stars were visible in the clear sky above as the cold began to grip them again and Meinhardt began to slow Klobig down. There was the sight of a village not too far away and though Dietrich was quick to assume it was some kind of enemy, Meinhardt gave him a grin and urged the horses on. They moved onto a clear path in the dirt towards the village, the horses plodding along as Igel was fast asleep beside in Dietrich's arms and Dietrich's body ached! As they entered the sight of the village, a small set of thatch buildings, and though Dietrich was trembling, grasping the hilt of his sword in preparation for danger, Meinhardt remained confident as a figure stepped out from the only stone building they reached in the whole village… a church!

"Father Constantine… its Brother Meinhardt of the German Knight's Order, sorry for the rude interruption, we were overwhelmed in the marsh and just escaped… but do you have room for us to sleep here tonight?" Meinhardt stated calmly to the figure in heavy, thick black clerical robs that stepped out from the stone building, a great crucifix made of wood hanging down his chest and his expression rather content until he spotted the knight. He seemed to stare at the pair of them, the dog and the amount of mud in total confusion before his big grey eyes widened and he quickly ushered them to dismount and come, not into the church, but into a small wooden shed near a building on the other side. A gentleman dressed in peasant's garb but looking tired and frustrated, looked towards the pair and gave a groan before suddenly throwing wood into a large fire and then taking several buckets away to fill them with water. Meinhardt though waved a hand at him. "Hello Johann... glad to see you're still wearing your crucifix and being a good convert even without your tongue!"

"Brother Meinhardt, please do not remind Johann of his penance... he has been a faithful Christian and though we are all grateful you and your Commander showed him leniency in not killing him like you did his father, you should not aggravate him when he is clearly being helpful." Constantine was Polish and he spoke in that language, which Meinhardt seemed to have total grasp over where Dietrich just stared from one to the other with a grimace of confusion as Igel tried to lap at his face in delight. Constantine was not looking at Dietrich at all as he beckoned Meinhardt to dismount, taking the reins from Klobig and patting at Meinhardt's shoulders. "Strip off and scrub yourselves down, there's only one tub but I will help gather the water and then when you're both clean, there are some robes I can lay out for you and you can come inside, have bread and water and sleep within the chapel. The horses and the dog will be fine out here."

"I'm very grateful, if Dieter here hadn't gotten stuck in the mud for a good while, we'd probably not have been stuck in a bad situation and ridden on through the night... but I think my southern friend is too cold... too use to the Sicilian climate!" Meinhardt snorted softly as he urged Igel off Dietrich's body and insisted he wait outside and be on guard. He then beckoned Dietrich to dismount and Constantine nodded his head before going to fetch water and Meinhardt insisted he would do the same so that his companion could be dealt with first. Indeed, Dietrich was trembling and grimacing upon his horse as he was beckoned off and when he dismounted and the damn black stallion was handed over, Meinhardt ushered Dietrich inside with a grin upon his face. "Get in here, see this wooden tub, big enough for two so you and me are going to bath together... I've always wondered what that would be like..."

"Incredibly smelly…" Dietrich grimaced, as he gave Meinhardt a firm look to say that it would certainly not be a romantic experience. Dietrich though stepped into the room, glad of the fire and quickly he shed his raiment as that appeared to be the smart course of action as he shuddered against the cold and then grit his teeth in fury as he watched Meinhardt gallop off. At least within the building, he did not have to be around the horses or that damned dog and with his clothes off and left to be taken away, save his breeches, Dietrich settled himself down by the fire. He rubbed his hands, scrubbed his shoulders and then groaned gently in frustration as he stared to the tub that was starting to be steadily filled up as Meinhardt shed his cloak and yet was grinning away. Dietrich looked to the callouses forming on his own hands and he gave a sigh as the building was emptied and he then lowered his eyes in sadness. "Eh… once they were so smooth and Meinhardt loved them…"

"I've always loved your hands but try to keep quiet… they know enough German to know when a couple are talking and they're suspicious." Meinhardt had returned faster than Dietrich had expected, and he was bright red in shock as Meinhardt then gently kissed his ear to make him jump in surprise. Dietrich was quickly huddling up within his breeches, feeling embarrassed over the fact that he'd been caught out speaking aloud to himself. Dietrich settled himself upon the floor for a while, breathing in deeply and trying to relax as he thought about the situation up here and just what he was likely to experience in this anxious looking place. Dietrich gave a sigh of frustration as he felt the cold reaching his body and watched as the wooden structure was being filled up with water. When it was eventually filled and Dietrich was more warmed up by the fire, the other gentlemen left and then Meinhardt stripped himself down right to the skin and patted at the tub. "Alright Dieter… hop in!"

"Alright… but it won't be romantic…" Dietrich scoffed softly as he shuffled out of his briefs and then calmly he pulled himself into the tub, which was only a little bit warmer than the cold water and shuddered as he dropped himself down and then groaned. He slouched into the liquid and watched the clear water turn mucky and brown as he groaned again before scrubbing at his body roughly. He pulled the water up in his hands, splashing it into his face to try and clean his beard and the rest of him that was covered in mud. Meinhardt waited for one more boiled bucket of water, beckoned Dietrich to shift to the side before pouring it in as Dietrich gave a soft little bleat at first. Then Meinhardt chuckled as he pulled himself into the water with a splash, dirt falling from his body as he then flopped onto Dietrich who gave a grunt at him. "Meinhardt!"

"Just a quick cuddle and a kiss… then I'll settle back down." Meinhardt chuckled as he looped his arms around Dietrich's shoulders, ignoring the hand pushed to his face to try and stop him as Meinhardt snuggled about him tightly. When Dietrich moved his hand, their cheeks were soon pressing together as Meinhardt grabbed at his lover's beard, musing that he'd managed to keep it quite clean considering as their lips pressed to each other gently. Then they locked their arms about each other tightly, holding themselves together lovingly as their lips clamped onto one another and they moaned against each other before Meinhardt pulled back. He stroked at Dietrich's hair, feeling for the scar hidden beneath as his blue eyes locked lovingly into Dietrich's own eyes and their lips came together softly again before Meinhardt purred. "You sure it is not going to be romantic?"

"The water is the colour of the quagmire and the longer we're here, the more it will start to resemble the place we just escaped… I don't think the priest would be pleased if the mud set in around us and locked us in this position." Dietrich stated with a sour expression although he sighed as he felt those familiar hard-worked hands stroking his face. He had to hold one quickly to his lips to kiss at those rough little patches before he lowered his hand and then their lips came together softly before Dietrich clapped at Meinhardt's hips. It got him not only a grunt but a gentle thump to the head for touching when he was not allowed to! Meinhardt sat back down and the pair continued to scrub away at themselves until the water started to get quite grotty and cool. Dietrich then pulled himself up out of the water, only to fall straight onto the floor with a grunt after giving a yelp because someone had dared to poke him somewhere rude. "Bastard…"

"Did you bite your lip? Sorry Dieter but I couldn't resist it when you climb out of a tub so… curiously." Meinhardt was grinning as he continued to splash about for a little more and then Dietrich seemed to rear up from the back of the tub, fury visible within his face. Meinhardt turned to look at him cautiously before he was suddenly grabbed at the back of the head and forced down into the water. It was only as he choked and spluttered and slapped about that Dietrich let him go and the pair growled and swore at each other until the mute man stepped in again with the available cassocks. Dietrich apologised, covering himself behind the tub before taking the robes as Meinhardt mused the fellow did not know a lick of German. All the same, Meinhardt got out and he pulled the robes on as well before they followed the fellow back into the church and were allowed to settle down to sleep. Meinhardt was quick to snore away, but Dietrich remained on alert… unlike his companion nothing about this landscape felt safe to just sleep, not even in a church!

When morning came, Dietrich had passed out and was being gently nuzzled about the face, he gave a grumble, swatting his hand aside and almost told Meinhardt off until he heard the heavy panting of a dog. Dietrich sat up with a growl, pushing Igel off him. The dog gave a booming bark and then galloped out of the church to where Meinhardt greeted him with some strokes and pats for him fetching Dietrich. Meinhardt was fully dressed in his knightly raiment and looking ready to go before he turned about and spotted Dietrich looking exhausted. With a groan, Dietrich pulled himself back off from the floor and then practically jumped in shock to find the priest hovering nearby and holding onto his clothes. When the pair eyed each other cautiously, the priest then gave a soft sigh of frustration before pushing the clothes into Dietrich's arms and pointing back towards the familiar shed as Dietrich grimaced… clearly they were not very fond of him here.

Dietrich dressed as swiftly as he could within the shed, rubbing at his cut lip and then grimacing that he was so shaken and frustrated after one bad day in this strange place. Once he was dressed he opened the door only to find Igel waiting to jump on him, coating his white cloak in muddy paws before his face was slurped by that hideously slimy tongue. Dietrich had to grit his teeth not to blaspheme as the dog then bounced away from him and then rushed at the horses, suddenly making the black stallion squeal and skip about in frustration before being steered towards Dietrich. When the stallion then trotted over to the shed and paused, nibbling at Dietrich's shoulder, Igel stopped and gave a playful bounce before galloping off to Meinhardt. Dietrich gave a heavy sigh as he turned to look at the stallion next to him, stroking his muzzle.

"I know… I feel exactly the same way about that dog, but hopefully tonight we'll get to Vogelsang." Dietrich muttered in frustration as he patted the stallion's shoulder and then swiftly mounted, although the animal gave a soft whicker of irritation. Then Dietrich gave him a soft kick, steering him towards Klobig who was grazing beside the worn path through the thatch village with a few flicks of his tail, leaving some free manure to make sure there was grass for next year. As the two horses met up, Meinhardt was still chatting away in Polish and then handing over whatever coins he had on his person to give to them in thanks for their kindness before he beckoned for Dietrich to trot over. Dietrich trotted over, holding out his hand to thank the priest, but the figure turned away from him immediately and instead just said his goodbyes to Meinhardt before he beckoned for Dietrich to follow. The pair of them lined their horses up to one another and began to trot together, hurrying down the path on towards the river that would lead them towards the castle, but Dietrich had to give a grumble. "Why was it they did not even want to acknowledge me?"

"You're accent... even to me it still sounds funny, to them it was hard to tell if you really were German. You're just... too foreign, also those lovely green eyes of yours... they're... they're very handsome and not common out here." Meinhardt grunted, but as he complimented Dietrich his face was suddenly bright red and he lowered his head in utter despair as he grimaced in embarrassment. Dietrich suddenly produced a sound of awe, finding it perhaps the nicest compliment he'd had from Meinhardt in a while, but he swiftly lifted his foot and gave Meinhardt a soft kick in the hip. It made Klobig give a grunt of upset, the two stallions opening their mouths as if to nip at each other before continuing on. Dietrich was suddenly looking towards Meinhardt with a swooning manner to make him go redder as he swatted his hand in Dietrich's face to stop looking at him. But then he hunched into his shoulders and gave a soft blush as he muttered to himself although Dietrich looked even more dreamily towards him. "I... I hope that when we get to the castle, Komtur von Landsberg will allow me to share my room with you. Then... then we can have a room just for us... as if..."

"...as if we were a married pair, is that what you... Meinhardt!" Dietrich chuckled until suddenly, Meinhardt kicked Klobig hard and the gelding began to gallop off in his strange lolloping pace with such a heavy body. Igel gave a bark of excitement and galloped right after the horse, his jowls flapping in the breeze of the chilly morning air with its crisp coolness as Dietrich felt his horse shudder and snort in frustration. He pondered whether he should let the stallion gallop, if only because he did not want to be left behind either and so, gently, Dietrich gave the horse a quick kick and he only needed the slight touch to charge off. Dietrich was soon clenching his legs around the speeding animal, its movement so fast and its legs so long it was soon overtaking Klobig as Meinhardt hollered out to keep following the path. Dietrich heard but he wished he could guarantee slowing down would mean Verbrecher would actually slow and not just stop to throw Dietrich!

As they galloped on, the cold air and the heavy feel of the knight upon his back as well as the uncomfortable sensation of the hard, stiff ground beneath his hooves began to slow the horse. The stallion was getting hungry and there was some green grass approaching them on the left of the track, so he dropped to a trot and then started to slow down, the sound of Dietrich's teeth champing together making his ears strain back in confusion before he paused to start eating. Dietrich was grimacing in pain, the saddle hadn't been strapped on as tightly as it should have been and it had given him a few jolts in the wrong places and he could recall why he'd been taught to stand when a horse went into trot. With a groan he slouched back against the saddle, he dropped a hand to his groin to try and shift the now bruised luggage within as Meinhardt's demonic cackle came cantering down to his ears as Klobig hurried to reach the grass and then Igel came hurrying over with a grunt of fascination.

"There we are Dieter... see that far hill in the distance and that stone structure, that is our new home. On the other side of this river to your right... that is Culmerland." Meinhardt stated firmly and proudly as Dietrich stared at him with a soft blink of confusion before looking back to the track behind them and recalled the marsh and the people there. He had been quite sure they were already within that landscape and quickly he looked towards his companion with a firm expression of confusion. Meinhardt blinked at him in uncertainty for a few moments before realising what he was confused over and Meinhardt quickly slapped his shoulder and pointed back to the hill. "You'll see the actual place called Kulm though they call it something different in Polish, but if its going to be our Order's new spot, it'll have to get used to our name for it. What we were caught out by was probably a raiding party, the kind of things Masovia wants us to get rid of and the best way to do it is raid right back. The Vistula here has a low point that a man can easily get a make-shift bridge over in the winter in the middle of the night or a heavy snowstorm and gallop over to cause chaos before getting back and removing the bridge before the enemies use it!"

"Is that what you've been doing then?" Dietrich gave a soft chuckle of amusement as he looked towards his companion and then Meinhardt gave him a proud sort of look as if he could not think of something to be prouder of... aside from Dietrich's love and his position in the order. It made Dietrich give a soft chuckle of amusement before he stretched out his hand to lay it upon

Meinhardt's arm. There were some things about those tactics that Dietrich did not quite agree to at all himself, but when he noticed the way Meinhardt looked so proud he could not help himself but grip at his arm a little more tightly before giving a soft sigh. "You know I love…"

Suddenly there was the massive fawn coloured dog leaping up and slapping his massive wet tongue across Dietrich's face as he swore out loudly. As Igel then clambered up onto Klobig's hips, Meinhardt was swift to start sniggering with that typical 'kse-kse-kse' sound as Dietrich grimaced and tried to wipe the slime from his face. Meinhardt teased that Igel was a guard against their lusts and Dietrich just glared at the big dog as it lounged, panting happily across the old grey gelding's hips. There was no point making a comment on that matter, Igel had made it quite clear that they were not to be naughty in his presence and then Meinhardt leant across his saddle and caught Dietrich's right eye with a soft kiss.

"I love you too… oh and, welcome to Culmerland!"

Five: The Warm Spring

The weather turned and warm winds finally began to clear the chill from the air and Dietrich learnt that the coming summer was the time to battle the pagans, but not just to raid. It was the time to go out and preach, to offer Christian healing and teachings to all that would listen and like all on the holy mission, step into villages that seemed possible targets of conversion and figure out if they would convert. It doubled as covert operations too, counting how many people, the locations of the villages of pagans and just how many men there were that would fight and women and children that could be sold as slaves. Considering what he had seen with Esther, Dietrich was not too sure he liked the thought of dealing with slaves, but things were busy and thankfully the pair of them were enjoying their time together.

Upon arriving at the castle, they were permitted to share a room, though it included the dog whilst the wind was still cold. Dietrich found himself taking notes to share with the squires and other troops soon to catch up with them and learnt too that there was a lot more Polish being talked around here than German. Only the squires from Thuringia seemed to have the difficulty in speaking the language and so Dietrich would sit with them when Meinhardt was out and try to learn the language with them. It was a difficult language and his own accent made it even more awkward... Danish seemed far less awkward in comparison, but Meinhardt tried to help him and they were amused to have a reverse situation with one another.

But there was something very pleasant that occurred because of their time sharing the room; though Igel made it damn awkward to do much more, they were able to embrace and kiss to say goodnight to each other. To have that ritual, some tiny reference to their secret marriage was paradise. It held more value than any passionate encounter as in this room they could sit beside each other, hold hands and just let time pass by. Every so often the dog barged in or ripped up Dietrich's bedding to interrupt, it was still bliss. Even the other knights would comment on how Meinhardt was certainly far less bullish around Dietrich and of course, Konrad was very fond of Dietrich too and the pair often spoke on ideas for storing supplies and the hopes of the other knights coming into the region. When it was warm enough for Igel to go outside with the horses, Dietrich and Meinhardt found themselves going out to assist the squires and the other men to build up the fortifications and plan a raid for the middle of spring, these being in regions they had thrust into during the late winter where they could build up another fortress.

Konrad was already thinking ahead on what might be needed and he had been in contact with the Sword Brethren in Livonia, gaining information on whether they would be willing to keep the pagans on their side of the country under control. With the thoughts of taking out the rest of the pagans and building in Kulm, Meinhardt and Dietrich were excited and worked extra hard, collapsing onto their beds at night and just managing to slap their aching hands together in a gesture of goodnight before they passed out. They were both getting very excited for the chance to step out into perhaps their own command somewhere and hopefully remain together. When Leonhard appeared to request Konrad's presence in Masovia to witness the new treaty that would allow them to claim Culmerland completely... several of the knights and squires left, leaving Meinhardt and Dietrich behind with no one occupying the rooms next to their own!

"Brother Dietrich... brother Dietrich! Your stallion's gotten in with the fillies again! Thankfully they're wearing the cloths but... he's feeling the spring I reckon!" One of the young squires, named Diethelm and very fond of Meinhardt, came storming over. Dietrich was busy sorting the armoury and trying to match up the rather staggering collection of left boots with the rather limited number of right boots. He was definitely not sure what had happened with these shoes, only to note from one of the older knights with him, Uwe, that a lot of boots were lost within the frozen ponds. It had led to a few chuckles over Meinhardt having decided to strap his boots to himself, but Diethelm's interruption was not welcomed as he quickly punched against Dietrich's shoulder. "Well, are you going to get out there and deal with him?"

"Be respectful, Squire... Dietrich is a senior knight and you should treat him as such, brat!" Uwe nearly grasped one of the belts ready to give Diethelm a beating, but Dietrich lifted his hand to prevent it. Instead he instructed the stroppy thirteen-year-old to carry on his work as he galloped out of the wooden shack. The squealing of Verbrecher echoed around the field and Dietrich grimaced as he stepped out onto the muddy courtyard in heavy boots that squelched and squished the muck beneath.

It was a typically misty day, even high up the mist of the Vistula still clung about the wooden structures and took the warmth from the breeze to keep the air damp and heavy. It was certainly different from the Alpine air, the Sicilian heat and well, it felt more ominous than Burzenland. Stepping over to where the mares were ignoring the prancing young stallion and the men were looking peeved, Dietrich whistled out but was ignored. He then barked at the stallion to come over, even locating a slightly sour smelling apple to try and tempt him, but Verbrecher ignored him. The servants were muttering at his ineptitude and Dietrich wished he had Kirk there to help when an idea came to him.

"Igel... Igel... Come here boy I have a job for you." Dietrich was glad Meinhardt was helping move stone with Klobig on the other side of the castle or he'd never hear the end of this. As he beckoned the great mastiff over with his wagging tail and lolling tongue, Dietrich noticed that Verbrecher had frozen and was eyeing up the canine aggressively. Dietrich had to accept the dog whimpering and lapping at his face as he then pointed to the stallion and grinned. "Bring him here, ja?"

This was embarrassing and he hoped that no one would report this to Meinhardt, but the dog's tail was wiggling about in utter joy before he galloped into the field and rushed straight towards the black stallion. Dietrich remained perfectly still, a little worried that Verbrecher might kick Igel in the head and kill him… though Dietrich doubted there was a brain within to damage, he was rather startled as the dog lunged at the horse with a snarl of fury. The stallion reared up with a scream, guarding his fillies as he kicked his legs out to warn the dog aside, but Igel ran right past him and galloped straight over towards the other end of the field. Verbrecher straightened up, a look of confusion on his face to match Dietrich's as the animal spun on his neat hooves, slapping his sleek ebony tail in irritation as the dog found an interesting looking stick and then galloped straight back towards Dietrich.

"God in heaven…" Dietrich whimpered as he heard the eruption of laughter from the men working, and the choking snorts as Igel lunged over the fence and then sat himself firmly in front of Dietrich, holding a mould cloaked piece of branch. Dietrich slapped his forehead, but to his relief, as he then gave a heavy sigh, Verbrecher's nostrils were suddenly twitching and he lowered his head in fascination, the big stallion strolling over to see what was going on. To Dietrich's own embarrassment and relief, the stallion seemed to sense his distress and dropped his thick lips to Dietrich's sandy brown locks, nibbling at them in appreciation with all aggression gone. Dietrich then grasped the lead rope in his hands, slowly swung it around Verbrecher's neck and then beckoned for the gate to be opened by one of the sniggering servants. He then led the stallion with ease towards the gate and then back out towards the field furthest away… Igel following after him and carrying the stick proudly as Dietrich groaned. "This is a test of humility… clearly I need to pray for forgiveness more."

Dietrich let his stallion go about to nibble the grass and curiously, Igel decided that his new job was to guard Verbrecher and so he lounged in the grass and began snapping the stick to pieces. Dietrich then padded off back to his job within the castle to check the storeroom. When asked he did not answer as he settled back to arrange the items in the right order, ensuring every knight and squire would be fully equipped. He buried himself there in total silence, filling out the scroll on what items were in stock and what needed to be replaced before he found himself sighing gently against the wooden shelving. He realised there was significantly less breeches and braies than the number of knights arriving. However, he was startled when Uwe gave a sudden grunt of interest as he speculated over the next steps for the order.

"Once the treaty is signed then we'll swarm Kulm and take over, billeting men in the locals' housing and requiring them to assist in building a new castle before sending men onward in more raids to stretch out and secure the land. I doubt it would take too long, the Komtur has already learnt that the terrain is too dangerous for big groups so several small raiding parties can be far more efficient, and we have Christian allies in little pockets throughout the villages including missionaries. I doubt this place will need to hold onto too many knights for long." Uwe stated and Dietrich had to agree with him, Meinhardt and Komtur von Landsberg had been suggesting similar things and indeed, it would be Konrad's intention to focus upon these tactics when reporting to Balk. But Dietrich was suddenly terrified as Uwe then gave a firm grin of amusement as he eyed Dietrich up and then gave a snort. "The way things are going and the rumours I've heard… you and Meinhardt might be getting a promotion to lieutenant… after-all, there will be several commanders in need for each raiding party. Meinhardt deserves a command truthfully, but alas, dukedom politics and blood still hold strong here."

"I agree, Meinhardt does deserve such a position… but there's the call for prayers and then dinner, we can pick up where we left off after." Dietrich stated and he marched with Uwe and the rest of the knights and squires to the large stone chapel. It was just big enough to fit them all in as the prayers began. He was too far away from Meinhardt to be able to discuss the situation, but even at dinner sitting together it was strictly a quiet meal. Dietrich was silent as he ate his broth, thinking only of how they would be separated again and this time there would be less trouble in communicating with one another for a while. Not to mention, it was far more terrifying to think of Meinhardt marching out into these lands where killers were more frequent than the Cumans had been in Burzenland.

Meinhardt noticed the silence and curiously, Dietrich held it throughout the day as the pair went their separate ways to work until night when Dietrich was sitting upon his bunk writing out the stock information and calculations as Meinhardt came in, bruised and black-eyed. It made Dietrich immediately shift his head up from his work and he shook his head at the sight of the injury. Meinhardt plopped onto his bunk with a grunt, pulling off his clothes and then sitting upon the fabric, stark naked and just staring towards Dietrich rather expectantly. Dietrich continued to work away, not that he had not noticed but he liked to make Meinhardt react. The figure was quickly standing up, stretching out his arms and his body, trying to make a point of being naked as Dietrich continued to ignore him. It was only after a few more attempts garnered no reaction that Meinhardt then lifted a foot up onto Dietrich's bunk and leant towards him, which got a grunt.

"You know I just need to lift my foot and your voice will get higher..." Dietrich grunted and tried to hide a smirk behind the papers as Meinhardt then knelt onto his bunk, and then grasped at the scrolls to make Dietrich freeze. He was giving him a sharp expression so he would not get ink on his fingers or hurt himself, or worse mess up the calculations and Meinhardt gave a snort before removing his hand and shuffling closer to Dietrich. His husband then finally settled the items upon the bed and then stood himself up, shifting off his clothes but then finding Meinhardt's arms suddenly wrapped around him. He was then easing up his tunic and kissing at the back of his ears to make Dietrich chuckle softly. Then Meinhardt helped him remove the undershirt before then leaning Dietrich to the side slightly to kiss along his neck and shoulder in firm clapping pecks that made Dietrich's face go red. "What's my husband up to?"

"Your husband wants you to share his bed tonight... we're not to be disturbed till the prayers unless the place is attacked. Come into my bed Dietrich... I want to sleep with you wrapped in my arms..." Meinhardt whispered softly, nuzzling his face into Dietrich's shoulder and then even trying to grind at his partner's backside to let him know that he wanted something passionate together. It made Dietrich chuckle at him as he then dropped his underwear and then jumped when he felt Meinhardt's hot form pressed against him. He noted how excited his husband was and trembled in excitement to then feel Meinhardt's sweaty face nuzzling against his shoulders and back. He sighed lovingly into him as his hands wrapped around to grasp at Dietrich's scarred stomach, breathing softly as he rocked his partner within his arms and then kissed at his back. "I don't like it when I'm not able to hold you for as long as I want… but I suppose holding onto you forever is impractical in warfare."

"Unless I'm supposed to be a meat-shield…" Dietrich chuckled gently, Meinhardt giving that signature little kse-kse snigger into Dietrich's back. Dietrich leant his head back for Meinhardt to straighten up and nuzzle against, their long noses brushing gently together as Dietrich grasped his hands about Meinhardt's. It made him snort to think how curiously loving and affectionate Meinhardt could be when such a romantic moment was upon his terms. As he nuzzled his nose against Dietrich's shoulder, kissing along the old white grazes of the whip and then just pulling him in a little closer, he muttered that he'd never use Dietrich like that. Dietrich gave a soft snort and then he stepped free of the arms and then lounged along Meinhardt's bunk with a sigh and a smug expression. "So… still in rut?"

"Was I ever out of it?" Meinhardt growled low, stepping to his bunk and then slipping onto it, swiftly lying over Dietrich and wrapping an arm about his chest as he kissed at his back lovingly. Dietrich chuckled as he lay himself out along the bunk and into the pillow. He turned his head to the side, feeling Meinhardt's soft lips clip at his as he swept the sandy hair back to kiss at Dietrich's head and ear before he then straightened up with his arms either side of his lover. He then traced his lips down Dietrich's broader back, licking and sucking at every scar, nibbling just a little and moaning loudly and wetly as Dietrich blushed heavily. Meinhardt was clearly enjoying himself as he could feel the warrior below nudging and pushing at his backside with each movement. It made Dietrich want to chuckle before he suddenly gave a grunt and rolled around to reveal his chest to Meinhardt, only to suddenly wheeze sharply.

Meinhardt's lips were clasping and sucking, pulling up roughly at one of Dietrich's nipples as he swung his arms about his husband, pushing a hand into

Meinhardt's head to hold him to his bosom. The tingles and tickles, the sharp little scrapes from the edge of his teeth shot into Dietrich's spine like needles to tug and scratch every nerve that screamed pleasure as he wheezed and hissed. Meinhardt was quite adept at this now, sometimes it was the only thing he could do, twisting and teasing, thumbing at Dietrich's nipples to just give him a brief bit of pleasure although it always drew Dietrich's thicker form to rise. As Meinhardt suckled at him lovingly, Dietrich gave a low moan that was almost of discomfort as he had to shift his legs to let his form lounge more comfortably against Meinhardt. Then his lover turned to him with a wicked grin and began to kiss downwards as Dietrich gave a soft moan.

"I know that face… you aren't seriously going to… but I never know if you like doing it… surely you prefer me to…" Dietrich had begun, throwing off Meinhardt's rhythm so he gave a soft groan, straightened up and then flicked Dietrich on the nose to silence him. Dietrich slouched back, his arm over his eyes because he was more comfortable but also to hide his embarrassment. He could not help it when he knew what Meinhardt intended to do and Dietrich shuddered, his whole-body tingling in total excitement as he felt that warm but rough-skinned hand lay upon his manhood. Meinhardt never had to do much to encourage excitement from Dietrich, just a slight stroke could bring him to the edge, and it was all because of the expectation. Meinhardt snorted, his husband was such a girl! "Meinhardt… you don't have to… you don't…"

"Alright… if I don't do that, I'll enjoy something else… no complaints! You made this decision!" Meinhardt grinned wickedly and Dietrich almost gave a grunt of shock when he was forced to almost knee himself in the head. Dietrich's backside was pulled into Meinhardt's lap and then up to his face, suddenly Meinhardt was burying his face against it, lavishing it and making Dietrich's whole-body quiver. He smothered his face, trying not to whimper for how good it felt but also how very, very bad it must be. Considering he had been the one to insist he would bear the greatest of the sins in their relationship, Dietrich always felt that this was something that his dear Meinhardt took too much pleasure in. It made Dietrich's body prickle, twitch, pulse and tingle in delight and sometimes it reached something that normally took fingers or Meinhardt's form within him to reach and always it caused Dietrich's belly to be soaked in precum!

"Meinhardt… please… can't stand it!" Dietrich groaned, suddenly dropping his foot to sit upon Meinhardt's shoulder and push him back slightly. Meinhardt paused, grumbling about it before he pulled himself away and then lay himself over Dietrich's body, rubbing his groin against his lovers before kissing at his neck and then nibbling at his ear. Dietrich gave a chuckle at him for such a touch, patting at his shoulder and whimpering that he was sorry for making him stop. Meinhardt grumbled wordlessly, he did not want to say that he was angry to be stopped, he did not like the thought of Dietrich getting upset with him and then he lounged against him with a soft chuckle of amusement. He started to nip and suck at Dietrich's ear instead, making him swat at him gently. "Meinhardt… I want you inside me already…"

"I was inside you… but then you said you couldn't stand it…" Meinhardt grinned wickedly, softly blowing air into Dietrich's ear to make him chuckle and suddenly itch at himself. Meinhardt kissed his cheek before stretching his tongue out to lick Dietrich's nose, even as Dietrich pushed him with his hand to behave. Meinhardt then kissed him softly, fluttering his eyes and then dropping his hand down to rub at his husband as Dietrich moaned and then Meinhardt gave a sudden smirk. "If you want it so bad… show me where… show me what you want me to do… Hengst…"

"You wicked…" Dietrich grimaced, but he knew what was wanted and he was far too eager to enjoy their time together as he rolled onto his back and lifted his legs up against the wall, making the bunk creak but Meinhardt grin mischievously as Dietrich then stretched his legs apart and then grimaced as he had to almost roll onto himself again. He then snatched Meinhardt's hand and placed it onto his buttock, forcing him to curl all but one finger down and then he grasped about the knuckles, Meinhardt letting him drag his hand to the now slippery hole and then prodding Meinhardt's finger at it as Dietrich glared up at him. "Imagine your finger is your… Stier… I want that to go in there, simple?"

"I love seeing how ridiculous you look when you're upside down and talking to me like I'm an idiot. It's such a paradox my lord…" Meinhardt grinned wickedly as he looked into Dietrich's scowling face before he then grasped his lover's backside to give it a pinch, only to receive a foot to the face. Dietrich grumbled and dropped his legs, swinging on the awkward bunk and sitting up with a grimace as Meinhardt then shuffled between Dietrich's legs and nuzzled his head whilst Dietrich was pouting over the embarrassment. Then Meinhardt gave him a loving kiss above the eye and gently pushed him onto his back, lounging over him and nuzzling at his face as Dietrich wrapped his arms about Meinhardt's body. They nuzzled and moaned as they cuddled up tightly to each other before Dietrich licked Meinhardt's neck, he shuddered violently above him and then whimpered softly. "I know when you're on your chest, I can get deeper and hold onto you more but... but is it alright if we cuddle as we're doing it?"

"Meinhardt... in every sense you are a pain in the..." Dietrich began until Meinhardt shifted his head, lifting it so Dietrich could only see him give those ridiculous puppy eyes. It made Dietrich want to smack him on the head and certainly cut him off as the green eyes rolled in irritation and then he spread his legs apart. He then gave a chuckle as Meinhardt then lifted his head to peck at Dietrich's soft lips, snatching them in quick little kisses and then nuzzling at his chest. Dietrich gave a soft moan as he shifted his body slightly and Meinhardt then shuffled into position, kissing and nuzzling at Dietrich's chest before he dropped a hand. He pressed a finger to the soft spot, making sure that it was still comfortable as Dietrich took a deep wheeze to relax himself and then smiled lovingly at Meinhardt as he stroked and twirled his finger around the ring. "You don't need to tease me, husband."

"I love it when you call me that..." Meinhardt chuckled lovingly as he stretched forward and Dietrich leant forward, their lips clapping each other firmly before he began to tease gently at Dietrich, making him sigh more lovingly. This was something Dietrich very much enjoyed as Meinhardt beamed down at him, love swimming in his eyes, he gently brought himself to that place. There was the soft sensation of a stroke, the burning heat that made Dietrich's stomach flip with anticipation and as soon as that familiar, firm form slid deep into his body, Dietrich had to give a deep suck of air and opened his mouth in a grimace to hold back the noise as once more penetration slammed him with pleasure. It made Meinhardt grasp him tightly, lying his body against the stain upon his lover's stomach as he clamped his lips about Dietrich's. Their tongues soon rolled and slid against one another lovingly as they then broke with a hot wheeze. "You are still so beautiful whenever you're like this Dieter... you still feel perfect..."

"Don't compliment me when I've already messed myself... just kiss me and make love to me without another word... except I love you." Dietrich grunted in response and Meinhardt gave a chuckle and he kissed him firmly again in response, making him gasp softly before he wrapped his body around Dietrich's and then gently, they began to move their bodies against each other. Both were soon gasping and moaning, their bodies pressed tightly together, the room filled with the sound of their clapping kisses, their streaking sweaty bodies, their moans and their sighs of delight. Every so often their mouths would come together, just to stroke at the hot air they exuded with their pleasure as one would mutter 'I love you' and this would lead to a deeper push, a tighter groan and their mouths locked together again. Their bodies were soon coated in sweat, the scent of one another mingling into a whole new one... eyes were filled with tears and they were unable to separate from one another, even when their bodies had given in their mouths still clasped, their hands still grasped and their eyes remained locked together.

"Meinhardt..." It was the middle of the night, probably not far from dawn and though they were both wrapped in each other's arms, beautifully hot, a little smelly but not unpleasantly so and the pair were utterly content, Dietrich had woken up. The words with Uwe were suddenly rattling around his head and he kissed softly at Meinhardt's ear, urging him to give some sign he was awake but instead the figure was still just snoring loudly. When Dietrich gave a groan that he was not getting anywhere with the big warm northerner hooked about him with their legs intertwined and a little numb, Dietrich shifted his hand down. As he kissed at Meinhardt's neck, making him shudder with pleasure, Dietrich then gently lay his hands upon Meinhardt's manhood, feeling it stir and practically lie into his grip as Meinhardt opened one glittering blue eye with a smirk.

"I thought you'd had enough... but if you're still eager..." Meinhardt grinned, suddenly swinging himself onto Dietrich as his partner gave a soft grunt and then almost slapped at him for hooking just one leg up and over his shoulder as he twisted awkwardly. Meinhardt was soon bent forward kissing at Dietrich's shoulder lovingly and curiously, though Dietrich might ordinarily complain that he was being stupid, he let his leg stretch and then gave a sharp shuddering gasp when Meinhardt joined with his flesh. Meinhardt was then smothering Dietrich's face in kisses as Dietrich was squashed into himself. Meinhardt's hips were soon moving rather fast and messily, their flesh slapping together loudly as Dietrich gave little hiccup like breaths as he tried not to moan too loudly but also to breathe. This position was something new and it was hitting him deeper than any other face-to-face, but it was quite awkward, and Dietrich could feel a cramp forming in his back already.

As he grit his teeth against the cramping muscle, trying to ignore the agony it caused and instead focusing on the pleasurable build up of pressure at the base of his spine, Meinhardt was quick to start leaning more into his leg. The stretching muscle was becoming just as uncomfortable and Dietrich had to close his eyes tightly and clench his teeth, resisting the urge to just scream at Meinhardt to get the hell off of him, but he was finding it far too pleasurable and when Meinhardt then seemed to speed up as if he wanted to hurry to come to his own end, he groaned over Dietrich! Dietrich gave a sharp gasp, the hot spurt within his body making him tremble as he then gave a groan that was almost pained as he reached his climax just as he felt Meinhardt's length start to pull back. With a groan Meinhardt pulled away and then slumped his face into the pillow as Dietrich panted but then turned to look at him.

"Not that I didn't enjoy it but... I actually wanted to ask you something..." Dietrich panted, only to receive a groan and a hand slapping at his shoulder for not telling him sooner. Now Meinhardt was going to feel bad for misreading the situation and he quickly hooked an arm about Dietrich, pulling him in close, kissing at his ears and whimpering pathetically that he did not mean to take it just like that. Swiftly he was smothering Dietrich in kisses and cuddles stroking at his backside and apologising for being pig-headed and not using his brain. Dietrich just snorted as he pushed Meinhardt off of him, only for that more sterner looking face to flop into his chest and whimper that he was sorry. Dietrich just gave a snort, stroking his fingers through Meinhardt's almost icy looking hair as he sighed against him. "I said I enjoyed it... to be fair, I don't think I could say no to you... ever. You are my husband and I do have my 'duties' to perform."

"Don't say it like that... you're not a woman expected to just sit back and pop out babies... though, I have to admit if you were a woman... I don't think you'd ever not be pregnant..." Meinhardt grumbled as Dietrich muttered about his lack of self-control before their lips came together in a loving kiss. They stroked each other's cheeks and nuzzled noses, snorting at each other before kissing again and then lounging comfortably against one another. Meinhardt still stroked at Dietrich's side, resisting the urge to just force his partner onto his side, lock their bodies together and just stay like that all night. It would be an interesting experience and yet Meinhardt was going to behave himself as he kissed Dietrich's chest above his throbbing heart. "What's on your mind? If its about where we're going next... I wonder about it too, but it'll be you and me, I know it!"

"But that's what I'm worried about Meinhardt... what if we're both made lieutenants and therefore sent to different areas with different masters and unable to be anywhere near each other? What will we do then? What if we're completely separated again? I… this… this I don't want to leave. God in heaven, I don't want to be away from your arms again!" Dietrich grunted and Meinhardt was grimacing into his lover's shoulder as Dietrich rolled about to face him and they were both looking uncomfortable. Dietrich then shuffled to wrap his legs around Meinhardt's, wrapping his arms around his shoulders and then pressing his hairier chest to Meinhardt's. His husband grasped him to sit more comfortably onto him, feeling his excitement growing despite the seriousness of the situation. Dietrich was looking miserable as he closed his eyes tightly and nuzzled his nose against Meinhardt's. "I think I would rather die than be away from…"

"Don't say it, by the holy father don't ever say you'd prefer death no matter the situation because I could not bear anything if I didn't know you were there. I'm strong because you're here Dieter… if you were not here, I'd never have coped this freezing winter without you. Dreams of you alone kept me sane." Meinhardt grumbled as he wrapped his arms around Dietrich tightly and pulled him straight into him, nuzzling him. But then Dietrich kissed his mouth lovingly, glad of his words and thankful that Meinhardt was so much more practical in these matters. But as they rolled into each other to snuggle and kiss some more, Meinhardt stretched a hand to Dietrich's backside and clasped a cheek whilst the other gave a grunt. "Uh… the only benefit to being separate for a while is that I won't keep jumping you…"

"What are you, a stud?" Dietrich grunted before he felt Meinhardt crawl over him and somehow manage to fall out of the bunk completely onto the floor and Dietrich chuckled. Meinhardt pulled himself upward off the floor and scrabbled to get back on the bed behind Dietrich as he sniggered. "You deserve that… I hope the floor is chilly enough to cool your ardour…"

"Like anything could cool my love for you!"

Six: Mission at Hand

"Dietrich... Dietrich... no one's awake just yet and Konrad's bringing everyone back today... do you think we can..." Meinhardt had woken up excited, his blood pumping as he rolled on his side to find Dietrich's back pressed against him. When Dietrich gave a soft grumble to say he was half awake, Meinhardt leant forward and kissed at his partner' shoulders, nuzzling and moaning at him, swinging an arm about to stroke at Dietrich's stomach scar to wake him up. Dietrich opened his eyes slowly and gave a groan, rolling onto his front as Meinhardt sat himself up expectantly and Dietrich just slumped over the pillows, pulling them under his chest and muttering to him that he could rub but not enter. Meinhardt gave a snigger, lying over Dietrich's back, hooking his arms under Dietrich's chest and then nuzzling his face into his head. He kissed at his ear and then his neck, making Dietrich chuckle before moaning softly as Meinhardt then gently began to grind his hips against his lover's back, becoming aroused quickly.

It would have been something rather sweet in Meinhardt's eyes as he kissed and nuzzled at his lover's shoulders, had Dietrich not given a sudden snore. Meinhardt froze with his eyes widened in shock and he then gave a groan before gently nipping Dietrich's ear, making him jump and then turn his head. Then Meinhardt stretched forward, kissing him lovingly and receiving a kiss back before grinding himself against Dietrich's plump backside again, before Dietrich then gave a soft groan and then mumbled that he was not into it this morning. Meinhardt paused, rolled back around and gave a groan before lying back and then asking Dietrich to cuddle him all the same. Dietrich rolled towards him, pulled him close and they nuzzled and kissed at each other, Meinhardt content and just settling back to sleep as Dietrich kissed him lovingly.

About twenty minutes later, Dietrich woke up because he was feeling the morning issue from his body straining towards Meinhardt and he was thinking for a moment that he should wake him and get intimate, when he heard the distant cawing of the poultry. When the birds started stirring, that usually meant that the rest of the world was about to wake up and with a groan of frustration, Dietrich sat himself up and then patted at Meinhardt's knee, urging his husband to sit upward. Meinhardt sat himself up with a soft grunt, spotting Dietrich's arousal and then grinning before dropping a hand to grasp Dietrich as his lover stretched out to grasp his. The pair were then kissing, moaning, their tongues stroking at each other as their hands stroked away gently and they sighed against each other, ready to enjoy themselves one last time before everything else became hectic and then Meinhardt began to moan at him lovingly....

"Oh Dieter... your hands are still so beautiful... I want them in my mouth..." Meinhardt groaned as their tongues stroked one another. But it was an odd request and Dietrich gave Meinhardt a curious look, just keeping his hand to Meinhardt's body as his partner then dropped his head against his shoulder. He moaned and whimpered softly, Dietrich could feel the heavy pulsing within Meinhardt's form, as always he was far too excited and Dietrich turned to kiss at his eyes, watching drool forming on the edge of Meinhardt's mouth. He was whimpering softly, his hands unable to grasp hold of Dietrich any longer as instead they moved to hold Dietrich's shoulders as he smothered his face into his body and then his partner gave a soft sigh.

"Don't turn away Meinhardt... I'd like to see your face when you... when you get there..." Dietrich whispered hoarsely, his whole-body trembling and he shifted his body so that they could put their forms together. Meinhardt gave a soft warble, looking at his lover with tears in his eyes and looking so very terrified that he might look awkward if Dietrich was watching him. But Dietrich gave a soft moan as he felt that pulsing between them, pushing themselves against each other until Meinhardt began to gulp and whimper softly, his eyes almost rolling back. Dietrich wanted to lean forward to kiss his beautiful face as Meinhardt looked so strained and scared, until there was a sudden stomping sound in the hall and a call.

"Brother Meinhardt? Brother Dietrich..." Dietrich froze but then he gave a gulp of shock as Meinhardt had grit his teeth with a hiccup and well, made a mess onto Dietrich's arm as the pair then turned to each other. That was Uwe's voice and clearly there was something wrong... not to mention they were very close to getting caught! Hurriedly, Dietrich lunged onto the other side of his bunk, grasping a damp cloth to clean at himself and Meinhardt grasped for his nightgown, jerking it on just as Uwe's fist rattled on their door! Meinhardt gave a mumble he was coming, but he almost fell onto his side with a groan of surprise as he pulled about to get to the door. He was feeling his anger rising for the interruption as Dietrich made a point he'd just gotten up to clean himself after a night of constant twisting. Meinhardt opened the door and then Uwe stepped inside, ignoring Dietrich's nibbled up back. "Brother Meinhardt, Komtur Konrad's just returned, he says we need to get everyone up and move out across the river as soon as possible... Meister Balk has already made arrangements for a massive raid to capture Kulm fully and the four villages out from it, also the little town further off where we have a church on our side. We've got to get up and move, now!"

Meinhardt patted Uwe's shoulder, insisting that everything would be sorted and that he should go and start waking everyone up. He was groaning in frustration as he watched Uwe leave and then calmly, he turned towards Dietrich who was already pulling his clothes on with a soft smirk. Meinhardt was then blushing as he realised that he'd not managed to satisfy Dietrich and swiftly he closed the door. He then hurried over to Dietrich's side but was suddenly grasped in a tight embrace, their lips coming together in a tight kiss before they nuzzled their cheeks as Dietrich heaved a soft sigh. Meinhardt was suddenly aware that this meant that their time was over... they were about to go on their own missions after this and Meinhardt gripped hold of him tighter than before.

"No matter what happens here, as we've agreed before... we're not going to forget each other or forget our vows... I'm your husband and you're mine... we made that pledge before God and it is only between us and him. Keep the secret and keep the promise to be together..." Meinhardt whispered, trying to bight his lip because he wanted to cry at the thought they could enter battle now and some brief accident could cost Dietrich his life. Dietrich held him tightly in response, nuzzling against him and then insisting it would all be fine as they separated and then finished dressing themselves. They shared one final kiss together, a short and sweet one, before they marched out of the room in full knightly regalia and then were hollering and thumping on the doors to ensure everyone was up and out!

Straightaway Dietrich marched down to the squires, aiding Uwe in beckoning them up and encouraging those still desperate to sleep to get up with a firm kick. The battle was nigh and they needed to be ready; hopefully just a show of force should do the trick, but there was always the chance that death could occur and so he beckoned them out as fast as he could to where the Ordained brother was beckoning for a sermon beside Komtur von Landsberg. Once Dietrich had rounded up the squires in their gear and brought them before the Ordained brother, they were on their knees as Meinhardt and the knights were also down and bowing as behind the men-at-arms prepared the horses and their own gear. With all the knights and squires present, Konrad bowed and allowed the priestly brother to make a blessing and pray to God on their behalf, all of them joining their voices to announce 'das Vaterunser'. Then, the prayers were said and the men brought the horses as the knights mounted up and followed Konrad to the boarder of the river where Balk was sitting upon his huge grey charger, steaming in the chilly air in preparation for the crossing created overnight by Balk's men. Smaller raiding parties had already moved off to the smaller villages and the task was nice and simple… like with fighting the Cumans, charging through and hitting down any opposition before turning around and surrounding the village.

The horses were getting as giddy as the riders as everyone was lined up and Dietrich found himself with the squires, watching Konrad lead Meinhardt to Balk's side. The group was soon ready, everyone muttering swift prayers and whispers for God to protect them and aid them in their Christian goal as Balk took a deep grunting snort and lifted his sword. There was no word given, the signal was clear enough and as the lead horses were urged across the swaying planks and then wading to the other side, the others followed suit until they were lined up on the other side of the bank together, stretched out wide and ready to engulf the town up ahead.

Once the majority of the forces were across, Balk lifted his sword again before the lead horses were kicked into a canter, the mounts behind moved like a herd, keeping nose to hip so that they were not separated from their friends as they charged the village. As the herd thundered towards the land, the sound like a storm coming in from the west, the town started to become alive with screams and hollers and men scrabbling to think to fight the invasion. The ranks spread out as they charged, small sections breaking off and seeming to gallop off in a different direction to every other group. These were to splinter off and take the villages to the side and hold them until the others joined up to build more fortresses. As they charged on through, to the town, the men who thought to fight back the charge came out with spears and other objects that would be of no use against the body of the horses crashing into them.

Dietrich and the squires were at the back of the charge, the whole rank quivering but ready for action that thankfully, did not come. The main body of the force knocked out any attempts for attack and the few spears and arrows that flew out towards them were easily deflected and even those that landed were hardly life-threatening, most pinging off shield or lodging within the mail. Dietrich felt a bolt skim past his chin, it cut and stung worse than on parchment, but the adrenalin coursing through his body to follow the charge and be ready to hack with his sword kept him from hollering out. His stern expression was welcomed by the squires as the other ranks funnelled through the main passage of the town and steered around, leaving the squires and men-at-arms most at risk. But Dietrich and the other older knights urged them to spin right around and charge through again, startling anyone that might think to come out and fight and thankfully, the squires followed and left the men-at-arms to set up some covering fire and a more useful hand-to-hand combating unit.

At reaching the other end, losing only two squires to well-aimed bricks thrown from the houses of the rebellious, Dietrich met them up with the main body and then other knights came in with lit torches. They were swift to take out the houses along the corridor, letting the thatched rooves do the work, the flames pulling out and spitting onto other rooves. They kept the fire contained to just a few houses, letting the populace emerge and run into the waiting men and knights, forcing them to cower together and accept defeat whilst those houses burnt were left to go until the majority appeared and then the men-at-arms were encouraged to put any fresh fires out. The time, the fear and the ruthless manner was enough and the people were defeated, trembling and then Balk was announcing the victory and the penance….

This was something rather more uncomfortable for Dietrich to witness, in the Holy Lands and against the Cuman it was clear that the enemy would not convert, they were protecting against the heathens, but this was stomach churning. He could see the women clasping their children; the children would be taught to convert and so they would be unharmed and possibly even sold as slaves, the same with the women… but the men were more troubling. They mumbled and growled and muttered but many of them agreed for the sake of their families to join the church. Those that did not, Balk was quite swift to come to his decision upon them. He beckoned the Ordained brothers to bring him the Holy Water and aid him in Christening the huddled masses of converters. They were all rather petrified at the sensation of the water flicking onto them, jumping and whimpering save those already baptised who urged them to relax and be calm. Beside him, Uwe was grumbling to the squires that the flinching was the clear sign of the devils within them being afraid of the touch of holy water, but Dietrich could tell it was just fear.

Then the worst part came, though Konrad had been harsh in dealing with pagans in strapping them to their sacred oak trees and either strangling them or slitting their throats, Balk had the men-at-arms prepare stakes in the square and gather what rubbish had not burnt from the buildings. The executions would be immediate, the non-converters were strapped up and the Ordained brother gave one more chance to encourage them to convert. Some did, too afraid of burning alive and they were blessed before being tied up aside from the main body to be sold as slaves. Those that did not, well, Balk dismounted his charger and gladly brought the flame to them, ignorant to their screams, stern and focused that this was the only way to purge their souls and grant them freedom from any further sin.

A mass was then performed, everyone blocking their ears to the sound of those men screaming, some praying louder just to cover the sounds. Those natives that were converted previously and curiously had not suffered damage to their housing, their family or friends were quick to lead the others in the words of the prayer in Latin, helping them save themselves. The words of Balk's swift methods of dealing with pagans were well-founded and Dietrich prayed insistently as those wounded brothers were healed and the bodies of the few who fell prepared to a Christian burial. It was not a pleasant start to the campaign here, but it was a mark of what was to come and Dietrich knew he'd have to stomach it and show mercy and clemency where he could and pray for an assignment that did not involve such harsh treatments... even if he knew they were necessary.

By evening the knights to stay in Kulm and prepare its castle were being billeted and assisted by the locals, Balk and Konrad were to return with a few squires and the Ordained brother back to the castle, but the knights present were being sifted through and given assignments and squires. It seemed those squads to have separated and gone further on were the new Komturs, each of them had their assignments and some would be going further out. It was for these Komturs that Balk was being toured around the other knights remaining, to choose who would be going where. Dietrich had been stuck around the squires still, listening to their anxieties and their excitement, or just their frustration that they did not even get to kill anyone! The various reactions made him feel uncomfortable, but he calmed them all the same and then felt the heavy flop of Meinhardt against his back, practically hearing him grin.

"That's a better way to fight? No needless killing and easy conversions… we hardly lost anyone and well, these are the tactics we'll use to convert these pagans, turn the tide and use their own manners against them!" Meinhardt was grinning, jogging Dietrich's shoulder as the broader knight gave a slight scoff, only to turn about and notice that Meinhardt's face was bleeding rather heavily above the eye. Dietrich groaned, did this fool never learn to keep his head out of trouble? He turned about to grasp his face and then look at the wound. It was a scratch across the forehead, a typical flesh wound but the skin was so thin there it bled easily and always looked worse than it was. With a sigh Dietrich then dropped his hands and grasped at the inside of his tunic where he'd kept a little paste for this kind of situation. He smeared it against Meinhardt's forehead though the other grimaced. "Stop acting like my grandmother… it was just a flesh wound!"

"Which means there's no excuse for it getting tainted because you didn't clean it. Quit flinching, you're worse than a child!" The pair grumbled between each other, causing a few haughty chuckles from others to see the pair acting like that. It was no secret that they were close and complete opposites, some even speculated they were an excellent example of the bonds of the order, but as Balk approached the pair separated. Balk was as intimidating as always and even with Konrad beside him, he looked like one point from his finger might bring down the wrath of God upon an individual, and it was incredibly troubling as he pointed straight to Meinhardt and gave a grunt.

"You… Brother Lehenman… you're to remain at Vogelsang with von Landsberg, your ability with the Danish mercenaries and the local Poles is invaluable and will be required as our forces increase. We're expecting some Danish mercenaries to join our band and Konrad says you've got friends in high places amongst those barbarians." Balk scoffed, his hatred of the Danes obvious and probably due to the fact he did not approve of the idea of mercenaries being involved in the manners of a Holy Order. But mercenaries had eyes and ears that were able to clue in to more places than for others and with them owning the lands on the other side of the Livonian Sword Brethren, they had knowledge of the areas and indeed of the Chutes and other native tribes further east. "You'll be promoted to Lieutenant and you will be given that troublesome fellow, Diethelm as your squire… you may be given another two at the end of the year if that is suitable… you'll also be given a contingent of thirty men-at-arms and work with five other full knights and their squires here. You'll be keeping an eye on Masovian movements and ensure messages are put through. Our new base will be here at Kulm until we find a better place further in."

"Oh, thank you sir... thank God too for such a great victory and lack of bloodshed today." Meinhardt sounded uncharacteristically out of sorts and his words seemed scattered. He could not think what to say as Balk casually performed the sign of the cross above his forehead before patting his shoulder firmly. The honour bestowed upon him to get to this was very important, he'd have to send off to his family immediately and well, they would be truly, truly grateful to hear he had such a grand job and was not too far from home. It also meant that more of God's grace had fallen upon his low-ranking household and he hoped it would play out favourably for his family. Dietrich was also pleased to hear it, but when Balk squared up to him there was almost a look upon him of disappointment, as if he'd assumed from build and the stories of his scars and previous achievements that Dietrich might have been more inclined to show himself off. But Dietrich could read from his eyes that Balk was thinking about the ancestor Dietrich showed some likeness to, and from it, his link to the emperor and as he spoke, Dietrich was almost angry.

"von Hohenflacherstein, you will be sent off to assist Komtur Rudolph von Lippe further up the banks of the Vistula, deeper into Pomesanian territory but still within our bounds. You'll also be gaining the rank of Lieutenant but you will be taking twenty squires with you to train up with young Ludovic Odermann, he was originally a novice, but his local lord put money in for him to have a chance to be a squire. Your ability to read and write is very important for von Lippe, he's working with the Ordained brothers to convert through literacy and it's having some success but for raiding parties attacking and kidnapping or killing the novices and apprentice men-at-arms. I'll give you thirteen men but no knights. I don't think much of this tender footed approach, but it's proven useful in developing maps and gaining names of tribes and their leaders... so that is where you'll be headed." That was all, Balk walked off and did not even give Dietrich a second look, it made Dietrich's skin uncomfortable and almost want to hide away, as if for some reason this master did not like him at all. Perhaps it was because of his heritage once again, it was still something the others could not quite overcome their prejudice with.

"There Dieter... both rising in the ranks now! Plus, you won't be too far away from me now and I'm glad... you'll be somewhere safe." Meinhardt whispered gently as he patted Dietrich's shoulder, but his lover was not too pleased about the idea at all. Though Dietrich was glad to be in a defending and teaching position rather than thrown into death's path over and over, somehow he felt it was supposed to be that way. He had the strangest feeling that his blood tie, though it should have been meaningless here, still meant that they wanted him kept alive. Maybe it was to do with drawing people in from the Swabian Court, he could not say but he had the distinct sensation still that Balk did not like him. Meinhardt then gave a curious sound of fascination as he realised something. "I think I remember Diethelm complaining about him… he turned up in a monk's habit but with his own horse and a man-at-arms and apparently though a novice, everyone tends to treat him very well. Diethelm said he asked his elder brother and he said Odermann's apparently the bastard son of someone very high in the Imperial Court. I think that's all nonsense… then again, he would not have to be a bastard to be a spare son shoved into holy orders… like the rest of us."

"Indeed… thank you for the information, but doesn't that make it all the more humiliating that I've basically been given the job of baby-sitting?" Dietrich grimaced in frustration and Meinhardt stared at him for a moment in confusion, his eyebrow curling in fascination before he stepped back. He patted his shoulder, insisted that they would be fine as he beckoned him to follow after their master and back to their horses. But upon finding their horses, Dietrich was soon grimacing in frustration as his stallion was showing off and trying to mount everything left-right-and-centre whilst the men were trying to hold him and getting thrown a few kicks. Dietrich groaned in frustration, wishing he could get rid of this damn stallion but he was doomed!

During the night, Dietrich and Meinhardt were in bed together for the last time, their arms wrapped about each other, stroking each other's shoulders and waiting for the sound of others outside to calm down. They had two more bunks in the room, they were being billeted with two more that were going to be turning up any minute now after they had finished scrubbing up from their own journey from Masovia with the last of the reserves. One of them was Leonhard, so it was not as frustrating as it could be and yet as the pair held each other, the mix of body heat and anxiety for what was to come was manifesting in lustful thoughts. Meinhardt could not keep his hands from Dietrich, stroking at his chest, grasping his breast to make Dietrich give grimaces before Meinhardt's smooth chin rubbed against his shoulder. Meinhardt wanted to leave a mark, some kind of bite that would take a while to fade but would remind Dietrich who his husband was… but they had no guarantee they would not be disturbed.

"Ugh… Meinhardt… do you think we could sneak out to the latrine and… and you know…" Dietrich grimaced, he'd never wanted to do something so lustful before, but considering he was about to go through another period of time, not knowing when they could even next kiss, it was awful. He hated feeling that he wanted something so much and as he turned within Meinhardt's grip, he leant over his shoulder in return and dropped a hand, knuckling near Meinhardt's form to entice him. Meinhardt sucked air in through his teeth, grimacing as he kissed at Dietrich again and continued to grasp at his chest. He was massaging and kneading against the flesh as Dietrich gave a groan and continued to knuckle against him, turning to kiss at Meinhardt's neck to make him moan. "I take it you don't think it would be safe?"

"No… it wouldn't… I feel so awful about this Dietrich. I feel like I want to do some terrible things to you, but it would not be a good idea at all. I mean… how will I cope being away from you for who knows how long? Its been hard enough these few years but, when you're so close…" Meinhardt grimaced, smearing his face against Dietrich's chest again with a groan before lifting his head. Their noses rubbed together, and they pressed forward, enjoying a soft kiss before Dietrich gave a chuckle; they had always written before and they could keep each other in their dreams at least. As Dietrich stroked at his face, Meinhardt gave a pout and then a grumble. "Shame we can't meet up once a week somewhere in the woods and…"

There was the sound of feet in the hallway to cut off anymore of their affections as Dietrich shifted across to lounge upon his bunk and pull the sheets over himself. He stared towards Meinhardt longingly, looking at how his companion was grimacing and grinding his jaw, clearly too excited all the same as he slumped back, revealing the tenting of his clothes before he jerked the blankets over himself. Dietrich stretched a hand out to hold his, they held each other until the door opened and Meinhardt automatically went to slap at Dietrich, making Leonhard roll his eyes as he and another stepped into the room and closed the door. Leonhard gave Meinhardt a clap to the ear to stop being a pain and then patted Dietrich's shoulder before slumping on the bunk right beside Dietrich.

His back bashed into Dietrich and Dietrich sat up and turned to watch Leonhard and his companion pull their tunics off, engaging in his usual conversations over what was going on and Leonhard was rolling his eyes. He was grumbling about how harsh Balk had been with the village, but the other interjected that the pagans were given too much mercy generally. The conversation continued as Leonhard decided to forego the nightshirt and just sleep in his braies, but then Dietrich leant against him, insisting he had some uncomfortable looking hairs coiling on his back into boils, so Leonhard froze to allow Dietrich to pluck them. But this made Meinhardt's eyes narrow and suddenly he leapt up out of the bed and grasped Dietrich by the wrist, giving a nasty snap towards Leonhard.

"Get someone else to sort it or cope... acting vain like that... anyway, Dietrich's got to help me with an uncomfortable boil... we'll be back!" Dietrich gave a grimace, of all the things Meinhardt had to practically shout at them, why did it have to be that? Leonhard was soon sniggering along with his companion, typical Meinhardt being self-conscious about something everyone had to deal with as they watched him drag the stunned Dietrich out of the room. Meinhardt pulled him into the washroom where there were toilets that emptied out down the side of the stone walls and into the ditches below. It was not a safe place to be, there was no way to lock the doors and well, it was just the way as everyone could go in and out but immediately Meinhardt had Dietrich pinned to the wall and was growling at him. "Why were you being like that with Leonhard... touching his back and..."

"Not the jealous streak! Meinhardt, envy is a sin and I would never do anything against you or to Leonhard... he's like a brother to me." Dietrich groaned, wheezing against Meinhardt's firm grip but then soon moaning as Meinhardt slammed his lips to his. The kiss was violent, typical of Meinhardt's reactions when he was jealous and Dietrich seemed to shrink down the wall into Meinhardt's grip as he pressed into him, lips parting to snatch breath before their tongues were rolling against each other. Dietrich's hands grasped his lover's hips, he tilted his own forward, enjoying the way his 'husband' would grind against him automatically, but then Dietrich returned to his senses and pulled away, making Meinhardt freeze. "We really need to behave ourselves... this time apart will teach us restraint once again. I'm sorry Meinhardt... but this is our last kiss for now..."

"I know... but it doesn't mean I have to like it."

Seven: Dietrich's Assignment

Morning came with misery, there was a fog and as everyone sat in prayers, Dietrich was feeling the despair grip him tightly at the thought he was going to have to leave what had been a pleasant sanctuary and go elsewhere without Meinhardt. It didn't matter that they were not 'too far' from each other as they had been when he'd been trapped in Swabia, but it was not the same. Being so close and yet barred from each other was more unpleasant than being sent all about the crusading world and Dietrich was worried something could happen to his beloved whilst he was away. As they prayed together he begged God to keep his love safe and to keep their hearts strong, but soon the sermon was over and Dietrich was packing his items and stepping to his horse.

The stallion was being distracted from trouble again by the dog, Igel rushing up to him and offering him a nice branch to play with that Verbrecher's lips nibbled at in fascination. The dog seemed convinced the horse might wrestle him for it, but the stallion gave a soft snort as the packs were loaded to his back. Although a few other squires had mounts to take with them, the majority of their supplies was mounted to a cart being pulled by a wheezing ox that the black stallion kept slinging kicks at, Dietrich was not having a good start to it already! But he was distracted from his thoughts and internal grumblings as he heard the sound of someone slipping into the mud and manure ridden yard and the other squires sniggering away at him for it. Dietrich turned, only to see the rather chubby and fearful looking form of who was practically his ward, Ludovic.

"I wouldn't laugh… or the first one to make a mistake will find themselves shovelling shit as punishment. You alright there Squire? I'm Brother von Hohenflacherstein, but everyone is to call me Brother Dietrich, understood?" Dietrich stated, swinging a finger around to point to all the squires, most of them younger teens except chubby Ludovic who was probably heading towards his twenties. As Dietrich stretched his hand out to him, yanking him up, it was accompanied with a sudden expulsion of vomit from the young squire that Dietrich put down to fear and the stink of the pig muck. It caused some stifled giggles but Dietrich patted Ludovic's back down and then beckoned him to get up onto his horse beside him, passing him some cloth from amongst the supplies and helping to wipe Ludovic's face clean. The figure did not look like he would sob however, he just seemed resigned to his fate and Dietrich could not help but recognise that look. "Come on… let's get going…"

Their guide appeared and the group was just about to head off when there was the sudden yelp from Meinhardt as he galloped down from his own group and straight to Dietrich's side. The squires were all looking towards Meinhardt in awe, somehow he was like a god descending amongst them as they straightened up proudly before Meinhardt heaved a sigh and then whistled for Igel. Dietrich found himself scowling at the dog, realising it was sitting in the cart as if it were a vital supply, but then Meinhardt started cuddling it. He was fussing and nosing at the dog and then swiftly he tied it to the cart by its collar and Dietrich was about to lift his hands and insist he was not going to allow such a thing, when Meinhardt marched to his side and then slapped his hip.

"Dieter… I had a thought… Igel is a good guard dog but also a smart dog… when you get settled, strap a note to his collar and tell him to go find daddy! He'll be able to give us reports to send to each other and find out how we're doing. That way, you and I can keep in touch and if its something really serious, tie a bit of cloth to him and I'll know to come straightaway, got it!" Meinhardt stated firmly, ignoring the way the youngsters were staring at the full brothers in fascination but also in jealousy. They were quite sure that this was something secret but important that they would not understand until they were full knights, yet Dietrich was swift to grasp Meinhardt's shoulder and scowl at him as Meinhardt gave a grin. "Just no poems…"

"You really are adding to my trials, dear brother… but alright, however I make no apology if I kick the dog in the arse…" Dietrich scoffed as he straightened up, only to be grasped at the neck and yanked back down. His nose was to Meinhardt's, the knight spoke threateningly about him even harming the animal, but as their eyes locked and he made all the loving expressions he could within them, Dietrich understood. This was Meinhardt's version of a goodbye kiss, well it was better than his idea of a nuptial kiss… which had been Dietrich kicked off his horse! When he was released, they patted shoulders and then the guide begged them to follow. Dietrich and the others started moving, the helmet being firmly affixed to Dietrich's head before he turned back to watch Meinhardt wave out to him. Igel was soon whimpering and howling for his master and for once, Dietrich envied the dog's ability to do such a thing!

The journey along the river was dangerous to say the least, though their guide insisted them it was just three days march during the day to get to their destination, it passed through dangerous lands very close to the Pomesanian boarders and raids were commonplace. The thought of using Igel to send messages to Meinhardt suddenly seemed to make a lot more sense but it was not a pleasant situation at all, the guide alone had stopped them marching into an ambush on the second day and they'd been required to travel at night. The landscape was no easier, the ground was still frozen and the river swelled and dared to snatch up bridges on its way up towards the sea. There were lots of wolves that howled at night too and they all huddled close to their fires, guarding them with their own forms because even in the woods there seemed either eyes glowing and staring at them or glimmers in the darkness to say others might be near.

There were no losses when they reached the worn road towards the village, but the sight of the village with its wooden church and half-stone barracks seemed out of proportion. There was a long wooden house like that of the northerners, dotted around it were smaller houses made of thatch, wood, but most a mix of wood and mud. They'd cleared the trees around them and in front of the long house was a large square between it and the church. However, there were few people out and about, most of them working to bring in timber or working on the few fields darted about nearby. There was also signs of fishing on the Vistula, ferries and well, the place looked to be slowly evolving into a more civilised looking place, but at the same time, something about it seemed too quiet, until children came running in from the field squeaking in delight and then Dietrich wheezed in relief.

Children running and laughing was the sign of growth, a sign of health and they were all drawn straight to the figure clad in the white raiment with its black cross upon his massive black horse. The guide let them stop and then moved towards the barracks attached to the church, thumping on a hard wooden door to bring out the Komtur and the ordained brother. Dietrich beckoned the group stop and then dismounted, the children rushing over to look at him fearlessly and to Dietrich this had to be a good sign for them not to be scared. He knelt down amongst them, lifting his helmet up so they could come over and look at him more, he strained out his gloved hand towards them and they clasped hold of him gently in giggles of delight. They all started grasping his raiment and his hair, tugging at his beard as he chuckled and let them inspect him. The squires watched in confusion until the door of the church opened first and a being, dressed head to toe in poor dark cloth with just the most delicate and elegant manner stepped over with his neat hands folded over a Bible and about his neck a series of prayer beads.

"My, it's always a good sign when the knight sent to us is gentle with children... we feared we might get someone a little more barbaric, but I'm glad to meet you. I am Father Allard, or Brother Allard for you my dear monk... Komtur Rudolph will be out soon, he's busy... cataloguing the native fish within our stores. Frightfully insistent figure, he demands a catalogue be as accurate as possible, variety, size and even level of freshness will be identified and sorted by. I dare say, with just the two of us here it's been a little dull." The priest had all the manner of his kin, gentility and sweetness, the children clustered about him and held his hands as he greeted the knights and Allard seemed curiously keen upon their attention as he stroked hair or gripped hands as the children giggled. He then beckoned them leave before beckoning the brothers to follow. He was old and greyed, he'd probably been very handsome in his youth and his slightly more eloquent speech informed Dietrich that Allard was from Tyrol as it seemed to ping with the occasional Italian sweeping motion of his hands.

Dietrich beckoned the squires and men follow to the barracks and they were led around the back of the half-wood, half-stone building to find the younger cousin of the old Kronstadt Master. He was bent double over a bowl of still living fish slapping about the place as he grumbled. He was trying to make notes onto a wax tablet with a stick, which made Dietrich almost a little concerned before he lifted a hand in greeting and introduced himself, only to be cut off by a lifted hand. Apparently, Rudolph was very busy with his work, far more interested in it than in saying hello to the recruits and instead Allard stepped to the door and beckoned them all in. Dietrich turned to the recruits and beckoned them to follow, insisting that once they had helped unload the cart and sorted their bunks, they would have a sermon, which Allard insisted he would perform for them all. Dietrich watched them leave, Igel then padding to his side to give a whimper before stepping over and about to sniff the Komtur's exposed rear, until he snatched the dog's collar and then Rudolph gave a grunt.

"You're von Hohenflacherstein... you look as I expected and I'm certain you can do the job of teaching the locals to read and write and what not but trust me... that is *all* that happens here. There is no action, no dealing with the raiders... you keep your sword on you but nothing much else. This is where we teach the squires to read scripture and do the stock and tax forms… too many of the lower classes coming in and knowing nothing." Rudolph grunted and curiously, Dietrich found himself just staring at Rudolph in total disbelief before Dietrich just insisted, he was eager to do his part to spread the word of God. It made Rudolph scoff and then he sent Dietrich in to go and see the priest. Dietrich came to the quick conclusion that Allard was probably the only person who actually knew what was going on here.

To Dietrich's great boredom, it was summer by the time he had a moment spare to write a message to Meinhardt and send Igel off. There had been no lies from Rudolph, though his lack of attendance to the prayers held late in the day and first thing in the morning was unusual, there was nothing happening here. It was not a bad thing, Dietrich busied himself in teaching the squires as much as he could and then in aiding Allard ministering to the locals and somehow, as Igel always seemed to escape the barracks, Dietrich would find him playing with the children and be forced to join in. The children were all very sweet and friendly, but he noticed that when they were about eleven, the children would go and spend time alone with Allard, apparently undergoing a 'second conversion' to ensure their understanding of the Christian faith. After this, the children would seem rather strange and unsettled and unwilling to go near Dietrich, but he noticed even the squires were brought in from time to time, the youngest mainly.

This was very concerning and even more so when there seemed to be moments were Dietrich would wake up in the middle of the night and hear one of the squires sobbing softly. On this occasion, Dietrich had of course pulled himself up from his bunk and stepped over to the boy's side, giving him a hug because the boy seemed to need it. The boy had insisted he'd been sinful, but he was too scared to confess to Allard because he would be so disappointed in him! Dietrich was aware of how unsettling it could be to think they'd done something wrong, but when he'd insisted, he could take their confession, suddenly a lot of the boys were eager to talk to him and it irritated Allard.

In fact, Dietrich accompanied Allard as much as he could, to learn of course but it seemed to offend the priest greatly and put Dietrich on edge. There was something remarkably wrong with the area, wrong with the building he slept in, wrong with the whole thing and he was fearful it was just his loneliness for Meinhardt. He had grudgingly even accepted sharing the bed with Igel for a chance to have some kind of cuddle but to his great dismay, the dog seemed to really love lapping his ear constantly at night, and every so often it triggered a dream of Meinhardt that would have Dietrich suddenly sitting up and pushing the dog off! The squires always seemed to know and would giggle about it! But when he had his note written for Igel to send off, Dietrich was worried about what was going to happen to the dog and whether he was going to be safe and Dietrich was almost upset at the thought of letting the dog go, but Ludovic came to see him.

"We're going to go across the river and just let him loose… you think he really would go all the way back to Vogelsang and find Meinhardt? Is he really that good of a hound?" Ludovic was marching beside Dietrich in thick grey cloaks, trembling against the chill in the air but anxious as to all the eyes watching him. With Rudolph finally taking the chance to teach the squires about his wonderful new system of stock control and monitoring, the only things he seemed interested in, Ludovic was the only other fully literate member of the order present. With Allard preaching to the locals as they were preparing to celebrate spring and needed to be weaned against the pagan worship, the pair were quite alone as they stepped onto the barge with the dog panting and whining in excitement. "Brother Dietrich?"

"I think that he'll either go to Meinhardt as wildly and happily as ever, or he'll run right back to me. But we shall see, if this works than it's a very useful system considering the path along the banks is wild on both sides between here and Vogelsang." Dietrich groaned, patting the dog's shoulder as Igel lifted his head up to look at Dietrich in adoration before his ears were straining forward and his jaw was tightening. The dog had the sense he was supposed to be doing something interesting and it gave Dietrich a little bit of hope as Ludo patted the dog's head, but Igel turned about to bark at him viciously. Ludo pulled back with a grimace and then the barge bumped to the bank and Dietrich pulled the dog across and then stood on the path, kneeling down in front of him and cuddling him. "Alright Igel… you wanna go see daddy, right? You wanna go find your daddy? Well go on… be quick and go and give him as many horrible wet sloppy kisses as possible and make sure you roll in some pig shit before you jump on him."

"Isn't that a bit mean?" Ludo questioned as Dietrich straightened up and swiftly shook his head, Meinhardt deserved it! But as Dietrich straightened up, he watched the dog just stand there for a few moments, looking towards him giving a few whimpers of confusion before he suddenly began to trot off. Dietrich waited till Igel turned around again to check him, before spinning about and giving off a few gloriously loud barks before galloping off. Dietrich breathed a sigh of relief as he watched him run and then turned around to step back to the barge as Ludo just blinked a little. "Do you think he'll swim back across if he needs to?"

"I don't doubt anything that dog can do… but aside from that, I bet you're eager to help me teach the squires this evening… I thought we'd discuss the book of Esther tonight and see how they interpret it for our current situations. I already have the Komtur's permission, so no matter what Allard says I'm in charge of that." Dietrich stated firmly as they stepped back onto the punt and it was pushed back towards the other side. Ludo nodded his head gently, understanding that there were issues between the pair, but then the man pushing the barge seemed to give a groan of pain and Dietrich stretched out his hands to hold the oar. He let the old man show him what to do and then gently he helped push the barge along with him, before the old man stepped back with an amused expression to watch the knight do the job for himself as Dietrich groaned. "This is harder than digging out latrine ditches in Sicily!"

"You are very strange… no one else would dare to do that, but I've noticed you're not like the other nobles… you gave up nobility completely upon joining the order, but I have never seen any of the others to have given it up." Ludovic stated gently, but there was suddenly a blush upon his face as he complimented Dietrich that made the older knight feel worried. He thanked Ludo all the same, but he was suddenly very aware of the familiarity of Ludo's actions and his own manner with Sigmond. He suddenly clasped his mouth, feeling a sudden desire to vomit for the memory of that night, the way he'd been saved only by Kirk, and Dietrich was thankful that the old man had returned to grasping the oar as Dietrich rubbed his face. "Something wrong, Brother Dietrich?"

"Just… I hit a pocket in the water that produced a rancid smell…" Dietrich feigned, which made the younger man nod his head though he was a little worried. Dietrich then looked towards the buildings in the distance, feeling concern but knowing he should just talk to Ludovic about this immediately and learn whether it is what he feared or if… or if Dietrich was seeing things he was missing. But that was what made him even more upset, he was missing Meinhardt more than he had ever felt before and more importantly, he needed to be held or just to know that they could communicate their feelings and worse…

he was already utterly pent up. There was no privacy and no discreet ditch with a village around… well, there was one but he was not sure he could really deal with going there.

Upon reaching the other bank, Ludo held his head low and then pulled his hands closer into his clothing, before turning towards Dietrich with saddened eyes and it bothered Dietrich greatly. But he could not have the conversation he needed right now with Ludovic and gently patted his back. He then thanked the man again and they marched back towards the lessons. Dietrich hoped that Igel would reach Meinhardt soon enough and that it would be a message returned… because right now Dietrich needed to hear something from another reasonably sane knight compared to the squires and the knight here!

Two days later had Dietrich leading the youngsters to a thin stream that was used for washing by the locals, he'd requested their permission to have the boys wash and that there would be no intrusions or interruptions. Rudolph thankfully could speak the local language with ease enough to inform them that no women should be anywhere near the stream and even on approach, there had been a few girls giggling before Rudolph had shooed them away. Dietrich had decided that he and Ludovic would stay out of the water on guard for the youngsters and ensure no foul play… the last thing Dietrich wanted was the youngsters hiding each other's robes! But as they were washing, the boys were asking Dietrich about the Holy Land and he ended up telling them instead about the blind man trick and they were all enthralled.

"But how could you tell that you weren't going to get killed for sitting there? It must have taken a lot to get the people to trust you too… especially if other knights had been harming them!" One of the youngsters had gasped before having his head dunked into the freezing water by his companion. Dietrich had then used the sheath of his sword to give that teenager a whack to the shoulder for being a brat, but he told them he'd known he was doing God's work to protect. The young men were startled at the fearlessness, but they spotted Father Allard approaching and all ducked deeper into the water. Even Ludovic looked uncomfortable and Dietrich was concerned as he then pulled off his tunic and hose to join the youth.

"Right… have a look at my scar… the grace of God alone spared me." The elder knight left only in his underwear drew the young men over to look at the hideous line. They all came to view it, even Ludovic and ignored the seemingly disgruntled priest, fingers pointed at Dietrich then he showed whip marks and other scars. The young monks were eager to ask what hurt more and if they would ever have to endure such battles, but Dietrich chuckled. "Have faith in our Lord that you will know devil from man and overcome all struggles."

"You take pride in your stories, Brother... you sound almost as if you were pleased to have entered into such a battle for our Lord... do you not think that killing is blasphemous?" Allard stated, a stern manner to his face that said nothing but his irritation that the younger monks were giving Dietrich such attention. Curiously, the youngsters looked towards Dietrich anxiously! But Dietrich could read that there was a challenge being thrown down by this being and it bothered Dietrich to think that this was probably the first Ordained brother to ever make him so angry. Dietrich though shook his head gently at him and then eased himself into the water, settling to scrub and the youngsters pulled themselves up onto the shore, covering themselves curiously swiftly as Ludovic brought them cloths to dry and their clothes, as Allard approached the water and Dietrich turned to face him.

"I do not think killing can be easily deemed good or bad in the matter of a holy war, brother. When you encounter an enemy, it is easy to see what is man and what is not and there are far more demons that claim their God is the greater to make your whole belief foolish. From what I learnt of the Saracens, to die in a war they believe is for their God means they enter heaven immediately as warriors of their faith..." Dietrich began, assuming initially that it was a barbaric thing to assume that for killing *his* people, one could gain paradise. But then Allard stared at him cautiously and Dietrich could feel the words bouncing about his head, wagging a finger and insisting that it was no different to what their Pope had promised them. But Dietrich did not like to think himself close to any Saracen, not when he'd seen them battle and with their terrifying methods. "Have you been to the Holy Land, Brother Allard?"

"No... I was sent here to convert and teach; I believe that is the way Christ would have favoured above battle." Allard stated, still eyeing Dietrich cautiously and though Dietrich would have loved to agree, he had seen that some pagans could never be tamed. The pair remained with their eyes locked, their expressions hard and Dietrich could understand why Rudolph hated it here and why it was probably just a safer place to hide out nobility. But then Allard gave a soft scoff and he spoke in a way that was unbecoming of a man of his position as Ludovic finished aiding the others in dressing as Dietrich casually scrubbed himself whilst still watching. "Is it truly by the grace of God or the grace of your bloodline that has meant you have survived, von Hohenflacherstein? Do you really think its as holy a mission within the order as you believe? If it were... why only bluebloods and why do the Thuringians dominate?"

"I prefer to be called Brother Dietrich; my surname is of no use unless there is another Brother Dietrich in my convent. Yes, the Thuringians dominate, what families have given more sons to this cause than those? I would not speak down upon members of our Order for the sake of blood." Dietrich growled, feeling suddenly as if Allard had just revealed something about himself that almost intrigued Dietrich. There had been many whisperings in noble courts about excess noble bastards being born in case real heirs fell, but those not suitable were pushed into the church. For years it was not looked down upon, but the German nobility had changed, and it was not made up of so few families anymore. Was Allard just one of those leftovers, maybe from one of those great houses in Thuringia? "Is that why you insist on taking the boys aside to talk to them? Are you trying to insist upon them that they should be ashamed to have come from families of renown or that they were given up because they were unwanted? I've heard of resentful priests, the old child sacrifices to the church, but I had not met one before."

"What is spoken between me and one of my flock is between us and God. My duty is to give them solace and purge their sins." This had gained a furious look from the priest, as if Dietrich had caught onto something. It had to be about the boys and when they all looked uneasy, Dietrich pulled himself from the water, standing naked and looking sternly to him. Allard's eyes could not help but look down to him, only for his whole form to shrink and turn away and it made Dietrich very angry. This fellow was a bully, he was scared of Dietrich because Dietrich was not scared of him and Dietrich gave a growl of irritation.

"Do not think that you have the power to force them to obey you... you are a priest, not a knight... your duty is to speak to the flock, not tend to individual lambs!" Dietrich stated, looking incredibly stern and wishing he could just thump his finger into this priest's chest but could not. All the same, the fact that he was shirking at the sight of another man's body was uncomfortable, it was just the way of things that the men often bathed and dressed in full view of one another. But Allard spun on his heel and marched off, only to pause and eye up Ludovic nervously as he brought Dietrich over the rag to dry himself. The priest marched off and out of earshot as Dietrich turned to look at the young lads in concern. "Does he always make you boys feel so scared? He should not, hmm… look, from now on if you have a sin to confess you come to me, do not feel you have to go to him."

"Thank you, Brother Dietrich." There was almost too much relief from the young squires for hearing this statement. It made Dietrich's skin crawl and he wondered about his own time as a squire once again. Sigmond had always said that Dietrich had not been his first target and now he began to wonder just how many similar beings like him there were in this world and whether situations like war and training the youth helped them do what they wanted. There were rules and there were morals set by the church and it upset his thoughts to feel so uncomfortable around a priest.

There was a sudden booming bark that made Dietrich start and turn about towards where the creek met the river. His eyes swelled in horror to see an Igel-shaped beast covered in something he could smell from the bank. Dietrich trembled and gave a hideous groan, knowing very well the dog was aiming straight for him as the squires stared in excitement.

"Oh God its covered in shit… oh no… Igel I beg you…" The dog launched upon him with a whimper of delight, covering the freshly washed Dietrich in muck. But, from his neck, Ludovic pulled a fresh piece of cloth were a small piece of paper was sitting within, simply stating 'in three nights', but though they were excited to know what it meant, Dietrich was being licked to death by the eager mastiff. "I HATE THIS DOG!"

Eight: Dietrich versus Allard

"After midnight mass I must go out to the edge of the village to the ditch and forest to meet one of our order's scouts. I don't know the reason, but it could be there's a raid planned that could be of trouble." Dietrich stated the third evening just after they had finished their meal for the day and been cleaning up, Rudolph beside him grimacing and grumbling that there was far too much to clean up! This was even though they were merely assisting the servants that not only cooked but did the cleaning after their masters. Dietrich was cautious not to say anything more but just await a response as Rudolph seemed eager to ignore him. It was only as he turned about to depart that Rudolph gave a grunt, curious to know what Dietrich thought of the matter and why he was being called. "Oh but sir, I am more expendable than you are… if it is a trap, my life is worth losing when you are needed here."

This made Rudolph chew his lip before he nodded his head in agreement and gave Dietrich the go ahead to depart. Dietrich was thankful, it meant he should be safe to go and not be followed by anyone. Dietrich's heart was already trembling in excitement at the idea of going to see Meinhardt tonight and automatically his mind was filled with thoughts of cuddling in the moonlight, kissing, holding hands and being rather romantic… though feminine. Indeed, as he pondered the thoughts over whilst assisting sorting the laundry with the youngsters, he found himself snorting at the thought of Meinhardt saying something so silly as how the moon made Dietrich look beautiful. His sudden moments of sniggering made the youngsters query and Dietrich had needed to insist that they did not need to worry, insisting that he was thinking of when he'd seen his previous commanders trying not to fall off his horse after it had been spooked! The youngsters did not really understand but left it at that and Dietrich continued his duties.

However, the mention that Dietrich was going to be absent for an important reason from midnight mass had been passed to Allard and the priest was bemused on the matter and concerned. His thoughts were to seek out the older student, Ludovic, for though this young man was too old to truly appreciate the abilities of the priest in guiding the young during their most crucial and possibly sinful stages, he knew Ludovic was very admiring of Dietrich. When he found the young man within the chapel praying on his knees and almost about to lie down in a display of total submission to the Lord, Allard was intrigued. Ludo had come from a monastery and been sent out here because the religious were as important as the soldier and of course, Ludo's father was still trying to apologise for the sin of creating the child.

"Such penitence is befitting of you, Brother Ludovic... but tell me, something troubles you greatly to be so devoted to prayer outside the masses... I do not judge, that is the job of our Lord, but I can be a helpful ear to your troubles. Tell me brother... confess to me and it may ease the burden in your soul." Allard knew the words to say, he'd never wanted to be a priest and never wanted to be involved in anything that meant he could not enjoy himself and others. But he'd never had the choice, he'd grown up forced into religion, tortured by dreams and desperate for a way to purge them and only when he'd gained the trust of others to be alone in teaching, had he found ways to enjoy the dreary, boring life. He was good at hiding his sins within the knowledge of other's sins... he was manipulative because it had been the best way to avoid beatings and he was hateful of people like Dietrich who seemed to choose the order after having his fill of 'life'. "Please... tell me..."

Allard knelt down beside Ludovic as he straightened up, tears upon his face because of the troubles he felt and Allard knew that Ludovic was desperate for an ear. But Allard was feeling a little... peckish... he had a thought on what the issue was and he would draw the sin out, gain a confession almost like an inquisitor might, but of course... he would never hurt anyone. His long hand stretched to Ludovic's thigh, patting it gently as Ludo closed his eyes and lowered his head in shame, only to give a gasp of fear. Allard stroked around the inner thigh, stroked it very close until he felt the shift and he had the sin he would exploit, whether Ludovic truly did suffer it or not, but of course he would speak. Ludovic turned to look to Allard with terror written upon his face and Allard remained affectionate and kind in his face and voice but on the inside he was cackling in delight.

"It is not unknown for a squire to admire his master... it is not unknown to fall in love with a master... but to have impure thoughts, it is not so common, and it is dangerous. Tell me, brother... the way you look to Brother Dietrich, I have seen it in others accursed with such a grievous sin. You dream of him do you not? Your body reacts to the touch of any man because your heart tricks you to think it is his touch... because your body is being overwhelmed by a lust you have never known before... not even once... and it scares you hideously."

Allard stated, his hand still stroking and feeling the power he held over the young man as Ludovic quivered and grimaced in anxiety to be touched like this. Tears trickled down his cheeks as they reddened, a sickening feeling had overcome him and very, very softly, he nodded his head and Allard stopped, holding his shoulder and then he leant in. "Then I will help you, but first, I request that you do me a favour and follow Dietrich tonight and keep hidden… he might be in danger out there and I fear he does not appreciate my concerns. Will you help him and then, I will help you and you may confess to me."

"Yes… yes Father Allard… I need help, I wish to aid Dietrich too." Ludovic stated, his head lowered in dismay all the same and his eyes clenched shut. The hand had caused something terrible, something the young monk had been trying to stop for years and Dietrich had made all the more profound. Of course, Dietrich must not know of this feeling, he must not know anything of this and it scared Ludovic greatly that maybe the priest might say something unpleasant. He straightened himself up from the ground and nodded his head, insisting he would go and do as he was told and Allard gave a soft nod of his head whilst hiding an inside smirk.

This was exactly what Allard needed, a way to knock Dietrich down a peg as he was quite sure something was going on, maybe Dietrich was meeting with a woman… the cad!

When the bell was tolled and the squires were pacing towards the chapel to attend midnight mass, Dietrich was dressed in simple plain clothes rather than his raiment as he stepped out of the dorms and off the grounds. He marched steadily with a cloak over his body and his face covered as he was alone in the dark, grim world at that time. Dietrich felt cold and anxious, there were shadows that felt like they were following him and Dietrich could not accept it. He kept turning his head around, his green eyes flicking all about the place as if trying to see if there was indeed someone following him tonight. The general sensation of disquiet was not easy to shake off and he was anxious when he marched towards the small line of trees and the ditch beyond.

He was impatient as he stepped amongst the bushes and the scrub, smothered in the shadows with just a small lamp to guide him through the darkness. He was not even being followed by Igel and that made him almost a little fearful not to have the animal's company and caution. But when he reached the woodland right beside the ditch, he spotted a figure in a grey cloak shuffling about and holding onto a sword. It was difficult to see who it was in the darkness, but Dietrich's hand moved to a dagger he'd brought with him and cautiously, he stepped towards the being, the dagger out and his arm straining out, ready to snatch his enemy. As the figure paced about the edge of the ditch with his sword, Dietrich managed to sneak behind him and gently he grasped the figure's shoulder and was about to put the dagger to the stranger's throat in warning, when he received a kick in the knee and he gave a grunt of agony that was recognised with a familiar kse-kse snigger.

"Heh… its going to take a few more years of my hearing going before you can get me from behind… Dieter!" Meinhardt spun about, dropping his sword as Dietrich dropped the dagger. He was grinning at him dumbly, something in his eyes just shining with amusement as he then checked about behind them before grasping Dietrich about the waist and pulling him into a hug. The pair chuckled as they grasped each other, patting shoulders and just glad to see each other before Meinhardt then stroked a little at the collar of Dietrich's jerkin. Dietrich looked into his eyes, there were a few moments just staring before Meinhardt leant forward to a soft kiss, only to get pushed back as Dietrich gave a growl.

"You just kicked me… I'm not happy." Dietrich grunted and Meinhardt gave a snigger that it was only a natural reaction to have. The pair then settled onto the ground beside the ditch, a small lamp lit between them both as they patted shoulders again before Meinhardt began to explain what was going on. There was nothing unusual to be expected of course, a raid was going to happen nearby and the order needed slaves to sell, so Dietrich would have to arrest any new arrivals into the town if they did not show signs of following the right faith. Dietrich gave a groan of frustration, surely this kind of talk would have been easier passed in a message, but Meinhardt insisted he'd wanted to pass it over himself because there were too many people stalking around pretending to sell information. "It seems ridiculous, but there are a few camps of our foe along the riverbank, so I can envision you being cautious… still, I'm glad you came to see me, I do miss you hideously no matter how long its been."

"Because you're soft, Dieter! But, I'll admit I missed you too, hence I came here alone where I thought we might have… privacy." The sudden pause coincided with Meinhardt hearing a distant twig snap and he looked out amongst the copse anxiously. In the dull light it was hard to tell if he could see anything more than darkness and vague shapes, but when there was the sudden hooting of an owl above, Meinhardt shrugged his shoulder with an unpleasant shudder and cautiously Dietrich held his hand, glad it was accepted. Neither of them could see that there was indeed someone watching them, someone now flat on their stomach peering out and seeing their outlines but not too much detail, Ludovic. Their ignorance to him was obvious as Meinhardt then leant inward and Dietrich moved forward, the soft clapping sound and the motions of their shadows so clear that Ludovic smothered himself to witness them kissing!

It was just a nice and simple little kiss, but very quickly Dietrich swung his hand up into Meinhardt's blonde hair, stroking and teasing the dirty locks as he pressed his forehead to his lover's. Meinhardt gave a soft sigh, his arms grasping about Dietrich's hips to hold him as their faces came together in another kiss. It was a passionate and longer motion, breathing through their noses as their lips clasped and pinched tightly about one another, whilst their tongues rolled and coiled as they both moaned lovingly and their hands snatched at each other, gripping tightly as their faces twisted as much as they could as their mouths and tongues tried to remain locked together. Then, they pulled apart, that soft little strand of spit glittering between them as Meinhardt licked his lips to clear it before leaning forward to steal another kiss. Dietrich moaned lovingly, melting into another passionate kiss as Meinhardt held his hot cheek and stroked near his ear before they both pulled away again.

"You've delivered your message... I'll report it back... we should leave it at this and depart..." Dietrich stated, his voice unconvincing as he practically dropped his tone, his hands suddenly stroking at Meinhardt's thighs. He could see the kissing had excited his lover and despite the fact Dietrich knew they needed to separate and escape now; he did not want to when he had been so desperate to feel Meinhardt's heat against his. Meinhardt heaved a sigh of irritation and gave a grunt, practically agreeing but then leaning in to steal another kiss. Then he shuffled right up to him, Dietrich still stroked at his thighs whilst Meinhardt's rough hand was quick to stretch to his lover's belly, stroke its way within the clothing as they kissed once more and Dietrich gained a more loving moan. They pulled apart their faces, but their hands were already touching and groping at the groin of the other, their lips pinching together once more before Dietrich gave a groan. "If you keep touching me, I won't be able to let you go until I've felt you inside me..."

"I want to be inside you... I don't ever want to break apart from you... if only our bodies could remain as entwined as our souls." Meinhardt grumbled and Dietrich gave a soft chuckle, his face turning crimson as his heart hammered away and he gently licked Meinhardt's nose to make him give a soft groan of excitement. He realised he'd said something ridiculously romantic and though he had not meant for it to come across that way, Dietrich nuzzled against him lovingly and Meinhardt knew that he now could not leave at all until he had satisfied his partner... he pushed Dietrich down immediately. He didn't want the hassle of time lost in trying to prepare Dietrich, but he could not imagine hurting him and so he lay over his lover as they both held and kissed each other. Meinhardt's hand then shuffled to get Dietrich's backside free of his garments before sticking his fingers to the wanted area and then teasing and twisting his fingers to please his lover.

Ludovic's eyes could not really see what was going on, but he could see that it had looked as if Meinhardt were attacking him, before he then watched a hand doing something and then his ears were echoing with terrible sounds. Ludo clenched at the ground, lowering his head and closing his eyes, he could hear Dietrich giving low moaning sounds, pleasant, satisfying noises as Meinhardt was teasing at his body lovingly whilst kissing at his throat gently enough not to leave a mark. Meinhardt groaned in pleasure against his partner, thankful that Dietrich's body still remembered him as it had so long ago and then, with a firm kiss to the lips, he threw Dietrich's legs around his waist before he shuffled and then managed to connect their flesh.

Once more Ludovic dared to lift his head and he knew there could be no mistake in the shadows he was seeing; Dietrich on his back, smothering his face whilst moaning lovingly, drooling and nipping at his hands in rapture. Then there was Meinhardt, his body firmly pushing into the point where their shadows conjoined, sitting up and groaning while giving deep breaths of relief. There was a smell that began to form in the air too, something strange, sickly, sweet but then wholesome in its curiosity and it made Ludo's body ping and twinge in an unmistakable desire that was making him want to cry. The squire pulled himself up, hearing those moans and wishing it could be something to do with him before he pulled up onto his feet and managed to escape the pair with the swiftest of movements, hurrying to find Allard... only to know that he could not tell him what he had seen!

Dietrich had missed morning mass, lounging happily within his bunk with Igel laying over his hips protectively. The dog could smell his owner around

Dietrich and whenever the squires had gotten close, the dog snarled and growled viciously, possessively guarding Dietrich so the squires had hurried to mass. Ludovic had not returned to his bed that night, he had been stuck in Allard's company, his mouth shut over what he had seen and merely passing on information, but of course Allard could not give the information to Rudolph in case it raised suspicions. However, Rudolph was quick to gather the squires around Dietrich's bunk after breakfast, a cane in his hands as Igel snarled at him angrily.

"Now my young squires… you see our lieutenant here was on a special information mission last night and that alone is why he has been permitted to keep resting. The manner of his guard dog informs you that it was a very risky situation and the animal was on guard in case someone tracked him back, but you can see from the content look upon his face, that he is a man with good news from the Order and clearly gained a thrill in experiencing something close to the purpose of us soldiers here." Rudolph grunted, standing up straight and looking incredibly irritated that he had not been involved in such an event. Ludovic was amongst them of course and grimacing as he looked towards Dietrich's happy expression… that morning Ludovic had been shown by Allard a forbidden illustration showing what he thought Ludovic had seen and indeed, there had been similarities and the image had appeared painful. He could not understand the happy expression and he was thankful when Rudolph jabbed Dietrich firmly in the back with the cane and the dog suddenly grabbed it, Rudolph dropped it and Igel carried it away for fun.

"Uh? Apologies commander… I was very careful when and how I came back. I had to take a route with my brother before pulling away and waiting in case of followers before I returned here. I am sorry I slept through the early morning mass. Which penance or punishment do you wish to prescribe for my sloth?" Dietrich stated, swinging his body off the bed and then standing up, only to wobble slightly for the straining and weakness in his thighs. His back was a little sore about the hips, but only because the ground had not been soft, but Meinhardt had been remarkably gentle, so it had taken longer but bathed in moonlight had given it a much more romantic atmosphere that Dietrich was willing to gain some kind of punishment for. However, Rudolph informed him to pass the information over and Dietrich straightened up to look proper. "Sir, a raid on a nearby village will occur within the following days, but with several neighbouring areas containing pagan foes, we have been requested to obtain and convert any strangers that arrive within our community within the next week. If they fail to convert, we are to relinquish them to the Brothers for use as slaves."

"Good, good… a shame we can't get involved in such actions, but its something. I'll discuss with Allard on how to deal with this matter, but I need you to prepare these squires for a potential hand-to-hand engagement. You can act as their target, that seems punishment enough." Rudolph chuckled softly, walking out of the barracks whilst getting startled by Igel in the hall. The dog presented him with the cane and Rudolph gave a chuckle before leading the dog off to go for a walk. The squires were chuckling in amusement, quite eager for a chance to beat him up with some sticks for a bit of fun, but surprisingly, one of the youngest of the squires, one of the many named Konrad, lunged into Dietrich, knocking him onto the floor.

With a grunt of frustration, Dietrich fell onto the floor and then swung his arm out, grasping Konrad and pulling him down, patting his chest and insisting he was dead now. But Konrad kicked Dietrich firmly in the side to be released before clambering up onto Dietrich's back as the knight straightened up and tried to shake him off. The other younger squires then joined in, grabbing his arms and kicking Dietrich in the shins as he grunted but accepted the beating from the youngsters. The older squires and Ludovic though began to encouraged the youngsters to pull Dietrich down without harming him, to trip him up and tie his hands back like they would an escapee! Dietrich tried to be a little more difficult to encourage the struggle before they pulled him forward and he gently knelt down and let them pin him before stepping on his back, though he gave them a grunt for being callous. The youngsters were all chuckling before Lorenz, one of the youngsters who had been prepping for the monastery instead of the order, gave a sudden grimace.

"That's what Father Allard did." The words came out with such a suddenly depressed expression that made all the squires pull up and step away looking scared. Lorenz realised he'd spoken and quickly he smothered his mouth, shaking and trembling in anxiety for daring to have said anything on the matter. The other squires though were looking upset and then one of them even started to sob slightly as Ludovic even looked scared. Lorenz then started to cry and Konrad joined him as Dietrich pulled himself up, glad when he'd come in at night he'd not removed his full clothing but just left a long shirt and his breeches on. He quickly stepped to Lorenz, laying his hands to his shoulders and kneeling before him… then softly questioning what had happened as

Lorenz gave a whimper of fear. "It was for confession, he said he didn't believe what I had said when I said I'd never had an impure thought and then... he pushed me down and pulled my arms back... he told me if I made a sound I would prove I had impure thoughts and God would be ashamed of my lies... then he... I can't say, I swore I would not say because God would punish me!"

"You don't have to say... is that why you've been sleeping in breeches lately? Konrad... is that why you were having nightmares at night... did Allard hurt you too?" Dietrich looked to the youngster as Lorenz looked so miserable, he almost expected the other to refuse to tell him anything, but Konrad gave a grimace. He lowered his head and insisted he was having trouble with sinful things with his body, that Allard said he would help... but he could only make gestures of someone touching him and Dietrich felt his blood boil with fury. Then he looked to other squire that had been in tears... when they'd first arrived the boy had suffered what he'd insisted had been a bad bout with his stomach and well, bloodied bowel movements were nothing new to the life of a crusader... but now Dietrich was scared as he looked at this squire crumpled onto the ground by his bunk. "You poor boys... how could he dare to do such a thing..."

"Because he knows we're sinful... how can we not be sinful with the thoughts of lust that plague our minds. He sees it, he sees it within everyone and he says he can remove it... but... but it always seems to come back and so we have to go back, no matter how scared we are." Ludovic whimpered suddenly, smothering his face and then sitting down on a bunk, sobbing away in despair at the thought of what had been happening to him. Dietrich was shocked and furious, anxious that someone of the church could do the kind of thing that Sigmond did... indeed, now Dietrich pondered about everything that had been happening lately. He pondered about the children of the town that rushed to Allard but feared him too, the way he seemed to be stand-offish with adults and how he had been scared of Dietrich's naked form. It almost made Dietrich want to be sick, but he straightened up firmly, only for Ludovic to grasp his hand. "Please... please Brother Dietrich, you know that the punishment for sodomy is being burnt at the stake, do not tell Rudolph... would you really wish to see innocent boys burn?"

Ludovic held his hand firmly, his rotund form shaking heavily as tears fell down his eyes and Dietrich felt furious and yet, he grasped Ludovic in a hug, patting his shoulder and saying sorry to him. Then Dietrich turned to each boy, holding them in turn, apologising to them and they all wanted to grasp hold of him for protection before Dietrich then beckoned them to kneel with him in prayer and ask God for his forgiveness and his guidance on what to do. But Dietrich's stomach was boiling with horror, how had he not realised that something so hideous was going on right beneath his eyes? Why had he not shown interest before? Was it because he'd been so distracted with his loneliness? If it was, then the Lord certainly had a harsh way of slapping him back into obedience and Dietrich ended the prayers before straightening up.

"I'm going to talk to him, ask him to confess to me and swear never to touch anyone again. In the meantime… all of you should go out and start your training, I want to see you practicing your hand-to-hand, so stand opposite each other, stay in your spot, and try to punch at the other you can see in front of you without really hitting them. Ludo… I trust you to ensure they obey a swift rule not to hit each other. I'll dress then join you all soon." Dietrich stated firmly, a stern expression upon his face as he looked at the collection of young boys with utter misery and despair. These boys were still too young and probably unwilling to kill and fight the way they would be expected to, but if they were to remain so timid, they could not protect themselves against a bastard like this priest. It made Dietrich want to vomit acid, it was such a vile and horrible thing and yet he could only feel guilt for not picking up on it straightaway.

With a grunt, he marched to the chapel where Allard was busy wiping down one of the religious icons with a soft humming sound. When the figure realised he was being glared at, Allard just produced a smug but soft smile as he turned about to face Dietrich and calmly requested if he wished to have mass now or wanted to help sweep the floor. Dietrich though remained staring harshly towards the figure and Allard was just curious as he pondered over what Dietrich might be assuming of him, only to step to his side with open arms. Dietrich remained glaring at him and though Allard was not comfortable with such a grown figure glaring at him, no one else had ever dared to treat him with such hostility before and so he thought to say the only things that came to his mind.

"Have you ever wished you were not a knight, Brother Dietrich?" Allard stated, but Dietrich shook his head roughly, he'd not doubted that this was the place he belonged or he would never have returned all those years ago. Allard was amused and then he queried if the story about having his brother's wife to produce an heir was true… Dietrich had nodded his head and insisted it had been a desperate situation. It made Allard scoff and suddenly he'd looked at Dietrich almost knowingly and wickedly, as if he could see that Dietrich was no different to someone like Sigmond, to other self-righteous knights that sneakily turned into barbarians under the assumption all sins would be forgiven. "You liked the carnal act, didn't you? I can see it in your eyes, I can guess that you dream of it regularly... you make such sighs in your sleep and you have none of the complaints of other knights. But you see... you were able to choose to indulge, most of us do not and when we are forced to just accept it over and over again, no matter how weak or wretched we are from it... in the end you just accept and beckon it in so it will be over faster. Huh... from your expression, I say that's probably closer to what you felt."

"I was forced, it was never willing and I prayed every day to be taken back for the sake of my soul. Eventually, God called me back and I was ever thankful." Dietrich stated, but now he was curious about what had been happening to Allard, what he was doing and he hoped this would be a confession for what he had done, but Allard just smiled to think they had something in common. He held Dietrich's shoulder, looked him right in the eyes and then Dietrich almost vomited at the words said, his heart trembling with terror and unsure how he could deal with this and claim he was helping the squires.

"I did the same... every day I was in the monastery... I prayed he would be kind and stop my neighbour leaving his cell every night to come to me. Its one of those curious things in the religious world isn't it? Utter redemption for past sins by dropping everything and accepting the will of God... but if you're already infected with the Devil's desires, how can you stop yourself? My Brother had come to the monastery a long time ago, in his previous life he'd done many horrible things to other young people... hidden amongst the monks so he could not be hung and then found it the perfect ground to find prey. Isn't that horrible? But you can't tell anyone, the person he was before is not the person he is now... children make up such silly stories because they are unhappy here... all cries for attention and God will be wrathful for your falsehoods." Allard chuckled, his face twisted with some kind of manic expression as if those memories were almost... nostalgic and pleasant. Dietrich was terrified, he'd never heard of such a thing before, he could never dream that any being within the priesthood could ever have been such a fiend. It made him sick and scared too, but Allard had not confessed to him what he'd done to the

boys and almost seemed to be saying these things as if they were any excuse.

"Why then hurt these children? Inflicting such horrors onto others because it was done to you… why do that?" Dietrich growled, restricting his urge to just snatch his hands about Allard's throat and choke the life out of him. But Allard just looked at Dietrich with a soft snort of amusement and then looked to the icon upon the table before looking to Dietrich with a soft sad expression.

"I was told… we cannot truly understand the suffering Christ endured for our souls unless we suffer ourselves…" With that, he said nothing more and then returned to his cleaning. Dietrich wanted to shake him down, make him confess that he had done these things so that he could drag him to Rudolph and have him dealt with. But the result would be burning and if Allard had been left to suffer as a child because of a being like Sigmond that had gotten away, was it really so righteous to judge him to death? Something about it all was confusing Dietrich, wounding his softened heart before Allard turned around to face him with a pleasant expression and almost seemed to want to laugh. "When Rudolph came here just after my fellow priest passed over in the bad winter, the people did not trust the markings of a knight, until I told them to respect him. The people here trust me above your order and without me… what would stop them from doing worse to those little boys?"

"Don't ever touch them again… or I will kill you." Dietrich growled, but it was half-hearted and Allard seemed to know it as Dietrich stepped away to join the youngsters practicing. He noticed that Ludovic was staring at him forlornly, almost as if he knew that Dietrich had gained no ground in this manner. Something about the way Allard spoke to him seemed to swim around his mind, some kind of depressed, morbid charisma that made Dietrich look past to the hurt boy beyond that no one had wanted or cared about. The accusation against others in the church too was disturbing and Dietrich could not wrap his head about it… he needed someone hard of heart and straightforward in their convictions to deal with this.

He needed Meinhardt!

Nine: Meinhardt's Assistance

"Watch for that axe Leonhard!" Meinhardt grunted, swinging his sword out to chop clumsily at one of the pagans that was trying to swing his axe into Leonhard's horse. As the figure gave a groan and tried to turn to face his enemy, Leonhard's steed barged back, knocking the man to the ground before a sudden charge from two other knights pulled the horses forward. The figure and others were trampled or crushed within the tight confines of the chaos. As the group crashed into the minimal attack force that had met them, the remaining people within the small village were already trying to run for their lives. Meinhardt had spotted Diethelm still wrestling away with one of the pagans that was clearly dead, but the young squire had never killed before and the reactions were normal. "Diethelm... get your sword out of that corpse and back on your horse!"

The sudden bark from his elder knight made Diethelm jump and pull his sword away, tears were streaking down his face, he did not like killing and he was so scared and upset his hands could not stop shaking. The adrenaline did not seem to be aiding him one bit as Meinhardt kicked his old horse back over to hook up the more mule-like animal that Diethelm was riding, and he pulled the horse over to the young soldier. As the young man remained standing there, trembling with the shock of having shed blood, Meinhardt swung the reins in front of him and then gave a soft ruffle of his hair, making Diethelm look up to him as Meinhardt growled to get up on the horse. Diethelm obeyed, pulling himself up onto the horse and grabbing its neck tightly as he screamed and sobbed into it, Meinhardt left the horse and squire there as he went to deal with the rest.

He urged his plodding old gelding amongst the group, helping punch and kick whatever beings were not already down, seeing amongst the mud and the churned up grass that the defence was over and the village was left to them. Though it had been intended to be a usual raid to crash in, smash and kill what they could before leaving, it looked like a rout for the poor villagers! His commander was accepting that this was now the case and swiftly, called for the knights to surround the village and then he hollered to Leonhard to go and get the men-at-arms to come in and secure the area. Leonhard looked too locked up in the churning mess with most of the other knights, so Meinhardt turned about

and barked at Diethelm to go and do the job; the squire was thankful to escape and galloped off!

Meinhardt watched him go and then he continued to kick down the resistance, knowing they'd become slaves if they didn't die. He then charged through the cluster of horses and fighting men, hurrying off amongst the village and then hollering out for all residents to surrender in the centre of the village or else! He took a bit of wood still burning from a campfire, leaning down the side of his old plodder to hook it up and then set fire to the thatch of one household. It was enough to send people running out of the homestead and he hopped off his horse, bringing his sword forward in case the people tried to attack. Instead they just kept running and then a little child fell over in front of his feet. The adults continued running, too scared to worry about it and yet Meinhardt hooked the child up around the waist, ignoring the babe's screams and cries of upset as he marched with his horse and the writhing baby towards the centre of the village.

Other villagers were gathering, seeing the knight holding onto a child, his face obscured by his helm and his armour coated in mud and blood with his grim looking sword... they were all alarmed. As the people gathered together, huddling and whimpering to each other, the mother of the child remained locked upon its squealing form. Meinhardt noticed the mother's eyes staring and without care he stepped over and gently eased the child back into her arms. The people were startled before they all shrank as he continued to bark in the Polish language for the pagans, who just about understood the language, to gather together. There was a rush as the men still alive hurried back to join their families, all of them weeping and bloodied up, the entire village looking horrified and upset as the Komtur stepped over and beckoned for the fires on the village to be put out for now. He called his knights to then search the buildings and bring people out as they surrounded them calmly.

"Meinhardt... how long till your squire will return?" The Komtur talking to Meinhardt was not *his* Komtur, this was another figure that had taken on Leonhard as his lieutenant and was more than a bit of a miserable Thuringian about talking to non-Germans, so Konrad had given him Meinhardt to ensure this raid did not become a massacre. Slaves were worth more after-all and if the Order was to make its foothold here, it needed land, revenue and people to work it so the knights could focus on the important things. When Meinhardt insisted that Diethelm was good when he had a goal in mind, the Komtur just gave a scoff about how irresponsible squires were. It could not be helped, most Komturs were in their forties and veterans of the Crusades in the Holy Land, they'd been so used to the youngsters dropping like flies that they'd become desensitised and hardened, hence the anxiety about massacres, though Balk had made it clear to only kill those who resisted and those who would not convert and couldn't be sold off.

With the majority of the villagers already out and crowding in the square, Leonhard pulled himself from amongst the five other knights and squires to help guard the people as fires were put out and houses cleared out. The village was small, but its position on one of the clearest paths from a nearby marsh meant it had strategic value in holding back the native tribes. A garrison here could easily help warn of incoming attacks from the east and a garrison further north could deal with that lot too, but the Pomesanians were a little tougher and the ones that Meinhardt's family had encountered before. But as the men settled, Meinhardt thought to try and lead a prayer with Leonhard encouraged to count just how many of these pagans understood they should copy.

As he knelt down as the fires were put out and the houses seemed empty, some of the squires dismounted and chose to join him. The Komtur noticed too and trotted his large and handsome looking blood-bay charger over to Leonhard's side as he watched the villagers reacting. The children were confused, not sure what to do and only a few women with babes pressed to their chests began to look towards Meinhardt's position and so they did the same, assuming it might just save them and their children. A few of the old people copied, trying to see if it would help them out and the Komtur grimaced... if too many started to do that, they'd lose out on slaves and he gave a grunt as he stepped towards the group and then started to grab the arms of everyone who took the position, pulling them up as they screamed out or cringed and then passing them over to Leonhard.

"Those that I push over to you, have chosen to be Christian and will be baptised when the Ordained brothers arrive, we can let the men deal with them... they'll certainly want the company... but those I'm leaving behind, we'll chain up and send back to the Master, understood?" The Komtur scoffed and it made Meinhardt grimace in frustration as he looked towards Leonhard who was giving the man a stern expression as if he might just hurt him. Meinhardt was starting to realise how very lucky he had been amongst his companions of the past and indeed how Heinrich had been a very tolerable and calm master. This seemed especially true where others who'd been pulled out of the Holy Land were more harsh and miserable than he could have thought possible.

As the Komtur continued to pull the women and children up, making them scream and grimace for his bullying, Meinhardt noticed how some of the villagers started to drop their hands as if they were not praying. Meinhardt continued to pray out loud as the women and children were pushed forward along with some of the men that were clearly showing faith in the action. It told Meinhardt that the commander's bullying was to make people drop their hands to ensure there were more slaves to be sold. It irritated Meinhardt greatly and he growled loudly as he watched the Komtur grab and pull one woman by the arm, almost making her drop her baby. Meinhardt stood up and then gave the senior knight a harsh look before insisting he should be leading prayer. The Komtur gave a grunt and then stepped back to do the same, wiping hands assumed dirty for touching these pagans upon Meinhardt's cloak. The northerner did not care, these people were used to treating the youngsters like rubbish and Meinhardt then gently eased those that were praying up to their feet and motioned for them, speaking in the Polish language to go to Leonhard's side. Many others began to pray when they understood what was going on and Meinhardt was able to pull out a good portion of the population, meaning that the village would not be completely emptied for the slaves.

"Good work." After finishing the prayer the commander stood up and then instructed the squires to tie up the remaining villagers who tried to struggle and when a few tried to run, the Komtur turned to one of his knights. The figure, broad and stocky and completely hidden in his armour, swung his sword up and dared to run after the escapee, clumsily chopping at him until the person was upon the ground. He dispatched him finally and the villagers could not stop the conjoined mourning, moaning, sobbing and wails of agony for their fate as they were gathered up, but the Komtur looked towards Meinhardt with irritation. "Brother Meinhardt… you did well on your assignment the other night… can I count on you to return to Komtur Rudolph for the next two weeks to instruct them of this conquest and how it should link the Order, happily back to them."

"I'll go as soon as you request." Meinhardt stated, straightening up with a firm stomp of his foot to salute the Komtur and take his orders. He had the feeling this Komtur just did not want to look at him anymore and the feeling was mutual as the figure dismissed him with a wave. Meinhardt stepped over to

Leonhard's side and insisted that he would need to help Diethelm out when he returned, which his companion agreed to. Then Meinhardt stepped towards his old plodder, grasped the edge of the saddle and swung himself up as he then reaffixed his helmet before looking towards those women and their children. He may not like women at all, but he knew the strength of a mother protecting her child and he hoped they would become good Christians and appreciate what faith could do, as he steered his gelding away and trotted off.

Dietrich was in a plight, he may have been able to keep the boys away from Allard by busying them in study and training, but he had found that the local children were targets too. In fact, Allard was almost flagrantly too tactile with them than was usual, but Rudolph did not care and it was clear he viewed the natives as less than other Christians. Dietrich noticed though that the boys were growing in their confidence around him and their studies, but they wished there was something they could do all the same to help Dietrich with his concerns on what to do next. Dietrich could only protect the children of his order because of the language barrier and could only protect them whilst he was here. But what ate into Dietrich's heart more than anything else was the fact that the only thing that separated himself and Allard, was that Dietrich saw innocence where Allard saw ignorance that needed to be corrected.

Dietrich was scrubbing the church properly with all of his young squires as they grumbled about roughened hands and breaking nails, he alone was wiping down the cross of wood upon the altar. He was praying to it within his mind for some kind of guidance and aid, to send him some kind of figure who could tell him what he needed to do and how to fight Allard. Lost in his prayers as he cleaned and prayed alongside his master, Ludovic noticed that there was a strange sound coming from the front door. As Ludo stepped to the door and opened it up, some of the locals were rushing over and pointing hands, begging for Rudolph and seemingly insisting that they had done nothing wrong and they were loyal Christians, constantly making gestures of the cross as if petrified that they were to be slaughtered. Ludovic spotted a mud-drenched horse with a fully clad knight upon it with a bloodied sword and drying splashes of crimson upon his white raiment... all the things the locals had nightmares over, steadily approaching the church!

"Sir... sir! I'm Squire Ludovic, please show yourself, this church marks our small barracks..." Ludovic skipped out to help keep the peace as he ran towards the massive grey-white horse that was standing rather calmly and snorting away. As he hurried over, there was a sudden furious bark from the courtyard and Ludovic froze in fear as he watched Igel come speeding around the corner. The knight turned around to face the dog and Ludo gave a yelp. "Brother Dietrich! Dietrich, Igel's going to eat a fellow brother knight!"

Dietrich was roused from his prayers and spun on his heel, bolting down the hall only to skid on a puddle and go sliding into some of the benches as the squires rushed over to him in a panic. As Ludovic stared out at the dog, the animal launched right from the ground and onto the lap of the knight! The horse gave a grunt of irritation, his tail swishing and head swinging around as Igel lay back, cradled in the arms of the knight and slurping messily at his helmet, whimpering and whining in utter delight! Ludovic just blinked in surprise as he stepped to the horse and then looked to the dog in confusion as the knight lifted a hand to grasp his helmet and jerked it off.

Steely blue eyes, alabaster skin, short pale blonde hair it was almost white, patches of it notched from around the ears to claim the helmet damage and an expression of pure villainy emerged. He looked like an executioner with that cold, stern expression even as the dog lapped at his face and Ludovic was trembling in terror. Even he could not think of something more to say, to even greet the older being that was slightly bruised around the nose from riding in the helmet and clearly had come straight from a battle. Even the other young squires poking their head around the door were terrified as was Rudolph as he stepped into the courtyard, not really willing to be given new orders or his steady life to be distorted by troublesome warriors. However, when Dietrich managed to get up, rubbing at his back and grumbling to himself as Allard and a group of villagers appeared to have a look at what was going on, the figure noted him with a grin.

"Ah! Dieter! I've got the right village then… sorry for the mess, came right from chaos and was tracking escapees whilst being sent here to assist in case trouble comes. Three fully capable knights are better than just two and a bunch of squires." The figure beamed, a playful boyish smile making his face light up but his sniggering laugh all the more terrifying. No one was calmed until Dietrich gave a soft chuckle and stepped over himself, stroking the muzzle of Klobig before gently patting his companion's leg and then getting given his helmet. "Only bad point, been riding so much I've gone a bit numb in the leg… mind helping your brother off the horse?"

"Surely you should just get Klobig to back you into the ditch… of course Meinhardt." Dietrich scoffed and then watched Meinhardt slowly swing his legs around to Dietrich before sliding down. The squires calmed, they'd heard the name and remembered the voice, some of them slapping themselves for not recognising him at all! Dietrich grasped him firmly about the waist, letting Meinhardt grasp his shoulders and if it were not for the crowds watching them, it would have been a very different moment. Indeed, their hearts were beating and they felt that magnetic pull that would have urged their lips to connect and Dietrich would have loved to pull his lover onto him and fall upon the ground, kissing each other and ignoring the universe… but of course they were instead blushing as Meinhardt wobbled and lost sensation in a leg, almost pulling Dietrich over until they both landed into a present Klobig had decided to leave for them to squish into. There were sniggers of amusement as they straightened up and Dietrich slapped the dung off his hands until Igel leapt off and tried to lick the mess from him. "Dear God, that's disgusting…"

"Awe… he just wants to check you're alright, didn't you Igel?" Meinhardt sniggered again, grasping the dog's slobbering muzzle and ruffling his fur whilst making faces at him. As the young squires eased, Rudolph stepped forward and spoke in his rather poor Polish to inform the locals that this was not something to worry about if they were good Christians. He was gruff as usual and Meinhardt turned to look at him in confusion as he pulled himself up from the ground and then just seemed to eye the commander up. Rudolph turned about to do the same, he had to admit he felt a little intimidated to see this fellow, but when Igel kept licking at Meinhardt and whimpered, Rudolph gave a chuckle as Dietrich finally got himself up.

"Huh… greetings, Brother Meinhardt? Well… squires continue your work, I'll put the horse in the stalls, Dietrich you can take your friend to scrub up in the barracks, we should have spare clothing and then you can appoint one of the squires to do the laundry. When you're cleaned up, I'll be ready to hear your report within my office." Rudolph stated and Meinhardt straightened in salute before handing over the reins as Ludovic beckoned the squires back inside and seemed to take over. Allard watched and he felt just as scared at the sight of Meinhardt as Ludovic had been, but Ludovic was trembling in anxiety at the thought that what he'd seen before would occur whilst they were cleaning up. Ludovic did not want Dietrich's soul to be damaged anymore, but what could he do?

Meinhardt was led by Dietrich around to the courtyard and then to an area where he could remove his mucky boots before entering the building, one of Rudolph's quirks about cleanliness in the barracks. Meinhardt removed the hefty metal catches around his heels and toes before easing the boots off too and then grumbling that he had a pool of sweat within! Dietrich insisted it was the sign of a man that valued his duty to God rather than his appearance and Meinhardt mused it was good to hear such things again. Clearly, he was frustrated and tired, but life in the Order was never easy and rest was deserved only on special achievements and at night. As the pair marched down the row of bunks of the main barracks, they then steered to the small washroom that was not much more than a small wooden cupboard with a bucket of water that had been sitting for a while and a scrubbing brush. It was really just for use when washing hands before prayer or breakfast, but it would do as Dietrich scrubbed his dirty hands free and then pulled his clothing aside, tossing it onto a large pile sitting on a nearby wooden box that smelt rather rancid.

"I see Rudolph likes to maintain humility by keeping you in the same clothes for an entire week…" Meinhardt scoffed, but he could accept it as an act of humility and pointing out that the order still maintained monk-like attitudes and considering they were not to shave or cut their hair, with a few exceptions, it fit well to wear their clothes till they were unbearably smelly or torn up. But he watched Dietrich reveal his chest and perhaps a slight slacking in his muscles to say this was an easier life, Meinhardt could not help but give a soft chuckle and as he peeled his layers away and found himself requiring help with the mail, he looked towards Dietrich with a coy expression. "How's about helping your husband undress?"

"How about a lesson in humility when I yank the mail straight up and remove a nipple?" Dietrich scoffed, but where perhaps there should have been humour in it at first, Dietrich felt suddenly sick and curiously scrubbed his hands again. Meinhardt just chuckled over the idea before he started to slowly ease himself out of the mail and kept watching Dietrich sort through a second collection of folded and fresher clothing with just his braes on. This made Meinhardt excited, it embarrassed him to think that since they'd first done it and agreed to be married in God's eyes alone, his libido had become something unconquerable and all he could do was desire to touch his partner. When he was down to just his breeches and Dietrich was distracted, Meinhardt stepped right behind him and swung his hands about Dietrich's waist as the other gave a gasp.

He felt Meinhardt's lips tracing the pale scars upon his back as he gasped and shuddered. "Meinhardt… this isn't a good idea…"

"I know… but we're alone and I can't help but want to ensure this body remembers the sensation of my lips when its not safe for it to remember our connection." Meinhardt growled softly into Dietrich's back and Dietrich could feel his partner's arousal. But oddly Dietrich was suddenly aware of a hand stroking at his front, not too close to his groin but around the scar on his stomach and suddenly it made Dietrich retch and pull away. Meinhardt pulled back suddenly, quickly checking that he had indeed removed all the clothes that were dirty before scrubbing his hands again in case that was the problem. But Dietrich was leaning around the wall with a shudder, his mind had suddenly been locked upon Sigmond and he felt horrible… his body felt like it was an enemy, his love for Meinhardt something vile! "Dieter… are you okay?"

"Mein… do you… do you ever feel that I forced you into this? That I was maybe holding bad ideas from the start and, just the meeting at night after your emissions…" Dietrich began, wanting to cry into his hands as he grit his teeth together and almost shuddered in front of his beloved. Everything Allard had stated was running through his mind, what these boys had experienced and what Sigmond had done. Dietrich was scared that he'd made this happen to Meinhardt… how could Meinhardt have gotten into this kind of situation when he clearly was the most devout and against these things. When Dietrich put a hand to his face as Meinhardt queried the matter, he rubbed at his face and then gave a whimper. "Meinhardt… what if I didn't realise but I made you like this because I wanted you to suffer like I…"

"Like you what?" Dietrich smothered his mouth suddenly, he had forgotten that though he'd hinted that Sigmond had made suggestions and perhaps touched him, he'd never told Meinhardt what had happened… twice! He did not want to say the first and then the second when he was older and should have been less afraid in case Meinhardt thought that he was indeed some perverted creature… a sodomite that they all knew was sinful and diseased and unwelcome…. "Dietrich, what's wrong?"

As Meinhardt stretched his hand out to Dietrich's shoulder, hoping to try and ease whatever was bothering him, Dietrich threw his hand off him and then the door opened. They were both startled to see one of the young squires barging in and quickly pulling his own shirt off. Dietrich closed his eyes and turned away as the boy grabbed a new shirt and then blushed when he noticed

Meinhardt was scowling at him. The young squire bolted off and left the door open as Meinhardt gave a soft grunt and then grabbed his new clothes and pulled them away from Dietrich. He didn't like the words his lover had come up with and quickly he scoffed but under his breath so only Dietrich might be able to hear his voice.

"I loved you when I first saw you… all those dreams were of you, never any woman and… and it was not the first time I'd dreamt of a man and had those kinds of reactions. But until the day I'd met you, the lover I had in my dreams never had a face." Meinhardt stated with a grunt and then stepped out to the bunks and pulled his knew clothes on as Dietrich heaved a sigh of relief and then dressed himself too. As Dietrich then stepped out and over to his companion, he gently kissed Meinhardt's ear, making him grunt for being suddenly touched before they held hands. They heard more feet stomping down towards them as one of the other young squires hurried over to grab Dietrich's arm.

"Brother Dietrich… I think I've got lice… can you check my scalp for me?" The youngster questioned and both Dietrich and Meinhardt cringed in disgust at the thought of such hideous parasites roaming around. It was not uncommon, Dietrich had caught them in the Holy Land like many others but constant washing and smearing his head in oil for a week, apparently had cleared it. But in ones so young, the best method was to shave the scalp completely and kill whatever could be grabbed and thrown onto the nearest fire… including the bedsheets! Dietrich gave a groan as he grasped the boy's crop of hair and brushed it back, checking for the familiar marks of red scalp from bites and eggs around the ears. He could not see anything clearly, but to his shock a flea leapt out and onto him as Dietrich shook his arm with a grimace of fury as the youngster looked up at him. "Still got fleas?"

"Yes young man… I'm afraid the fleas are still present, but there is little that can be done to prevent them, they are everywhere." Dietrich stated with a sigh, patting the boy's shoulder and letting him hurry back to continue cleaning whilst Dietrich flicked his eyes towards Meinhardt, he'd have thought the squires would have gotten used to the fleas by now, there were few places even in the richest castles that did not have fleas and mainly because of the dogs. That made Dietrich look at the bunks and grimace as Meinhardt looked at him curiously. "I think we'll have to keep your dog out of this room, its unhealthy to have him sleeping on my bunk all the time."

"Ah… that's because he misses me and you smell the most of his master… and I want you to always bear my…" Meinhardt snorted in amusement, swinging an arm around Dietrich's shoulders and pulling him down a little. Dietrich's face was going red before another one of the squires turned up. Straightaway Meinhardt just ruffled Dietrich's hair, grumbling that it was starting to go brown in old age as Dietrich pulled himself out of Meinhardt's grip whilst his companion glowered towards the older squire to arrive, then insisted that he wanted to know what bunk to prepare for Meinhardt to stay in and suddenly Meinhardt gave a grunt. "I'm sticking beside Dietrich; we've shared before so we can share again."

"But… we have a spare bunk…" The squire stated in confusion as Meinhardt's face became even more irritable and Dietrich gave a soft chuckle. He insisted that they would indeed be giving Meinhardt the spare bunk and then the squire went to get the items. Dietrich then grasped hold of Meinhardt and jerked him out into the corridor where thankfully there were none of the others around to see anything. Dietrich gave a sigh and then grabbed hold of Meinhardt's jerkin and pulled him close for a firm and loving kiss, it made Meinhardt give a sudden grunt of pleasure before they separated and Ludovic arrived in the hall, only for Meinhardt to give a growl… too many interruptions.

Dietrich was thankful there were no more odd things happening the rest of the day and that their worship and chores went through without issue. Meinhardt was soon settled into discussion with Rudolph over his works and indeed the current mission and thankfully Rudolph was far more understanding of the kind of issues that he was going through. Rudolph was eager to hear it all and the missions he was missing, but he was happy to know he had someone to talk to that revelled in battle and the need to protect those who were faithful, though Rudolph's opinions of this particular place were unpleasant. But Meinhardt joined them in their prayers, kneeling beside Dietrich, his companion felt calmer for it and happier.

That night, Dietrich and Meinhardt would have slept longer and deeper just like everyone else, but Meinhardt was feeling something tickling him awake. He was aware of the fact someone kept approaching the barracks, someone in robes that would stand by the door and hold it, he could hear it and every time he did, he heard one of the boys whimper or Igel, who was at Meinhardt's feet, give a low grunt. Meinhardt did not know who it was, but he had a bad feeling about it and he was quick to find that his own discomforts were keeping him from settling. With a groan Meinhardt slid himself out of his bunk and as Igel relaxed back into the bed with a wag of his tail, Meinhardt shuffled over to Dietrich's bunk and gently stroked his shoulder as he whispered.

"Dieter… it's just me, can I shuffle in with you for a minute? I can't sleep…" Meinhardt whispered gently into his ear as Dietrich jolted in shock and then rolled around to face him with a scowl. As he did so, Meinhardt lifted the blanket and slid under, gently hooking his arms about him and snuggling against him without a noise. Dietrich's eyes darted about, fearful that something had happened to wake the youngsters before shuddering in pleasure and leaning back to Meinhardt. His lover kissed his shoulders and neck to make him lean his head down and kissed at Meinhardt's ear tenderly. They hooked their arms around each other gently, their legs stroking at each other and hands stroking one another too before they nuzzled noses and held each other tightly. "I love you…"

"I love you too… but this is bad… have you cuddled enough? If you have, go to your bunk now…. Aaah, Meinhardt don't do that…" Dietrich grunted as Meinhardt's fingers teased against the fabric and stroked at his nipples tenderly as he groaned softly against Dietrich's neck. His lips pecked and stroked up his partner's flesh, his fingers teasing as Dietrich seemed to crunch up looking embarrassed as his body started to react to it. Then Meinhardt's hand slipped down to cup around Dietrich's back, stroking his lower back whilst his other hand dropped to stroke gently at the scar on Dietrich's stomach. He could feel his partner reacting as Meinhardt smiled lovingly at him but Dietrich blushed. "Meinhardt… we can't… someone's… someone's hurting the boys here like this…"

Dietrich almost smothered his mouth as soon as he felt Meinhardt freeze and drop his hands away. For a moment, he feared his beloved would attack him over the matter instead, but Meinhardt grasped Dietrich's face and they locked eyes, before Meinhardt whispered calmly if that might be who was pondering coming into the rooms. When Dietrich nodded his head, relieved that he was not being blamed and then Meinhardt's scowl appeared as he whispered Rudolph's name, Dietrich shook his head. Meinhardt then sat up from the bed, sitting on the edge of the bunk so that he seemed almost as if hovering on the side and had not been within the sheets. But when Dietrich could not say the name, terrified that if he claimed it was a priest, he would then think the boys or Dietrich were lying about it all, Meinhardt grimaced and stepped back over to his bunk and then cuddled up with Igel. Dietrich was concerned that his partner was not reacting to this anymore and then, to Dietrich's surprise, Ludovic pulled himself out of the bunk and insisted he was going to use the latrine outside as soon as he realised Dietrich was awake.

When Ludovic stepped outside, Dietrich was staring towards the squire's departure forlornly and Meinhardt gave a grunt, insisting he was going to the chapel to pray. But when he noticed that this made Dietrich's eyes joyful, as if it were the right thing to do, Meinhardt had all the information he needed on what was going on. As he stepped up and out into the hallway, he followed a little way behind Ludovic to watch him take the right turn to the latrine whilst Meinhardt marched onto the chapel. He was rather concerned to see Father Allard sitting calmly upon the floor, as if he were expecting someone. But when the priest turned his head about to look, he literally jumped in surprise at the sight of him and then he turned away as Meinhardt settled down and began to pray.

For a good hour, Meinhardt remained praying and the priest was forced to pray beside him, the knight could sense the fear this being had to have him sitting in the chapel and seemingly preventing anyone else from coming into the building. At one point, he was sure that Ludovic had approached the door until he had spotted Meinhardt and made a point to return to the bunks. Meinhardt remained aware that Allard was indeed trying to think of some way to get the knight out of his chapel, but time had run out and when Allard realised it was nearing midnight, he stood up and then began to ring a soft bell that Rudolph would hear.

With the call to mass, Ludovic woke the others and Dietrich helped them out of the bed, hooking up the youngest that could hardly wake and carrying him awkwardly to the chapel. Meinhardt watched in fascination, almost finding it adorable to see Dietrich carrying in an eleven-year-old that was clinging onto him like a baby, no matter how Dietrich was wobbling and having trouble with balancing. As everyone settled down to listen to the sermon and pray together, Dietrich was careful to look to Allard with an irritated glance that the priest ignored as he presented the blessings to end the mass and then the others were sent to bed. He seemed to hold back around one of the younger ones... the one with fleas... but Dietrich beckoned him on to go to sleep and Allard looked irritated.

Meinhardt though seemed slower to get up and depart to bed too, but something inside Allard had seemed to click on possibilities and he held his hand out in front of Meinhardt. Allard was quite sure that this being had some kind of power over Dietrich; though Allard was not afraid of the other knight when he'd been able to silence him so easily, he was curious as to whether he could remove the troublemaker completely from his view. As he steered Meinhardt aside, they watched everyone else depart completely before Allard turned to look at Meinhardt, hoping to lock eyes and use his manipulation to take hold, but instead he found that those steely eyes were too difficult to deal with and so he'd turned his head aside and attempted to whisper.

"Brother Meinhardt… I have a concern that I know a well-versed knight like yourself, who is in more favour with the likes of the Meisters, would be the appropriate person to report my concerns to." Allard stated calmly, but around someone that made him feel so inferior, he dropped his voice down and his head, making himself meek. It was these kinds of aggressive knights, these men that were willing to kill whomever offended them, that revelled in removing pagans that Allard feared the most. These were beings without mercy, but someone like Dietrich who was obviously too soft and tender had been easy to manipulate and catch out upon their feelings of mercy. Allard had heard too about Dietrich having saved Sigmond's life and it was curious how Allard, Sigmond and a handful of others knew and understood each other and held their tongues.

"What concerns you, Ordained Brother?" Meinhardt stated, straightening up and staring towards Allard in fascination as he looked to the floor in anxiety. Meinhardt was curious to find out what the priest was going to say, whom he was going to accuse and somehow he had a bad feeling that this little figure in front of him was going to say something that Meinhardt's anger might not be able to take. He sucked in his fury, preparing to hold back the fist he could feel clenching as Allard then lifted his head with a blush and Meinhardt was quite aware that he was going to have to make a big risk to his soul once again to save someone he loved.

"I have suspected for some time since his arrival, that Brother Dietrich has been showing too much fascination in the young men, even to the point he will not let anyone near to witness when they bathe save himself. I have also heard from one brave squire who was willing to speak about it, that Dietrich's meeting with a fellow brother in the dead of night was a salacious rendezvous that might have including an act of the most heinous manner." Allard stated, looking anxious and shocked as Meinhardt almost felt his hands moving on their own to grab his sword and cleave this being in two. But he knew to act more cautiously, he was going to have to take the accusation seriously so that he could deal with it and gently he lay his hand upon Allard's shoulder.

"I will need to speak to this witness and yourself to fill out a full report before I can deal with this… hideousness."

Ten: Ludovic's Resolve

Meinhardt did not sleep the rest of that night but pulled Igel into his arms in a tight hug as he considered the accusation, Dietrich's anxieties and exactly what had been seen. He was sure that no one had seen them together, otherwise that priest might have known Meinhardt to be the other man involved, but he was still petrified, and his thoughts were locked upon the chubby little monk that had collected the information. It made Meinhardt very anxious and upset to think that anyone could dare to assume so much of Dietrich, when he knew Dietrich would never hurt anyone. But then it made him ponder as he'd held the dog close to him until the next sermon, still unable to sleep, just how much did he really know about Dietrich?

It was easier before, he always had Kirk around to tell him that Dietrich was not getting into any trouble and to protect them both, but around here there was no one he could trust like that. There was no one here that could be relied upon to protect Dietrich from the danger of rumours and it made Meinhardt hateful. As he remained in the chapel after the sermon to pray a little longer, Ludovic had held back slightly and thankfully, Allard had disappeared to sleep. Meinhardt was aware of the young squire's presence, but he was rather startled when the figure settled down calmly right beside him and then turned to him with a curious expression.

"Can I ask you something that's dangerous, but I know you will understand?" Ludovic questioned and when Meinhardt looked towards the pudgy face that he currently wanted to crack beneath his gauntlets, Ludovic looked to him calmly. There was some kind of strange truthful conviction within his eyes as if to say that he was going to say something important that could get him killed but was determined to say it. Meinhardt was suddenly thoughtful over what he had seen with the priest earlier, the priest had shown a curious interest in Ludovic and now, with these thoughts in his mind it was making something very dangerous leap into Meinhardt's brain. But when he looked at Meinhardt firmly, his words almost brought hands to his throat. "I believe I am in love with Brother Dietrich and I do not know if its because of his kindness or because I want to kiss him."

"And you're telling me…" Meinhardt hissed through clenched teeth, utterly furious and thinking how he wanted to throttle the young man already, he wanted to rip his stomach open and pull his organs out, screaming that Dietrich belonged to him and no one else was allowed to touch him. But as Meinhardt awaited the explanation, it was clear in Ludovic's eyes that he knew everything. Meinhardt's hand suddenly hooked around the boy's throat and Ludo's eyes swelled in horror as he was pulled in close. "What have you said to the priest? What had you said about my Dietrich? You had better hope its not the conclusion in my head or I'm going to take you out and slice you to ribbons and string you up for the crows to peck!"

"EEK!" The sudden squeak from the young man reminded Meinhardt of the boy's age, but it also made him loosen his grip. Ludovic had gone frightfully pale and it was clear that Meinhardt had made his point and, he'd found out who'd said something to the priest. As Meinhardt curled his lip and repeated his question, Ludovic began to shiver and his shame was obvious as he lowered his head but then whispered to the elder knight. "Dietrich knew that Allard was doing things to us, Allard wanted something to use against him... he sent me out to follow him and I saw you two together and I... I wished I was you because Dietrich was so happy and you looked so... so beautiful... but I never said it happened or that it was you... the priest just guessed it happened as Dietrich confronted him to protect us. But now Dietrich can't help us because the Order will believe a priest above someone like Dietrich."

"You... you thought it was beautiful? Eh... yes, when Dietrich is wanting to be embraced, there's this kind of presence around him that makes him shine and almost makes him look holy..." Meinhardt turned his head to the side, suddenly blushing and nipping at a knuckle when he realised he'd said such a thing out loud. He could not help it, when he thought about the way Dietrich sometimes held a hand out to him, gripped his arm and then looked at him with that beautiful expression to say he wanted something as gentle as just a hand stroking the scar on his head, it made Meinhardt swoon. He certainly was not going to admit to that, it would be emasculating to think that he got so enchanted by his lover, but Ludovic was looking at him in awe as Meinhardt then growled. "...but that's not the point... I do not know your priest, but he seems to not understand my relationship to Dietrich, so you'd better keep it that way."

"Is there anything you can do to save him? I would rather that I, one with impure thoughts who has permitted himself to be so tricked, would be the one in such a dangerous position. Rudolph may be a little lax in his command here, but he trusts Allard and its clear, if he were to think that there was danger from someone committing such a sin, he would execute them himself." That did not surprise Meinhardt, despite his own relationship with Dietrich, he did not perceive that any other pair of knights performing such an act to be similar, to be so immune. He would have no problem in such a task… unless it was to his beloved! But the words made Meinhardt ponder and swiftly he patted Ludo's shoulder and gave him a thoughtful expression as the young man stared at him in misery.

"I have a thought; we'll use this against Allard. I'll inform Rudolph that I've been sent to conduct a brief interview with the young squires and ascertain any suspicious behaviour here. If I have it all in writing and make them feel like we're taking this matter seriously, then Allard's victims can speak to me and I will solve the problem!" Meinhardt stated firmly, he was not sure he could really do such a thing with Rudolph, that man might insist on being right by his side when he interviewed and asked questions, but if he just gave him the idea it was vague and just something Balk was ordering as some kind of stocktaking for all those here. With rumours that the Sword Brethren were going to be absorbed into the order too, it might make sense. But he was not too sure and then Ludovic held his shoulder suddenly and Meinhardt turned to look at him with a scowl.

"If it will stop the pain and keep Dietrich safe, I'll do anything." Ludovic stated, looking up into Meinhardt's face with such adoring eyes that, for a moment, made Meinhardt want to throttle him again. But Meinhardt could understand that this figure was very much in awe of the only person that was listening to his upsets and showing him kindness. It was one of those things that made Meinhardt feel a little frustrated with Dietrich, he had a curious way around children and was good with them, but of course that was why the priest was picking on Dietrich! It made Meinhardt so angry, but he gave a soft sigh and nodded his head towards Ludo before encouraging him that they should head back to bed.

Together, the pair marched out towards the barracks with one another, Ludovic marching ahead of him as Meinhardt moved very slowly with his head down in thought. Each of his footsteps were slow, steady and deliberate as he made sure to give Ludovic the time to settle down into bed whilst he could go in and give Dietrich the kind of affection he wanted to give him. Well, the kind of affection that was not anything more than a hug and a kiss and well, just to snuggle into him would be wonderful now that he had an idea of what to do for him, but then Meinhardt froze as he heard the sound of an owl fluttering around outside. It made him think about the first night he and Dietrich talked properly, the beginnings of their relationship and it made him growl.

"God… I need your guidance and also… though I will do what I have to do, I will not seek your forgiveness for it, but only wish that my punishment would not be enough to kill me, because I need to stay around as long as I can protect Dietrich." He whispered softly to himself, speaking more through the movement of his mouth rather than the actual utterance of the words. Meinhardt knew that he was going to do something that was indeed terrible, but his reasoning would be accepted by the order as long as he had the right kind of information. But he was sure there would be retribution for what he would do to offend the lord and he was willing, he just hoped he would not lose his husband in doing so.

With a sigh, he then began to walk back to the building and slowly he opened the door and then stepped inside that long corridor of bunks where all the squires and Dietrich were sighing away in sleep. Igel had even returned to lounge onto Dietrich's bed, head over Dietrich's shoulder with his thin tail waggling about in happiness. The sight made Meinhardt snort in amusement as he stepped into the room and carefully closed the door before stepping over to Dietrich's bunk, calmly sitting down and patting the dog's backside. The big fawn coloured animal lifted up its black muzzle, snuffling and lapping towards Meinhardt's chin before he patted the dog and beckoned him to push off. Igel gave a groan and then steadily slid off the bed to slink onto the floor beside the bunk, hoping to gain Meinhardt's attention later.

Meinhardt then gently peeled the sheets up as he then eased himself onto the narrow bunk and barged Dietrich rather clumsily when he was trying to be gentle. Dietrich did not make a sound, but he was awake and rolled around, pulling up the blankets and opening his arms out to let Meinhardt cuddle into him if it were wanted. Ordinarily, Meinhardt was cautious to lay his head to Dietrich's chest, knowing that it made him appear weaker sometimes but on this occasion, he cuddled into him. They looped their arms about each other tightly as Dietrich gave a sigh, kissed the side of Meinhardt's head and then fell straight back to sleep. Cuddled against his warm body, Meinhardt was pleased that his lover was sleeping so soundly, and he hoped that he would always be this calm as he rested.

For a little while, Meinhardt remained cuddled against the warm body, listening to the soft sound of his breath as much as he listened to his heart, sighing heavily at the fact that his lover seemed to be careless in his affection at this moment and glad that the earlier discomfort was lifted. Somehow, that earlier caution had been unlike Dietrich and it was only thanks to the information from Ludovic and the actions of the priest, Meinhardt's head had been turning and he'd come to the conclusion that his mate had been bullied by this figure. It made Meinhardt angrier at what he had heard, but he was also more content to know that Dietrich had not been rejecting him earlier because he had fallen out of interest. Meinhardt nuzzled up against the warm chest one more time and kissed towards the heart before heaving a sigh.

"I'm going to deal with it, Dietrich... please understand." Meinhardt whispered softly, pulling himself up and ready to go to his own bunk before he froze. This situation felt familiar and his eyes looked towards the ragged pale mark on the scalp that seemed to have made the soft sandy brown hairs around it grow in a different way to the rest. He recalled the decision to go after those beings, to murder them for their injury to Dietrich and he leant forward, pressing his lips to the scar before climbing out of the bed and to his own, almost tripping on the dog but just keeping his balance. Meinhardt had been this firm in his resolve before, but he was hopeful that Ludovic would help the younger members of the group to speak to him when the time was right, glad that they all trusted Dietrich but knowing they needed to trust him when he spoke to them.

With a sigh, Meinhardt settled back into his bunk with a new resolve and yet a heavy heart as he closed his eyes and considered the task ahead. He was going to have to pray that Rudolph would not try to get involved and just let Meinhardt do this job, after-all, his Komtur had mentioned something that could easily have been interpreted as routing out the damned amongst their order. It made him heave a heavy sigh as he heard the low mumble from Dietrich across from him stating 'I love you', seemingly to the air but Meinhardt knew it was to him. As he settled down in delight, before suddenly hearing the dog straighten up and waddling over to him, claws clacking on the floor as he whimpered and then clambered up onto Meinhardt's bed.

"Oof... Igel..." Meinhardt groaned as the dog flopped onto him, snuggling against his hip before Dietrich grumbled on automatic.

"I hate that dog..."

Meinhardt was on a mission and deadly one at that, he woke up to get on with his duties and he was so silent and his expression so firm and harsh that the young squires, and even Dietrich, were a little concerned. His manner was firm, his mind locked upon his resolve to deal with this problem! Meinhardt was quick to get the cleaning duties he'd been given done, helped Dietrich and Rudolph training the squires to use swords and even forcing them to run around the building for a few laps to build up their stamina! Thankfully, Dietrich joined in with the running to encourage the youngsters to join and, they were so sweaty and frustrated afterwards, that they were deadly silent for their studies, thankful for the masses and at lunch, they were calm. When Meinhardt then left Dietrich to get the squires to learn the reason for the current tactics of the Order, Meinhardt went to Rudolph's office with a firm expression and knocked at the door.

When Rudolph gave a soft grumble, Meinhardt opened the door and stepped in as the Komtur was busy writing down a selection of notes regarding a curious looking insect he'd managed to catch under a glass and seemed to be examining. He had a very strange series of habits, but Meinhardt had no real care about the bizarre studious nature of the figure as he stood in front of the desk and awaited the chance to speak. Rudolph was quick, finishing off some notes on the colour of the insect's carapace, before he settled his quill down and then straightened up to look at Meinhardt. It was curious to see how neat his wording was, let alone how beautiful his characters and more importantly, Meinhardt could see that Rudolph had probably intended to be a proper monk working on transliterating works from the other worlds to something more suitable and Christian.

"Komtur von Lippe... I've come to talk to you about a delicate matter that my masters were suggesting I look into whilst I was here. Considering this place's position as 'accepted' by the local people who have been comfortably converted, it was believed this was a good place for squires to focus on their scripture and train before they were thrown into the battles, but as we have only sent the youngest or least experienced here there is a problem. This problem is something I'm sure you will recall was rumoured in the Holy Land and why we were very focused on the training in Sicily first... the well-being of the squires and whether they are being treated and taught correctly by their brothers... let alone, dealing with a much more serious matter involved in their 'vows'." Meinhardt was not sure he was strolling around it in circles much more than he should on the subject, but Rudolph was suddenly looking straight up and staring at him firmly. He was quite obviously uncomfortable with the subject, but he knew it was important and as he straightened up, Rudolph stretched his hand to a cloth and gently lay it over an icon that looked curiously from the Holy Land, to cover it from dangerous words.

"I see… I must admit, I was considering that it would be time enough soon that such morals would be looked into. When Allard was assigned here, there were concerns for how he was with the locals and I have to admit, I do not want the squires to become so close to the locals and forget what they were supposed to be here for. I also had my suspicions when they sent Dietrich to us with the youngsters, clearly they want to make this place more strategic and that means ensuring I become stricter with my methods." Rudolph grunted in frustration, Meinhardt almost began to grind his teeth in irritation to hear such things. Had Rudolph suspected something with Allard before and not dealt with it? Or did he suspect that Dietrich had done something wrong? But Rudolph then gave a soft growl of frustration before shaking his head gently and looking towards Meinhardt firmly. "I've been lax, what is it they wish to do to punish me?"

"You may have been putting your trust too much into others' hands… but my job is rather more simplistic." Meinhardt almost grinned, he now had the perfect thought on how to work this out and encouraged Rudolph to give him privacy. Clearly, Rudolph had been ignoring his duties a little in favour of these strange habits on studying the insects and was assuming he was under some kind of review and Dietrich might replace him. Meinhardt would prefer such a thing, it was safe here and Dietrich was calm enough to deal with the manner and good enough with the youngsters. However, Meinhardt stood up and folded his arms across his chest, knowing his work under Komtur Konrad would allow him to handle this easily. "I am to interview all members here on anything they feel is unsuitable or vows they feel have been broken. I will produce a report and hand it to the seniors. I will require a room and full privacy to discuss with each squire as long as I need to in order to discuss these situations. I wish to start with the Ordained Brother first before the youngest to oldest of the squires before Dietrich and then yourself. I will need ink, paper and water on hand… I will make sure to attend the masses, but I will be doing this from dawn till dusk…"

"I see…" Rudolph stated with a sudden expression of shock and concern falling upon him as he looked around his office and then lifted a finger to pull at his lip. He then stretched out a hand back to the image under the cloth and lifted it so the icon would almost bear witness. It seemed his faith was strong as he performed the sign of the cross above his head before standing up from his stool and looking towards Meinhardt with a firm expression. "If it is the request of the Order, it is a request from Our Lord… whatever you need, you will have. If we prepare the room now, at the next mass I will request that Allard come here after to speak with you. Then I will send in the youngest squire… but in order to maintain the secrecy of such an important matter and not scare the youngsters, I believe each squire will send in the next one. Will you assume it as taking confession and keep the information confident… if it is harmless."

"If it is harmless or merely a lack of dutiful behaviour then it will be something swiftly dealt with. However, if it is more serious, it may require more unpleasant work." Meinhardt stated in irritation as he considered the subject, before heaving a soft sigh. Rudolph nodded his head and then beckoned Meinhardt to help him sort out the office in preparation for what he needed as well as preparing an appropriate oil lamp for when it was ready. Meinhardt's only concern was that he'd have to write words very simplistically.

It was late in the evening when Dietrich had realised that something was off and the squires were looking oddly anxious. Though it was the late mass before they settled to bed, he noticed that Meinhardt had arrived with one of the other children before he'd settled down and his expression was utterly exhausted. It was clear he was up to something strange and Dietrich was not sure he wanted to ask about it, but he could sense that something was up and he was eager to learn what was happening. But the squires were quiet, Rudolph seemed on edge and Allard seemed utterly smug. When Dietrich thought to ask Meinhardt, he was informed that he was delaying his work and so he was ignored. Dietrich was anxious about it, he was not very sure what was going on with his lover, but clearly it was serious and Dietrich could not help but feel depressed.

His sensation continued through to the next day as through the night, Meinhardt seemed to be locked away and Dietrich did not see him come to the barracks to sleep. Then even during the masses through the night, he barely had a moment to even catch Meinhardt's eyes and Allard's expression had been permanently smug. Dietrich wished he could understand just what was going on at this moment with his beloved, but when it came to the following night, Ludovic stepped to Dietrich's side and beckoned him to go to Rudolph's office.

It was then that Dietrich had realised that everyone within their little commune had been to the office for a short time and he could not help but wonder just what Meinhardt was up to as he knocked the door, was beckoned in and then closed the door firmly behind him, even locking it on request until he gave a jolt of shock!

"I've missed you… don't worry, his eyes are covered, and we've got all the time we need!" Before Dietrich had a chance to react to the matter, suddenly he was pushed against the door, enough to lean his arms against it to brace himself as Meinhardt hooked around him. Meinhardt kissed and licked at his neck, making Dietrich give a gasp of shock and concern as he pulled back from the door and felt the hands stroking up and down his tunic in search of an opening. Dietrich grasped his hands gently, peeling them away for a moment with a chuckle of amusement before he turned around to sit in Meinhardt's arms. Meinhardt's hands fell calmly onto Dietrich's backside, pinching and grasping him and squeezing them as Dietrich blushed and gave a soft moan of surprise. However, Meinhardt nuzzled in close, kissing that bearded chin before lifting his lips up to Dietrich's as the smoother hands clasped Meinhardt's cheeks and they held each other together in a loving kiss as they moaned softly before relaxing back.

"Meinhardt… its not that I'm not happy we can have this kind of moment but… what are you doing in here?" Dietrich questioned curiously, giving Meinhardt a sceptical expression as they remained holding onto each other. Meinhardt stared into those beautiful greenish eyes for a moment before giving a soft grunt and then leaning forward to kiss Dietrich's lips again. Their lips clapped loudly in the room that was dark save for the oil lamp, small, but there was enough space on the floor to enjoy themselves properly. When Meinhardt just lifted his finger to Dietrich's lips and gave a playful wink that startled Dietrich, he pulled his hands away with a soft scoff. "I'm worried now…"

"Let's say… I'm dealing with a problem and tomorrow it will be solved… hence I need your affection now to give me strength." Meinhardt groaned, sounding curiously pathetic as he cuddled around Dietrich again and nuzzled his head into his shoulder. Dietrich was still concerned, but if Meinhardt was asking him for courage than he would give it and gently, he grasped the bottom of his tunic and pulled it up off his head. Meinhardt copied before the pair slipped their hose down and shed the rest of their clothes before settling onto the floor, Meinhardt sitting back against the long seat that doubled as a storage box as

Dietrich leant over his body. Their lips came together in soft, slow drags as they sighed softly and then Dietrich lowered his head to Meinhardt's chin and throat.

The northerner gave a soft groan of pleasure, feeling his body tremble and shudder as his hair stood on end and moaned as he felt the kisses touch his skin. He stroked his arm upon Dietrich's shoulder, sighing lovingly and letting Dietrich then kiss lower down his neck, stifling Meinhardt's breath as Dietrich then gently pecked and puckered down the centre of his chest to make him shudder. Meinhardt pulled his hands back to cover his face, moaning and gasping softly to feel the kisses rushing up his chest and back to his neck again as he growled into his arm. Dietrich chuckled in amusement, looking to where he was clearly aroused and shuddering softly in pleasure as Dietrich then kissed down towards it with a soft chuckle.

"Would you like this?" Dietrich whispered softly and Meinhardt blushed before then beckoning for Dietrich to spin around so he could play with him a little. Dietrich smiled lovingly before swinging his naked form against him, trying hard not to just smack his backside into Meinhardt's shoulder and wind him. But as Dietrich bent down to gently open his mouth and slurp up the tip lovingly, moaning as his kissed it with his lips, dragging it in as he then suckled at it. Meinhardt moaned lovingly, his shoulders dropping as he leant back against the box and then brought his fingers forward, kissing and sucking at his fingers, moaning from Dietrich's attention before he gently brought his fingers to caress and tease. "Uh… aaaah… gentle Stier… you've grown talons over the past few days…"

"Understood, Hengst… just keep a mind on your teeth…" Meinhardt snorted through a grimace, leaning forward to kiss at Dietrich's hip before his fingers were dancing and delving to soften his lover and give him pleasure. He had to be careful, both of them were enjoying the damp too much and likely to moan too loud, but with the darkness enveloping the only window in this seeming cell, the pair gave in to their pleasures and the heat. They sighed and kissed at each other's flesh, chuckling softly and moaning how much they loved each other, before Dietrich lifted his head and then turned himself around, straddling Meinhardt and towering over him as their wet lips came together in a loving caress. "Don't ride me like that damn colt of yours… take it slow, I worry this will be all we have for a very long time."

"I fear the same… a quick kiss or squeeze to the hand we might be able to steal in secrecy, but this is a little harder…" Dietrich stated, stretching a hand back to lift Meinhardt's rock hard form into position before he squatted down and kissed at Meinhardt's lips. They kissed even more lovingly as Meinhardt's arms wrapped around Dietrich, grumbling he'd gained weight for being boring, as Dietrich lowered himself onto his lover. With a soft sharp sound, Dietrich then sat back into his lover's groin, letting his own pleasure sit and show itself as Meinhardt lay a hand onto it, stroking it tenderly as Dietrich gave a soft sigh and then steadily began to roll his hips and squeeze with his body. The pair then began to pant and sigh lovingly, their bodies together and gently they were moving up and down together, hips rolling and dancing against one another.

"Dieter... so tight... so beautiful..." Meinhardt growled at his lover, pulling his arms around him and nuzzling into him. Dietrich gave a sharp wheeze, enjoying the sensation of everything within being stroked, rubbed and sent into a spasm for excitement and pleasure that was almost painful but utterly absorbing. He hooked his arms around Meinhardt tightly, nuzzling his face against Meinhardt's shoulder and neck, his beard trickling at his sensitive skin as Meinhardt shuddered and seemed to thicken with the excitement. Every time either of them touched each other, their bodies would sing, but when they were so intimate like this, their bodies were in such a rapturous uproar that simple things like breathing could become laboured as all focus went upon giving the other pleasure. "I love you Dietrich..."

"Love you... Meinhardt..." Dietrich grumbled as he then gave a slight groan, clenching to feel Meinhardt's hips roll up against his body, shuddering as they rolled down again. He gripped his lover more tightly, nuzzling against him desperately and whispering happily that he loved him again. Meinhardt's lips then caressed and dragged themselves against Dietrich's body, moaning for the pleasure he was gaining and giving as he grasped hold of Dietrich's backside, pushing in with himself more as Dietrich groaned. He nuzzled against his lover, utterly desperate to just be engulfed within the soft scent of his sweat and the warmth of his body as they continued to move.

As they began to move faster and Meinhardt's body focused more upon the thrusting motions, reaching the end of the building pressure within that was desperate to rip out, Dietrich was moaning against him, grumbling softly that it might be a bad idea. Certainly, it was going to be awkward for Dietrich to clean himself from this, but Meinhardt grit his teeth together with a groan of irritation as he thought it over. He did not want to think it over, but it was too late at night for Dietrich to go somewhere to have a proper wash and though they'd had such risks before, there was the possibility of the next mass within at least the next half hour or so and Dietrich would certainly be having trouble with walking comfortably in his clothes! As Meinhardt continued to move in and out, scrunching his body around Dietrich's, he gave a soft snort and then looked up at Dietrich with an exhausted expression.

"Dieter… if I'm not inside you… you won't feel as good, but I'll touch you… take me out, let me go between but not inside…" Meinhardt groaned softly, he really did not want to leave the absorbing warmth where he melted and merged into Dietrich's body and yet he moaned softly as he realised he was going to have to. Dietrich grimaced as well, he did not really want to lose the good sensation within when it was feeling so perfect, but it was clear his concern about the mess was going to be understood by his lover for once and slowly he pulled himself up. He dipped down a little, making sure to keep the momentum going before both he and Meinhardt gave soft little shocked gasps to be utterly separated. Then Dietrich sat down, stroking his body against Meinhardt's, but making sure there was not another penetration before they both continued their movements as Dietrich rubbed himself against Meinhardt's abdomen as Meinhardt continued to thrust.

Only when Meinhardt swung his hand out to ensure it was grasping, stroking and squeezing at his lover's form did Dietrich give out a sharp gasp that was almost too loud. Meinhardt gave a low growl for him to keep his voice as Dietrich quickly smothered his mouth. As they continued on their journey to ecstatic fulfilment, Meinhardt's hand became wetter and he could feel himself nearing an end as he felt his lover's throbbing form mimic his own, but he wished he could be back within the constant warmth. They hurried on until Dietrich gave the cough first before he brushed himself backwards and rubbed his backside firmly against Meinhardt, attempting to give a clench that was enough to make Meinhardt moan in orgasm as the fluid splashed up Dietrich's back. The pair then separated, spinning around so Dietrich could lean into Meinhardt's chest for a bit, ignoring the stains upon their bodies as they caught their breath and their reddened faces came together in a loving kiss once more.

"Meinhardt…" Dietrich whimpered softly as he snuggled up against his lover, their lips clapping together softly again as Dietrich just seemed to collapse weakly upon him. Dietrich heard him give a soft groan of curiosity, but it did not matter what Dietrich thought he was going to say just then. Right now, knowing that he was with Meinhardt again, knowing their love and their pleasure was mutual and thinking in his mind that Meinhardt alone made him excited, he knew that there was no similarity between himself and Allard whatsoever. It had taken mutual understanding, mutual love and just that extreme bond that they'd built up from jealousy to trust to total affection before Dietrich had ever thought to let his body join with Meinhardt's... he'd not forced this! "Meinhardt... I'm happy you're here...."

"Heh... is it that boring here?" Meinhardt chuckled softly, but he kissed at Dietrich's ear and decided they could take a few minutes to breathe more freely before they should redress and clean up. He guessed that what had been going on with Allard had certainly upset Dietrich a lot, just the details he had asked for had been horrendous and cruel. But then it had made him ponder about why Dietrich had not told him straightaway, why he'd been so upset about it in the first place. He wondered too about the way Sigmond always attacked Dietrich and he pondered just how much of the pains these squires had gone through, his husband had gone through.

It was after the first sermon the next day that Meinhardt called Allard and Ludovic aside from the others during the meal. He was looking pale and upset, making Rudolph stare out to him in anxiety for how grim he was as he beckoned them to join him outside the compound. This fascinated Allard, Meinhardt was dressed in his full robes and obviously looking incredibly pained and even Dietrich was anxious at the nasty expression that Allard gave him, something almost smug. Then the trio stepped out on their long march towards an area of ground that was in the woodlands and Ludovic was trembling in anxiety as they approached an area that looked suitable for the one thing that Allard was certainly expecting.

"I see... you have found proof of a culprit... it would make sense that you would bring me here, this will be the site? I am glad I brought the holy water so I can consecrate this spot. Will you be intending to build a pyre? That is the traditional punishment for the crimes that... Brother Dietrich has committed, isn't that right Ludovic?" Allard stated softly, taking out the little bottle of water as Meinhardt nodded his head and then waited for the ground to be consecrated. But Ludovic was looking terrified as he turned from the priest to Meinhardt, waiting for the correct situation before the figure pulled out a piece of parchment and then he pulled out his sword. He looked to them both as Allard tilted his head to the side in curiosity, he'd never seen this before but he was very curious as he looked towards the knight. "What do you wish with that, and the parchment?"

"There will not be a pyre, I only need the offender to kneel... you are looking at your death warrant... for your crimes. Ludovic is here as witness, shall I read out the charges of sodomy and blasphemy for claiming that the Devil influenced you to harm the squires... or shall we deal with this quickly?" Meinhardt stated firmly and Ludovic looked towards the knight with a heavy gulp but a gentle nod as Allard then did something completely bizarre. He looked towards Ludovic with a curious expression before he looked towards Meinhardt's firm face, then he considered exactly what had been going on with the young squires all stepping in and out of the office as well as the actions of Rudolph. He could not stop himself from giving out a firm laugh before gently kneeling down upon the bare ground where he had splashed the holy water before he looked up at Meinhardt with a chuckle.

"Then, I shall go as a martyr... don't forget, I'm a victim of this devilry too." Allard stated, turning to look at Ludovic so viciously it was almost as if he were placing a curse upon Ludovic for the rest of his days. Meinhardt said nothing though, he waited patiently as the figure knelt down and then began to say his prayers, Meinhardt and Ludovic both joined him in prayer before they asked God to receive this sinner and give him proper judgement. Ludovic was sure that mercy should have been included in those words, but Meinhardt looked too stern to say such a thing as he then swung the sword and in perhaps the hardest but swiftest hit, the sword was buried halfway into the head. Allard fell forward as Meinhardt jerked the blade back out and took a second swing to ensure the deed was done before he then turned to Ludovic with a sharp expression.

"Take the letter to Rudolph and..." Meinhardt stated firmly, but to his shock, Ludovic turned to him and then grasped the sword in his wrist and stared up at him pitifully. Meinhardt knew that Ludovic was going to say something stupid but courageous before he was able to threaten him if he should put Dietrich in trouble, but even he was shocked at the young man's resolve as Ludovic then looked up at him with a sharp expression.

"Pease use your sword to remove from me what a monk does not need so that I may never become like Allard and I will take a vow of silence in penance." It was a bold request and, Meinhardt was not against granting it.

Eleven: The Dane

As much as they were shocked and, that there had to be an official enquiry as to the events surrounding Meinhardt's claim, there was no doubt that Rudolph was appreciative that he had not been in trouble himself. There was a real move to keep the information secret from the majority of the order and to claim that the death and Ludovic's genital mutilation was the result of pagan attackers and that Meinhardt had arrived in time to save the boy. The warrant and the contents of the confessions that Meinhardt had collected were damning enough, but the fact they had no confession or information for Allard himself, considering Meinhardt had interviewed him first, had meant there was still some disquiet amongst the commanders who were the only ones permitted the information. Meinhardt was arrested, but instead just given a month of hard labour for carrying out an execution without orders… but though he completed the month regardless, Leonhard and his Komtur had admitted to their own orders for him to go there and root out trouble… which they agreed could have easily been misinterpreted.

Dietrich was grateful that there was no chance Allard would return and hurt the youngsters again, but unfortunately it meant that he now had to take over a more fundamental role as assisting all new ordained brothers to come to the group, but Ludovic's own training in a monastery came to the fore. Rudolph seemed to realise with the scare too that he had to man up and so he used scouts and various members of the community to help him and Dietrich learn more of the language to communicate better. Dietrich was trapped here, but Meinhardt deemed that a suitable place as he found himself teaching even the locals to start reading scripture and with that, they would be able to find more opportunities for themselves. Meinhardt though was passed onto a different Komtur who was doing most of the raiding jobs, all of them dangerous and terrifying as Meinhardt dragged Diethelm onto these missions.

No one spoke of Allard again… no one was to acknowledge it if it were brought up. Anyone that did ask, they were informed there was an incident and he was attacked by a pagan and decapitated… this fuelled fervour that the pagans really were venomous towards the Christians out here and in the end, it worked better for the order to claim an Ordained Brother that had been well liked by a community he'd been converting would have died in such a way. It was true that he became a martyr in this respect, but that fact was something Meinhardt could live with, though Dietrich and the youngsters were not sure of it.

The landscape around the area was building up with the order, more villages were being connected up and communication was getting better, there were problems during the height of summer with lots of small attacks, but thankfully Dietrich's position made a perfect hospital and many of the worst injuries were taken to him and the squires were taught much more useful tricks for the field. In fact, Dietrich was grateful that the new priest to join them, Brother Bernhardt, was also a skilled healer with extensive knowledge of local plants and, a northerner. He was jovial and talkative, eager to learn everything he could and thankfully, his accent made Dietrich's heart ease as the time between his meetings with Meinhardt were reduced and Igel was no longer allowed to go wandering on his own after chasing one of the local bulls!

For Meinhardt, the situation was perhaps a tad more miserable, he thought of Dietrich at night, he thought of him when he ate, when he prayed, whenever he was not focused on slaughtering the enemy or scouting, there was only Dietrich in his mind. His squire was not much help, Diethelm had gone through all the worst parts of knightly training with a sensitive stomach and it had taken a very close brush with death from a man with a club to actually get him to use his sword. Meinhardt had been badgering him about it for months, but when autumn came along the youngster had finally gotten used to the fact he had to use his weapons. It was just in time as an early winter heralded a time for raids and there was a surprise when Meinhardt and Diethelm came back from one such raid with not only good stores for winter but slaves.

"Ah… Meinhardt… you look to have had some luck, I'm pleased to see you remembered to capture some slaves this time… oh, but I need your assistance, someone's turned up with a letter of well… it's almost a letter of reference from the King of Denmark and your name is mentioned in it." There was still issue with the Danes, whether it was the constant warring over the northern regions of the marches or their patches in Livonia, they would be peaceable one minute then return to their more quarrelsome Viking habits of trying to exploit the situation in seeking coin for not interfering. Most of the Komturs left the matter for Balk and the other Meister to handle, they just got on with their jobs and whenever they saw a good opportunity to hire Danish mercenaries, they would pull them in and pay them well. The mercenary system was common, the Danes still liked an excuse to cause mayhem and this worked well for the winter raids, so at this time the Danes were helpful allies but troublesome vultures in summer!

Meinhardt was confused by the fact he'd been requested, but his weird association with the Danish royalty was still something that cropped up from time to time. There were rumours too that in a recent battle, the king had apparently been rescued from near death by an anonymous German knight and the Germans neighbouring them had been quite sure it had perhaps been a member of Meinhardt's family. Meinhardt hadn't heard such a thing, but from the sounds of it even the Danes did not know and were not even confirming if the rumour was true... so it probably was not. But still, Meinhardt had a good grasp of the Danish words that did not match up with German and he strolled to Komtur Geiselhart, known as the Grim Komtur with his wizen face, shrunken cheeks and long grey and white beard. Once in here Meinhardt received a shock at the sight of a being that looked to be nearing seven foot, broad and muscular in every sense wearing mail and armour and a helmet that must have been a relic to his Viking ancestors... the Dane before him looked like the pagan warriors of yesteryear and Geiselhart pointed at the being with a grunt.

"He's called Magnus, apparently he's a mercenary who believes God has sent him on a mission here to aid us... his uncle apparently knew your father and lost an eye to him in battle once... so he knew you were here and this was a good place to use his sword. Its either here or he travels to Kiev." The Grim was looking as grim as his nickname, staring out to the bulky being in the wooden fort with a look to say he had probably assumed the being to become his assassin. Certainly, the fellow was terrifying and more than well armoured he was wearing an array of weapons on hand, but Meinhardt knew that the Dane mercenaries tended to carry everything on themselves when they sought a place to join, seemingly enjoying the exercise in carrying and the practice in living off only the most basic. Until they found a town suitable enough to get drunk in. It was a bit of a surprise, but Meinhardt approached and threw out an arm.

"Gud dag, Magnus?" It was not dissimilar to the German, but it still sounded weird to Geiselhart, but the being gave a hearty laugh as he yanked the helmet from his head by its seemingly leather flaps and slapped it to the table. He then stretched out an arm as if to shake but hooked Meinhardt about the waist, pulling him into a tight bear hug. Even the Komtur grimaced as he watched Meinhardt wriggle and writhe within the grip as the figure clapped his back and then began to chatter away in Danish as Meinhardt growled and swore at him until he was released. Meinhardt adjusted his raiment, looking vicious until he turned to his master and a grin split his face as he gave a snort. "Sir, Magnus is going to help us with the winter raids… he knows some of the local language and suggested having a Dane in this northern area was safer in case we bump into their turf. Magnus, Geiselhart here is our Komtur, he's the boss."

"Ja!" Magnus stated, a grin splitting his bearded face, as Geiselhart eyed the figure up, he could almost say that the man had Germanic features, his skull was shaped in a similar way, the chiselled jaw too, but something was fatter, his body stockier but curiously, his nose just a little longer and he looked more how the southerners in the Holy Roman Empire teased the Northerners of being… sharp and straight, not an inch of fat or a kind smile amongst them. But as the figure continued to try and wrestle with Meinhardt, Geiselhart almost laughed, they could have been brothers! But before they departed, the Komtur raised a hand and Meinhardt turned towards him expectantly, almost like a hunting dog awaiting the leash to be loosed.

"Brother Meinhardt, we will be expecting your friend Brother Dietrich next month for a few days to sort out some of the medical supplies here. When he arrives, you might want to hand him your squire for a bit so he can learn some ministering. Diethelm's been very slow to his training so he might find a niche in healing that would be useful for us all. Now, if you'll see to our Dane… in three days I've got a plan for the next raid and it will be a big one." The Komtur grunted and Meinhardt straightened to salute him in excitement whilst the Dane just swung a hand in seeming interest before strolling after Meinhardt and towards the bunks. The wooden hut that was filled with three other knights, two more squires and a spare cot would have to house the Dane, the fifteen men-at-arms were pretty packed into their tents and Meinhardt doubted the burly figure was going to be eager to help build any wooden buildings for them.

"You're lucky Magnus, we captured this pagan village a month ago, it's got prime track through the marsh to connect us back to the rest of the order with room to expand out to the neighbouring pagans. We're working on raiding during winter when they don't expect it, taking food or slaves and burning a hut or two. They're getting nervous now but whenever they think we're going to come back, we move on to the next place, make them weary then hit them again just when they calm down. Of course, if they convert the situation is easier, we don't burn and we bring them back here to the Ordained Brother and secure their village. We've already garrisoned two knights and men at arms in one of the nearest villages we just wore down. The winter here's come in fast though and in white, we really do hit them with surprise." Meinhardt began, grinning from ear to ear as he led the brute over to the spare bunk, which happened to be one that he would be sharing with his back to Meinhardt. Meinhardt thumped the hard frame firmly with a grunt. "We just got the barracks here up last week so space is a premium but better than a tent. You'll be sharing with me... or on the floor, your choice."

"Heh... is all good, nice to get a little company, better if it's a lady though... heh, wait, you knights are all you know... like eunuchs, right?" Magnus laughed heartily as he slammed a fist into the wood as if to ensure the frame was secure, but more to show off. Sleeping in a room where there were sex starved religious folk was hilarious to him, especially when he would go seeking a haughty widow the first chance he got. But when he turned to look at Meinhardt, he could see that Meinhardt was not embarrassed but giving him a look as if to say he could compete with him in that level of manliness and this intrigued Magnus. He rubbed at his red-brown beard, growling to himself that Meinhardt certainly had something about him and Meinhardt gave a snort of amusement. He then turned and beckoned him to follow, but now Magnus was intrigued and he then gave a sly chuckle. "So... you're a naughty monk huh?"

"Huh? Naughty? What kind of childish notion is that? Urgh... is it that obvious?" Meinhardt growled, he hoped it was only obvious because the Dane had said such things first and Magnus nodded his head with a splitting grin upon his face. He then wiggled his hand, gesturing he wanted details on this woman and Meinhardt jolted back slightly, his face going bright red in surprise. He'd never told anyone anything before, there was only him, Dietrich and now Ludovic who knew the truth and well, Ludovic had castrated himself! Something inside made him want to tell someone, sometimes he wanted to sing about how much he loved Dietrich as if he were singing the glory of God... but if Dietrich heard that he'd laugh at him. Meinhardt stared at the Dane in confusion for a while before blushing and rubbing at the back of his head, he'd have to make out that Dietrich was a woman. "Well... she's... she's got these really beautiful green eyes, this big nose that I like to tap because they make a funny face, lovely sandy brown hair that I envy how long it can grow and well... she's so kind and loving and... and mine. MINE! Don't get ideas..."

"Heh… you are naughty… but tell me more about the body… what kind of beauty is she? Eyes and hair, that's nice but what about the breasts and the body? I can tell you've had your experience because you're looking even more shy… naughty monk." Magnus grinned, so toothy it could have belonged to a demon in a painting and made Meinhardt grimace. How could he describe Dietrich as a woman when everything he liked about his body were all the masculine features? He certainly could not say how much he loved doing things to Dietrich's manhood… or even his backside… that was too embarrassing that even when he did it Dietrich panicked! Meinhardt grit his teeth, trying to think it over as he tried to describe him.

"Well… she's taller, by a little bit… and I say you could call her 'plump'?" Meinhardt had the thought if Dietrich ever heard this conversation, he'd throttle Meinhardt for even saying such a word. He'd been thinking of his backside at the time, even making a groping gesture and then pulled his hands away and behind his back as the Dane had just looked very intrigued by the thought. He begged him for more, gesturing about the bosoms and Meinhardt froze… he did like Dietrich's nipples and he'd groped his breasts a little like they were a woman's… they were surprisingly quite the handful. "So beautiful… such gorgeous nipples I just love to flick them and squeeze them just a bit to hear the sound… ah, but kissing is the best, even if the beard can tickle."

"I see… heh, you like a woman who can carry a pig under her arms huh? Matches what I heard about your father! Just be careful… Meinhardt… you can trust Magnus to keep your secret but its not good for a monk to know so much…" Magnus chuckled in amusement as Meinhardt covered his mouth and was swearing to himself. He'd mentioned the beard, how could he have done that? Now he was really worried… if Magnus was around when Dietrich turned up, would he guess? Meinhardt grimaced as he nodded his head and then steered Magnus towards a place where he could get some decent food and better conversation, but the Dane gave a hearty laugh. "I like you Meinhardt, you've got balls!"

"Currently…" Meinhardt whispered to himself… Dietrich would kill him!

Three days passed, Meinhardt and Magnus were surprisingly quick to become friends, they were very close and even sleeping beside each other they seemed to compete over who snored the loudest. It increased the jealousy that Diethelm held for anyone gaining more attention from his trainer, but he was so scared of Magnus he said nothing. Many of the others were weary of the Dane, but the seeming devotion to Meinhardt kept them calm as Meinhardt would indulge him in arm wrestling and in fighting practice. Already Meinhardt had been defeated in two wrestling matches with the second landing him in the horse muck, but it was enough to band everyone together and the Grim Komtur had made no comment on it. On this third day though he laid out his plans for a raid into the boarders of the Pomesanian patch, a region that was dangerous because it could lure in attacks on the order from other tribes that the Livonian branch were still battling. It was a very difficult raid requiring utter stealth and the Dane's presence would be useful as the Komtur laid it out.

"Horses are to be left in the woods overnight, not to be ridden in, we're to do this raid with as much secrecy as possible and get as close in the dark as possible. This tribe we want slaves from, we also want to burn as much as possible so the whole group will be attending bar myself and those garrisoned elsewhere, plus I will retain twenty men-at-arms in case we have problems. You will have from midnight till dawn to do the damage and then run… we need whatever we can get from this mission without casualties. Balk has confirmed that the upper echelons of the order have agreed that slave trading is permitted and vital to build up money for supplies and mercenaries when the land here is not as viable as in other regions." The Grim being muttered with a look upon his face as if someone had forgotten to remove whatever leech was draining his body dry. The knights all present and the Danish mercenary nodded their heads firmly in understanding, glad to have another straight-forward mission to work on, but one that required their utmost stealth. With fresh sprinklings of snow falling in the region, their white cloaks might help them move around the village on foot and the presence of the Dane would throw them off. The plan was hopeful and the Grim gave a soft grunt. "With a feast day approaching, what better way is there to celebrate than through the removal of such pagans?"

"Do you believe they might have some stolen relics in their possession, Komtur?" One of the elder knights spoke, one who'd clearly battled in Jerusalem for the idea of recapturing God's property and assuming there must be something to be said about it here. One of the other knights mused they might have the head of a recent martyr with their reputation and a few snorts and whispers of intrigue ran through the knights and were bound to bounce to the squires. Meinhardt did not take part, he did not want to throw out random ideas that could not be compounded or give a reason for the soldiers to dawdle in their actions looking for a relic. But with that news out and the Komtur sending them away, there was a buzz of excitement within the group and when Meinhardt met with Diethelm, the young man gave a soft grunt at the commands.

"Isn't it wrong to make the squires believe we might be rescuing a holy relic? Why should we put such a heavy investment of faith into something that could potentially backfire and lead us to a slow death and a botched raid?" As always, Diethelm spoke like he was decades older, a grumpy old man that felt he knew more about the world than anyone else around him. It vexed Meinhardt to hear the grumbling, but he had to admit he was not too sure on the situation either. He had to trust in the Komtur's thoughts on the matter and hope for the best just like the others would. He did not believe there was a relic, but Geiselhart's refusal to deny there was one could cause trouble and Meinhardt gave a groan as Diethelm rushed to his side to walk proudly with him out to the chapel for prayer. "I'm ready for the raid this time, sir... I won't disappoint you again."

"You didn't disappoint, you annoyed and embarrassed me a little... but it takes time and some squires take longer to really know how much danger they are in. You haven't come from a position where you're on the edge of a battlefield all the time and you haven't been let loose in the Holy Land to try and figure it all out, so I know it's still too new. Besides, one should never get used to death." Meinhardt stated with a firm expression that said nothing of his true feelings for the boy's progress; the truth was that his anxiety reminded Meinhardt greatly of Siegfried and how empathetic that squire had been. Of course, Brother Siggy was doing well and stationed south on the edge of the Masovian territories and when he called Meinhardt or Dietrich brother, it truly felt like a family bond. But as they approached the chapel the burly Dane was right beside them. "Coming to worship, Magnus?"

"Looking for my good friend Mein... simple question but best for dark corners ey?" Magnus was wearing a massive grin that made Meinhardt's skin crawl as he stepped aside. The big heavy arm of the being fell upon him with the weight of judgement as he shook him gently and pulled him aside. In his tattered clothes and scraps of leather armour about his chest, he looked like the stories of the dread Vikings to have spawned him and Meinhardt knew he wouldn't like the question coming. Shoulders hunched as they leant into a walk and the Dane gestured with his hand, the Teuton was close to throttling him.

"So... with your lady... how do you not risk pregnancy?"

"If she were to get pregnant it would be hailed as a miracle." He growled and gave the Dane a strange stare that practically begged him to push off. However, Magnus gave a few random blinks as he looked at him and then shifted his gaze about before making a sudden suggestion of, 'the other entrance' as Meinhardt's eyes widened. Though initially, he'd had a slight thought in his mind of how cute it might be if he and Dietrich could somehow have a child together, the sudden thought was too blasphemous to linger long and easy to swat aside before this suggestion. Meinhardt's face went bright red, even his ears were going red and his neck and shoulders as he suddenly thought of that beautiful place where they had such wonderful interactions, where their bodies connected and he looked towards the Dane in horror. "How dare you even think of my... mine's... special place...."

"Heh, that's a very childish way to put it, interesting place to stick it too... is it better than the other... OUCH!" Magnus found himself being kneed firmly in the gut and then pushed down onto the floor with a growl. Meinhardt was standing over him looking as if he might be about to stab him to death with his eyes alone! He looked down at the bulky figure on the floor groaning and rubbing at his stomach in amusement. The sensation had been curiously painful but he'd had the thought it was better it hadn't been the full force, Magnus pulled himself upward and then grinned at Meinhardt's sneering face as he gave a snort of amusement. "Sensitive? Is she a nun then?"

"Yes. Now, to mass!" Meinhardt barked in frustration, as he turned on his heel and stomped towards Dietleib and grasped hold of him, jerking him on down the corridor and into the chapel. Magnus straightened up with a grin of amusement, he would love to see whatever poor woman was the kind that had to deal with that ridiculous and violent being. Clearly, he was very possessive of this person and that only made Magnus all the more intrigued by who it might be that had captured Meinhardt's heart. For the knight however, he was praying and even ended up lying on the ground to pray and be closer, begging for forgiveness over what he had said and hoped that it would not affect the coming raid as they prepared for the storm.

It was pitch black, but even so the winter wind had whipped up the snow from the ground to smother all vision as the knights and their horses remained tucked amongst the pine trees, staring out across the plain of churned up mud and frost towards the distant flickering lights of fires within huts. The gathered knights were wrapped in their great white cloaks with helmets covering their faces, reducing their sight but making them more obviously ominous like phantoms staring through the trees. There was an aura of total doom around them as they stood within the shadows of the trees and waited for a relax in the weather so they could move forward and raid them. The horses were quiet and expectant, it was only when Magnus approached from his own bit of scouting that alerted them all to the time.

"The time is right, the weather's got the entire village inside and the majority of suitable slaves are closest to us. I can sneak back over there and set fire to a few of the buildings to flush them out towards you, then a few of you can find what you need." Magnus grunted to Meinhardt as he threw the information over to the others as Diethelm trembled nearby and the senior knights nodded their heads. As Magnus scampered off into the swirling winds of snow, the knights then stepped out to the low ground, moving carefully and swiftly as they walked towards the huts with the wind whipping their faces and swirling about them, pulling them backward as if warning them not to do what they intended to.

As they reached the huts, Magnus slid off towards the homes that were suitable to be burnt whilst the knights gathered around the doors. They squatted calmly and quietly, Diethelm and Meinhardt looking to each other calmly as they stood beside one of the huts and waited with the snow swirling about them, their cloaks flapping about to add to the white of the world. As the distant sun was visible as a lighter line of blue in the distance, the Dane calmly lit the thatch of several of the huts and then calmly waited to grab the first person he could. As the fire began to grow and the villagers clambered out giving hollers of fear and anxiety, others came out and swiftly, swords and clubs hit the men that stepped out as other beings began to scream and were grabbed.

Meinhardt hit the back of a man's head with his sword, Diethelm hit the second and when a young boy came out, younger than any squire, Diethelm was instructed to hook the boy up and he did, going and rushing back int the snow, wrapping his cloak around the screaming figure that bit and kicked at his armour. Meinhardt stepped into the hut looking at a mother and her children, choosing to leave her but take one of her other sons that looked old enough to work. He hooked the boy under his arm and then almost walked into a blade before the axe of Magnus crashed into the body trying to bar him. There was a rather haughty looking woman biting, kicking and screaming in fury on the Dane's shoulder as he beckoned them to head back. Meinhardt was startled but the boy in his arms was weeping and Meinhardt grit his teeth in frustration before wrapping his cloak around the boy and whispering to him.

"Don't worry, you'll go to your brother and everyone you leave behind will be fine." Meinhardt did not know if the boy understood as the knights hurried off, some with food and others with things that would be useful. He noted too that one of the older seniors was running out with a large box in his arms that had apparently the head of a saint within it. Everyone hurried off with their captives, leaving the villagers to put out the fires, tend to the dead and wounded as some tried to hurry after and rescue the captives, but the wind seemed to throw the snow out to help them escape. Meinhardt hurried on with the boy sobbing to his chest as he grit his teeth and just held the boy close to him, confused why he wanted to comfort the boy as he reached his horse. He placed a hood over the boy's head as was done to the other captives, they were also tied up before everyone mounted up and departed.

The raid would go down in history for the order for apparently securing the head of a martyr, though details on who, when and how were altered later on for the official records, Meinhardt found himself uneasy over these thoughts and more so when the slaves were taken away to be sold elsewhere. As the winter became worse and colder, Meinhardt, Magnus and Diethelm became closer with each other over their concerns for such a blasphemous claim, and Meinhardt prayed for Dietrich to arrive sooner and give him a different focus.

Twelve: The Pomesanian Problem

The winter was hideous, it was not only cold but the snow melted suddenly when the sun came up only to freeze in to cold air to turn mud into ice. The stone seemed to shimmer with a slimy, freezing layer that meant the first on duty in the morning was ordered to keep a broom by their bed to scrub the ice aside. It was not a nice winter at all and sharing his bed with a Dane that expelled a lot of gas and snored loudly beside him, all Meinhardt could do was think about how much he was looking forward to Dietrich's arrival. This was just as troubling as Meinhardt would find himself reacting as he lay back-to-back with the snoring, groaning hulk that would occasionally swing an arm and smack his face. Meinhardt would wake up terribly aware how dangerous his situation was, slipping out of the bed to march to the latrine, only to slide about on the ice and thankfully lose all the sensation that had been bothering him!

The snow was falling relentlessly and with it the supply chain was awkward and there was news about something big being planned against the Pomesanian tribes and their allies the Pogesanians There were thoughts it would revolve around some work in spring upon a ford in the Vistula. The commanders were all expecting to be called in already to discuss the situation with Hermann and Konrad, but there was no news in Meinhardt's neck of the river and he assumed that Dietrich was likely to be coming with the information. The bad weather meant most of the knights, squires, men-at-arms and even the Dane were spending their time scraping snow away from the roadways and areas that could be damaged by it. This gave them all some kind of distraction, but without new orders there was a sense of restlessness and anxiety clinging to the fortress.

Then, there was a break and though the air was bitter and the sky grey, the snow stopped falling and their Komtur ordered a new raid for supplies more than slaves. This time everyone was going to wipe out the entire village that sat between their last raiding site and the river route. This area was risky, dense forest and the locals could run for help from the other tribes easily. There was also a very big encampment of their enemy in that region who were building up for battle against the order in spring. The thought of a dangerous raid made Meinhardt unseasonably concerned and Magnus mused over it with him as they were settling for sleep.

"Riding out tomorrow afternoon, you should be excited for another chance to slaughter the foe. Raids are good for the spirit of the troops, also keep the non-monks happy." The Dane chuckled on the bed with a sudden yawn and Meinhardt grimaced, he did not feel up for that kind of battle and he stayed sitting up in thought. He'd already prayed to ensure Dietrich's safety in travelling to see him, but he was anxious that he should have asked for protection too. He had never before considered the idea of having to leave this world and Dietrich alone! That almost made him upset as he rubbed at his chest and sighed. The Dane grimaced at him, not quite sure what was on his mind but he yawned loudly. "Your friend might be traveling to us soon, good healer is he?"

"Not a surgeon but he doesn't blanche at cleaning wounds unless leeches are involved. But I was concerned about him, what if he travels during the raid or when we've raided and the roads become more treacherous?" Meinhardt grumbled, grasping his jaw and squeezing just a little with a groan. What if Dietrich got hurt because of them, he'd never be able to forgive himself! But the Dane just patted his back and beckoned him to go to sleep and the other knights grumbled that it was wise to do so. Meinhardt accepted their advice but as he curled up, he closed his eyes and thought of Dietrich.

Lately his thoughts could be so lewd and strange about his lover! He kept thinking up curious nonsensical scenarios where they were somehow reunited and able to explore their passionate sides. He blamed the winter's cold for it, missing the hot flesh of his partner, the rich cinnamon curls of hair to nuzzle into, the smell of his sweat and the feel of Dietrich's body reacting to him, quivering breath and that deeper heat within! He'd ended up imagining them finding each other lost in the snow, making a camp and spending all night with bodies entwined to gain heat. There were scenarios where Meinhardt was bathing in cool water and Dietrich would ride up to snatch him and take him to a wooded area where Dietrich would present himself against the trunk of an oak tree and beg for him. But by far his more embarrassing preference was to rescue Dietrich from their pagan foes trying to soil their captive Knight and Meinhardt saving him before anyone could touch his lover!

It was unsavoury and certainly could get embarrassing, but it sent him to sleep and gave him food for thought. As they prepped for battle Meinhardt could tell the cold was affecting Klobig and though it was unpleasant to consider the truth of the matter, it might be the last season for the gelding on campaign. Still, he prepared his weapons and Diethelm was more prepared for the situation with his younger horse giddy for adventure. Magnus and his sturdy

Nordic pony with its strange wild looks pulled up beside them as the figure played with his axes. Meinhardt then joined the group prayer and they marched along the track ready for battle, making sure anyone seeing them would assume they were gathering elsewhere and not involved in a raid.

The day was freezing, a steam hung around the caravan like a clinging mist made from man and beast. The atmosphere was ominous and heavy, a cold chill of expectation ran through every man and the dark hours looked about them. As soon as the darkness came, the units separated, with one lot swinging off the track to come at the village from the side whilst the main body continued until forest loomed to their right. They slid down amongst the sullen pillars as the forest seemed to become deadly silent as if a deep breath was being held in.

The sensation squeezed the chest, every soldier moved into position with horses being brought together in preparation to charge in, cut down and burn what they could. This village was less primitive, they were not huts as much as homes with thatch roofing and stores. It was for this reason they were chosen as they were the sort to have better supplies. The knights believed their God would rather the fruit of his work was shared among his holy warriors rather than those who knew not of him.

The troops were in position and they waited in silence as the village was still loud and busy. Eyes searched through narrow visors on helms that bore shapes that almost seemed demonic. The heavy featureless helmets turned all the knights into faceless entities that might as well be demons to their enemies for their ferocity would be such. When the signal was given as the sun began to sink, they charged in total silence and crashed into the community as if going through a barbarian camp.

The defence was quick, arrows flew at them but mail and speed meant there were few casualties as the riders cut down men close by. To the edge of town, the second group of men-at-arms fired their bows amongst the men that came to fight and even those that fled. It did not take long for the thunder of hooves to die down and the screams, shunting clangs of metal to metal or flesh mixed with the squeaks of the horses and the crackling of fire, breached the silence. Knights dismounted to subdue all that wanted to fight, favouring their axes to chop into flesh or mailed fists to thump beings to the floor. Like thugs they mowed their way amongst the Pomesanians and cut to pieces any being that did not fall to the floor in fear. In a matter of hours the village was subdued and the people enslaved and gathered up to be converted or chained. Many of the men had been wounded and to the credit of the villagers they had killed ten men-at-arms a squire and badly wounded several with arrows and brute strength. They were tough people, but as Magnus put it, even his own ancestors had known the purpose of their kind in naming them Slavs.

The spoils were gathered and to Meinhardt's great shock, he watched the Dane and some men barter with the Komtur before grabbing some of the sobbing and screaming women to take aside. He immediately marched to his commander, questioning if he knew what they were doing but the Komtur just looked at him as if he was an imbecile.

"They didn't convert and we all know these pagans have coming of age ceremonies where their virginity is given to any number of men. Heathens and their orgies, the exact reason we must purify the world of their kind." The boring old figure grimaced but though Meinhardt could agree with some things he could not agree with just accepting the rape of women to satisfy the non-brothers as acceptable.

"We would let Christian men poison their bodies with an action no different to the actions we blame upon pagans? This is not right, I will write of it to the Meister!" Meinhardt growled, knowing a Komtur only feared the process of administration and discussion rather than the actions of a fuming low-blood officer like him. He would tell Dietrich for sure and have him write something up, but the reaction from his usually vacant Komtur shifted. Suddenly Geiselhart had a look of pure displeasure upon his face and his eyes seemed to darken as if to dare him. Then he made a soft snort as if remembering that this knight was still quite illiterate, and he then stretched his arm to suddenly push into Meinhardt's saddle. The younger knight gave a sharp gasp, he'd not realised how bruised one knee was from a hit there with a club, the saddle pressed down near the tender flesh as Geiselhart sneered at him.

"Its almost as if you are questioning your commanding officer, it's a good thing you didn't get your knee chopped off thanks to that Dane. I would advise you take hospital rest until your knee is not the colour of charcoal!" The vicious expression was mostly from his teeth and Meinhardt winced in agony as his Komtur pressed down on his knee so that it seemed to creak and groan as if it might snap. Then the usual Grim expression returned to Geiselhart as he released Meinhardt's saddle and then gave him a blank stare. "Say as you wish, but I would think anything that reduced the money paid to these mercenaries would be welcome. Now, fetch your Squire and get on with leading the converted back to be blessed by our ordained brothers."

"Yes sir." Meinhardt almost growled it but lowered his head and joined Diethelm, who was sporting a gash to the head and thankful his smashed helmet had taken the worst of a potentially fatal blow. He looked through his swollen eye to Meinhardt as his senior grabbed some snow, wrapped it in cloth then slapped it to his face to make him wince. It seemed the student had found his confidence and was raring to do more, when Meinhardt dared to tell him his thoughts, the squire had stared at him blankly before giving a scoff.

"If they don't convert, they have no souls so they're just wild animals." The words seemed to bother Meinhardt, but only because rape was not something done to an animal! He would admit though that it might have been kinder to kill the women then allow them to fall further from grace. But he had his orders, and he would have to wait for Dietrich before he'd hear sense from anyone!

The snow came again but it was not thick and the temperature had risen so it barely settled. Meinhardt remained limping up and down the pallets of the hospital corridor aiding his companions. Their Ordained brother Peter was trained to heal, but once he'd done the necessary he'd left the rest to Meinhardt. Most had been gashes, broken or dislocated shoulders and some had been looking at risk of gangrene, so they'd debated keeping the limbs or not. Being in the quiet of the hospital as it slowly emptied was oddly soothing and reminded him of Burzenland and of those he'd lost there. He sighed softly often, thinking about how much he'd fussed at Dietrich touching him and how unfair he'd been because he was scared.

It was a good place to reflect his choices and Meinhardt hoped he could stay just a little longer as he continued to limp and do the washing of the fabric all within this confined space. But he was irritated when he heard the only door to the main barrack open and he was expecting another being to come in and complain his poor abilities with bandages had made them get infected! But he was startled when a new patient walked in with a black eye, bloodied shirt and yet a loving smile upon their face.

"I'll be honest with you, the black eye was Verbecher rearing and smacking his neck into my face and nose, but the rest was a Pomesanian attack. The mail took the brunt but Geiselhart ordered me to rest up in here till morning." Dietrich did not want to be smiling so obviously to be near Meinhardt again but it was impossible as his beloved hobbled over to him. They grasped each other in a gentle hug as their lips clapped together in several loving pecks before they just sighed. Then Meinhardt snatched Dietrich's garb and yanked it up.

Seeing a slice so close to one of the precious nipples and fresh blood on the stomach scar, Meinhardt shuddered in fury. He blamed his group for having performed a raid on the main route, but Dietrich said nothing. He let the slacks be removed and then just lounged along a free bed, curious to feel Meinhardt do the healing this time. Though he might have expected a tad of tenderness, Meinhardt was characteristically himself, finding a fresh cloth rubbed salt into it after rinsing it in some lukewarm water before slapping it on! Dietrich gave a groan and grumbled away as Meinhardt washed his body roughly before he then kissed Dietrich on the lips. He then kissed down from clavicle to the top of his braes with soft, loving pecks. He then found some poultice and prepared a patch for Dietrich's face.

When he brought it over, he slapped it to the black eye with a grunt and then awkwardly swung himself onto the bed beside Dietrich. He gave a sudden grunt of irritation, Meinhardt was heavier than the bed could really cope with as it creaked and groaned, threatening to collapse if he moved too much. The pair argued briefly over the space until the younger swung his arm around Dietrich's neck pulling him in and forcing a very sloppy kiss. He felt as if doing so might just make Dietrich a little less angry but he was sadly mistaken, as Dietrich swiftly pushed his hand into Meinhardt's face.

"I came here to be healed, not to be groped by you, or at risk of the bed and my neck breaking." He began but rather quickly he received another loving kiss, less sloppy but this time to the ear to make him shudder as Meinhardt wrapped his arms about Dietrich lovingly. As the fool northerner gave groans of love and adoration, Dietrich rolled his eyes and lifted his hand to stroke at Meinhardt's neck to make him give a squeak before he was given a loving kiss on the lips in return. The pair sighed, lounging happily on the bed together as if the world did not matter as they kissed each other softly time and time again. Their hands stroked each other's shoulders and the bed seemed to stop its threats. The pair sighed lovingly, foreheads pressed together and hands locked as they sighed and nuzzled a little while longer.

"Is it obvious I missed you? I hate the soppy stuff, it's not manly nor what a knight should do but..." Meinhardt had grunted, eyes closed at first as he'd nuzzled against his lover's face until he'd realised that Dietrich's hand was not gripping him tight. He opened a speculative eye, noted the scowl on his lover's face and considered his words before heaving a sigh of irritation. He might as well mention work whilst they had total isolation in this room for the night. He took a deep breath of frustration before kissing the swollen skin of Dietrich's cheek before stroking the familiar hairs on his lover's chest like stroking a dog. "I am going to ask you to write a formal letter to Balk for me. The other day my Komtur permitted the rape of captive pagans to some mercenaries to reduce the payment and this seemed to be like the Order prostituting them and potentially damaging goods. We're monks, we should deny this behaviour to aid others to follow the righteous path."

"You know, for what you did for me it would be the least I could do and I thank God to allow me a chance to repay your actions on behalf of my boys." Dietrich stated, focusing on giving a positive then asking more questions or bringing up a subject neither of them could quite cope with discussing. Rape of the lower class, the slave was often flaunted in a court as the privilege of higher rank and after what his brother had done, Dietrich could never allow such actions to go unquestioned again. He stroked his husband's cheek softly, luring him in for another soft kiss before Meinhardt gave a chuckle, referring to those little brats as 'his boys' made Meinhardt snort in amusement and Dietrich had to laugh as he explained it. "It's just how things have turned out, they treat me like their mother... if I'm being truly honest and they all want to hear my stories about your bravery! They all aspire to be as forthright."

"Heh... I like it, they are wise to have such trust and faith in you. I must admit for a moment I was scared our raid had led to you getting the fall out but, sometimes I forget that when that krankhaft Sigmond isn't around, you're a great warrior." Meinhardt teased as Dietrich gave a scoff at his words, only to feel those hands trailing down his stomach. Tenderly Meinhardt was spiralling his fingers around Dietrich's belly button, making him shudder and then an awareness came to Dietrich. He should have guessed the reaction would have happened, but it still always seemed a shock as Meinhardt slid down to lay his head on Dietrich's belly whilst staring up at him lovingly yet possessively. "Sometimes, I think how interesting it would be if I somehow got you pregnant... if I could put life in your belly... marriage is supposed to make children after all... but I don't think I could share the love in my heart with anyone but you."

"You sure no one's bashed you on the head, Stier, only I'd say that was rather unsettling until you made your point and... and your point was oddly pleasant." Dietrich blushed as he then reaffixed the patch to his sore face. But even with one eye he could see clearly what Meinhardt was doing and, not since he was drunk in Kronstadt, had Dietrich seen him acting coy. His husband was undoing his breeches, easing them down slowly and kissing and nuzzling into each inch of flesh that was revealed. It was making Dietrich's body start to swell in anticipation as Meinhardt wheezed that his 'wife' had such a lewd body. Dietrich gave a gasp as his swelling phallus was revealed and Meinhardt nuzzled against it lovingly, sniffing gently and sighing in utter joy as Dietrich's body seemed to dance for the attention. Meinhardt gave him a sultry look that Dietrich had never seen on him sober before as he kissed that place and then made a salacious sound as his mouth enveloped the length.

Dietrich did not know what to do with his lover, his legs strained out, knees bending to let Meinhardt's fingers grasp about his buttocks as he drank his lover's flesh. Dietrich could hardly believe how terribly lustful Meinhardt could be and yet even now if he tried to touch back it could earn a smack. Heat poured in steamy wheezes from Meinhardt's nose onto Dietrich's skin as he covered his mouth, nipping at his knuckles to stow his voice as he groaned at the exquisite massage motions of Meinhardt's mouth. It felt so wonderful and it felt new though it was not and as Meinhardt slid the swollen and twitching length from his mouth, he thought to lavish below as he suckled at them gently to make Dietrich give a sharper gasp.

"Meinhardt... it's to open out here... someone could barge in... No! Not there, dear God that's so dirty you idiot!" Dietrich had stretched a hand down, beckoning for them to both be more aware but Meinhardt's icy eyes had held him still. Then, his cheeky husband had dared to indulge his tongue with a pleasure that made Dietrich's body quiver, his breath catch but his mind spin in disbelief and shame. Yet that tongue rolled and lashed and dipped into such a dangerous spot as Dietrich's legs began to crunch upward, willing for a more satisfying penetration. "Meinhardt, I surrender just... just is there a way to hide or go between the beds?"

"The floor is freezing, but I think we can wobble to the laundry room, there are some cloths in a pile we can crash onto... hurry Dieter, I'm limping for two reasons now!" Meinhardt grimaced as he pulled himself from Dietrich's body, only to lift his leg up and give his calf a bite to make Dietrich yelp in shock. Then Meinhardt turned and wobbled steadily towards the back of the room, one hand dropping down to hold himself, trying to keep calm otherwise this was going to be a much more awkward situation. He opened the door and then shuffled in patting down the fabric pile in anticipation before he waited for Dietrich to join him. Here in the narrow room, next to the cauldron filled with dirty rags and a lot of sweaty clothing, it was not the right kind of atmosphere but that did not matter when they were together.

Dietrich had steadily pulled himself off the bed and felt it creak dangerously as he stood up and then groped about for the clothing. He then walked after Meinhardt with one hand pressing the poultice to his bruised eye and then he stepped into the cupboard, grunting that he had to barge into Meinhardt to get in and then Dietrich's backside was grasped hold of. As he gave a sharp gasp, Meinhardt ensured that Dietrich was completely naked and their clothes lay on a pile on the floor. Meinhardt stripped his own lower half but maintained his long shirt that just covered his backside from the cool draft whistling around the entire building, he then spun Dietrich around and pushed him back onto the pile as he gave a grunt of shock.

"Gentle... I..." Dietrich began, but he soon had Meinhardt lying over him, holding onto his shoulders and kissing his lips lovingly. Dietrich gave a soft groan of affection, stroking at Meinhardt's head gently before he then hooked his lover up to lie more onto the fabric before he grabbed his legs. Dietrich repeated the word gentle and then found himself being beckoned to grab under his knees and hold them up, spreading himself and blushing heavily for how awkward it all looked before Meinhardt grasped at Dietrich's shaft. He was soon stroking at it gently to make him gasp and moan, Dietrich turning his head onto the unswollen side and giving a soft sound of pleasure before Meinhardt then pressed closer to him.

"I'll touch you more, then when I put myself in, you can put your legs over my shoulders..." Meinhardt groaned softly, leaning forward to kiss his lover again before he brought a hand back to Dietrich's sensitive backside, stretching it and stroking its insides with his fingers, teasing and twisting as Dietrich gasped in shock. His whole body was heating up and he was straining out in arousal, not sure if he might just embarrass himself before he'd accept Meinhardt's full form into his body. But as Meinhardt gave him another loving kiss, letting his tongue probe into the soft chasm of welcoming flesh, Dietrich moaned deep and then Meinhardt growled by his ear. "I wish you weren't so embarrassed when I kiss you down there."

"If you know it makes me feel so awkward, why mention it... you can be so pig-headed…" Dietrich growled gently in frustration before he was gasping and moaning as Meinhardt pumped his fingers inside. Soon he was huffing and panting in shock as his body seemed to open out, gripping at Meinhardt and he beckoned for the penetration already. Meinhardt's face was bright red with excitement and swiftly he gently eased his form into the puckering hold as Dietrich's mouth juddered. He moaned, almost arching his back to try and feel more comfortable on the stinking pile of rags. Once penetrated, Meinhardt paused inside, moaning and sighing to feel him being grabbed, to feel that tightness before he bent forward and let Dietrich's knees bend onto his shoulders, hooking his arms around him and kissing his lover. "Eh… Meinhardt…"

"I love you Dietrich… I thank God for every day I know that you love me too… just leave it to me… being joined like this… its beautiful." Meinhardt sighed lovingly, kissing Dietrich's cheeks and then his lips as Dietrich groaned, feeling his husband deep inside him. When Dietrich muttered that he was in fact being ridiculously loving and Meinhardt grumbled, he started to thrust into his lover. His movements were deep, slow, making sure every spot was stroked and every chance of Dietrich's body to squeeze around him was gained. He groaned and sighed, panting as he moved in at a steady pace as Dietrich began to gasp and moan, releasing one of his legs but then slapping a hand over his mouth. He tried to smother the sounds of the moaning as Meinhardt thrust in and out of his husband's body as Dietrich was moaning softly. He made sure to put all weight on his better knee and he groaned lovingly as he could feel his body swelling inside and Dietrich's body was pulsing around him as he moaned against his wrist. "I love you… I love you…"

Magnus was watching the brothers go to their religious service and he gave a soft snort, he was quite intrigued to find where Meinhardt was. He shuffled to where he'd been told the hospital was, hopeful that whatever had made Meinhardt thump him the other day was cooled down and they could have a decent conversation. He stepped in with a gentle smile and without any thought, only to pause to see it was empty, only to hear heavy pants and smell something obvious in the air. Immediately the Dane was excited, he hadn't known any nuns had come visiting but he was certainly interested to know if Meinhardt's lady was present. He shuffled silently to the end of the room, a grin on his face as he spotted the doorway was partly open, though he was almost embarrassed. He had to stifle a laugh until he heard the sudden groan of pleasure from something that made him worried as the pair seemed to reach their end and Meinhardt groaned.

"Ah... Dieter... you wouldn't believe me... but right now you look the most erotic I've ever seen you..." Meinhardt groaned lovingly, as he pulled out, grabbing a rag, and wiping himself before pausing to stare at Dietrich. Dietrich was lying flat on the pile, his face sweaty and red, his whole expression one of exhausted ecstasy as he lay there with his stomach glistening from his pleasures and beneath him, dripping slightly from between his legs was all the signs of Meinhardt's adoration and every other part of his work on full display. It was arousing for Meinhardt to see what he had done, to see it all still reacting as Dietrich gave a soft moan of pleasure and then Meinhardt leant forward to kiss Dietrich's lips. It was at this time that the Dane opened the door, peered in and then gave a scoff.

"I thought Dieter wasn't a girl's name..." The pair had never known themselves to be caught before, there was no way to explain this as anything else, but Meinhardt felt fury and fear twisting and tangling within his body as Dietrich just stared at the stranger, almost about to burst into tears that someone knew and this person would hurt Meinhardt!

Thirteen: Unpleasant Pleasantries

"NO!" Meinhardt suddenly leapt onto Dietrich, wrapping himself around his lover protectively and glaring at the Dane that was suddenly leaning against the doorway. Magnus' arms were folded across his chest and he was giving them both a look of utter amusement, in fact he'd had to agree with Meinhardt's uncouth assessment of how his companion had looked coated in such sin... very alluring. But Magnus could see parts he didn't like much and hair in the wrong places, he just snorted as he looked at the way Meinhardt was wrapped so tightly about the shameful, red-faced Dietrich who was too scared of what would happen to do anything as Meinhardt growled towards Magnus. "I'll kill you... you say anything or it you touch him..."

"If I touch him?" Magnus stated, almost wanting to chortle out loud but he could only snigger. He was rather bemused, but he regretted it as Meinhardt suddenly launched forward and pulled Magnus into the closet and against the wall. His hand wrapped about Magnus' throat and he squeezed mercilessly as the bigger being just choked in shock. There was a dead look in Meinhardt's steely eyes, a look that said killing was all too easy and the real Meinhardt was already asleep and letting this warrior take hold. It startled but impressed the Dane to see, though he choked and wheezed before Dietrich grasped Meinhardt's wrist, squeezing it softly and then wrapped another arm around Meinhardt's waist, leaning his head down onto Meinhardt's head and making him aware of his shorter height as he loosened his grip.

"No Meinhardt... he was not threatening us or saying anything like our enemies would... he was just surprised. Hear him out, we should show mercy and forgiveness you know..." Dietrich stated softly, knowing that if this was God's design for them to be seen and punished, then it was the will of the lord. Meinhardt was rather more unwilling to make that kind of merciful decision but when Dietrich kissed his neck, the Northerner gave a yelp, releasing Magnus and turning around to smack Dietrich's shoulder, until he realised he was still naked and then returned to wrapping himself protectively around Dietrich, still growling that he would kill Magnus. The Dane just chuckled in amusement and then rubbed at his chin as Dietrich lowered his head. "You're a mercenary? We don't have much money given by the order... but is there a service we can give to pay for your silence?"

"Heh… such a noble air, and that accent, I can hardly understand that German, but I understand money for silence. Hmm… Meinhardt, your Dietrich clearly knows how to talk to my sort… but what to ask for…" Magnus grunted with a cheery tone, his face in a big grin before he then grasped a pair of breeches from the pile of clothes nearby and passed them to Dietrich, encouraging him to dress. Meinhardt's mouth opened as he turned, ready to bite Magnus but the Dane pulled his hand away with a chuckle, patting Meinhardt's head like he was a child, making the shorter man between the three sneer. But Magnus then sat himself back against the fabrics with a thoughtful expression as he rubbed at his bearded chin and Meinhardt turned to Dietrich, growling at him sharply.

"We should kill him, friend or not this is a serious matter and your life could be on the line! I couldn't allow someone to put you at risk or to dare to ask things of you! Curse my impetuousness!" Meinhardt growled in fury, only for Dietrich to loop his arms around him and pull him into his chest, patting him firmly and smiling as he whispered into his lover's ear. There was no reward for turning them in, mercenaries were always out for money and preferred blackmail to murder if it could help them later. Besides, he knew they were religious monks and he would probably ask for nothing more than a few prayers or a request to sell him passage into heaven… the Dane did not know anything about what they could do only what he'd seen thus far and Meinhardt grit his teeth before Magnus yawned.

The big Dane stepped out into the infirmary and Meinhardt hobbled after grabbing his clothes, pulling them on hurriedly as Dietrich continued to dress himself in return. The knights then marched to their seats and Dietrich was quick to look for a damp cloth to swiftly wipe whatever of the mess he could get rid of from his body. He felt utterly disgusting all the same, wiping his groin and backside on a bed as gently as possible as Meinhardt squatted on the end of the same bed, making it creak but seemingly protecting Dietrich again. Magnus was utterly intrigued by this situation, it was clear that Dietrich really was the one Meinhardt had been talking about, but Magnus could not really see anything 'feminine' about the other German to make him the slightest bit attractive. Maybe it was just something strange with this race… Germans had always seemed not too dissimilar in looks and battle menace, but it was obvious up close that they were very, very strange. Maybe this interest in the same sex was quite common among the warriors, some way of being even more 'masculine', Magnus could not even figure out a way to consider it at all, it did not make sense to him but with so many men stuck living together and not allowed to take women, maybe it was natural?

"I have decided… just three things… nothing too big. Firstly, that I always sleep in a bed on my own, I don't like sharing sleeping space. The second is for you to pray for my soul, I'm not scared of death but, if it may help my potential the same way as placing money in a man's palm, then pray for me." Magnus grunted, his mercenary brain showing through as Meinhardt nodded his head firmly in acceptance, although he was worried for the third part as Magnus rubbed his chin and then gave a soft snort before he leant in, curious to see Meinhardt's reaction. "It gets lonely as a mercenary… perhaps you can find me a suitable companion that's not afraid of death and battle!"

"WHAT!" Meinhardt growled again, standing up off the bed and recalling those poor slaves they'd pulled in from the raids. Going into battle, saving other Germans, fellow Christians from the foe like in Burzenland and the Holy Lands was different to this, up here it was slaughter or slavery and it was getting to him. Meinhardt did not want to trade a life to this being that would only be treated poorly or worse, for soothing those barbaric urges of this northerner. But Magnus did not change his serious expression, he knew he wanted something worthwhile that would last a lifetime and he liked Meinhardt, he thought Dietrich might be reasonable too but he was eager to see if they would be cunning and amuse him with their choice, or if they would just be angry as Meinhardt was.

Dietrich though was swift to give a chuckle and then insist that they wait there. He wobbled and seemed uneasy as he moved, Meinhardt almost leaping over to aid him but Dietrich waved a hand for him not to follow. Calmly, the elder knight strolled in the least amount of uniform needed towards the kitchen where the men-at-arms were preparing their meals and the stew that was to be given to the knights tonight. For a so-called 'Grim' Komtur, their Geiselhart was very keen on meat in his meals no matter the time of year and with the snow falling outside, this would no doubt be a very salty stew! Dietrich stepped in, only to be pinned to the ground as something huge and slobbery, stinking of foulness was snuffling and lapping at his chin in delight with his tail wriggling in total joy.

"Alright Igel… alright… now calm down, God in Heaven… that offal must have been on the edge of turning, yet you still ate it? Dear me, you smell so foul!" Dietrich still could not quite cope with this damn canine, it was the most frustrating being he'd been around for years and yet, finally the canine had a chance to prove his worth. This boar hound was very much a war dog and very eager to make friends, if Danes were anything like the men from the March like Meinhardt, then there was no doubt that he would be very keen on a canine companion. Hopefully, Igel would be eager to make friends with the Dane too as that figure was more than likely going to get him the kind of food he'd enjoy, let alone have the time to play and cuddle with him. Dietrich might finally get rid of this damned dog! "Come on Igel… follow me and don't get distracted… we've found you a new master."

Igel gave out one of his voluminous barks as he galloped down the hallway, ignoring Dietrich immediately and running down the various passages of the hall. Dietrich grimaced in frustration, beckoning him to come to his side already but the canine was ignoring him and continued to bark away as Dietrich groaned and hurried back to the infirmary. Once he stepped to the door, he opened it and then looked at Meinhardt who was sitting on the bed looking furious whilst Magnus looked bored. When Dietrich then loudly greeted Meinhardt, there was a sudden shrieking squeal-like bark and the sound of nails clattering down the stone corridor as the canine galloped towards Dietrich, looking like a stallion hurrying over to him.

"Wait… is that my baby! IGEL!" Meinhardt shrieked, wishing he could go onto his knees to grab the canine, as the dog heard his call and came hurrying over. Dietrich closed the door behind the mastiff as it charged right up onto the beds and into Meinhardt's lap, pinning him down. Meinhardt was rolling upon the bed, making it creak and splinter as the canine lunged onto his master's chest, drool covered tongue smothering Meinhardt's face as he cackled away, cuddling his dog with the joy of a child. With a sigh of relief, Dietrich limped towards Magnus and sat down on the opposing bunk, noticing the way the mercenary was grinning towards the massive dog in amusement. He gave a soft whistle to greet the dog and Igel paused, turned around to look towards Magnus before suddenly giving an aggressive groaning growl before spinning and lunging. "IGEL!"

There was the usual sound of Dietrich's discomfort and then his disgust as Igel did not jump Magnus but instead jumped Dietrich, knocking him flat on his back and then crouching over the knight in the most amusing but unpleasant of positions as Dietrich swore to castrate the beast. Igel was giving his snorty low barks and growls of warning towards Magnus, clearly guarding his favourite toy from the seeming stranger before Magnus gave a chuckle and leant forward. He stretched an arm out, fearlessly daring to lay it upon the dog's head despite the obvious risk of injury before Igel then snuffled at his hand eagerly, slurping it in greeting before crouching over Dietrich again protectively.

"I hate this dog… so I thought you'd rather find more use for him, Magnus. A mercenary has more places to travel, more need for a guard dog and more money on hand to keep him fed well. Besides, if it's just you two, then you will have all the companionship needed to keep him content. He's fine with horses, but when he realises you're his friend, Igel will guard you with his life." Dietrich stated from under the dog, groaning in frustration over the smell of the animal let alone the horrible items that were close to his face. Meinhardt though was grimacing and then patted his lap, beckoning for his dog to leap to his lap once again as he gripped the dog to him lovingly, nuzzling his face into the dog and growling to himself as Igel was whimpering and panting, confused but excited as Dietrich sat up and glared at Meinhardt. "Meinhardt… think about it, Igel is a good boy and he will come to us if ever he's in serious danger and he will look after Magnus very well and with it, our secret."

"But… he's like our baby… he's so silly and affectionate, like you… but when there's danger he's all serious like me. He's such a good boy, he's so happy and cute and… he's mine." Meinhardt growled in frustration, nuzzling his face into the dog's body and groaning as he patted at the chest of the big animal, which suddenly decided to give a loud belch. Magnus though gave a soft chuckle as he straightened up and then stepped over to the dog, pressing his big hand against the dog's shoulder in a heavy pat. The sudden sensation made the dog turn its head and then straighten up to look at the Dane curiously before lifting his big paws up to Magnus' shoulders, leaning into the grinning figure before snuffling at him eagerly in fascination. "Igel… are you betraying me?"

"Nei… this boy's good. He will do for my companionship and well, I could use a good hunter… unless one of you wants to show me a little companionship instead…" Magnus grinned toothily and Meinhardt gave a sudden gasp of shock, leaping back over to grasp hold of Dietrich, practically hooking him in his elbow and keeping him choking and unable to do anything in response. Meinhardt was clearly trying to guard Dietrich from anything, the thought that the Dane could not possibly like him completely lost upon Meinhardt. However, the Dane just cackled away in delight, patting the dog's shoulder as Igel continued to waggle his tail and became rather content with the big figure patting at his back. "Relax friend... I told you before... I like my larger ladies...."

"See Meinhardt, Igel will be fine and we'll be fine too. We can rest assured that he will look after... our boy... very well and besides, Igel spends more time pacing around the building than actually doing anything constructive and with what's to happen soon... we may not even know what will happen with our own assignments." Dietrich sighed in frustration as Meinhardt finally released him and then looked at him cautiously. They stared at one another in anxiety before the Dane gave a soft chortle, mentioning that the other mercenaries had been thinking something big was coming for the spring. When Meinhardt looked at Dietrich expectantly he shook his head, lifting his hand flat to beckon them not to ask further as he gave a soft groan, only for Igel to lick his hand. "Tomorrow I'll explain it to everyone, as I am supposed to do."

The next afternoon after the snow had been moved out of the way and everyone had not only eaten their lunch but finished their prayers, they were beckoned to the courtyard. The courtyard was still icy, but Igel was bouncing around with random sticks and his seeming enthusiasm to be around so many other humans encouraged them all to settle down and just listen to their grim looking master. The old Komtur looked miserable as he stood at the front with Dietrich at his side, the ordained brother was unwell and so Geiselhart was taking control of that matter and looking more tired for it. He gave a groan as he finished giving everyone present a blessing, then turned towards Dietrich with his arm stretched out.

"This is Brother Dietrich; he's been sent to us by our master Balk to inform us of the great plan ahead of us... our spring campaign against these pagans." The grey figure grunted in frustration as he looked towards Dietrich with a bored expression and then towards the rest of his group. The few knights were visibly tired and unhappy about being out in the cold weather, whereas the younger squires were looking about the snow and watching the dog in fascination. He hated how ridiculous these damn youngsters could be, never paying much attention to a figure that was clearly being seen as important enough to pass information around. Meinhardt though was staring fixedly at Dietrich who was standing there patiently, Diethelm could see it too and was trying to look as respectful and serious too. But Diethelm still did not like

Dietrich, he could only explain it as a jealousy no matter how sinful it was to experience such a thing, because Meinhardt looked at that person so much and talked to him but did not with Diethelm. "If you'd explain the situation…"

"Of course, Komtur… it has been decided that our troops will be gathering for a winter assault on a large community of pagans. It will be to secure the entire area for our control, a new castle is planned to be built there and this conquered side of the bank will soon be home to other Christians looking to settle in. For this, we'll need the majority of our knights and squires on hand as well as all mercenaries. I have been given a list of all those who will be reporting to von Landsberg and will need to join with the other forces moving back there at the end of the week. This includes all squires and three of the knights here. We'll need to prepare to leave soon, following me. I will have to depart now myself to reach the next grouping and collect their knights to leave too." Dietrich stated firmly, reading through the battered and gnawed scroll in his hand. He'd already stopped at two other groupings of knights and mainly it was to round up the mercenaries for the assault that was to come, but he was already feeling anxiety for the camp one of his young squires had been sent to go to at the same time as him. He did not let his anxiety show but simply passed the paper onto the Komtur and then encouraged everyone to pray to God so that he knew his faithful were working in his name to rid the world of heathens.

With that over, the Komtur insisted it was time to go back inside and dedicate themselves to some study in the warmth and just as he turned his back and went inside, someone threw a clump of snow where the Komtur had been. The Komtur continued in but the knights were quickly looking amongst the curiously quiet and nonchalant looking squires. Igel stopped chasing about with his sticks and then hurried back to the stables where someone was calling him for food. The knights looked at the squires carefully, should they punish them all for disrespect or let it pass and just go back inside? Most seemed to look toward Dietrich to decide the matter because he was at the front, but when Dietrich turned about to leave, another clump of snow flew in the air.

It clapped him in the back of the head, cold snow slipping down his neck as he gave a girlish shudder of shock before turning around and noticing that every hand was pointing at Meinhardt, who was grinning wickedly. Dietrich had a moment to decide on whether he would be mature and just order them all in or whether he should dare to give into his childish side and start a fight with the snow. He knew, if he'd been back with von Lippe, he'd certainly have started a snowball fight to keep the youngsters motivated, but right now they needed to be sombre and consider that lives would be lost and the knights would be at great risk. It was a serious matter, a serious battle… but he was suddenly hit by another ball, from Diethelm and that childish part took over.

With a sudden series of cackles, everyone picked up the snow they could and just tossed it around in the courtyard, the mercenaries either walking off at such a childish display or deciding they wanted to enjoy the fun. There were laughs and a few grumbles but everyone was careful not to scream, not to run about too much and not to swear! They only had about ten minutes of fun before the Komtur returned and gave a hideous snap of fury. Everyone froze and to the shame of the knights and squires, they were all punished for their disobedience by no food for the rest of the day and that any further reactions would have them tied to a post and whipped. Everyone apologised and departed, stepping inside the building and finally settling down after a good rub with dirty linen before switching into fresh linen, whilst Geiselhart requested that both Dietrich and Meinhardt would get stuck with the job of the laundry and then Dietrich could depart.

They did as was asked in silence, but once all the clothing was in the big tub soaking after its initial scrub against the boards, Meinhardt shooed Dietrich off to go and do whatever he needed to do. Dietrich was thankful, though still anxious about what he knew was to come when they met up again, before gently kissing Meinhardt's lips and then holding his hand. They bent their foreheads together, whispered their vows to each other and God again, thanking him for Magnus' kindness and both prayed for Magnus and Igel to do well together. But then they departed and as he stirred the washing around, Meinhardt was thankful for the steam of the warm water and the foul smells, they helped cover the tears that began to fall as he realised there was a possibility this time that Dietrich might die….

Hermann Balk was not the kind of man that anyone would want to stare at too long, though he had an attitude that made him perfect for the job, a devotion to Christ that could never be questioned, his demeanour could only be described as fanatic. This was not a bad thing, they all wished for the fanatical devotion and dedication to their purpose here and in the Holy Land that Balk's words could fire up within the knights and squires, even the mercenaries could feel they'd joined a good place that offered not only money but a pinch of absolution for some of their antics here. However, whenever the knights were gathered in his presence, they were forced to always look up at him on the back of his horse rather than on the ground and hear him bellow out as they prepared for the assault.

"We're crossing the Vistula... once we're over, we will not cross back... this will mark the first permanent point of command for our Order in this land. From this point, we will spread over these heathens as a holy wave, purging those that will not see true faith. As we march through this depraved land, we shall join up with other brothers in Livonia and end the terrorising methods of these pagans against all good Christian fellows. We have been sent here by God to a land ignored, overrun and closer to home in need of feeling his judgement. Our victories here will protect our homes, families and the future of all those under the Holy Roman Emperor and the Pope from all these beings!" Balk bellowed out, his voice making everyone tremble and they buried themselves into the hearts of all beings. To know that their efforts here would protect those they'd left behind, was something even more intriguing than before and then Balk closed with the lines that made every heart swell. "Victory here, even death in battle, will ensure your position in heaven as soldiers of our Lord!"

Everyone suddenly seemed to bark out in salute to the Almighty and then Balk began to conduct a mass as the gathered soldiers bowed down on the hard ground. The warm spring wind had come and melted the snow, the rivers had swelled but there was a decent and large enough crossing point in the Vistula near this region in Culmerland that Balk referred to as 'Thorn'. This land was to the south, a decent sized settlement, pagan like the rest of Kulm and this was where Balk had decided that they would make their first true fortress and castle. It was going to be their base from now on; Kulm would be secured from the enemy... it would encourage the migrants, farmers and the development of the large hunk of land between the Vistula and this road.

Dietrich and Meinhardt listened calmly as they prayed amongst the other knights different squads. But though Dietrich would be safe with the majority of the forces and with the mercenaries, Meinhardt was joining the knights that would secure the roadway and he was stuck with Sigmond as his Komtur for this job and even Diethelm was scared of him.

Fourteen: Meinhardt's Bad Luck

"I bet they're having fun up there... what a job... guard the roadway between Kulm and Thorn!" The knights were not impressed with the current situation for themselves. They were all imagining some glorious and epic battle with their Master slamming through waves of heathens and cutting them down with total ease. They were hungering for battle and yet there was no way they would risk Balk's fury! However, the unit of four knights, four squires and twenty men-at-arms felt oddly inadequate squatting along the roadway. Their horses could sense the trouble and were pacing about in anxiety, they were just hoping to see Leonhard cantering down the road to tell them the battle was won or that they were required.

It was far more pleasant than being on the ground as if in camp with the horses grazing in boredom then jumping every time someone made too much noise. The men were comfortable just making fires and cooking, but the squires were the most unsettled and amongst them Diethelm seemed the most unwilling to just accept that this was life. But as he sat with the other squires and two of the other knights, waiting for Meinhardt to return from his current mission to check the south passage of the road, he was aware that one of the knights was someone that Meinhardt did not like at all and as he looked at the figure, he felt slightly sickened. The man was bald, tall, lean and his face was ravaged with scarring from hideous boils some said were due to the heathens from the Holy Lands using black magic against him.

He was called Sigmond, he was well known for having an unpleasant reputation as a thug, more so than other knights, but the fact Meinhardt had warned Diethelm to keep clear of him only seemed to intrigue the figure. It made Diethelm wary as he stood beside his rather worn nag, hoping that Meinhardt would return soon enough. Indeed, his total unwillingness to pay attention to the sharp eyes and the predatory expression of the senior knight had been intriguing enough for Sigmond to wonder what was being told to the boy. He was also eager to put Meinhardt on his toes, still angry for the various interruptions to Dietrich he'd caused and with a soft chuckle, Sigmond stood up and stepped over to Diethelm's lonely fire. He settled beside him as the squire looked at him with a desire to look anywhere else but the pox-ridden face.

"You don't like me, do you? I bet it's just because you see your trainer looking at me like I'm a villain and that's what you've assumed. Or maybe you don't like me because Dietrich's told you that I'm not to be trusted, that's what he's told Meinhardt and why he won't listen to me. I can't stand Dietrich; the princeling should have never been permitted back into the order after he was sent home to commit incest... who sleeps with their brother's wife with the intention to get her pregnant after-all?" Sigmond grunted, settling down rather calmly with Diethelm, not bothering to act like he was trying to get him to like him. He just seemed to be curious and yet his words caused Diethelm, the men and the other squires to look to Sigmond in shock and the figure then chuckled. "It's true, isn't it Franz?"

"Very true, I saw the first letter when it arrived in the old commune in Burzenland. Apparently, his brother had become impotent due to someone getting revenge for his previous infidelities and with their line due to perish, they jerked the monk back to do the task. I can understand it being permitted because of circumstances, but to pardon Dietrich and send him back here to the Order... they could only have insisted upon that because he 'enjoyed' the task too much. He's always had perverted notions, Meinhardt used to be at loggerheads with him all the time... but now they are both strange together." Franz stated, spitting at Dietrich's name and the mention of Burzenland as the younger knights looked to the elder in utter fascination and shock for this information. Franz was someone they all felt they could trust and Sigmond was a Komtur, clearly there was something in this to be trusted. Franz then sat on the other side of Diethelm, shaking his head and then patting the guy's back. "Must be hard, I'm sure you've noticed the way Dietrich looks at Meinhardt so lustfully... maybe they thought it was better to come here and lust over his friend then his brother's wife."

"Lustful? Wait... you mean... you mean Dietrich has thought of men and women? But... but it's blasphemous isn't it?" Diethelm gasped and Franz and Sigmond seemed to share a glance with one another that spoke of their desire to stoke more hatred for Dietrich. They nodded their heads grimly at him, insisting it had been this way since the Holy Land and that it was probably something to do with the Saracen wound to his belly, spilling out ideas that it might be cursed! They spewed out strange and horrible statements that made Dietrich sound like a wolf in sheep's clothing amongst their kind and, the squire could only look despairingly towards his contemporaries as he thought of his poor master's involvement in it all. "And... and... and Brother Meinhardt's situation in all of this? Is he safe or… why is he so loyal?"

"Dietrich and Meinhardt have a strange relationship, Dietrich lusts for him but thankfully Meinhardt would never let such a thing happen, he knows his companion's issue and for the sake of us all he keeps him in check. But it won't be much longer and then it will all burst out and he will be truly sorrowful." Sigmond stated firmly and Franz nodded his head at the thoughts, though he hated the idea that his friend Meinhardt could really be stuck in such a situation, though he certainly would never allow himself to be touched at all. As if on command the sound of the old gelding calling from far off alerted the horses and Franz patted at Diethelm's back, about to state that things were going to be calm soon enough, when they heard a shout to get to arms!

Everyone was up and to their weapons, heading down the road to see Meinhardt and his horse galloping with a flurry of arrows and a collection of angry looking locals behind them. Clearly someone amongst these tribesmen had realised that something was going on and they'd not been happy to find a knight guarding the road. Klobig was not doing well, he had a bad slash on his flank and his near white body was creasing with blood and his nostrils were steaming and red-raw. He was still going though, ignoring the pain though one leg seemed almost unable to even touch the ground and it was clear he was not going to make it onto any other mission. Meinhardt had been smart enough to take a shield with him and wear mail, it had done its best to stop arrows hitting his arms and he'd thrown the shield behind him to cover his shoulders, neck and head, but each thud clapped his ear and he was feeling worse for wear and stressed.

He'd walked right into the contingent on a bend, heard the sounds of others approaching but not expected them to criss-cross through the forest and he'd been surrounded. Thankfully, they'd been too startled at first and he'd hacked his way out with Klobig's huge weight barging many out of the way as they'd hurried on. Now the old war horse was flagging just as the men-at-arms came rushing down the road to join the fight, one well-aimed hit from an arrow scored the back of a leg and hit into something not only laming but painful and Klobig tumbled right onto Meinhardt! He gave a roar, swinging his shield around to cover his face from arrows as he'd fallen from the saddle but not far enough away. The sudden weight of the heavy animal onto his left leg caused a scream of agony he'd hardly realised had left him. The horse tried to pull itself up but a few more arrows hit and the animal thrashed about in agony.

Meinhardt managed to use his arms to kick his other leg free and push the horse away long enough to get his leg out, but poor Klobig became little more than a shield of flesh as arrows kept flying from men mounted in the woods and the men-at-arms were being felled. The knights finally got involved and charged through the trees on their horses to cut what must have been just six fine archers down. Meinhardt lay behind Klobig, the animal wheezing and snuffling, prone on the floor and loosing too much blood from the axe wound to his flank to be able to live. Meinhardt tried to steer his body around to hold him, to comfort his beloved old friend but his pelvis ached and he was scared. He was truly scared in this moment as he had never been scared before and all he could do was stroke and pat the withers and whimper to the dying horse.

Diethelm was quick to come over, insisting he was going to meet up with the fourth knight who should be heading back now to join in and then go on to Kulm to find a physician. He wanted to yank Meinhardt up and drag him away from it all, but there was no way it was a good idea when Meinhardt could hardly pull himself up to sit or stretch forward without a wince of agony. But Diethelm patted his shoulder and insisted he would get help as he mounted up and kicked his horse on and hurried off. Meinhardt groaned in agony as he heard the last few yells and clunks of sword to flesh before the men and the squires remaining were ordered to follow on up the path and ensure there were no more coming. It seemed a strange order indeed, but when there was not the sound of other men groaning and just the steady, hard footfalls of Sigmond over to his side, Meinhardt realised he was in serious trouble and he almost wanted to curse his bad luck on this whole mission.

"Well now Meinhardt… I don't think you'll be walking for a while, looks bad but we might get you back in time to clean it before the foulness stinks the place up. Maybe… but you know, I'm very angry that you keep protecting Dietrich like you do, you have no true understanding of what he is or how dangerous he can be if you don't treat his malady in the right way. Its such a shame there's no redemption between us except… well, to make you understand why you've made a mistake." Sigmond stated with an expression of smugness upon his face before he grasped Meinhardt by the chest. Meinhardt swung his arms, punching at him but swearing as he was rolled onto his front and then Sigmond held a blade to the side of his neck and smirked down at him. "You really are hard-headed, maybe you don't comprehend exactly what Dietrich is, but you will. Franz… show me you're a man or I'll show you what will happen if you ever question my methods even once."

"Question you? But I would never do such a thing, I'm utterly loyal and I believed everything you told me about Dietrich, it made sense to me that he was some hideous sinful fiend. But… but you told me that you intended to help Meinhardt, to make sure that he understood the danger that Dietrich held…" Franz was suddenly anxious, he was clearly made more pallid and fearful as Meinhardt looked up to him with the most vicious expression imaginable as if daring him to be just like this being. Franz just continued to stare fearfully as he tried to think of a more suitable kind of excuse not to hurt his friend, but Sigmond growled and grabbed him by the waist, yanking him down beside Meinhardt and then grasping him somewhere inappropriate as Franz gave a bleat. "No please! I've never even… please for the sake of my chastity!"

"You will be forgiven, you're going to save Meinhardt and yourself from the hideous lust… you'll do it Franz, because I'll do it to both of you then kill Meinhardt if you don't." Sigmond stated and Franz seemed to look at the being for the very first time as if he could see the monster he truly was and yet, he was too afraid of disobeying his Komtur and potentially getting killed compared to something that… well, if he did not enjoy it, it was not a sin, surely? Meinhardt though looked at them both and managed to spit at them before he snarled in fury.

"When I'm able to heal up… I'll hunt you both down and slaughter you!"

Thorn was proving a successful choice, there was a firm resistance from a much more capable local force than they were used to, but as always cavalry held the advantage. They had taken a few squires out with arrows and taken out a few horses, but for being there they were rather surprised how eager to battle the people were and yet how they seemed more targeted on the horses and failed to guard their heads, backs or necks from the swords. Some of course had grabbed knights, tried to yank them down whilst surrounding the horse, but distracted, the mercenaries had ploughed through and the knights had just chopped what they could. The last few skirmishes were finishing up, anyone wielding a projectile was quickly charged down or hacked whilst the mercenaries routed the buildings and more than two fires had started to drive the people out.

It was strange to witness for Dietrich, these tactics were as thuggish as the barbarians to the east and in Burzenland that had just raided and ransacked for grazing pasture, yet this was God's will? He assumed it was because these beings were pagan and would have to be treated as dangerous as any of the other pagans Dietrich had encountered. But they seemed almost between the savages bothering the Hungarians and the sophisticated heathens of the Holy Lands in their abilities but chiefly… they did not appear to be the ones crossing over the Vistula to raid into Masovia, at least not to Dietrich. But he was fighting with as much vigour as ever, locked into every scene of his brothers being pulled down or attacked and reacting to it. His mind was blinded in the need to protect his fellows but as it had died down, so this dangerous thinking had ensued. It was the aftermath that was causing more frustration to him and some of his companions as Udolf looked towards their master in concern.

"He's calling for the people to be rounded up, converted, enslaved and all the tribal leaders to be burnt at the stake. I can understand it, but why bother converting when enslavement pulls money into the order? He should forget about the need for money and just burn them." Udolf had never been a very gentle being let alone merciful, but it seemed curious to those around him that he was so angry because the order needed for money. However, Dietrich knew that anyone hearing his quibble might assume he was against slavery, but Dietrich knew that Udolf's real frustration was as he said the need to burn them. He had already murmured over how easily anyone might disown their faith in fear of the sword and recent converts could not be trusted. They never were, mainly because they were not German-speaking and Dietrich was aware of this and that Balk was probably of the same mind. He gave a grunt as he dismounted and moved in with a sword to a house that was half-burnt but needed to be checked for life.

"Have you questioned him on it? Perhaps our master's of the same mindset but is under bounds…" Dietrich questioned, but then there was a sudden bark from the mercenaries near the roadway that caused everyone to quiet down. There was a knight approaching and though Udolf and Dietrich looked ready to go that way and talk to them, it was von Landsberg that pulled himself onto his horse and then kicked it off, apparently following after Magnus, his horse and his dog. Balk gave a grunt for a few of the men-at-arms to go on up the roadway and clear the route to ensure that no one was going to trouble their victory. With the other mercenaries already helping to clear the houses and being careful not to do anything that this ruthless religious master might actually respond to, the locals were all out to the squares and some of the men were building a bonfire.

It looked a little worrying as the men were all beckoned forward as the mercenaries were encouraged to secure the area completely and kill any of the locals that emerged now or tried to run. With everyone brought to the square again and put upon their knees, with children, infants and women crying alongside the elderly and even some of the men of this township, Balk insisted they hold a mass and of course he led them. Everyone, even the pagans were bowing their heads and accepting the prayers as the motions were made to bless the land and then Balk cleared his throat to then inform them of the plan and everyone was startled.

"The Lord has granted this victory, but it is a victory that now marks the development of a land for our Order to grow and protect our fellow Christians. You have all done well, but our work is just beginning and we shall commence with the production of a castle here. It has been decided that instead of selling slaves from this community, they will be granted their lives and conversion in lew of building the castle along with our construction teams to gain God's favour and retain their homes and duties…" Balk stated and everyone was quite surprised as they looked towards the startled locals that were not really as primitive as many of the knights had expected them to be. However, these villagers did look curiously relieved at the thought of going back to normal before Balk then looked towards the men that were considered the head of the village, his eyes narrowed upon them. "However… your leaders will be placed upon the fire for their pagan ways and so will any of you that dare to go against this mercy that God has shown upon you this day. Now, you will be baptised as we deal with your pagan masters."

With that, everyone in the order was rather surprised and relieved at the thought of Balk showing such kindness, but they were intrigued too. Clearly Balk wished for a castle made of stone, the first castle to be built in their new territory and they were all rather curious for the thought that this was indeed a good beginning for the order here in the lands beyond Masovia. But there were many enemies around them and creating a castle here and perhaps building a more secure fortress in Kulm might ensure that they would be able to keep their section of land safe and give them good grounds to move forward from. It was also exciting to think that having this land might be able to lure in more to the order and even Germans to come and work the land to help the order survive. The thoughts of having a place better than Burzenland where there could be no quarrels over them being here was exciting and they were all eager to consider that this was a gift from God to help them all.

However, Dietrich had a very uncomfortable feeling that something very bad had happened and he gave a sudden shiver of pain that crawled into his back and made it twinge. He felt suddenly sick and then even seemed about to faint as he knelt beside Udolf, only for the older man to grab him and steady him. He then looked to the various bruises and points on Dietrich's body where their battles had led to wounds and then he gave a grunt. There was blood coming from around the side of Dietrich's head near the old scar and he gave a soft grunt of frustration as Dietrich then fainted. The only word to come from his mouth was a soft whisper for Meinhardt.

Fifteen: Judgement

It was the screams of pain from a familiar voice that roused Dietrich from where he lay on a straw bed in one of the houses in the community of 'Thorn'. He groaned in frustration, listening to a squire opposite having a wound sewn up as he was being told to stay perfectly still and had already dislodged the stick from his mouth to bite on. There was a mercenary beside him, holding him down for one of the Ordained brothers to help him out and yet it sounded like nothing was going quite right at all. Dietrich felt sorry for the teenager, clearly he'd taken the brunt of the aggressions in the battle but some squires were just crazy like that. Dietrich remembered that well as he gave a soft groan and was startled to see how much of his own body was wrapped up in bandages before he noticed Udolf standing nearby with a big grin on his face.

"Look who's finally woken up… only the little princeling could be so lazy to spend nearly two days unconscious, not even flinching when he was patched up. You're really something Dietrich… even Meinhardt was awake and snapping branches in his jaw like a dog whilst he was being patched up... though Konrad had him taken back to Kulm with him this morning." Udolf grumbled in frustration, as he yawned and settled down calmly onto the straw bed on the ground, turning to the figure with a grin. But Dietrich gave a jolt and sat up immediately at the thought that Meinhardt had been hurt, before he suddenly felt his whole body becoming weak and then he fell straight back. He had urged his hands to grab, opened his mouth to speak, but he'd felt himself being pulled back down onto the bed as he groaned and began to pant gently as Udolf gave a snort of amusement. "God in heaven… you're startlingly weak, now I can see you've been made even softer under Rudolph's care, probably making you spend all day recording him trying to figure out patterns on leaves…"

Dietrich groaned softly, lying flat and just taking in breath, realising that his chest was very tight and it was painful to breathe but not impossible. He could tell too that there were wrappings around his head again and above one eye was stinging as he felt something almost splitting because of it. Dietrich was startled, he hadn't realised he'd gotten so bashed up, he remembered being hit off his horse and slammed in the chest by some wood that was then struck at his helmet, but he'd carried on after that. Dietrich pondered if that old rage of his had blocked out the pain and that was why it had taken a while before his body had realised everything. He was not sure, but his own ailment did not matter as Udolf brought the water to his lips with a chuckle.

"Worry not… I have already enquired about the matter, poor lad met the enemy and had to lead them to the others… only for arrows and axe wounds to bring down that old horse right on top of him. He's a bit broken, but thankfully nowhere that won't heal… he's lucky, god was with him." Udolf grunted and rather suddenly slapped his big heavy hand onto Dietrich's shoulder, making him give out a sudden cry of agony. The old knight pulled his hand away, insisting he'd forgotten as Dietrich found himself going cross-eyed and falling straight back, pain overriding his senses and throwing him back into a daze. He groaned a little as the old knight then squeezed his nose, causing him to choke and come back around before Udolf lifted up a wooden bowl with water to his nose and Dietrich gave a groan. "Come on, have something to drink before you pass out again, you can have a prayer with me too for your fellows."

Dietrich's eyes rolled, he really did not feel comfortable, but there was no arguing with Udolf otherwise he'd have to listen to him calling him a pathetic princeling forever. Besides, Dietrich was now concerned about the matter of Meinhardt and he was able to pull himself into a gentle lift, grabbing with his bad arm and groaning before Udolf hooked around him and yanked him upward. It was painful, muscles and limbs being tugged against rough clothes and mail as Udolf rarely removed his battle gear, but he was still thankful for the attention as Udolf brought the bowl to his dry lips. When the water splashed onto his dried mouth, Dietrich could hardly remember a time he had not loved the sensation more, groaning as he was given a sip and swig before another to wash about his mouth before swallowing back. He was permitted to sip half the bowl empty before Udolf then helped him lower back down, though left the last inch to gravity so Dietrich grit his teeth once more, but, with the other figure no longer screaming and the other master making a point the treatment was over, the old knight brought his hands together in prayer and it was welcomed.

"Oh Lord in Heaven, who watches over us and guides us on our journey to purge the lands of the north from the heathen infection, we beseech you to watch over our departed brothers in heaven, to guide those suffering to your mercy and to aid all others in their healing. We give thanks for this kind victory and pray we will always remain in your good graces and our mission here is completed swiftly and in your honour, amen." The Bavarian's grunts were greeted with an echo of 'amen' from the other three in the room before Udolf straightened up. He then ruffled Dietrich's hair and went to check the squire, letting Dietrich groan back and yet confusion and upset gripped hold of Dietrich as he considered it all.

He never feared when fighting beside Meinhardt, when he fought anywhere in fact and yet, by curious luck and good grace, Meinhardt had never been so badly hurt he'd been in need of going elsewhere. The thought of him having been crushed beneath his horse too, not to mention understanding that Klobig was now dead made Dietrich's chest ache. He felt a terrible dread overcoming him that made all the injuries upon his body tingle as if they were little more than illusions compared to the pain he must imagine Meinhardt to be in. What if it was so bad that Meinhardt could never walk again? What if he could not be a knight, would he remain Ordained instead? What would happen to his beloved?

Suddenly, the overwhelming sensation of depression, fear and sympathetic pain towards Meinhardt as well as a profound sense of sudden loneliness overcame Dietrich. He started to sob gently, almost laughing as he sobbed and whimpered in despair that Meinhardt was hurt and he could not be beside him to comfort him. The sound rather startled Udolf, he was not quite sure he could remember a man of Dietrich's age ever sobbing before and he shook his head with a groan. He then lay his hand gently to Dietrich's mop of hair, stroking it tenderly before he whispered quietly to him to calm down.

"Don't be fearful now, God is with you and with Meinhardt... you'll both live." Live perhaps, but there was one thing that had bothered Meinhardt before that Dietrich had promised never to do and that was to leave the Order after he'd returned. Now he feared that this was the fate of his beloved and he shuddered to think that God was placing such a test upon them. Was this then maybe a punishment for daring to turn against Allard and letting Meinhardt kill him? Was this what they deserved for their constant sin of lust and sodomy? Dietrich shuddered in despair, his tears ebbing but he felt exhaustion overcome him and he closed his eyes and gave a gasp of pain as he mouthed Meinhardt's name though no one looked to see it.

Mentally, he found himself begging God to let him see Meinhardt, let him feel him and know the pain he was in and share it. The thoughts were strange, abnormal perhaps but he was quite sure that if he begged he could gain some kind of link to him, spiritually. He lay back as flat as he could, let the weight of his body just fade away till he felt like he might be floating when in fact, he was merely daydreaming to try and understand what his beloved might be thinking or feeling in that moment. He still loved Meinhardt so greatly that he could easily see him lying on a bunk and growling as he ground his jaw about being told to stay down in bed and rest!

Dietrich would have chuckled at the thought, but his body was locked in the daydream as he imagined Meinhardt seeing him and grumbling to him not to worry. He could hear the slew of confidence but irritation to be fussed over, telling Dietrich he was too soft about such things and that if he saw him cry, he'd hit him. He could imagine that pout on his lips so clearly and as Dietrich felt himself falling into the dream to sleep, he imagined himself bending to gently press his lips to Meinhardt's in a soft display of affection and confidence in Meinhardt's recovery and then, Dietrich was back to sleep and he was smiling.

Meinhardt's eyes shot open, his lips tingled from a weird clinging sensation and he spat and sputtered in case it were a harvest spider walking across his mouth. He had strict orders not to move, his whole body was still aching and he had to keep wiggling his toes to remind himself, despite the pain and bruising, that he had not been crushed completely. He grimaced as he looked around the dusty and cold dungeon that was being used as the safest place for someone with his injuries to remain secure. He'd been shocked at first to be brought here after the surgery, but his physician had given him the kind of questioning look when he'd dealt with the areas bleeding that had said he might have assumed something had happened. Meinhardt's lips were tight on the matter though, he was not a woman so saying he had nearly been raped... he wouldn't let anyone know this and for it, placement in the dungeon seemed suitable.

Of course, luck had it the physician had bleated that the bleeding might have meant Meinhardt's innards had exploded and were coming out, so they'd hovered around him the first day in case he'd suddenly died and well, he'd been happy not to be alone and yet bitter to think that Franz had been forced into it and done such a piss-poor job that Meinhardt was glad he was much more affectionate with Dietrich. But it had reminded him of how difficult their first time had been, though drunk in the mood he'd recalled the speckles of blood, the soreness of his partner and then every other time when he'd been a bit rough and should not have. It upset him to think he'd been put into such a position for the sake of revenge but also, that his friend had betrayed him and Meinhardt grit his teeth as he whispered to himself.

"If we can ever be together again… I'll be honest with Dietrich and tell him just what happened… he'll understand… he did warn that…" Meinhardt began in his whispering, only to freeze and shudder in thought. Dietrich had warned him about Sigmond, he'd seen Sigmond go for him twice and the second time that ridiculous dog had been the one to rescue him when it had looked like he might have raped Dietrich. Meinhardt's fists clenched, even if his knuckles were swollen and tight from having attempted to brutalise Franz when it had happened. He was soon terrified as he thought of that bald bastard Sigmond, of what might have happened with Dietrich… why hadn't Dietrich told him the exact details of what had happened between them? But now of course, Meinhardt's mind could only think of the young Dietrich he'd first met who'd always looked on the edge of tears when bullied, being forced into bad situations and it made him want to roar.

His shame however only grew for his own predicament when he heard the soft sound of feet shuffling his way and he knew it was time that he was fed the horrid gruel-like soup that was being made and had something to drink. He was annoyed by it, he had to be tilted upward with the utmost care and then had to just drink because it was easier… but you could hardly drink a soup that had more lumps in it to chew then a decent stew! But when the rather unpleasantly familiar form of the bruised and disquieting face of Franz came into view and was clearly alone, Meinhardt curled his lip and gave an expression that Franz could only liken to a cornered wild cat hissing!

"Touch me and I'll kill you." Meinhardt snarled, but Franz lifted the tray to show the food he'd brought with him, but Meinhardt continued to give a snarl towards the flat plank of wood. Franz grimaced, he did not expect that Meinhardt would ever forgive him, nor understand what peer pressure was, but Franz also felt Meinhardt should be grateful it had not even ended properly because he'd panicked too much. Franz wanted to do some kind of penance, there was not enough water in the universe to clean himself where it had been stained, but he assumed Meinhardt was of the same opinion. Franz felt the guilt and shame equally, he'd realised afterwards that he'd been humiliated just as much and Sigmond had been proving that even in his sickly state, he was far more manly than any of the men in his charge.

"I know you will, but you need to build up your strength to do it, so you might as well accept water and… whatever this grey stuff is. It looks more like someone swung a bowl in the moat." Franz scoffed in bemusement and though Meinhardt did not want to, he could not help but give a little one of his odd sniggering sounds. It frustrated him though, once Franz had been his friend and they'd shared their sarcastic humour with one another and their distinct belief regarding the order and God's will in dealing with pagans. Only Dietrich had come between them, it should not have been such a big item to pull them apart but this... it was shocking they could still be in the same room. But Franz placed a hand to Meinhardt's back, let him swing an arm around his neck and accepted the sudden headlock as Meinhardt growled.

"You're a coward Franz... when you condemn others so harshly, thinking you're more righteous, you then commit a sin because you're afraid of Sigmond. At least for being unwilling, my shame is more a reminder to have shed pride." Meinhardt snarled, his lips curling as he tightened the squeeze in his elbow to make Franz choke a little more. But then Meinhardt relaxed it and let Franz feed him, making it awkward and a mess on purpose to teach him a lesson on what he'd done. Franz was obedient and silent though, he could not deny that Meinhardt was correct and he was almost relieved that his friend had not revealed it to their elders, because he knew Meinhardt would be willing to face death for the revelation if the crime against him was dealt with. But Meinhardt growled again when he was settled back down, Franz had a much more unpleasant job to do and he was scared of getting near that area again as Meinhardt snarled. "Still a coward, too afraid to see what you did and own up to it... why should I protect you?"

"If you were any other brother, I would have no fear to aid you in this... I shouldn't be afraid but... but I am, I am a coward because I did not want to hurt you... but Sigmond... Sigmond is too..."

"Coward! Coward! Christ was not a coward and his burden was greater!" Meinhardt snapped, thoughts in his head were spinning around at Franz's upset and paled expression. The fool wanted to try and get himself out of it already but there was no possibility to do so, he grimaced as he just helped ease Meinhardt to his side, peeling back the cloth and then bringing the bowl to him as Meinhardt sneered. It was unpleasant and hideous for both of them, for Franz it was worse than what had happened but Meinhardt revelled in the sound of his disgust. He was still so furious and yet, he found himself sneering even more. "You have always been unkind to Dietrich, why is that?"

"Before... before it was just because he was some important son that...

well, he made everyone look bad in comparison. But then when I was with Sigmond, I overheard his men laughing about how Dietrich cringed around him and then one said 'that was HIS Dieter wasn't it, his favourite little friend in the Holy Land that had the soft mouth and hasn't stopped offering it to him'… I couldn't understand, but then I dared to ask Sigmond and he admitted that Dietrich was… was one of those filthy creatures… that he'd joined the order because the family suspected it and… and he'd done his 'service' to Sigmond when they met up again, but then Dietrich became interested in you." Franz stated, wiping his companion and shaking as he did so because he could feel the air around Meinhardt starting to boil with total fury and Franz trembled. He did not know how to react to this, what else could he say but the truth and then he knew to say something that almost seemed rather pointless in light of what he'd done. "But I knew… I knew you'd never let Dietrich do that to you and if anything, around you he was better, less foolish but then Sigmond says he's still… still seeing Dietrich covet you and…"

"It's a LIE! SHUT UP, FINISH YOUR JOB AND LEAVE!" Meinhardt spat in fury. He could not believe that Franz would believe something like that and yet his heart was clenching in more pain than in his aching hips. Tears were in his eyes and he was glad of the broken bones and the pain, it covered the fact he felt like a criminal here, especially upon hearing those words and knowing Dietrich's fear. He considered what he'd done, the way he'd pushed back amongst that straw and Dietrich had obeyed, only for him to have gotten drunk and forced himself on Dietrich. Considering it, now he remembered the upset and Meinhardt snarled as he was gently eased back and Franz lowered his head before Meinhardt snarled. "I'll keep my mouth shut, if you believe me that Dietrich was forced by Sigmond and that is why I protect him. You were forced to do this to me, don't you think it would have been just as easy for him to do it to a frightened young boy?"

There was silence, Franz left and Meinhardt was hopeful that the fellow had been given the glimpse into the true nature of Sigmond that he'd needed. But upset still bit into Meinhardt and he let the tears flow a little more easily as he was left alone in the remaining agony, unable to really sleep but not really wanting to either. He would use this pain as penance, he'd done terrible things to Dietrich and this was his punishment, he would have to remain and pray for Dietrich the rest of his time here, but anxiety gripped him too… how long till he would heal?

What if he never healed?

A booming bark greeted him and he shuddered in relief to hear the sound of Igel bounding towards the dungeon and then crashing into the door. He scratched and scraped until Magnus gave a haughty laugh and then opened the door. He let the dog in and Igel rushed to lick at Meinhardt's face as Meinhardt heaved a sigh of relief. Magnus approached with a smirk, but he noticed the tears and made sure the door was closed again before he settled on a stool nearby and then gave a grunt.

"You're lucky… many a king and nobleman have been crippled by a horse, you will heal well. I talked to the person to wrap your body up, I'm still amazed at what you went through, one side of your body is still black and blue… but your swelling is easing, the leeches are helping… but I'd say there's a few breaks but nothing that would have made your stomach fall out of your ass. Maybe you've just had the trots and the shock of the pain made you have an accident." Magnus stated as he sat there, knees almost to his cheeks as the stool was too short for him to really be comfortable with. Meinhardt just smiled and beamed at the affections of the dog, Igel was such a happy being for never judging a human as anything but good or bad… no grey areas or morals for a dog! But as Magnus rubbed at his beard and whistled through his lips, his eyes turned towards the door and he gave a grimace. "…I heard parts of your talk, but I left after that talk of your Dietrich. I believe I know enough about a being when I look at them to know the kind of people they are… besides, even I was startled by how such a masculine fellow like Dietrich could look so enticing when in that position."

"If you've been using that interruption as material to dream about, I'll order Igel to bite your balls off!" Meinhardt spat, making Magnus give a cackle to hear that his friend had not lost his humour. But Meinhardt settled back more comfortably as Igel moaned and whimpered as he snuffed at his body. He did not really want to say anything right now, but his Danish was coarse enough that no one coming by could hear it perfectly and he gave a soft sigh of frustration as he locked eyes with Magnus as the Viking-like Dane turned to him with a nonchalant expression. "You heard what he did and what was done to Dietrich… I cannot pay you anything for this but… perhaps someday I can find a way to…"

"Say no more… that one and, Sigmond, right?" Magnus' face slipped into something demonically wicked and yet, Meinhardt was determined that no matter what this was the way things should be. He could not kill a fellow brother, but Magnus was a mercenary and when the figure straightened up and placed his hand to Meinhardt's shoulder, he gave a soft chuckle to the soured expression. "No payment needed, just pray for me and uh… let me consider that face of his at least when he was like that. I still haven't seen anything close on a woman."

"You never will. But I'll allow it, all payment for an oath of silence." Meinhardt snarled and, though he was considering whether a vow of silence might be suitable for himself, Magnus gave a low moaning yawn of frustration. Meinhardt guessed it was because he had information to give and he looked to Magnus carefully before he considered that Dietrich had been in a battle too. He gave a grunt but the Dane just chuckled again as Igel bounced against him for another cuddle and to have his slobbery jowls ruffled.

"Dietrich got hurt but not enough to kill him… bit less blood but, he'll be up and about soon enough. But you've got a problem… I've got to report your condition to your father, he might not be happy about this and might drag you back home." Magnus stated with a sly expression and Meinhardt's eyes widened in surprise and then complete understanding. His elder brother had been aided in his troubles by a Dane mercenary hired by his father and it seemed that mercenary was still working on his father's orders. Meinhardt did not want to think how his father could have bought this loyalty, but he was terrified all the same and then gave a soft growl as he looked to the cross pinned to the wall of the dark, cold cell.

"The Lord is my father… I am a Knight of the Teutonic Order… I am not a son to man anymore…"

Sixteen: Father's Love

Spring hurried on and the cold weather just became chilly and wet, intermittent sunshine seemed to fall upon the developments as a castle was wanted in Thorn and the Pomesanian's in the area were all soon found, wiped out or converted. Their neighbouring tribes began to take interest, but there were ponderings from some of the members of the order about whether to expand or not. Communication between the order and that of the Livonian order had meant there was some view expansion should continue out to reach Riga. There were quibbles though over the agreements with Masovia... old concerns from Burzenland were quick to surface.

Something rather strange happened during the spring too, Magnus and a few of the other mercenaries decided to head home for a bit, abandoning the knights and when they departed, strange news came that they might have attacked one of the Komturs in the night. Rumours spread that someone might have paid them to do it, whether pagans or maybe the neighbouring kingdoms to the south with their tempestuous relationships with one another and the Germans. But the Komtur to have been slaughtered, apparently completely chopped apart alongside his lieutenant had been Sigmond, his lieutenant having been Franz. It was news that was taken as just part of the matters out here in pagan lands and working with mercenaries, especially when some mercenaries mentioned how Sigmond had not been careful with what he said to some men.

It was a relief to Dietrich to hear that his oldest tormentor had finally passed although he understood with Franz dying too, it was more than likely a raid and the mercenaries just looted camp on their way out. As one group of mercenaries left more came in and with them came the usual migration of German-speakers eager to take land and work it. Men to work on the castles came and yet, Balk put them to work on smaller structures of stone and wood to make their presence more known. When he was reminded of the matter with Burzenland and the concern that the order might overstep their boundaries, Balk always said the same.

"We have an agreement for this land at the very least and the Livonian Sword Brethren have its order which will join with our works... we'll just be connecting them and securing our own position. Stone is harder to burn then wood or bury unlike earthen mounds."

It was a firm statement and no one in their right mind would refuse the thoughts of the commander, let alone when his orders were passed down from the Hochmeister. As much as they were concerned there might be some note on the agreements made with Masovia on this point, the thought of being able to keep hold of a territory completely was rather exciting. There was a lot of news too about the situations to the south, the terrifying monsters that were exploding out of the east to overwhelm other Christian nations and prevent the Crusades in the Holy Land out of desire to protect their own lands. There was a growing concern about those beings and their ferocity, stories coming in from those trading on the Silk Trail that the region of the Caucasus had been overwhelmed. There was a lot developing and yet, Balk made no point of this as being of any interest to them in the Baltic whilst the Brethren were doing well in Kurland and slowly drawing towards the Teutonic position.

There were thoughts too on whether the Bishop of Riga truly was as eager to link with the Teutonic Order's presence, but there were words that the agreements with Masovia and trouble from the Swedes had meant that the Livonians were not as stable as they might be. They also had their concerns regarding the beings east of them across a huge lake in a place where the Christians were deemed the wrong sort of Christian. They did not recognise the bishop and yet the Teutonic knights did… but that was all the usual speculation running around the lower ranked members of the orders as the German-speaking farmers, masons and smiths began to migrate into the land as eagerly as they had Burzenland and the order was feeling invincible against others trying to push them out.

In settling some of these beings, Dietrich and the squires were out of the church and with Rudolph in control they were guarding the road from Masovia past Vogelsang to Kulm, ensuring that the settlers passed over and for this they were to be billeted in Kulm. Here, Konrad was still in charge whilst Balk was stomping around Thorn and sending letters to Riga, and Konrad was glad to know that Dietrich was present as he was now quite sure that seeing a friend might cheer Meinhardt's heart. Dietrich was busy sitting on his unruly black horse against the rolling mist of the morning with his white cloak flapping in the chill wind, when Konrad rode up to him with a thoughtful expression upon his face.

"The wind is warm at least… did you sleep well, Brother Dietrich?" Konrad questioned, seemingly out of the blue as Dietrich jolted in surprise as he turned about to notice that the Komtur was easing his bay horse over at a gentle trotting pace. The animal picked its way carefully towards the black horse, both turning heads and Dietrich being forced to turn around completely and greet his master, his ridiculous stallion was nuzzling and nibbling at the mare. Both Konrad and Dietrich tried not to notice, after-all it would be more than a little embarrassing if the mare was in heat and Verbrecher might just try to take the opportunity. Dietrich pulled his reins up, steering the stallion to the side and Konrad did the same so that they were facing out whilst giving a soft cough of embarrassment. Konrad was looking a bit gaunt and pale; he'd had a bad chest over the winter but still worked through as best he could and Dietrich made a point of this as he chuckled. "I was content, I've had more time to rest with Meinhardt being sick in my stead... he's been entertaining company as always and he can certainly read and write well, he even wrote his own letter back home just before the injury."

"I see... I'm thankful you've aided him in his learning, I heard he's been using his time on his back wisely to read the Bible cover to cover... but I'm not sure he's aware of the language difference." Dietrich stated in amusement as Konrad nodded his head with a soft grunt, thinking of how Meinhardt had looked at words and then looked at his own sentences and been confused they were not the same but he knew the sounds of both words. But that was what made Dietrich thankful, even if he were to be crippled, Meinhardt would be kept as a monk to read and preach and perhaps one day chronicle their works, or even just to write to dictation or read out letters. It was not great work, but he could still be useful and Dietrich lowered his head gently. "I know it might be presumptuous but..."

"You two have a curious bond, he healed you when you were at your worst in the house of your family, I'm sure you can probably heal him here. I guess you should spend the afternoon with him, do you have any issue in helping bathe his body or changing his dressings? There's not much to change just the few patches that are slow to heal... you know, he's moving his feet and arms with no problem, just jolts when he makes his hip jump... I don't think he'll be completely crippled, just a bit lame." Konrad stated and Dietrich heaved a sigh in total relief to think that he could be of such help to his beloved Meinhardt. Konrad was quick to grin, he was glad someone else was willing to do the job as the few squires they'd tried to get to do it had been shouted out or complained at for being too gentle or too rough. Konrad just beamed as he looked towards the position of the sun and on time, there was the ringing of a bell and he steered the mare away. "One of the men can take the guard duty from you after prayers…"

"Yes sir." Dietrich stated with a slightly higher tone of delight within his voice, not that he wanted anyone to really notice it. Konrad nodded his head, his face shifting into that brief little smile to say he understood very well and the pair moved off back towards the castle. They reached the yard and the men were waiting to take the horses, though Verbrecher was quick to try and drag himself back towards the mare for a greeting. The two knights then stepped into the hall, removed their boots and their mantles for the men to scrub free of mud before they joined the procession of the squires and the two other knights that were on hand in the castle.

With Vogelsang now just the meeting point before crossing the Vistula to Kulm, there was only a pair of full knights needed and with word that another batch of knights would be sent to them, instead of the Holy Land, there was more chance that Vogelsang would eventually be forgotten in favour of Kulm completely. For that, the group of twelve sat within the chapel in the cold, hands together as Konrad led them in prayer and they were all quick to settle into the routine without too much need for guidance, making Dietrich relieved that the time in the monastery with him and Rudolph had taught this bunch of youngsters to remain calm and consistent in the midst of prayer.

As they prayed, Dietrich's eyes were watching the youngsters carefully, Diethelm was amongst them and since Meinhardt's injury, he'd been incredibly quiet. Not once had he thought to be unkind to Dietrich or even to say anything to him, clearly he was just uncomfortable because he felt he'd contributed to his trainer's injury, though that was a foolish thing to think! Still, Dietrich just prayed and thanked God for everything he'd given him thus far and this chance to be with Meinhardt again and know what had happened to him and give himself some hope that they would not be separated.

When the prayers were over, the others went to their meal and Dietrich was sent to collect items from the kitchen to take down with him. He had some soupy broth that was more water than meal, as well as the next best thing to a chamber pot tucked under his arm and then, somehow managing to take another pot of water with him and a rag to clean him up, he was off. Even though it was an awkward amount to carry, somehow Dietrich clutched it to his body and made his way down the stairs without more than a few skids and jumps to the heart. He wanted to be quiet, not give away that it was him, but as he approached, he was almost laughing to hear Meinhardt trying to read the Latin out loud and then repeat the sentence in German. Meinhardt was confused by the word translations and he grumbled about knowing what it meant all the same, but it made Dietrich smile.

"Ugh… why isn't there a version of this in German? Komtur von Salza used to have versions written in other languages no matter how poorly translated that he'd commissioned himself. If I can't compare, I can't read!" Meinhardt growled to himself, lounging slightly to the side and growling that he could not read the tattered bible within his hands without getting confused. It made it clear to Dietrich something he'd never realised before… Meinhardt had always read by heart, but he'd even memorised what others had read to him. Dietrich wondered if their old Komtur had always known that and when he stepped into the dungeon, where a rat rushed past his leg and made Dietrich's spine tingle, Meinhardt didn't even want to turn around. "I know you're there, don't worry about being rude just… just do what you have to and pray for me as I'll pray for you. Forgive me for humiliating you like this, Brother."

Dietrich was a little confused until Meinhardt grasped the cloth from his body and pulled the itchy woollen quilt aside to reveal his backside. As much as Dietrich was aware it was to ensure some cleanliness was maintained, he could not help but start sniggering as he approached because Meinhardt hadn't guessed it was him. Dietrich would have loved to just give him a poke in the rump the way Meinhardt would always poke him, but jolting would be painful and he was here to look after his partner… like a good wife. With a sigh as Meinhardt was gritting his teeth over the sniggering, assuming it to be another man-at-arms who had no respect, Dietrich stepped over and placed the chamber pot beneath him as Meinhardt then swung an arm, instinctively grabbing Dietrich's shoulder and pulling himself into a sitting position. Dietrich automatically held his shoulder, standing behind him and noticing the tears now streaming down from the clenched up eyes as Meinhardt pushed his form into the pot and the natural processes took hold. He was incredibly embarrassed by it, but carefully as Meinhardt kept his eyes shut to stave off some of his shame, Dietrich eased him to lie on his side against the pain when it was over, placed the pot aside and then calmly began to wash Meinhardt as he trembled in misery only to give a soft snort.

"Brother… your kindness and silence are appreciated; your hands are soothing… thank you." Meinhardt was snorting and sucking in the despair and the pain he felt, so utterly ashamed that he could not do this task himself. But when it was done, Dietrich wiped his own hands and then knelt on the bunk and kissed Meinhardt's cheek, making him growl before he opened his eyes and the most contorted expression fell upon his face. It was clear to see he was so happy that the gentleness had been from his lover, but then the embarrassment had burnt to the fore and he was about to yell at Dietrich when the soup bowl was pushed to his mouth. His stomach grumbled to insist it needed it as Dietrich fed him, stroking his belly gently. Meinhardt growled as he drank, but clenched up all the same, feeling weak and pathetic around the one person he never wanted to be weak around.

Whilst sitting here waiting to heal and praying over and over that he would be able to walk and be a knight still, Meinhardt's steady recovery and mending bones had given him hope, but he'd gained a new resolve. That resolve had been a promise of total silence over what Franz had done, of what he'd heard had been done to Dietrich because he loved him too much to ever make him feel pain. He also did not want his pity, not for something so humiliating to him… and he did not want to ever make Dietrich feel like that, a thought that made him nervous to do anything more than let himself be held by Dietrich. Dietrich sensed that the weakness upset his partner, but fearlessly, once he'd been fed, he placed the bowl aside and then lay Meinhardt back onto the bed before leaning down to kiss him lovingly.

For Meinhardt the kiss seemed more healing than anything else he'd been given, his hands lifted to stroke through Dietrich's soft sandy brown hair, feeling for that ragged line and letting their tongues caress as their bodies longed to. Fresh tears fell from his eyes, but his face was christened with Dietrich's own tears of joy as he stroked the face of his beloved and together they just sobbed softly with one another as their lips parted. They held each other for a time, feeling confused that their situations could be so reversed and yet joyful to have the chance to return the favour of healing. But then Meinhardt gave a growl as he stroked Dietrich's face with a frown.

"I know I can be prideful about my strength and that I like to boss you around and claim its my role to protect you, but God made it clear I had to learn humility. I will walk again, I know this much because I will not allow myself to be a cripple depending on you to… to… wipe my arse… but it will take time still before I'm strong enough and Konrad has been saying I should be sent to Germany to heal. I do not want to go… I will not allow myself to go, because I can't leave you alone here." Meinhardt growled, gripping hold of Dietrich's hand as the pair nuzzled against one another gently and then Meinhardt sneered. "I don't want you to feel lumbered with me either…"

"How can you think that? After-all the times you've saved me, all the times I've come to you for help with my problems and all those times I've leant on your strength… its about time I share the load and help you. It won't be a burden to me, I would have thought you'd understand that our love is a heavy enough burden to wipe out all other pains and problems… especially when it comes to each other." Dietrich stated, only to watch Meinhardt's face scrunch up with confusion of the ambiguous use for the word 'burden' and Dietrich could not help but snort and laugh into his shoulder. Only Meinhardt would take everything literally and Dietrich could not love him anymore if he tried as he kissed Meinhardt's cheek tenderly with a soft sigh and then sat up. They looked at one another with eyes that shone with their total love and then Dietrich bent forward as their lips pressed together again and he whispered into Meinhardt's ear with a chuckle. "Its not like our marriage could be annulled…"

The pair suddenly sniggered together, chuckling away and Meinhardt felt joy overcome him for the first time in a while as he gripped Dietrich's hand in his. It was so good to be around him again, so wonderful to know that he was not completely alone in this dark, dank, silence and that there was indeed a reason to heal. He felt like he could do anything with Dietrich standing beside him and his will to heal and walk again was growing even greater. However, as they nuzzled noses again, the sudden bark of frustration from two deep voices echoed from the top of the stairs and the pair pulled apart. Dietrich looked to be cleaning up as Meinhardt just skewed his face up in confusion once more over the familiarity of the voices. One was certainly Konrad insisting that someone did not have authority, the sound of something being clattered against the steps and heavy boots, but more fearlessly the heavy booming voice of someone that made Meinhardt surprised.

"I will not hear of it, you're order may claim to adopt the sons of noble families and make them a new family, but unlike those rich arrogant lot looking to curry favour with the lord by passing off a spare child… I love my children! The Lord may be the father to us all, but here on earth a father still has duties to his own, no matter how old they grow or what religious order takes them in!"

The great booming voice echoed around the room and Dietrich straightened up with a look of concern as he watched Konrad hurry down into the dungeon with them. Meinhardt turned, only to suddenly pull the cloth over his head to hide himself from someone that made Dietrich feel tiny. He'd never seen any human nearing seven foot, with a bald head from chainmail ripping the hair free, no beard at all, but so tall and muscular and just so huge in armour, with a massive bear skin wrapped about him as a cloak, scowling down at Meinhardt. Behind him, two attendants appeared with a palette to carry Meinhardt away and Dietrich was shocked as the towering figure stepped over to the hiding knight and he gave a grunt. "Well, Little Mouse, you've certainly caused some trouble. What have you got to say for yourself, boy?"

"Uh…" Meinhardt shrank and Dietrich just looked from Meinhardt to the giant and back again as he considered who in their right mind would ever call Meinhardt something such as 'Little Mouse'. However, as he looked to the piercing blue eyes and the pale hair just visible upon the figure, their sharp noses and that familiar accent, Dietrich realised that there was only one person that this could be and he was shocked and terrified as Meinhardt bowed his head. "I take it… I'm going back to Germany, father?"

"By God you are, not to any monastery either, you're coming back home and once you're walking you can come back here with the mercenaries. I've brought some here to join the campaign for summer so they won't be lacking, but you're coming home whether you like it or not." It was clear to see why Konrad had not been happy about it, but Meinhardt was blushing and nodding his head like a nervous child. Dietrich was startled but as Konrad went to his side and muttered to him about not wanting this, Dietrich and Meinhardt's eyes met with a clear understanding that they would be separated yet again by family. Dietrich then watched the giant hook up Meinhardt to ease the palette beneath him and then… he was taken away.

Seventeen: Seeking Distraction

There was nothing but despair as the days and weeks trickled by and, as summer came into the fold, the fighting became more vicious. The native beings of the land began to be more active in their attempts to fight the Teutonic knights, but now the raiding parties were being joined by young princes from nearby kingdoms as news that the Crusades in the hotter climes were fading away under the threat of beings from the furthest east. There was only one or two incidents, young masters low down in family ranks looking for a bit of adventure and bringing their bands of fighters to join a brief raid, spend a fortnight living like the monks and then return as if it had been a pilgrimage.

The order had been startled by these arrivals, but Balk had insisted that they brought attention to them, as well as some money and trade for the slaves these masters helped them collect. It looked to prepare the order for an alternative to the Holy Land and made their claim to the region firmer. It was clear too that their growing success was causing some upset within the Masovian Courts, clearly not quite sure what lines they'd drawn out for the Teutonic Order to use. The mumbles about the 'Burzenland Fiasco' was echoing around again, they were frustrating, but time just continued to trickle along for the order and for Dietrich.

Somehow, being within Sicily and having those months between meetings had seemed easy, even here in the coldness, there had been chances for them to meet and yet now, Dietrich had no way of knowing what would happen. Indeed, Dietrich was filled with misery at the thought that back in the Holy Roman Empire, Meinhardt was alone, in pain, angry and yet miserable that he could not do anything to reach out to Dietrich. In dreams he thought about him time and time again, as months began to fade as the activities of the order increased and Dietrich became harsher, meaner to the enemy that had caused this separation and yet… gentler to the new squires and to the sickly.

"You're working your way towards a proper promotion there Dietrich, you might have climbed higher in ranks to a master if you'd only been born in the right place. But you've done well as my lieutenant and with the more territory we gain, there's more talk about your potential to be a Komtur of your own group." The words were from Rudolph as he and Dietrich were reunited once more for the late summer to raise up a new group of squires, but it was clear to see that there was an added hardness to Dietrich's expressions. Once, he'd been more eager to smile and quick to laugh, his expression to his brothers always welcoming and yet now, he was distant and harsh to look upon. A new scar crossed Dietrich's chin, something that worked with his stubble but only made him look harsher, a typical wound of any man forced to snatch a blade aimed for the face. Dietrich was looking like a proper warrior and yet his heart seemed… lost. "Does it not please you, brother?"

"I am honoured, but anything more than that might risk the sin of pride. In truth, I am not worthy of such advancement when my past is still whispered amongst the commanders. I am no more than a man trying to pay penance in this order, so I will be content with whatever responsibilities they grace me with." Dietrich spoke in his high tone, sounding more like a commander and making Rudolph's lips wrinkle in frustration to hear such a high and mighty tone, and yet, the right kind of words. Rudolph nodded his head gently in agreement with the words, but he could see that Dietrich's eyes were ever westward, beyond the Vistula and it made the older Komtur give a soft grunt and actually decide he might try and speak for once.

"You're not unique in feeling that way. My cousin was the master in Burzenland, and I was placed in what they thought was a 'comfortable' position, up here away from the order initially because others thought nepotism had given me rank. I was actually trained as a treasurer in my father's household, I had intended to take on that role when I'd had a religious calling and my cousin invited me to the order. But still they assume a lot of spoiling… but if you speak to those that know me, they'd rather insist that I'm the most annoyingly precise grain counter going… they love to envision me as counting every grain sent to my stores and then writing up a long letter of disapproval when the right amount is not given." Rudolph stated with a soft snort and Dietrich turned his head to look at him in fascination, he had not known how Rudolph had joined the order and had sadly believed it was thanks to Theodoric von Lippe's aid. But it made Dietrich give a soft grunt of appreciation as he considered the situation himself and gave another groan. Rudolph looked at him and then suddenly gave him such a hard clap to the back that Dietrich gave a wheezing cough of horror.

"WHY?" He gasped, his stern expression lost to choke and cough loudly over the side of his horse, Verbrecher giving a few snorts and grunts of irritation to be jogged around. Dietrich lifted his head to stare at the older, fatter figure with the rather thicker beard but the most unamused expression going as he shook his head at him. "What was that about, sir?"

"You've been miserable since your friend was wounded and went home... its disturbing. You should have faith in God that he will be healthy, and he will be with us again soon." Rudolph stated firmly and Dietrich nodded his head gently, only to grasp his chest and heave slightly with pain. He did not understand the logic for the big slap, but clearly he was being reminded to keep some faith regarding Meinhardt. Dietrich was also embarrassed that someone might have noticed that he was missing Meinhardt, but Leonhard had also mentioned that he was looking as miserable as Meinhardt had been at their first separation. Rudolph though just gave a soft chuckle of amusement as he steered his horse to the left and beckoned Dietrich to follow after him with a soft groan. "If you do well in the last of the summer campaigns, you might get a chance to go on the recruitment rounds in winter..."

"Are you trying to give me hope?" Dietrich questioned as they moved cautiously towards the next bridge on the river where they still had the occasional pagan try and launch an attack or sneak around. However, they saw no sign of movement and Dietrich gave a soft grunt of irritation as he watched the mist slinking back into the banks of the river. He had to keep locking his eyes on the lapping water, the hidden edge of the bank making him flashback to that night in the Holy Lands and making him growl. Somehow, he was finding it difficult to hold back those bad memories and the terror they brought without Meinhardt around and Rudolph gave a soft grunt over the matter.

"I'm going to request that you go in for recruitment, I think they'll accept it if you can really impress the nobles coming. It would seem they'll include some French youngsters needing a bit of experience that they're bound to push to either of our care. I'd of course send you out with them on a raid or a battle, depending on what's happening." Rudolph grunted and Dietrich nodded his head, feeling a sudden jolt of excitement at the thought of getting a chance to go out and be away from the harsh winter and also to be around a few different faces. Lately, the main subject of conversation at bedtime was about how long everyone's beards were getting or about the nasty way the skin on their feet was cracking, splitting or developing hideous blisters. It nearly always led to a monthly check on the health on one another and the binding of wounded feet and a lot of pissing on the boots that would be brought out, half-frozen and intending to be used. There was always a desire to see home again, but then

Dietrich's heart was trembling in utter delight as Rudolph snorted. "Leonhard put the thought through… he said he would have been going to visit with the residents in the Nord Mark to find out about the Danish situation, not to mention a chance to meet Meinhardt… so he suggested it to me to pass on to you and so I mentioned it to the Komtur's and of course, von Landsberg was in agreement of it."

"You mean… I could have the chance to check on whether he will be returning to us and indeed on his health? I can… I can see my brother again?" Dietrich questioned, a softened expression forming within his pretty green eyes at the thought of getting a chance to go to Meinhardt's home and see how well he was doing and how much he'd missed him. Dietrich pondered if he'd get the same sort of reaction that Dietrich had given him, before he grimaced at the thought of how ill and quite mad he'd been during that time. "Even if I'm just to go there for information and not to go on recruitment, I think I would accept a vow of silence for the chance to see how my brother has improved."

"Hmm… unfortunately, your voice is needed to teach the students… but I'll make a mention of it." Rudolph chuckled softly with a snort of amusement before kicking his horse on. Dietrich followed after him with a slightly dreamy expression upon his face and yet he wondered also why these two Komturs were being so kind to him in this matter. Perhaps they just did not want the so called 'Princeling' around for a little while, or maybe they were thinking he'd be able to make a good figurehead for their position out here. Dietrich could not think of the answer, but he was content all the same with the thought of a chance to see his dear Meinhardt once more.

The late summer was shockingly warm, so warm that the men sweat under their raiment and the horses were constantly trying to steer themselves into walking into the marsh lands for water. The quagmires of the region dried out quickly in some parts and here, the soil was quickly craved by the peasantry for the crops. The section of the Pagan lands that had been claimed by the order were completely secure and the castle in Thorn was starting to show more shape. There was also a sudden migration of Saxon peasants and more from the Nordmark to move across and start working to improve the landscape. They were quick to build up their homesteads and pay tax to Balk, not to mention put in offers to take on extra jobs to reduce tax where they could. It was turning into the Burzenland again, but these were hardier peasants that could stand the cold and understood the soil. They were hard looking people and not above agreeing to get involved in fighting if needed.

As they marched on, with them knights were hired to aid their passage through Masovia, the master of that land was starting to get antsy with Balk and there were rumours that the pair were not getting along, but that the internal strife in the regions below were too important for Konrad of Masovia to get involved in anything more with the order. Balk's plans for expansion were growing and when the migrants brought a collection of two French noblemen looking for adventure, an English noble and indeed two Germans, Balk had welcomed them in and the money they offered to the holy order to gain not only honour but the kind of penance the ordained brothers could give them for joining the crusade. The five nobles were eager to live just like the warrior monks and eager to talk with whichever knights had stories to tell them and, with the new scar upon his chin, Dietrich was a favourite, especially with the English noble.

Dietrich found himself being followed on his rounds in his white raiment by the colourful patterning of the Englishman with his entourage of eager lackeys and soldiers and his hunting dogs. Dietrich took the nobles on hunts along with the squires, insisting it was permitted in their order because of the harsh terrain and the need for the squires to get used to dealing with blood young. The nobles adored the situation and were always eager to have the chance to hunt and save the knights of the order from the hassle, as well as giving them a chance to inspect the terrain. There had been several incidents of chasing deer into the bogs that were still wet and regretting walking back coated in mud that dried quick and became heavy to wear... a lesson in humility if ever there was one.

But Dietrich's chance to prove himself for the winter wander came when there was an incident with Balk. His thoughts were made clear that there was something big a foot as a group of a thousand men came with a German Duke for an advancement towards the next river by the order, stepping through Pomesanian land and into the Pogesania regions. Balk had his eyes on another river point to connect them closer to the landscape of Livonia and when this duke and his group were present, a huge series of raids and battles were planned. The raids would cut down the Pomesanian's in the north that were still awkwardly trying not to convert and the Pogesanian's would be drawn into battle and it had the various nobles excited.

"Ah… brother Hoey-flak-stin! Dietrich! Brother Dietrich hold on a moment, I wanted to talk to you again!" The English noble was as bad as the French for getting Dietrich's surname wrong, let alone for constantly getting all of the German names wrong. He spoke French wonderfully, language of the courts it was said, but whenever he tried to speak German his tongue seemed to twist, even though there had been musings of how the English language was more akin to the Germanic… however, the Englishman would always scoff that 'English' was for the peasantry! As always his colourful blue, red and gold coloured clothing stood out amongst the white of the order and his fancy state of the art chainmail always seemed to make the loudest chink sounds as he galloped faster than a man should with a grin on his bald, long face with his flat nose and his big blueish eyes that looked more the colour of a rainy day! "Dietrich!"

"Please… Sir, if you keep running like that, I'll have to make you sit and scrub the mud from your mail. We do not shout in the order; we are more polite." Dietrich grumbled softly, trying not to be angry but he had a lot to do in preparation for the battle he was going to enter. But the Englishman, who had insisted that Dietrich was allowed to call him Roland, was not going to give up and as he galloped over and still spoke too loudly compared to what Dietrich had hoped. The Teuton ended up straightening up and turning around to look towards the figure with a sigh of frustration as Roland stopped beside him with a soft pant of surprise before grinning as Dietrich just glowered at him. "You should be saving your energy; we're heading off to battle first thing…"

"I know, but I'm concerned about the situation… will I be in the same position as the other nobles or will I be pushed to the back because of the Duke that's here? I expect to be somewhere worthy of fame and renown!" Roland stated, pouting visibly as Dietrich rolled his eyes and gave a soft groan in German about the boy's arrogance. He was quite sure Roland should understand the sin of pride by now, but it seemed the knights outside the orders in both the Holy Land and now coming here were not there for the sake of God but themselves. Dietrich shook his head gently, feeling fury build up like bile in his throat and quite sure he should be like Meinhardt and head-butt the being to teach him a lesson, but thankfully the bell for prayer sounded and Dietrich gave a sigh of relief as Roland grimaced. "If I join you in the service, it should make a better impression, shouldn't it?"

"I think you should join us to learn the sacred art of silence and worship. If you want to know about tomorrow, I insist you sit and meditate with me in the chapel after the service… I have to pray for God's favour upon our battle as well as for my brother's health." Dietrich stated, his heart clenching once more as he considered the sad fact that he might not do well enough to visit with Meinhardt in the end. The Englishman looked at him with a skewed expression before stepping over to the flagstones on the path into the barracks. It was filled with knights and men at arms, so many that only a fool would mistake their movements as not being invasive, but on the stone Roland wiped the mud from his feet and then looked about for some kind of fabric or some lower ranked individual to wipe his hands on before Dietrich suddenly ripped a ragged corner of his underclothes off and pushed it into his hands. "Hurry up now."

With that and a quick thanks, Roland was cleaning his hands up with a grin before he strolled, with that stupid look of delight upon his face, after Dietrich and then gave a scowl when he spotted Leonhard and one of the other younger knights with the French nobles. The two men were looking cool, calm and confident as they followed the knights to the chapel, their swords gone and their expressions serious as if they had no issues with the religious life at all. Dietrich wished that the pair of them had hooked to him more, but it seemed Dietrich always had the liveliest men clinging to him and it tended to start whenever someone asked if he'd been to the Holy Land. Roland tried to suddenly look more serious as Dietrich rolled his eyes and then stepped amongst the group.

They crowded into the wooden chapel with its wooden floor, all of them standing up shoulder to shoulder and filling the room as Balk and his lieutenant stepped forward to begin their sermon. As he spoke, he made no mention of the matter of battle but instead continued the usual praise of the lord, reading of the scriptures and then a lecture on the righteousness of their presence here. He did make a brief mention that the Masovians had shown contempt and claimed some of their establishments were illegal, but he gave a firm grunt to swat the idea away… the Teutonic Order were staying in the Baltic and that would be it. Dietrich listened to the sermon, pleased to see Roland did not question any of the talk in German but knew the prayers to obey. Then, when the sermon was finished and they were permitted to go until the next, Dietrich stepped to the altar, bowed and then stepped down to kneel and then lay himself on the floor in front of the altar.

Balk noticed as did a few others, but a few of the older knights did the same and the German Duke followed with his bodyguard kneeling and praying at his side. Roland looked about anxiously, not quite sure what they were doing until one of the Frenchmen leaving noticed his expression and then gave a chuckle. He tapped at his shoulder and then whispered into his ear that it was a way of meditative prayer that was most commonly seen in monasteries. It showed not only humility, but a desire for total connection to the lord instead. Roland looked at the figure in confusion for a while before giving a grunt and then plonking onto his knees, looking at the muddy floor and then slumped himself down with a grimace of discomfort as he tried to shift his weight to be comfortable and Dietrich was quick to grow irritated.

Had Dietrich always been this irritable? No… he must be starting to turn into Meinhardt the more time went by. He tried to ignore Roland shuffling about in discomfort and instead, Dietrich heaved a soft sigh upon the ground and closed his eyes. He took the time to pray to the Almighty and to whichever of his heavenly host would grant him aid to help him with the growing battle. He prayed too that he would be able to see Meinhardt and that he would be healed and not injured as he had been before… that he might return to the Order soon. He thought about it and let it roll around his head before he felt his whole form relaxing and he tried not to sigh too loud so the other praying would know how he felt, but he was embarrassed as Roland asked if they'd prayed enough yet…

One could never pray enough in a religious order!

Balk had kept quiet until the last meal where the Order remained in silence, but he spoke to them all and expected they would understand the obedience required. It was revealed that only his most trusted knights with a few men-at-arms would be performing the raids on the road whilst the main force walked into enemy territory. It was clear that they were to expect a serious amount of walking and encouraged to rest well and prepare for the confrontation as their enemies were massing already. With that, Dietrich was relieved to know he would be in the front as those doing the raids would be expected to raid and split in half, letting one of the two knights in each group lead the spoils back to Kulm, some of the men-at-arms would secure the raided village and then the rest would join the group again! Thankfully, Leonhard was one of them and Dietrich could focus upon the fight and upon keeping Roland safe alongside his large retine.

It was a cool morning, there was mist clinging around the quagmires upon the route march and the men moved in silence. The horses snorted and whickered every so often, but did not startle or make too much noise as even the hunting dogs had joined the party to take on the role of war dogs. Dietrich was almost surprised that he and Verbrecher were being surrounded by the big mastiff dogs that drooled and looked up at him lovingly and he even missed Igel. They moved along the worn paths that had been used by the tribes for years, the best guide to where the force would be massing to fight them. The knights were sure that there had been spies from the already converted tribes to give the warning and that Balk had been smart enough to encourage this thought, especially when he was expecting a battle good enough to gain renown.

As they marched on steadily through the growing brightness of the summer day, the mist to cling to their bodies began to hiss away and heat overcame their bodies as a growing tension filled the air. There was a sensation of anticipation rolling down the column of marching men as they cleared the forest line and the edge of the old swamps, coming into areas once inhabited by locals collecting plants growing on the edge of the mire. It was here there was the sound of horses galloping and the front of the group halted as everyone shifted and hands went to swords. The anticipation grew with men clenching muscles and jaw, holding onto their anxiety and prepping to battle, until the shriek of a horse was greeted by one amongst their group and then the column began to move on.

As they moved, the men were able to see a group of bloodied and muddied soldiers pushing into line amongst them, the first of the raids had been successful with few deaths and an air of expectation and excitement fell upon them. They were feeling relieved and prepared for more good tidings and indeed, Dietrich could feel the heat rising off the men as the tension was lost completely for anticipation and the thought of glory. As the march continued, more clouds of dust joined the column as the other raids returned, some dirtied but in good nick, others quite bloodied and bashed but grinning from ear to ear. When Leonhard's group returned to them and he drew himself to the back, looking exhausted and bruised with his horse bearing a few scratches, Dietrich felt relief as they came to the crest of a wide plain that showed the signs of having been used for crops, but was now left to dry in the sunshine for battle.

They could see the Pogesanian army already building up on the other side of the field, a force close to the number of knights but no horses. Their weapons were varied, consisting mainly of clubs and axes with a few swords, but there was always the possibility of archers hidden amongst them. But that was why the German Duke had insisted upon his war dogs and the hunting hounds, as the men gathered up with the knights forming a line together. Roland and Dietrich lining up with them, some with lances but Dietrich with a mace, the dogs were brought up with their handlers as Balk was practically beaming in delight. As the pagans seemed to tense up and pull in together, ready to battle, they were oddly anticipating the advance of the knights and that generally told them all that they wanted the knights to move first… clearly they had a trap!

As Dietrich tensed, the Duke turned his head towards a massive dog the height of Igel but slimmer and bearing a massive, spiked collar, drooling and frothing with its ears back and head low, ready for battle. The handler was holding the dog's collar, jogging him back as the dog pulled forward, revving him up for the fight and the other handlers were doing the same. Dietrich, like others, had heard the stories of where the mastiff dogs had been used by Romans in coliseums to fight beasts and used as well for war, but it was strange to see so many lined up about the mounted knights and looking very eager to fight. Balk looked to the Duke and lifted his sword slightly, using it to almost flick forward and keeping it low, a sign for the dogs to go as the Duke gave a whistle, the dogs were released, and Dietrich's eyes stared in disbelief.

The dogs were quiet at first as they charged in and for a moment, the locals in their tunics and slacks were scrabbling to grab shields, not sure what to use against the dogs before one of them encouraged the hidden archers to react. However, the dogs were faster than the horses or men, the arrows only hit the hesitant hunting hounds but the larger dogs crashed through into the people and then there was the noise. The sudden loud sound of the snarling dogs ripping and smashing into people, biting everything their teeth could, twisting, snapping and grabbing was hideous as many of the men pulled away from the dogs and the archers were exposed. The hideous noise almost put Dietrich off, until Balk ordered the charge.

A few horses shrieked in excitement, one or two rearing under the sudden jerk of the reins as the cavalry ran in. They took the moment of confusion to cross the field before the archers could try to get them and as the archers tried to fire, the dogs were rushing them and grabbing at them. Accuracy and confidence was lost as Dietrich and Roland crashed into the men first, knocking a few about before swinging their weapons. Roland's sword thunked and slapped against shield or mail, blood coating the end as he chopped randomly from side to side, kicking his horse to just keep barging through the people. His men were soon rushing behind him to keep him free and the others were crashing into the group. Dietrich was swinging the mace carelessly about him, feeling that rattle up his arm and the hideous thud when he made contact with flesh as his stallion roared and seemed to stomp and stamp at people, chasing people. The dogs were quick to hurry around Dietrich and seem to keep him safe.

Dietrich growled and clenched his teeth, snorting messily through his nose as he swung his tiring arms and the sweat began to form upon his forehead. He tried to keep his hips angled into the saddle as he had to draw his sword and try to fight in the melee without falling from his horse. As he crashed and attacked the people, feeling clubs swing past his legs, thankfully it was only the occasional body he barged into as the other knights barged in. The cavalry forced themselves through to the back of the crowd, the dogs were rounding people up and as the cavalry ploughed through, the men on the ground were forming behind and the cavalry was ready to spin around and charge through again.

The smell of sweat, mud and blood was filling the air, there was still the constant hideous sound of the aggressive dogs, the screams of injured horses and the squealing noises of humans being ripped apart or smashed. It was terrifyingly exciting as Verbercher slid on the mud, making Dietrich jolt before falling off and into the sludge. The stallion though continued his charge, bucking and screaming and madly kicking out at anything near, knocking people and keeping anyone from getting close to him until he spotted Leonhard's mare and was quick to hurry to her side. Dietrich lay in the mud, but swiftly a bloodied-up mastiff rushed over to him, licking his face as Dietrich pulled himself up before someone with a club, that was almost half a tree, came rushing towards him aggressively.

Dietrich's eyes swelled, he reached about for a sword, ready to impale the figure, but when the man came at him, the dog lunged. The huge brindled beast stood up on his hindlegs, bloodied and wounded from various other hits, he wrestled about the man's body like a bear, the club was dropped and they fell into the mud. The dog was soon savaging the human, worse than when Dietrich had seen a wolf ripped apart by hounds as entertainment in his youth, so he picked up his sword and dispatched the human out of pity. He then jerked his sword out and hurried straight into the fray with the dog limping to his side as he patted its head and he returned to the battle.

He swung his sword into anyone that got close, using it more like a club than to hack and slash as he made his way, the dog rushing around him and grabbing people, towards Leonhard and his horse. The mud was splashing everywhere, turned from dust to swampy with the horrid fluids of scared and dying beings, it clung and grew heavy, but tripping over the bodies of dogs and humans was just as unpleasant. As he reached a toppled horse carcass, slashing one man in the face and being forced to punch another firmly in the jaw before the dog tackled the man, Dietrich paused and steadied himself against the carcass. He took a few pants of relief and ignored the mucky sweat dribbling into his eyes, the dog was right to his side, lapping his trembling wrist that was bloodied from the punch before it noticed trouble.

With a violently loud and screeching bark, the dog launched up from the carcass and slammed into a human that was hurrying up to attack Dietrich. As it pushed him down, wrestling and biting his face and making that hideous shrieking sound of canine excitement, Dietrich pulled his sword around to stab the human in return, but as the human fell, he managed to stick a blade into the dog, making it shriek in agony and leap aside. Dietrich chopped down at the man's neck to ensure his death before he turned to the panting and whimpering dog as it limped onward but was bleeding badly. There was froth in the dog's mouth and something foaming out past the blade wound in his ribcage and Dietrich knew what it was, and how the dog was going to drown in its own blood that was filling its chest. He'd seen it with people before and quickly, he ducked behind the dead horse and beckoned the dog over, he stroked the animal's side as it wheezed and whimpered and then gradually, it seemed to choke and gasp within his hands before Dietrich thought that maybe, he should show the same mercy to the dog, but for how it slowly licked at his hand.

As the dog slowly died in his arms, the battle continued and seemed to be ending around him as Dietrich gripped hold of the dog that seemed in pain but happy all at once. It was only when the smelly breath stopped wafting into his face and he could not hear the bubbling anymore, that he knew the dog had passed. When he settled the dog down, he got up and launched back into the battle, feeling a renewed hatred and something different he'd never thought about before… he owed Meinhardt a war hound!

Eighteen: A Moment

"You got a puppy from the dog that saved you on the battlefield? You're a funny one Dietrich, not long ago you seemed to hate these damn animals." Roland was beaming in delight as he rode calmly through the dirt tracks, which made the streets of the first town in the Nordmark they'd reached. There was no snow here but it was bitterly cold and there was ice and frost that was making the ground slip under the shod hooves of their horses. Verbrecher though had grown accustomed to snow and accustomed to moving around people, but some things were still new to him and he was not very keen on the pigs that would suddenly be run ahead of him on the path. He was calm under Dietrich's control, but within the thick mantle and stuffed within the rest of his knight garb around his belly, a little dark brown puppy with fawn-coloured brindles was snuffling and sneezing way against cold and making Dietrich smile.

"I have a reason… I owed someone and finding out that war dog had sired a few litters was a miracle. Besides, it won't be returning with me, it's going to be staying here once I get to where I'm going." Dietrich chuckled, he had another new scar to his face, this time a little notch out of his nose after getting into a bit of chaos removing some mail and having surprising bad luck. It wasn't the first time he'd done something like that, but this time the notch had become more obvious and he was amused that he was looking forward to the lecturing on the matter. As they pair continued on through the melee of busy peasants selling what they could and gathering whatever they could afford, the pair spotted the group of dressed soldiers in the town square waiting for them and one knight upon their steed looking slightly familiar as Dietrich gave a chuckle. "It looks like we'll be separating here... it was good to meet you, Roland."

"Good evening, Brother Knights… I was informed to collect a member of the order and bring them back to our house, these gentlemen to take the nobleman visiting from England to the Lord's lands. I am Bartholomew Lehenman, which brother of the Order am I addressing?" The figure on the stockiest big bay horse came trotting over to their side, followed by the other rider who translated to French to greet Roland, who said his goodbye to Dietrich and steered his horse and his followers to the left of him and a different path. The soldiers that had been waiting in the square departed with them and

Dietrich was left with a figure whose name alone had startled him. Dietrich looked to the face and saw familiar sharp ice-blue eyes staring back at him with an edge of fury that almost made Dietrich's heart flutter.

"I am Brother Dietrich von Hohenflacherstein…" Dietrich began, only to gain a surprise when Bartholomew practically lunged off his horse to grasp Dietrich within a tight embrace before slapping his shoulder hard enough that Dietrich choked. As he saw him closer in the grey light, Dietrich was able to see a broader form than Meinhardt, taller and certainly chunkier around the belly, but with more rounded cheeks and a softer edge to his face and nose that did not quite suit Meinhardt, or indeed the face of his terrifying father! But Dietrich recalled a younger brother, this man was probably just into his twenties and a freshly made knight as his hair, a darker shade of blonde with brown roots, clearly had not been chopped up by wearing too much mail and he sat too comfortably upon his horse. The figure was grinning at Dietrich as he queried if he were the brother named for the monk and with a loud 'hah' and a big grin that came to his face naturally, Bartholomew nodded his head.

"Ja… that's me! Mein told us he'd made a friend that was a Princeling… your accent is starting to sound more like the others in the Order, so you don't sound as 'southern'. But it's a pleasure to meet with you, Brother Dietrich, come with me… I'm looking forward to all your stories about what you've been doing the past year or so, you've got a few interesting scars there… Mein said you had one from the Holy Land too!" It seemed Bartholomew was a talker, a constant talker as Dietrich trotted beside him and the pair marched through the dirty tracks and roads with the puppy still asleep against Dietrich's belly. He was a little relieved to be listening to German this time and not having to listen to conversations switching between French and bad German that would make his head spin. He really had been thankful to be away from the court for so long and yet as he was walked out of the sight of the town, he realised that this was not something he was expecting at all. He'd expected to be steered towards some grand stone house, but instead they were moving out amongst farmland and then along the river towards a slight rise with a bridge that led into a large set of stables, livestock pens and several large wooden buildings with only one small section that appeared stone.

It was busy, it was smelly, steam rolled off the thatched roof of what looked more like a grand hall than a household of such an important family. Dietrich could see the clear differences between his childhood in a castle compared to what was more akin to a household of two hundred years ago! He was worried as he was led to a stall for his horse, trudging in mud and the stable boy was not even going to ask for the reins but yanked hold of them and tied the horse up. Bartholomew hopped off his horse without question and beckoned for Dietrich, only to get a surprise as a little puppy was suddenly plopped into his hands. The figure looked at the dog with a mix of confusion before suddenly giving a snigger in a familiar hissing sound that eased Dietrich's heart as Bartholomew passed the puppy back to the dismounted knight.

"He's still so soft to dogs! Eh... my terrifying religious brother still goes on about that dog he got and complained you gave it away because it would help a friend. This an apology?" He snorted as he tapped the wriggling puppy's nose as it whimpered within Dietrich's grip. He nodded his head in response, cuddling the puppy close as it calmed down and lapped eagerly at Dietrich's shoulder as he followed Bartholomew to two sloppily dressed guards keeping the door. The figures opened it without question and they stepped into a large open room with a roaring fire that felt like something from the tribal past, not too much different from some of the places that Dietrich had been going into for conversions. It was curious as he noticed the huge dogs lounging on the floor chewing bones and the household seemingly sitting at a large table, the massive and terrifying form of Meinhardt's father spotting him and standing straight up with a seeming bellow of greeting.

"Aah... a knight of the Order... hmm... I recognise those eyes, not those scars... eh, Meinhardt, which brother is this?" The master of the household was as bald and tall and terrifying as ever as he stood up and marched over to Dietrich's side, grasping him by the shoulders and towering over him even though only by a few inches. Everything about him was just awe inspiring, even Balk couldn't give as much intimidation as this figure did in just one meeting. But Dietrich's heart leapt into his throat as the big figure looked over his broad shoulders towards a seat near the fire where a person was hunching in a pale greyed tunic, enjoying the heat with a wooden crutch pressed to his chest. Dietrich spotted the pale blonde hair and then the turning of their sharp profile towards him, the ice blue eyes and then the way the figure straightened up with a groan.

"MEINHARDT!" The word leapt out of Dietrich's mouth with such delight and joy he couldn't hold it back. Obviously, his lover had assumed that it was just going to be Leonhard or someone he didn't know and want to know, but he'd jolted and even wobbled with a grunt of pain at the sudden bleat. Meinhardt's father slapped Dietrich's shoulder heavily, though it was meant to be in a reassuring manner as he stepped out of the way so that Meinhardt could look at the figure. When their eyes locked, a mournful expression slid onto Meinhardt's face that made Dietrich suddenly very anxious and fearful that maybe they could not have the same relationship as they should have had!

But, as Dietrich waited and watched, Meinhardt pulled himself up onto his legs, hooking the crutch under his shoulder, leaning onto it and then wobbled towards Dietrich. One leg was only lifting slightly, just enough to stop the foot dragging, but it put his balance off and he soon began to hop instead, only to stop with a grimace of pain. Meinhardt swore softly under his breath before dragging himself forward using the crutch once again, his father grunted that he was just getting used to walking and moving around more. Dietrich was not sure if he should go forward to hold him and steady him, but he was not going to make Meinhardt look anymore uncomfortable than he already was as he reached Dietrich and gave a grunt before his eyes locked onto the puppy and immediately, he brightened up and stared at it eagerly.

"Hah! Dieter you… uh… what are you doing holding onto a puppy like that, its clearly cold and hungry." Meinhardt leant his crutch to his father who took it eagerly, Dietrich was expecting himself to be given a hug or a pat to the shoulder in greeting. However, Dietrich was disappointed as the suddenly shivering pup in his arms was hooked up eagerly by Meinhardt, who managed to keep his balance and swing himself about with the pup, pulling it right into his chest and nuzzling into it. He gave a few loving sounds of delight, kissing and nuzzling at the eager looking puppy that gave a yelp of glee and was trying to lap and snuffle at his face eagerly. Meinhardt ignored the crutch and limped with the seemingly heavily leg dragging slightly towards the warm spot by the fire. He put it down, wrapped it in a blanket and then grasped a large bone with meat still on it from one of the huge and vicious looking dogs under the table, which gave a booming bark of dismay, and dropped it down for the puppy with a chuckle. "There."

"Well, I'm glad to see my gift was received well…" Dietrich groaned in frustration, looking towards the crutch with an anxious sensation of despair, as if everything between them had been destroyed because of this injury and nothing would ever be the same, but for Meinhardt's love of dogs. However, Meinhardt was ignoring him in favour of the puppy and when his father queried if a certain duke had been fighting with him during the summer, Dietrich nodded his head. He then strolled with the crutch over to the chair where Meinhardt heaved a sigh and sat down, only to find Dietrich beaming beside him. "Of course... its father died saving my life in a very unpleasant battle, the Duke offered the pup because I asked about it. I thought you could use some company whilst you heal."

"It's a lovely puppy, I'm not sure what to name him... maybe something heroic or just cute... look at him rushing over to get some food." Meinhardt beamed as the waggling little puppy with a tail almost as long as his baby legs seemed to sway over to the meat and began to growl and tug at the meat desperately. The big dog it had been robbed from, some greyish blue mastiff with heavy jowls and the sort often seen in noble halls to fight bears, strolled over to give it a sniff of fascination. The pup snarled at him furiously to stop him from trying to take his meat as Meinhardt gave a chuckle and patted the two dogs gently. He then noticed the way the household was standing there expectantly towards Meinhardt for the proper introduction and Meinhardt just gave a scoff as he pointed towards Dietrich. "Ah, family, this is Dietrich the Swabian, my brother in arms and well, practically everything but blood. Dieter... my family."

"Its an honour to meet such a family, I've heard so much about you and fighting beside Meinhardt I've much to praise you for in raising him well. I also owe him my life a few times over, so I owe you for that too!" Dietrich stated, bowing his head to them all as the group of various beings gathered around the table together. They settled down and it was clear that the three younger men were Meinhardt's younger brothers with their startling blue eyes, but the two young girls present were softer-eyed, but their hair was almost white-blonde, and they certainly did not look like they would ever take on the roll of a wife so... comfortably. But amongst them the short, slightly dumpy woman with her blonde hair going grey-white and her expression gentile, beckoned to one of the seats with a beaming smile upon her face.

"Nonsense... sit yourself down, eat what you wish and sit close to the fire." This was Meinhardt's mother of course, but even taking the time to look at her properly, it was still astonishing to think that this tiny little woman and that giant man had produced such an array of children. It was something that was making Dietrich stare at her a little too much and Meinhardt pulled himself up with a groan of irritation before introducing his mother properly. Dietrich stepped over to her, held her hand and planted a gentle kiss like any knight. However, there was an immediate low series of growls from behind him and Dietrich was quite sure it was not any of the dogs but the humans in the room. Dietrich pulled away and then sat himself down as Meinhardt pulled himself up and then settled himself before his mother spoke again sweetly. "Perhaps you can tell us a story and…"

"He is cold and needs food as well as to pray, do not hassle our guest." Meinhardt growled protectively, making Dietrich blush slightly and then Meinhardt clapped his cheeks. He made a point of the redness showing the cold and Dietrich was thankful, though Meinhardt kept clapping his cheeks firmly as if to scold him. It made Dietrich feel relieved though, thankful that he was getting attention from him and more importantly, that Meinhardt seemed to be showing off his possessive streak when his little sister suddenly leant over the table to look to Dietrich's belly, querying to see the scar but Meinhardt grunted. "You sit back down; he's not exposing himself to anyone!"

"Yes brother… but at least he could give us news from the Crusades to the east." The sister stated, sitting back down but then sticking out her tongue gently. However, Dietrich's eyes bulged to see how swiftly the mother's fingers pinched around her daughter's tongue, only to glare down at her with a villainous expression that made Dietrich feel like he was shrinking into the background. Now he could see where Meinhardt's own sadistic nature came from, before the mother released her daughter's tongue, beckoned the servants to present the food properly to them and their guest, before turning to Dietrich and asking if he would 'indulge' them with a story.

Dietrich found himself unable and indeed unwilling to resist against such a powerful woman, let alone to refuse the offer of rest with them for at least a week. It was certainly something he would not have ignored and probably would have begged for, but there was a realisation of how small this place was and how much he wanted to be alone with Meinhardt. He told them all about the latest news and the desire for next summer's offensive to bring in men from all over the Holy Roman Empire and beyond for a huge push. It made Meinhardt's brothers and father look eager for the chance to go and they even mentioned Meinhardt might be healthy enough for such an adventure then. Dietrich was glad to hear it, but still a little anxious over the thought of being pulled away from Meinhardt for so long!

They were a lively bunch and despite Dietrich's best efforts after the meal, he found himself being forced to show off and tell the stories of his scars. The old Saracen wound was a crowd pleaser and even the guards and servants were beckoned to sit down and listen to the story, something that made Dietrich feel a little more comfortable with talking to them all. He'd then told them about arrow bolts from the Cumans, his scars from the Prussians and then he told them about the incident with the dog. It made Meinhardt give a gasp of disbelief and even shed a tear for the mighty dog, yanking up the puppy from the floor to cuddle him, nuzzling him and then insisting he would have to have a brilliantly strong name so he could become a war dog too! It made Dietrich almost laugh, before he told them the story of the scar of the back of his head that Meinhardt had saved him over and how he'd come to him when ill to save him from fever.

The stories with Meinhardt in pleased the whole household and everyone seemed eager to insist that Meinhardt was not normally the sort to speak about his experiences in battle, save what used to happen in Burzenland and training Diethelm. Dietrich could understand, it was clear that the only things that Meinhardt might want to talk about within that time were moments with him, but how could they explain that… they could not! However, Dietrich made it clear that they got along well and talked regularly too, building a close friendship to be as close as Meinhardt had stated they were. His family seemed satisfied and joyful for the company before Dietrich found himself sharing a room that night with Meinhardt and Bartholomew.

In that small room with its three bunks tightly pushed together, Dietrich found himself lying in the middle on the bunk close to Meinhardt, learning they'd been put close because Meinhardt would roll to try and get up sometimes. He learnt too that the door could not be locked so Meinhardt could crawl out to the bathroom if needed, because he did not like using the chamber pot. Dietrich was not surprised, Meinhardt was still very particular about such things and it seemed he had only started walking around the place since autumn, originally crawling more than walking but all because the leg would drag. Bartholomew insisted that Meinhardt had been lucky that it might be he'd only limp a little, something easy for a knight to deal with and not a full cripple. Considering he'd barely been able to sit up without great pain or roll over, it was a great improvement and a joyous thought that Meinhardt would not be forced to use the crutch forever.

But that night, settled in the bed together, Dietrich waited till the lamp went out before he shuffled a hand under the blankets beside him. He was grateful to feel a hand stretching out for his and they gripped together tightly before both turned their heads to look at each other. They could not see in the dark light, but Dietrich knew to shuffle closer and bring his lips to Meinhardt's. It could not be a proper kiss, just the gentle brushing of the lips, no pursing but just that tingling sensation to make Meinhardt give a heavy sigh and squeeze Dietrich's hand tightly… they still were in love with one another.

"Bartholomew… Dietrich's going to spend the day with me in the stone building. We'll be there till the morrow… we will only have bread and water and observe a day of prayer." Meinhardt had announced two days into Dietrich's visit and seemed to decide that he and Dietrich had to indulge in praying nearly all day separate from the household. Dietrich had to admit he was not playing to the rules of prayer and he was sure that Meinhardt was trying to scold him over the matter, but Dietrich was curious when Meinhardt's youngest sister made a laugh over it. She'd mused that Meinhardt did it once a week, always praying to have his leg and hip fixed more and so he could keep to the rules of the Order. Dietrich was glad to hear it was not unusual, but he'd spent his second day still debating names with Meinhardt and his family over the puppy as well as to get to know them all. He'd never experienced such a joyful and talkative household where even the servants had been with them for years and treated as much as friends as Dietrich had treated Kirk.

"I hope that's not an inconvenience for the rest of your family, but I've been neglecting my prayers since I started the journey, so I should in fact fast today completely in penance." Dietrich stated to Bartholomew as they got up, he was grimacing at the thought of it all, before he shrugged it off and insisted it was perfectly fine as long as tomorrow, they went on a hunt with him. Dietrich nodded his head, glad tomorrow was not a feast day before Meinhardt scoffed that he had no issue riding his horse and wielding a sword, so Dietrich would feel better for seeing him back to himself. "I'm pleased to hear you're still the ardent warrior monk, Meinhardt… but, don't rush yourself with such an injury, God has smiled on you thus far, don't get too bold."

"I would not… I have prayed for healing and it has happened, I wish to return to the Order soon and aid you in the conversion of the pagans!" Meinhardt scoffed as he limped out of the room where the youngsters had been showing off their writing skills to Dietrich. Dietrich had learnt that Meinhardt had been learning and teaching with them, but as he padded calmly after his lover, it was clear they were not going to a chapel built into the structure of the household. In fact, Dietrich had learnt that the family had decided long ago to own only what they needed and could move easily, too many incidents fighting in the Mark for them to be completely secure at the idea of building a stone fortress. There was also the comment that Meinhardt's father refused to own a household more lavish than his master and of course, Dietrich would not argue with that.

The pair paced out into the courtyard and then away into the grounds, following a path of random flattened stones that led up a slight hill to a copse. Meinhardt hobbled onward on a mission, his body seemingly aware of the route as he panted and grunted, his balance failing every so often so he would have to straighten himself. Dietrich would stretch out his hand to him on occasion, carrying with him a flask of water and a loaf of bread, but Meinhardt would make a sound like an angry dog chewing on a rat to prevent the assistance. Dietrich remained patient, the pair of them carrying on until they reached what was little more than a stone cell with a small window bearing two firm wooden bolts between it and a door that was easily locked. It looked like a prison, but inside there were blankets and rags on the floor and a collection of letters... letters addressed to Dietrich but never sent.

"I see you come here for solitude?" Dietrich questioned, following Meinhardt inside the room that was filled with warm bright light from the morning. Meinhardt gave a grunt of acknowledgement, panting as he pulled the door shut, locked it with a firm bolt and then wobbled onto a collection of rags, throwing his crutch aside and then flopping back onto the fabric with a groan of dismay. Dietrich was waiting for his companion to start off their prayers, but Meinhardt picked up some of the letters, passing them to him so that Dietrich could look at them. The figure gave a sound of fascination, reading through the ridiculously adorable series of letters confessing loneliness, adoration, desperation, longing and the simple fact that Meinhardt wanted to return because he could not stand being away from the person he loved most. "I've been so lonely and so afraid for you; I've prayed every day for your health and then buried myself in battle. Almost the entire Order seemed to believe I was lonely without you... though, I don't think anyone knows our secret."

"If they did, they've seen nothing to suggest... not to mention how many of them joined after dubious deeds in the Holy Lands... or did not stop even in the order... like Sigmond. I'm glad he's dead." Meinhardt growled and Dietrich found himself nodding his head very slowly as he settled down and gathered up the letters himself, stuffing them under the fabric to keep them hidden before then shuffling over to lie beside Meinhardt, glad not to be wearing his full raiment but his own dulled, rough tunic. They sat together calmly, Dietrich rolling onto his side to look at Meinhardt's tired face carefully before he leant over Meinhardt and kissed his lips. However, Meinhardt lifted his hand to stop any more as Dietrich smiled down at him, only to see his face look miserable. "I'm going to tell you what happened to me and you won't like it… but I need to be honest with you and… I will expect honesty in return."

"Of course." Dietrich stated, though part of him was now feeling scared that something terrible was going to be said. Meinhardt heaved a sigh of frustration and then his face wrinkled in fury and embarrassment.

"I'll say it straight… why paint a picture and torture us both… but Sigmond told Franz to rape me to prove a lesson, Franz did not, he tried but panicked. Then he came to apologise for letting himself be led and suddenly he said he was then aware of the situation you must have been in with Sigmond as a young squire. He told me what Sigmond did to you then, what he forced you to do regularly and how you only just avoided it getting worse when you kicked him back and screamed out that he was going mad. Then I was told, in Burzenland… that meeting you had with him, ended in him forcing you to do it again… that was why you came back so ill, so willing to die… willing enough to kiss me." Meinhardt stated bitterly, a sour expression upon his face as if he feared that this was the reason Dietrich had finally shown himself. It was clear to see that the question was plaguing him, Meinhardt now seemed to understand all his wrong moves in Kronstadt and how much his own libido had put them at such risk it had been no less coercive. He seemed to ignore Dietrich's own libido, own desires when they were together and Dietrich sighed heavily, sitting up and kissing his lips again, this time stroking Meinhardt's cheeks as he felt tears forming and could see that Meinhardt was trying to fight off the shivering panic within him.

"It's the truth that all happened and… and I was always too ashamed you would claim me a deviant or pervert because I was too scared to not… only Kirk ever saved me from it." Dietrich whispered anxiously, looking depressed and yet he kissed Meinhardt's lips again, Meinhardt looked at him with the same anxiety still etched upon his face. Dietrich knew the question and then nuzzled against his chest as he lay there for a moment, giving a soft and loving sigh before bringing his face back to Meinhardt's, their noses coming together in a soft rub before Dietrich sighed. "That moment I thought I would kiss you because there could be no way you were feeling the strange attraction I did and I wanted to die... I thought, you always looked at me, you always seemed to hate me... I couldn't help being drawn to you over and over and so... if you hadn't kissed me back, I'd never have had a reason to keep fighting or anything...."

"I see... its strange you say I hate you... I thought I'd made it clear the moment I met you I was scared because I wanted to be around you. But... I'm sorry Dietrich... I'm sorry I never killed Sigmond when I had the chance." At first Meinhardt seemed sorrowful, but then as he'd made his growl, it was obvious that Meinhardt was happy again as he suddenly swung his arms around Dietrich and held him so tightly that Dietrich gave a gag of surprise, gaining a series of soft pecks to the face before Meinhardt heaved a heavy sigh. It must have been on his mind for most of the year and Dietrich was saddened that he'd never said anything before, that he'd not been as honest with Meinhardt as he should have been. But then he sighed and kissed Dietrich again before blushing heavily. "I should probably let you know that... I often come here once a week... all day, not just to pray but to think about you and well, it's shameful to say but... you used to say to deal with it 'discreetly', back then."

"Meinhardt... I've just been taking lots of dips in freezing water myself, but you should come back to the order soon!" Dietrich chuckled, sitting back up and then grasping the bottom of his tunic and pulling it up over his head. Meinhardt gave a scoff of amusement, how could they both always go from serious to salacious in a flash? It would be their only time to be together until they returned to the Order; Meinhardt made no question of it as Dietrich then removed his braies before bending down to kiss Meinhardt again. Dietrich then slid a hand down to his groin to stroke him into life as Meinhardt shuddered before Dietrich sighed heavily, his beautiful body seeming to glow in the morning light that filtered through the bars. "I'm going to make sure that you and I don't die till we're creaking old knights... I promise that."

"I'll keep you to it too... I love you Dietrich." Meinhardt shivered as their lips came together to seal this new promise.

The End

Look Out for Part Three
"Glory of the Father"

In 1257, the rumbles of Crusades back in the Holy Land and the Livonian Order, attached to the Teutonic Order, were continuing to cause chaos and concern for the campaign in the Baltic. A new shift in leadership keeps the order shuffling, but with lands now being awarded to knights and migrants moving in and pledging tax and loyalty to the Teutonic Landlords, things are changing but the battle to convert continues.

Twenty-five years have passed and with troubling neighbours and wounded pride from recent conflicts, the order is digging its feet in and those nobles from the surrounding landscapes that do not join the Crusades in the Holy Land are still flocking to the Baltic. In the north, Dietrich von Hohenflacherstein is now the Komtur of his own area not far from Wehlau, preparing his knights and soldiers to push further along Curonian Lagoon to link up with the Livonians in Memel. It has been a busy time and now into his later years, Dietrich is looking forward to a summer shared with a special recruit, Reinhard von Hohenflacherstein, his own son. But with the situation with the Prussians still steaming, Dietrich will be facing many challenges, but for the first time since their days as fresh knights, Meinhardt Lehenman will be at his side.

This book is the last in the "Sons of the Order" trilogy.

If you're interested in this story or any others, please look about or sponsor me on Patreon where this series as well as others including the Viper Clan are uploaded as soon as a draft chapter is written and available to read but for the last two chapters of a book.

Sponsoring on Patreon not only gets you early access before the rest of the world but allows you to see what else is in the works and comes with lots of extras no matter what level you sponsor at… including a short complete story (non-edited first draft), each year at Christmas.

Keep up to date with Patreon, the first chapter of this FINAL story will be uploading in August!

http://www.patreon.com/ClareSMKeating

Thank you!

Ingram Content Group UK Ltd.
Milton Keynes UK
UKHW021947040723
424555UK00014B/1535